DAYWORLD
REBEL

DAYWORLD REBEL

Philip José Farmer

An Ace/Putnam Book
Published by G. P. Putnam's Sons
New York

An Ace/Putnam Book
Published by G. P. Putnam's Sons
Publishers Since 1838
200 Madison Avenue
New York, NY 10016

Published simultaneously in Canada by
General Publishing Co. Limited, Toronto

Library of Congress Cataloging-in-Publication Data

Farmer, Philip José.
Dayworld rebel.

Sequel to: Dayworld. c1985.
I. Title.
PS3556.A72D4   1987   813'.54   86-25432
ISBN 0-399-13230-9

Typeset by Fisher Composition, Inc.

Printed in the United States of America
1 2 3 4 5 6 7 8 9 10

Once again, to my wife, Bette. I was very lucky
when she married me.

1

He had been seven men.

Now he was one man.

The woman whose office he visited for an hour every day had told him that. Until then, he had not known about it, though she claimed that he had once known. According to her, he still might know and probably did. He had no doubt that she was wrong about that. No matter. If he wished to live, he had to convince her that he knew nothing of it.

That was indeed strange. "I'll tell you what's so. Then you try to make me believe that it is so."

If he failed to convince the authorities, he would not be executed, though what would be done to him would be almost as bad as being killed. Unless, and it was a very slim unless, somebody in the far future decided to make him alive again.

The woman, the psychicist, was puzzled and intrigued. He suspected that her superiors were equally mystified. While keeping them so, he might stay alive. Living, he could always hope to escape. He knew, however, or thought he knew, that no one had ever escaped from this place.

The man now calling himself William St.-George Duncan sat in a chair in the office of the psychicist, Doctor Patricia Ching

Arszenti. Having just become conscious, he was still a little confused. Breathing in truth mist did that to anyone. A few seconds later, his senses, jigsaw pieces, fell into the proper places. The digits on the wall chronometer told him that, as always, he had been under the mist for thirty minutes. His muscles ached; his back hurt; his mind quivered like a diving board just after the diver had sprung.

What had she learned in that time?

Arszenti smiled, and she said, "How do you feel?"

He sat up straight and massaged the back of his neck.

"I had a dream. I was a cloud of tiny iron particles swirling around in a wind in a vast room. Somebody thrust a huge magnet into the room. I, the cloud of particles, flew to the magnet. I became one solid mass of iron."

"Iron? You're more like putty. Or thermoplastic. You shape yourself into another—or an Other—at will."

"Not that I know of," he said.

"What shape was the solid mass of iron?"

"A two-edged sword."

"I'm not here to psychoanalyze you. That image, however, is significant to me."

"What does it mean?"

"What it means to you may not be what it means to me."

"Whatever I told you," he said, "has to be the truth. Nobody can lie when they've breathed in the mist."

"I've always believed that," she said. She paused, then said, "Until now."

"Until now? Why? You could tell me why you think I'm different from all others. Rather, you should tell me. I think you won't because you can't."

He leaned forward and glared at her. "You have nothing but irrational suspicion to back your statement. Or you've got orders from your superiors, who are crazy with suspicion. You know and they should know that I am not immune to truth mist. You have no proof otherwise. Thus, I'm not the persons arrested for daybreaking and belonging to a subversive organization. I'm not responsible for their crimes because I'm not them. I'm as innocent as a just-born baby."

"A baby is a potential criminal," she said. "However . . ."

They were silent for a while. He leaned back, relaxed, and smiled. Arszenti sat as motionless as a healthy adult could, her twitches and shiftings almost undetectable. She was no longer looking at him. Her stare was at the window. Though she could not see the big yard and the high wall beyond it, she could see the right side of the street and the building beyond the wide sidewalk. At lunch hour, the junction of Frederick Douglass Boulevard and St. Nicholas Avenue was crowded. Pedestrians jammed the sidewalks; bicyclists, the street. One-seventh of Manhattan's population was out enjoying the early spring sun. They should be outside. Of the approximately ninety obdays of this season, they would know only approximately eleven days of it.

Timehoppers, he thought. A grasshopper clinging to a weed bending under its weight flashed through his mind. With it came pain. Or memory of pain? He had no idea why he should envision a grasshopper and feel grief. Nothing in his memory connected them to him.

Suddenly, a fly tearing herself loose from a web—a web also of memory?—Arszenti jerked her stare from the window and leaned forward. She looked fiercely at him, which only made the big handsome blonde even more attractive. Her large white teeth looked as if they were about to bite him; they shone like sun on prison bars.

William Duncan grinned. It took more than that to scare him.

"I don't know how you did it," she said. "You integrated seven different personalities. No, that's not right. You *dissolved*, repressed beyond detectability, let's say, the seven personae. You became an eighth person. You even have some of the memories of that eighth person, your present persona, though they have to be false. But you can't change your fingerprints, odorprints, bloodprints, eyeprints, brainwaveprints, all that declares that you are still Jefferson Cervantes Caird, the Tuesday cop, and all those others, Tingle, Dunski, Repp, Ohm, Zurvan, and Isha-rashvili. The personae you changed, but the body . . . you're no Proteus."

"Until you told me about them, showed me all those tapes," he said, "I'd never heard of them."

"That seems to be true," she said. "*Seems* is the operative word here."

"For God's sake! I've been under the mist many times, and you've also monitored me with blood chemistry and brainwave tests, or so you said, and you haven't found the slightest indication I'm lying."

"But there is no William St.-George Duncan in the records. Therefore, there is no such person. We *know* who you are . . . were, I mean. And . . ."

She leaned back, her wrists on the edge of the desk. Her glare had softened to puzzlement.

"I'm authorized to tell you that the official opinion is that you may be unique. May be. They're not sure there aren't others who're also able to resist the truth mist."

He smiled, and he said, "That must really panic them."

"Nonsense. It could, let us say, ripple the fabric of society, make things uncertain for a while. But it won't shake our society to the roots of its being. It'll just take some flexibility to adapt."

"The bureaucracy, which is the government, doesn't have flexibility," Duncan said. "Never did; never will."

"Don't be amused. You'll be subjected to a long and intense experimentation. It may be emotionally painful for you. It'll determine if you *are* resistant to the mist. And, if you are, why."

"Well, at least that'll put off the time to stone me."

She leaned forward again. Her elbow was on the desk, and her chin was in her hand.

"Your attitude bothers me. You're so cheerful and unafraid. It's as if you expected to escape—soon."

Still smiling, he said, "Of course, you asked me if I planned to escape?"

"Yes. That bothers me even more. You stated that you had no

plans, that you knew no one could break out of here. That . . . I can't believe that."

"You have to."

She stood up. "Interview is over."

He also rose, his long lean body straightening like a jackknife.

"You showed me some of the interrogation tapes. I don't know what this elixir is you asked me about. But it must be something apocalyptically important. What is it?"

She paled slightly. "We believe you know full well what it's all about."

She called out, and the door swung open inward. Two big men, uniformed in green, stood in the hall, looking through the doorway. Duncan walked toward them. Just as he was going past her, he spoke out of the side of his mouth.

"Whatever it is, you're in danger just because you know about it. See you next Tuesday . . . if you're still here."

There was no point in scaring her, because she was only carrying out her duties and had not been brutal to him. But it gave him some satisfaction to threaten her. That was his only way to strike back. Though it was a small way, it was better than none.

As he walked down the corridor, the two guards behind him, he wondered where his optimism came from. Logically, he should have none. No one had ever, not ever, escaped from this place. Yet he thought that he could do it.

He passed along the hall on the thick light-green carpet, seeing but not taking in the sea- and mountainscapes the TV strips showed on Tuesday's walls. Near the end of the silent and empty hallway, he was halted at a command from one of the guards. He stood while the other guard punched the code on the button-panel by the door. The guard made no effort to keep him from seeing the sequence of numbers punched. The code was changed once a day, and, sometimes, in the middle of the afternoon. Moreover, a TV eye was on the wall opposite the door, and the human monitor downstairs also had to punch in a code before the door would open.

The guard stepped back to allow Duncan to enter. Though

the escorts carried no weapons, they were skilled in martial arts. Even if a prisoner could overcome two men, he still would be locked in. Both ends of the hall were closed with doors that could only be opened through the same procedure that opened Duncan's door, and his every step would be monitored.

"See you tomorrow," Duncan said, meaning next Tuesday.

They did not reply. Their orders were to utter only commands to him and, if he should try to give them information of any kind, to shut him up. A kidney punch, a blow in the solar plexus, a chop on the neck, or a kick in the testicles would stop him. That such treatment was illegal would not bother them.

The door slid out from wall recesses behind him. He was in a room thirty feet long, twenty wide, and ten high. Shadowless light had come on as he entered. The floor was thickly carpeted, and the walls were lined with monitoring and entertainment strips. At the north end was the door to a bathroom-toilet, the only unmonitored room. Or so he had been told. He suspected that he was watched as closely there as elsewhere. Near that door was the bedroom entrance. That room held one bed suspended by chains from the ceiling.

Along the west wall, starting from the north wall, was a row of seven tall grayish cylinders. Each had a plaque on its base and a circular window three-quarters of the way to the top. Behind all but two windows appeared faces and shoulders. They were motionless as stone. In a sense, they were stone. The molecular motion in their bodies had been considerably slowed. Result: they were "stoned," in a state of suspended animation.

Tuesday's cylinder was empty because that was Duncan's. Wednesday's was also vacant. Its occupant was gone, probably because he had been taken to a warehouse and stored away or because he had been released. The man had been there when Duncan had come here. This morning, when Duncan had been destoned, the man was gone. Next Tuesday, Duncan might find it occupied by another patient. For *patient*, read *prisoner*. The empty cylinder was one of the things Duncan had been hoping for. It could not, however, be used as yet, though it must be used tonight. It was now one o'clock in the afternoon.

Duncan pulled a chair up to the huge round window in the middle of the outer wall. For a while, he more or less amused himself by watching the pedestrians, the cyclists, and the electrically powered buses. At two, the sky became hazy with thin clouds. By three, it was shut out by the dark gray clouds. The newscaster predicted rain by seven that night and said that it would last, off and on, until past midnight. That pleased Duncan.

Later, he watched two programs. One was about the early life of Wang Shen, the Invincible, the Compassionate, the greatest human of all history, the conqueror of the world and founder of modern civilization. Another hour was filled with Chapter Ten of the series titled *The Swineherd*. This was *The Odyssey* of Homer dramatized from the viewpoint of Eumaios, Ulysses' chief pigtender. Its main tension derived from the conflict between Eumaios' loyalty to his king and his fierce resentment of his lowclass station and his poverty. Though it was well done, it was spoiled for Duncan. He knew that swineherds in Mycenaean times had high prestige, and a reading of Homer's works would reveal that Eumaios was anything but poor or without authority. Moreover, in that era, it would not have occurred to anyone to resent his allotted place in society even if he disliked it. Also, many of the actors looked very unlike ancient Greeks. A viewer who did not know the story or could not understand English might have mistakenly guessed that it was about the first contact between Europeans and Chinese.

Duncan had no idea how he knew that the play was historically inaccurate. It was just part of his memory and without attachment to any recall of teacher, book, or tape.

After sitting for two hours, Duncan did his exercises. Though he had earlier put in an hour of running and swimming in the institution's gymnasium, as required by law for prisoners, he had been alone, except for two guards. Though this was definitely illegal, the authorities had ruled against his having any chance to talk to other inmates. The reason was obvious. He must not pass on knowledge of the *elixir*. Yet the only thing he knew about that had been told to him by his psychicist.

After somersaulting across the room in many directions, Duncan assumed the lotus position in the center of the carpet. He closed his eyes and passed into a state of transcendental meditation, or so the monitor would be assuming. Actually, he was going over and over his escape plans. After an hour of that, he walked around the room for thirty minutes, then watched a documentary on the current restoration of the Amazon basin from desert to jungle. That was followed by a half-hour show depicting the horrors resulting from the latest drilling to reach the earth's core. Four such holes had been successful, and the heat tapped was being converted into thermionic power. But the drilling equipment for the Dallas project had been destroyed in an eruption of magma, molten white-hot rock. Two hundred workers had been killed, and the magma had spread over fifty square miles before halting. Fortunately, the comparatively few inhabitants of the county had been safely evacuated. The city of Abilene in next-door Taylor County was no longer threatened.

At 5:30, he watched an hour of news, most of which was devoted to the meeting of the All-Days World Government Council in Zurich, Switzerland, the capital of the world government.

After that, he went to a panel in the wall near the southwest corner and pulled out his supper tray. This had been inserted from the hall outside the room. He placed the tray in a destoning cabinet box, turned on the power for a second, opened the door, and withdrew the tray. It went into the microwave unit, and he took it out and set it on a table by the window. While he ate, he looked at the street through the window. Rain was beating against it; there was not much to see except the boat-shaped blockhouse across the way. Most people, like him, were dining, and the rain would have discouraged shoppers, anyway.

From about midnight of today until six in the morning, Duncan had slept. The morpheus machine ensured that four hours of sleep were enough for his body and mind, but he had set the alarm for later because he had no need to get up earlier. Now, though he did not feel tired, he went to bed anyway. If events went as he hoped, he would require a lot of energy. He placed the band holding the electrode to his forehead around his head, closed his eyes, and was voyaging into a sea of dreams. Most of them, though pleasant, were about people whom he did not know yet felt that he had somehow known long long ago.

At eleven-thirty, he was rocketed midway from a wet dream into lonely and dry reality. He got out of bed sluggishly, stripped off the covers, sheets, and pillowcases, put them into another wall panel, and showered. Feeling somewhat better, he left the bathroom. By then a wall strip was flashing and clanging, notice to him to get ready for stoning. Throughout the city-state of Manhattan, throughout this time zone, the warning was sounding.

Clad only in shorts, very aware of being watched by the electronic eyes, he walked to the window. If the rain had stopped while he slept, it had started again. Two men and a woman, blasted by rain and wind, were hurrying bent over along the sidewalks. The street lights were flashing bright orange.

Now and then, lightning curdled the night. Thunder must have been keeping it company, but the thick walls and windows shut it out. Within his mind were also thunder and lightning, though a physician would have described them as a storm of electrical impulses, hormones, and adrenaline, among many million other interactions, excluding that of the brain. Duncan, however, would have told you that he considered himself to be, not a robot, but a human being. The son of the sum was more than the whole.

Now, he tensed. A fist seemed to be squeezing down on his heart. Looking calm (at least, he hoped he did), he walked to the Tuesday cylinder. He opened its door outward, knowing that a red light would be flashing on the panel before the monitor stationed on the first floor of the building. That would notify the monitor that the prisoner was about to enter the cylinder. However, the monitor was responsible for twelve rooms. Not all of these might be occupied. Duncan hoped that all were. The more the monitor had to watch, the greater the chances for Duncan to fool him.

He shut the door on the Tuesday cylinder. Now, an orange light would be flashing. All the monitor had to do was to look at the screens showing the interior of Duncan's rooms. If Duncan was outside the cylinder, the monitor would send guards up to make sure that Duncan was put into the cylinder.

The next few seconds decided whether Duncan would get away with his plan. He strode to the Wednesday cylinder, grasped the handle of its door, swung it open, and stepped inside. Then he shut the door and crouched down.

Several things could be happening down in the monitor room. The man at the station could be bored and not paying much attention. His eyes could be elsewhere than where they were supposed to be. He could have turned his head during the brief time that Duncan had strode from the Tuesday cylinder to Wednesday's. He could be talking to other monitors. Duncan had a dim memory of having been in that room more than once, though he did not remember who he was then or when he had been there. Probably when he had been Caird the policeman, the organic. The psychicist had mentioned that name.

Whatever was going on down there, Duncan knew that he would find out very quickly. If—oh, he hoped not!—the monitor was carrying out his duties, he would be closely watching the twelve screens. He would notice that Duncan was trying to pull a fast one. Within two minutes, guards would open the door of Wednesday's cylinder. Like it or not, he would be thrust into Tuesday's.

No light would be flashing on the panel for the cylinder Duncan was hiding in. That cylinder was Wednesday's business. When its personnel took over, a button would be pressed to switch monitoring to that day's circuits. Thus, the monitor now down there would not be notified that someone had entered the wrong stoner.

Duncan thought, the wrong one is the right one for me.

At least two minutes passed. By then the stoning power had

been automatically applied within Tuesday's cylinder. If he had been in it, he would be unconscious now, every molecule in his body slowed so that his body was the hardest substance in the universe. In that state, he could be hurled into the sun and sink to its center, and he would not melt in the slightest.

OK, he thought. Now the monitor has seen the light indicating that I'm stoned. He'll scan the twelve screens and make sure that none of his charges are hiding in the bedroom. He'll also press a button that will activate a mass detector to make sure I'm not in the bathroom. I hope he doesn't look closely at the windows of the cylinders to be certain there's a face behind Tuesday's. He might do that. Duncan was counting on the carelessness borne of yawn-making routine.

He began counting the minutes. When five had passed, he knew that his deception had worked. For the next fifteen minutes, he would be free to do what he wanted to do. The city was stoned, out of its gourd in one sense. His monitor and the guards had entered their cylinders, and it would be twelve minutes at least before Wednesday's came out of their stoners and took up their duties.

He had some extra time. The lights for this cylinder would not be on. Wednesday's monitor had no reason to check out this room.

However, Duncan wanted to get out of this place before today's citizens were awake. He had to be long gone, relatively speaking, before people appeared on the streets.

He stood up and pushed the door open. He stepped out. He felt strange because no one would be watching him. He was free of the ever-watchful eyes, but, at the same time, no one cared about him. He was really alone.

"You have to be nuts," he muttered. "Here you are, you've gotten what you wanted, and yet you're feeling panicky."

Conditioning, he thought. He'd been conditioned to feel that he was safe as long as the government was watching him and making sure he didn't harm himself or anyone else.

There was no time to ponder the implications of the irrational. He began the hard and heavy work needed to get him out of this room—if indeed he could get out of it.

The cylinders were paper-thin because they were made from paper. They, too, had been subjected to stoning power, and their molecules were also slowed in their motions. Hence, they were heavy. He uncoupled the power connection to the cable coming up from the wall behind Wednesday's cylinder, and he began wrestling it toward the big round window. He had to reach up and grip the edge of the top and lean it toward him. Not too far because then it would topple, and he would have to jump out of the way before it crushed him. Once it was lying on its side on the floor, he could not lift it upright again.

He rolled the tilted cylinder a few inches to his right on the edge of its round base. Then he rolled it a few inches to the left. Each maneuver got the cylinder about one inch toward his goal. Roll this way. Roll that way. Meanwhile, the wall chronometer flashed ever-increasing digits. Time, he thought, while he grunted and groaned, sweat coating him. Time was the greatest of the inevitables. Also the most indifferent of the indifferents. Perhaps Time, capital time, was the real God. In which case, it should be worshiped, even though it would be ignorant of that and uncaring if it knew.

At last, panting, eyes stinging with salt, he settled the cylinder on its base. He walked away from it to the end of the room. Now he could see where its end would strike if it were to be toppled eastward. He cursed. Its arc, the curve described by the top of the cylinder, would not strike the center of the window. Cursing because he had cursed and so wasted breath he needed, he ran to the cylinder, got behind it, pushed until it was tilted slightly toward the wall, worked around it, got his shoulder under, gripped with both arms and rolled it slightly. His muscles yelled at him to take it easier. He puffed and panted but got the cylinder a few inches forward.

Another run to the southern wall got him the perspective he needed. He smiled, though wearily.

Ten minutes left before the city came to life.

Actually, Manhattan was not entirely asleep. There were a few civil servants, police personnel, fire fighters, ambulance drivers, and others who were authorized to be destoned earlier than the rest of the city. These, however, would be few and not near, and they would not know that an outlaw daybreaker was on the loose.

On the loose!

His smile reflected his knowledge that he was not as yet free. And, if he did get out of this place, he might not stay long out of it.

Though he needed to rest, he had no time for it. After going to the west wall, he set his back to it, against the area in front of which Wednesday's cylinder had been. Then he crouched like a runner, his right heel against the base of the wall.

The starter's pistol went off in his head, and he was up and running. A few strides and he leaped high, his torso falling back. Both his feet struck the back of the cylinder near its top. He shouted at the same time as if his expressed wish would somehow aid his weight to topple the cylinder.

He fell back, rolled, and landed on all fours.

He turned around. He groaned. The cylinder might have leaned over from the impact of his feet, but it had not been enough. It stood upright, not showing in the slightest that it had been disturbed.

He rose slowly. The lower part of his back felt as if it were about to have a spasm. If that happened, he was done for. Forget the plan. Say good-bye to all hope.

He walked swiftly to the bathroom and ran cold water into a glass. Having drunk that, he walked just as swiftly to Thursday's cylinder. With a mighty effort that took him five minutes, he rotated the cylinder away from the wall and at an angle toward the one by the window. When he had it lined up with that stoner, he rested a minute. Four minutes left before the island came alive.

Friday's cylinder took another five minutes to get to the exact place where Wednesday's had been. Now he had three cylinders in a line. One near the wall. One halfway across the room. One a few feet from the window.

The labors of Hercules were nothing compared to mine, he thought. And the ancient strong man had a lot more muscle and a lot more time to get his work done.

The pain in his back told him that he might not have any time left. It was now one minute past time for destoning for Wednesday. He was behind schedule. This was, however, no time to push his body. Like it or not, failing or succeeding, he had to repair the damage. Slowly, he eased down on hands and knees while the back muscles quivered and burned. When he was on his back and was staring at the ceiling, his legs stretched out, he closed his eyes. Immediately, he went into the state of mind he called SEARCH. He had been training himself so long in this procedure, five to ten minutes at a time, two hours at others, any spare time he had (or so his memory told him), that he had only to think out the code letters. They hung in his mind like curiously shaped comets in a dark sky. When the last of the nine digits were there, he felt himself sliding down, down, shooting in and out, turning sharp bends in his body. It was like riding down a convoluted and murky tunnel, a safety chute.

Then he was flying through more darkness, but somewhere below him were enormous dully glowing blocks. His back muscles.

No time today to do more than say hello to the latissimus dorsi, the lumbar fascia, the serratus posterior inferior, the rhomboideus major, the infraspinatus, and all their close allies and friends.

Pain, hot and savage, struck him across the lower part of his back. It lasted for a half-second and was gone. Sweating even more, he rose. His muscles, for the moment at least, were in superb condition, violin strings ready to pour forth the music of Beethoven or his favorite composer, Tudi Swanson Kai.

His room was quiet. In other rooms in this building and in thousands of other rooms throughout the city, there would be noise. People, just destoned, getting ready for Wednesday, their seventh part of the week. Many of them would at once go to bed to sleep under the influence of the morpheus machine before rising to get ready for whatever time their work shifts started. In this building, the first shift would be sitting down to eat. Some of them would breakfast in front of their monitors, eating and at the same time watching the prisoners. His room would be unmonitored. It was possible, though, that a prisoner would be brought in and assigned to this room. That did not seem likely to happen immediately.

Outside, it was still dark. Rain struck the window. There would not be many people out on the streets as yet.

He went behind Friday's cylinder, put one foot against it, and, his back against the wall, worked his way upward. When he was opposite the top of the cylinder, he was in a fetal position, his knees against his chest, the bottoms of his feet against the cold gray substance of the stoner. Then he began straightening his legs. His face twisted with the effort; the cylinder started slowly, very slowly, to lean outward.

Suddenly he was falling. He slid back against the wall, turned, and landed on his side. That jarred him, though not so much that he could not get back on his feet at once. By then Friday's cylinder had struck against the back of Thursday's. Advancing in a short but heavily weighted arc, it struck Thursday's on the upper fourth of its height. And that, as he had hoped, tilted Thursday's and sent its top crashing into the back of Wednesday's upper quarter area. And that sent Wednesday's leaning, and it kept on leaning, and its upper front edge slammed into the center of the great round window.

The plastic window shot out of the incised retaining area in the wall like a retina detached in an airplane crash. It screamed when it did so, plastic rubbing against stone. The tumble of the three cylinders was as loud as the fall of the temple pulled down by Samson. The floor shook three times and vibrated like the earth in a quake. Rain spat through the opening. Now, he could hear the thunder.

He wished desperately that he had been able to do all this

before destoning time. The people in the building might not hear the fall of the cylinders, but this side of the building would have shaken considerably. It would take them some time to track down just where the vibrations had originated. A time that should be all he needed. Even so, it would have been far better if the opening were not to be found until much later in the day.

He picked up the mattress he had taken from his bed and shoved it through the round hole. The rain cooled his face. Leaning out of the opening, he saw by the streetlights and yardlamps that the mattress was lying somewhat canted on the bushes at the base of the building. The bushes would bend beneath the mattress and soften the impact of his fall. He climbed into the large O of the opening, gripped its sides, and leaned out. He felt as if he were in a spaceship's airlock and about to venture onto a little-known but undoubtedly dangerous planet. Gauging the distance to the mattress, he leaped.

2

He landed on his back, and the mattress and the springlike bushes absorbed the energy of the impact well enough. Unhurt, he crawled out of the bushes, stood up, and waited a few seconds. Rain soaked him, and the lightning lit up the yard so that anyone coming up the walk to the building could have seen him. No one was there.

He was the first ever to get free of the building. Now, he would find out if he could be the pioneer to escape entirely.

He shoved the mattress behind the crushed bushes and dropped the plastic window behind them. He plunged into the bushes as he saw a car stop by the curb. A man and a woman got out and, heads bent under their umbrellas, ran up the sidewalk to the front door. The car pulled away. Duncan walked slowly through the yard to its northeast corner, turned onto West 122nd and walked toward the Hudson River. He strode along as if he had legitimate business. Any organic patrol car going by would stop, though. Bareheaded, without raincoat, he would look suspicious.

He got to Riverside Drive West without incident, though a few pedestrians and cyclists did look at him. He slanted southward to go around the tip of Grants Park, a long narrow pile of rocks and dirt covered by trees. Grants Tomb had been destroyed during the first great earthquake of an obmillennium ago and never rebuilt. He crossed under the high pylons of Riverside Drive West and entered Riverside Park. It took him a few minutes to get to the bank of the Hudson River. First, he had to climb a long high flight of stone steps to get to the top of the dike that kept the river from flooding Manhattan. The sea level was now fifty feet above the lowest point of the island, and the polar ice caps were still melting.

The top of the dike was at its narrowest a hundred feet across. He crossed it and went down a flight of many steps to the dock area. The larger buildings were store and office areas for the commercial boat companies. Between them were small boathouses for private citizens, mostly government elite. He went into the closest, found a rowboat, opened one of the doors, and rowed out onto the river. The rain was as heavy as before, and the current angled him far down to the opposite shore. When he reached it, he was tired and cold.

He had to drift along high banks for an hour. Meanwhile, the rain ceased, and the clouds began to disappear as if by fiat of Mother Nature. Begone. You've had your fun.

There were also more boats out, magnetohydrodynamically powered electrically driven vessels pulling or pushing long strings of barges, and some early fishers. They could not see him, but he could see their lights.

When he came to a comparatively flat place, he beached the boat, got out, and shoved it away with an oar, after which he threw the oar into the water and plunged into the forest preserve of the state of New Jersey. The upper third had been set aside as a national park, and there were perhaps a hundred thousand people in the whole area. Seven hundred thousand counting all seven days' populations. These would be mostly forest rangers, zoologists, botanists, genetic engineers, organics, trades- and service-people, and their families. There were some farmers, here and there, though these lived close to the villages.

Now that the clouds were gone and the thunder and lightning had ceased, the monitor satellites would have a clear view. Not of him, though, as long as he stayed under the trees. These dripped cold water on him, and the bushes and the rising and lowering of the ground hindered fast walking. After some blundering around in the dark and scratching his face and hands on thorns and bark, he found an overhang of rock. He crawled as far back under it as he could and slept badly, waking often, shivering. Dawn found him also hungry.

He left the shelter and went southward, or toward what he thought was the south. For the first time, he thought of the chance that he might starve. He was a city man and knew nothing of wilderness survival techniques.

By the time that he could see the midmorn sun through openings between trees, he was warm. That helped him feel better somewhat, but his hunger and tiredness more than canceled that. He decided that he should go eastward toward the coast. That increased the chance that the organics might see him. On the other hand, he might find a village or a farm and be able to steal food.

Ten minutes later, he flattened against a tree. Something green had moved across a gap between two trees, green against the blue sky and the darker green of the leaves. Though he had only glimpsed it out of the corner of his eye, he thought that it had to be an organic aircraft. It made no sound, and the occupants would be listening to very sensitive sound detectors and watching the monitor screens of their infrared detectors. They would also be using a dogsnose machine, a device that could detect one out of a million molecules flying off a human body.

The craft had been moving eastward. It was probably making large circles and was probably in communication with other nearby organic vessels. This manhunt would be far larger and more determined than most. He did not know why he was so very important, but his sessions with the psychicist had convinced him that the government considered him to be so.

He slid around the trunk of the tree to keep it between him and the searchers. He did so very quietly. The directional sound detectors would have to be zeroed in at the narrow area he occupied. And there were numerous bird calls interfering with the sound reception.

He jumped, slightly startled, when a crashing noise came from behind him. He turned. Had the organics landed and were they now coming after him? His heart beat hard. Then he forced himself to relax a little. They wouldn't be making that much noise. Something big and careless was moving through the forest. A moment later, he saw it, though briefly. It was a huge black bear ambling, swaggering rather, unafraid of anything. The beast showed on top of a hill a hundred feet from where Duncan stood. Then it was gone, concealed by the heavy vegetation.

He hoped that the organics had identified it and were moving on to another area. Anyway, he was going to follow it. Maybe the hunters would think that he was another bear.

He had just stepped out from behind the tree when he saw, again out of the corner of his eye, the green bulk overhead in the gap. He moved back quickly, clung to the trunk, and peered around it. The craft had stopped, and he could see its long needlelike shape and the two men sitting in it. It looked much like an Eskimo kayak except that the cockpits were larger and much more open. Seeing the emblem on the fuselage, he sighed with relief. It bore the brown symbol of the forest preserve department, the ranger's hat, Smokey Bear's, used by all the days. The two were probably tracking the bear through the transmitter attached to its collar. He had not seen the collar, but he understood that at least half the bears in the area had been anesthetized and then fitted with a collar and transmitter.

That did not mean that these two were not dangerous to him. The organics had undoubtedly radioed the rangers and told them to be on the lookout for him. It was even possible that they had been drafted to join the search.

His sigh of relief was followed by a sigh of anxiety.

Then he felt better. The vessel was moving away.

He did not move away from the tree at once. It was possible

that their instruments had shown some body heat even though he was behind the tree. They might be pretending to go on but actually hoping they could draw out whomever or whatever was behind the tree.

He counted sixty seconds and walked toward the hill. He still was going to track the bear. Bears were always hungry and knew where to go to find food. He was even hungrier than the bear and did not mind sitting down to lunch with it. As long as he did not sit near it.

When he reached the top of the hill, he found a pool of rain water in a depression in the ground. He drank deeply from it before continuing the trail. That was not hard for even a city dweller to follow. There were, here and there, pawprints in the mud and bent bushes or pieces of fur caught on thorns. Duncan envied the bear. It did not care whether or not anyone knew it was here; it did not worry about being caught. It cut a swath through the woods as if it owned it. Which, in a sense, it did.

The bear had gone over the hill and down a rather rugged slope. Duncan kept from falling by hanging on to bushes or bracing himself against trees. Near the bottom was a wide creek, and beyond that was a steep bank that gave to a wide meadow slanting upward. Duncan stopped halfway down the hill when he saw that the ranger craft was hanging about fifty feet above and to one side of the bear. One of the occupants was photographing the bear with a small camera.

Duncan waited behind the tree, drawing his head all the way behind the tree when the camera swung toward the hill. The bear was standing almost body-deep in the water near the shore and was watching the water intently. Suddenly, its right foreleg moved, and a fish, caught by the paw, rocketed out of the creek and landed on the shore. Making piglike noises, the bear waded out of the water and began eating the fish. It was sizable, perhaps a foot long. No fisher, Duncan did not know what species the fish was, but he was sure that it was very edible. Just now, he felt that he could eat it raw.

Having devoured its prey, the bear went back into the water.

Five minutes passed while the bear and Duncan did not move. Now and then, the cameraman would sweep the forest. He would stop sometimes, perhaps to zoom in on a bird. Two antlerless deer came down to the stream about fifty yards to the south. After eyeing the bear, they drank daintily and then disappeared into the greenery.

Venison would be a better meal, Duncan thought. However, he did not have a knife. In any event, he doubted he could ever get close enough to a deer to use even a club.

Presently, another fish was scooped out of the creek and was flopping on the shore. After eating that, the bear ambled across the water, swimming at one point for about ten feet. It walked slowly out of the water, its black fur clinging to the skin, shook itself, drops flying like pearls in the sunshine, and then it veered to the left into the bushes. The ranger vessel turned and flew northward.

Duncan knew that a monitor satellite had its cameras pointed at this area. Anyone in the open would have been photographed and the pictures transmitted to the organic headquarters in Manhattan and in the state capital of New Jersey.

Duncan wanted to cross the creek. He had no intention of doing so unless he could find a place where he could make the transit under thick cover. He went back under the large trees and made his way slowly through the bushes and brambles. Following alongside the creek, he walked uphill and down for approximately five miles. He heard many birds, saw some, and also glimpsed a few animals, a raccoon, a red fox, something gray that disappeared quickly, and a large rabbit that watched him, its nose wiggling, until he was about thirty feet away, then hopped into the bushes.

He thirsted, yet he could not drink. Nowhere was there enough leafy overhead for him to get to the creek without being observed. A satellite straight above him might not photograph him, but the swarm poised above the atmosphere would have some placed so that they would take angle shots. It would make no difference if he crawled out and kept his head down. Anyone unidentified would bring the organics, the "ganks," to the location shown.

His belly was rumbling with hunger, and he felt slightly light-headed. He was sweating even in the comparative cool of the shade. His mouth was dry, and the pebble he was sucking did not bring forth saliva after the first few minutes.

Perhaps they might find him someday, but he would be bones gnawed and scattered by the beasts.

When he saw, through a small opening in the branches, that the sun was at its zenith, he sat down with his back against the trunk of a huge sycamore. He closed his eyes to think about his situation, to consider any way of getting to the creek that he might have overlooked. When he awoke with a start, the sun was no longer shining straight down. He rose, his body and legs stiff, and walked on. After a while, he saw the sun again. At least two hours had passed since he had leaned against the tree. He did not feel rested, and his body lusted for water.

Just as he was thinking about getting a drink and to hell with the consequences, he heard something that made him stop in midstride. It was a low rumbling, no, a deep droning. It sounded like a dynamo, a rapidly rotating generator of elec-tricity, in the distance.

Whatever was making the sound, it had to be a machine. No animal, as far as he knew, would utter such a sound. However, there were some strange beasts in the preserve, products of genetic engineer—biologists. In any event, he was not going to ignore it. His curiosity was too much for him, even though the noise might come from something dangerous to him.

He slipped from tree to tree, moving slowly so that he would not make a loud noise in the bush. The humming or droning came from the northeast and away from the creek. Presently, it became so loud that he was sure that he was near its source. When he looked around the side of a great cottonwood, he was surprised. The dynamolike sound did not come from a machine but from the rapidly moving lips of a man. He was seated cross-legged under the branches of a tremendous oak.

He was naked and rather fat, big-paunched. His skin was a light brown; his head, large and round. The broad cheekbones were topped by slightly Mongolian eyes. His hair was black and fell behind his back and over his shoulders. He was staring straight ahead, but if he saw Duncan's head he gave no sign of awareness.

Duncan stepped back behind the tree and listened. After a few seconds, he recognized the content of the droning. "Nam-myoho-renge-kyo!" Over and over, so swiftly that only someone who had heard it before would know what he was saying. The man was uttering the phrase which the Nichirenites, a Buddhist sect, chanted to put themselves into phase with the Bud-dhahead. The phrase ensured good karmic cause and got rid of the bad karma.

Or so Duncan remembered, though he did not know where he had gotten this information.

However, though the huge man's hands were held together, palm to palm, opposite the chest, a large crucifix dangled from the string of beads attached to it. He wore necklaces from which were suspended a seal of Solomon, a crescent, a tiny African idol, a four-leaved clover, a four-armed, fierce-faced figurine, and a symbolic eye on top of a pyramid. Jewish, Muslim, Voodoo, Irish, Hindu and Freemasonic.

The droning ceased. A few seconds passed. Then the man began chanting in Latin, a language Duncan recognized though he could not read or speak it. Duncan eased down behind the tree and listened. He also considered the implications of this man's presence and his exotic garb, or lack of it, and his be-havior. Whoever or whatever he was, he was not a gank or ranger. Those professions were barred to the religious. The government did not prohibit the worship of any deity, but it certainly did not encourage it, and it did make it difficult for those who followed any religion.

The man could be a worker of some sort, perhaps on a nearby farm or ranger or biological station. He might have sneaked away to practice his obviously rather eclectic faith.

After a while, the Latin chant was succeeded by a Hebrew chant. And then, while Duncan grew thirstier, hungrier, and more impatient, and also angered at some large flies that bit him savagely, he heard a different sort of chant. It sounded somewhat like the Hebrew but was throatier and harsher. That must be Arabic.

"To hell with this!" Duncan muttered. He rose and walked around the tree trunk. There was a slight pause in the chanting when the man saw him, but it picked up again. He kept his gaze on Duncan.

Duncan stopped a few feet in front of the man and looked down at him. In turn, the chanter fixed his eyes on the area of Duncan's navel. Duncan inspected the man, his hugeness, the folds of fat around his middle, the sweat filming the brown skin, the hairless chest, breasts which were large enough to be a woman's, the bulging belly with a glinting jewel stuck in the bellybutton, the enormous penis, the dirty feet, the pale green eyes, surprising in so dark a man, the slight epicanthic folds, the long thin nose, slightly bent at the end, the hairy ears, the redness under the black of hair when a sun ray suddenly struck through the gap overhead.

Suddenly, the man raised his right hand from the beads holding the crucifix and gestured swiftly to the base of a cottonwood about forty feet away.

Weirdness in the wilds of New Jersey, Duncan thought. He walked to the tree indicated while the man changed his Arabic to some language Duncan did not know but suspected was West African. In which case, it would be Swahili, the tongue all sub-equatorial Africans now spoke.

3

By the side of a half-exposed tree root was an area of loose dirt. Duncan dug the clods aside with his fingers and revealed the side of a canvas bag. He lifted the heavy container, opened the flap at the top, put his hand in, and felt a smooth cold vessel. It was a metal canteen, which he did not hesitate to open. After all, the man had in one gesture told him to be his guest. The only trouble was that, when the cap came off, Duncan smelled whiskey, not the water he had hoped for. He groped around in the bag for another canteen, found none, and drank. He had to have some kind of fluid.

Great God!

The liquor burned his dry throat and brought tears that he had thought his dehydrated body could not give. But it also gave him a sense of not caring and a giddy optimism. And then a desire for water twice what he had had a second before.

A smaller bag offered him cheese, onions, and bread. He ate half of all but the onions, hoping that he was not abusing the man's hospitality by so doing. The food eased the choke of whiskey and shrank the hollow in his stomach. His ache for water was even stronger.

He turned, and the man, still not looking at him, took his hand from the beads and finger-stabbed at somewhere past the tree. Duncan, dazed though wondering why he was so obedient, walked past the tree. After wading through some waist-high bushes and being raked by thorns, he came close to the edge of the creek. Here was an opportunity that he would not have seen if he had kept to his original course. A great tree growing close to the bank had been uprooted and was lying across the stream. Here was a bridge above which arched other branches, which formed a canopy. Here was the place for which he had been looking all day. He smiled, threw up his hands, croaked, "Ah! Thank God!" and got down on all fours. Crawling, he went down the sloping bank by the northern side of the many-rooted trunk and into the water. He drank greedily at first, then forced himself to stop. After a few more sips and submerging himself to the waist in the cold water, he crawled back into the forest.

Coming into sight of the man—the chant was now in another language—he stopped. A chill not caused by his recent dip rippled over his skin; an icicle formed on the eaves of his belly. Sitting on top of the man's head was a male cardinal, a feathered clot of blood. It darted glances around, then flew off. Immediately after that, a male deer walked into view, stopped, saw Duncan, but did not run away. It trotted up to the man, poked its wet black nose into the man's ear, licked his face once, and then bounded away.

What have we here? Duncan thought. A latter-day Saint Francis of Assisi?

The man, who had been chanting in some harsh language, suddenly became silent. He dropped the crucifix, which swung slightly back and forth, slipping on the thick sweat over his chest, then stopped. After crossing himself, he stood up. Reared, that is, his body seeming to rise and rise like a creature from the black lagoon films. Fully erect, he was at least eight feet tall, making Duncan's six foot seven inches pygmyish. Weighs 450 or more pounds, Duncan thought. A monster. A lion of a man. The behemoth and bull of the woods.

"Can you hear the music of the trees?" the man said in the deepest voice Duncan had ever heard.

"No, can you?" Duncan said. The man was certainly awesome, but Duncan was sagging-tired and his thirst and hunger were still unslaked, and he also was afraid of no man. At least, that was what he was telling himself.

"Certainly," the man boomed. "At this time of day and with the present weather conditions, it's in D Major. Allegretto."

Duncan grinned and said, "Are you always this full of shit?"

"Haw! Haw! Haw! Hoo! Hoo! Hoo!"

The laughter was like the bellow of an enraged bear, its effect softened by the big smile. The man held out a hand and enfolded Duncan's. The grip was strong but not too much. No show of domination here.

"Shake, friend. I surmise you're a fugitive from what the government calls justice?"

Duncan said, "Yes, I am. And you?"

He felt as if this were unreal. He was on a stage with some very strange sets and an exotic character. He was playing a role without a script, improvising.

What most surprised him was that the man seemed to accept unquestioningly that this stranger was an outlaw on the run. Wasn't he wondering if he could be an organic pretending to be a fugitive?

It was also possible, Duncan thought, that this man could be an organic pretending to be an outlaw so that he could catch the real outlaw.

"I'm William St.-George Duncan. Wanted very much by the government. I'm a danger to you because they're looking for me."

The man was striding toward the bag under the tree. He turned his head and said, "I'm Father Cobham Wang Cabtab. Padre Cob, for short, though there's nothing short about me."

Returning with the bag in one hand and a giant sandwich in the other, Padre Cob spoke with his mouth full. "What's your day?"

"Tuesday."

"And you escaped. . . ?"

"From the Takahashi Institution in Manhattan."

The giant's bristling black eyebrows rose. "A famous first. I'm

interested in how you did it, but I'll hear that later. Come with
me, Citizen Duncan. Or may I call you William?"

"Bill will do."

"Too common. How about Dunc."

"Fine."

Padre Cob lunged toward the north, and Duncan followed
him. When the man stopped to drink deeply from the canteen,
Duncan caught up with him.

"Where we going?"

"You'll find out when you get there. Stay by my side. I don't
like to talk with my neck screwed around like an owl."

For all he knows, I could have a transmitter planted under
my skin, Duncan thought. But then, for all I know, he could,
too.

As they followed a curving path around bushes, Duncan said,
"What's your day?"

"Thursday originally. Now it's Thursday to Thursday. As God
and Nature want it."

"Human beings are part of nature. Anything they do is natural. It's impossible for anything in nature to do anything unnatural."

"Well put," Padre Cob rumbled. "No argument. So, I'll say
that daykeeping is bad for humans. How's that grab you?"

"Right around the testicles of my mind," Duncan said.

Padre Cob chuckled, or made a sound that might have been a
chuckle. He stopped and held a hand up. Duncan halted. By
the priest's attitude, Duncan could tell that he was also to be
silent. He could hear only numerous bird cries, the loudest of
which were from crows or ravens. Perhaps these were disturbed
by the same thing that had caught Padre Cob's attention.

Presently, something dark-reddish appeared briefly between
two trees in the distance. Straining, Duncan heard a crashing. It
sounded like a big and heavy body moving carelessly through
the bush.

"OK," the giant said, softly. "It's a bear. If it comes this way,
get out of its sight."

"It'll attack?"

"Not while I'm with you. But I don't want it to see us. Some bears have been fitted not only with transmitters by the rangers but with tiny TV cameras. What the bears see, the rangers see. They see us, the ganks'll be here pronto."

The sound lessened and died. "Maybe its camera saw us, maybe it didn't," Padre Cob muttered. "Maybe it didn't have a camera. We'll proceed as if it didn't. *As if.* The bread and butter of human beings. We live by it."

Duncan did not ask him what he meant by that. Facts, not philosophy, were the meat, at that moment, anyway, of the present. Bread and butter were for leisure times.

"May I ask where we're going?" Duncan said. "And when we'll get there?"

"You may ask, but you'll get no answer."

Padre Cob softened his words with a big smile.

"I realize you're taking a chance with me," Duncan said. "But . . ."

"*As if* and *but.* Two of the eternal verities, humanly speaking. Is there any other way to speak—unless you're a dolphin?"

Not waiting for a reply, which Duncan did not intend to give, the man lurched forward. For a while, the undergrowth was so thick that Duncan had to walk behind the padre, who bent the vegetation under him. Though he looked as impervious as an ancient wartank, he did bleed from the thorns. And, as if knowing what his companion was thinking, he said, "There are paths we could take, but in this area we're better off not taking them. Now and then, here and there, trees along the paths conceal cameras. We know where those recently installed are, but—the eternal *but*—they keep adding them."

Duncan noted the "we" but said nothing.

At about four o'clock, Padre Cob stopped before a dead oak. He reached into a hole about six feet up the trunk and brought out a bag. "A cache." The bag held three canteens, a box that he said held medical supplies, and a bag full of cans of irradiated bread, milk, cheese, vegetables, and fruit.

"I could eat all of this and still want more," Padre Cob said.

"But you and I'll take only half of it. Others may need it some-time."

Duncan marveled at how Padre Cob could find the cache in this, to him, bewildering trackless woods. He did not ask him whether he had found it by memory or by some sign. Duncan doubted that Cob was willing to reveal all his secrets.

When they had eaten and drunk and reluctantly put the re-maining half back into the tree, Padre Cob, after a bearlike belch, spoke.

"We'll push on until dark, then we'll sleep. Up at dawn and onward. Excelsior!"

Duncan groaned softly and said, "Do we walk all day tomor-row, too?"

"We certainly don't ride," the giant said, and he laughed deeply but not loudly.

Then he reached out and grabbed Duncan's wrist. He said, very softly, "Don't move or make a sound."

That warning did not keep Duncan from rolling his eyes upward. Something dark was moving slowly over the treetops. Though he could see only parts of it, he knew that it was an organic craft. Presently, as the patches moved out of sight, Dun-can sighed relief. But Padre Cob, leaning over, whispered in his ear.

"They might be coming back. If they've detected something suspicious, they'll go on. But they'll be back, this time, near the ground. They'll find a place where the plane won't be blocked by the branches, slip through them, and come back close to the surface. They'll have the odor-sniffers on then."

Duncan nodded. Though it was cool in this place, he was sweating. His stomach gurgled. The food there, which had been digesting quite peacefully, was now shot with acid, and gas was forming.

"Sometimes," Padre Cob said, "they come back like a rocket, break through the branches, try to catch us by surprise."

Minutes passed. Everything seemed serene. The birds called or sang. The sound of running water came faintly from the

creek. Duncan breathed easier; his heart was beating at a normal pace.

Padre Cob rose. "It might or not be all clear. We're going on
anyway. If they should make a crash-attack, don't run away.
Charge them!"

Duncan rose. "Charge them with what?"

"Bare hands, my son."

"Are you crazy?"

"More than some and less than others. Just do what I do. You
up to it?"

"I hope so," Duncan said. "If I were in the city, I'd know what
to do. Out here . . ."

"If they're close, there's no use running. You might get a little
distance away, but their sniffers will pick up your odor, and the
mud is so soft they'll see your footprints. Just do what I do.
Follow the leader. Be my ape. You got it?"

Duncan nodded.

Padre Cob smiled and said, "I doubt they've detected anything. But, just in case, be prepared."

They walked on slowly, moving around bushes, stopping now
and then to listen. And then Duncan heard the explosions,
branches bending and breaking. Though he wanted to dive for
cover—where?—he did not. He looked at Padre Cob, who was
looking upward and to Duncan's right. Then he saw the needlelike vessel, painted in green-and-brown camouflage bands,
heading through the branches for the south. Where he and the
padre had been, not where they were. He glimpsed the two
men sitting, one behind the other, in open cockpits. They wore
light-green uniforms and helmets. Then they were gone.

"They'll be back!" the giant said.

He began running along the trail they had taken. Duncan
sped after him, though he thought that Padre Cob was not
acting rationally. After running, crashing noisily through the
bushes, for about a minute, the giant stopped. Duncan almost
ran into him.

"Behind that tree!"

Padre Cob jerked a thumb at a cottonwood to his right. He wheeled and ran to an oak about twenty feet from the tree behind which Duncan had hidden. The giant, seeing Duncan's head, mouthed silently, "Do as I do!" He tapped his chest with an enormous finger.

The organic craft had gone to the place where their detectors had first zeroed in on Duncan and Cabtab. Or so Duncan assumed. Now, it was moving above the trail taken by the outlaws. Its keel was just a foot above the ground. As soon as Duncan saw the needle nose appear, he withdrew his head. The big tree trunk would, he hoped, shield his body heat. The sniffers might pick up his odor by the tree, but they might not be able to distinguish that from the traces on the trail.

If this craft was like some others he had seen, it would be armed with large proton-accelerator guns. The two men would be carrying stun-sticks and small proton-accelerators. Moreover, they had probably radioed in for backup.

The nose of the vessel, moving at about five miles an hour, thrust into his line of vision. He moved back around the tree. A bellow startled him. He jumped, then ran out from his concealment. Cabtab had shouted, which meant that he was attacking. The bellow, designed to freeze the two organics, was also Cabtab's signal to Duncan.

By the time that Duncan reached the craft, Padre Cob was on the back of the craft and his arm was around the pilot's neck.

Duncan leaped up just as the man seated in front of the pilot turned. His hand was pulling out a proton pistol. It fell when Duncan slammed his fist against the man's jaw.

The fight was over. The pilot, his face blue, was slumped unconscious. The other man was lying against the side of the cockpit, his head lolling. Then the vessel slammed into a tree trunk.

4

Cabtab did not let go of the pilot, but Duncan shot out of the cockpit backward and hit the soft earth heavily. His breath knocked out, he gasped for a few seconds, then rose unsteadily. By then, the padre had unbelted the pilot, dropped him onto the earth, and was now doing something with the controls. The craft, its nose only slightly dented, was drifting backward. Duncan stumbled after it. Before he could get to it, it stopped.

Cabtab seemed to be enjoying himself. He was grinning, but he spoke somewhat harshly to Duncan. "Get that man's weapon!"

Duncan turned, chagrined because of his oversight, and rolled the pilot over. The man's face was still blue, but he was breathing. Despite the pain of his left hand, Duncan removed the gun from the holster and shoved it inside his belt. He searched through the pockets of the man's jumpsuit and found two charge-holders. These he put in his pockets.

Padre Cob had now taken the other organic from the plane and laid him out below it. "Hell of a punch you pack," he said. "I think you broke his jaw."

"I almost broke my hand, too," Duncan said.

"Action and reaction. Exchange of energy. Always some loss of energy during the procedure. Where does all the lost energy go? Into some kind of elephant's graveyard?"

Duncan ignored that. He said, "What's the situation? I mean, what do we do now?"

"I've turned off all transmitting equipment," Cabtab said. "I've also erased all the recordings. But it's safe to bet that these two didn't radio in that they were going to try to take us by surprise. We might've had a receiver and listened in on them. But the transmitter has been on continuously so that HQ can know its location at all times. I've turned that off. That means that other craft'll be on the way to find out what happened. Too bad we had to do this. No other way out, though."

Duncan gestured at the two bodies. "You're not going to kill them?"

"You want me to?"

"No."

"Good! I'm against all killing, all violence except as a last desperate means of self-defense. Although I must admit that I feel great just now! Exhilarated! The old ape is enjoying himself; he's been caged up too long."

Duncan said, "It did feel good. Striking back . . . I mean."

By then the pilot's face had almost regained a normal pinkish hue. He groaned, and his arm lifted.

"Get in," Cabtab said. "We're going to put some miles between here and there."

Duncan climbed up by means of a folding step into the front cockpit. "Belt up," the padre said. Duncan, however, was already pulling the retainer across his chest. "You know how to fly one of these?" Cabtab said.

"Yes, I do. But I don't remember being instructed."

"Here we go."

The craft lifted to six feet above the ground and then eased forward. Presently, it was going at about twenty miles an hour. Cabtab steered it around the trees, coming closer than Duncan liked but never touching them. After about twenty minutes, the

craft slowed and sank close to the earth. The two got out. Cabtab, standing by the vessel, set the controls. Duncan, watching
him, realized a second before each setting just what Cabtab was
going to do. Somewhere, sometime, he had learned all about
this kind of organic machine.

Cabtab said, "There! Go, little bird, and decoy the hawks!"

The craft lifted, pivoted, and headed back. Its sensors sent it
around tree trunks, forcing a winding course. It was soon out of
sight.

Cabtab said, "We've got about three miles of footing it. Follow
me."

He went to the left. The sound of running water became
louder. When they came to the creek, which ran over piles of
rocks for some distance, making a shallow rapids, they were still
under the cover of the branches. These extended halfway out
over the water, on both sides. There was a gap in the middle
over the creek, which they avoided by walking close to the right
bank. Ankle deep in the water sometimes, other times knee
deep and, once, waist deep, they waded northward.

"They might pick up our traces where we got out of the
plane," Cabtab said. "But they won't know if we went up the
creek or down. By the time they pick up our trail, if they do, we
should, I hope, be long gone."

"If they catch us before then," Duncan said, "what's your
policy? You shoot at them or give up?"

"What do we plan to do?" Cabtab called back. He said,
"Oops!" as a foot slipped on a rock. He went down on his
knees.

"Shoot," Duncan said.

The giant, wet all over, got to his feet. "Shoot it is. I escaped
once and so did you. Once, I think, is about all you can expect.
God, Allah, Jahweh, Buddha, Thor, et alia have blessed us a
single time re escaping. But if we're stupid enough to get
caught again, they will no longer smile upon us."

They did not speak until they came to a small tributary on the
right. Cabtab turned up this and walked for a half-mile. Most of

the way was covered by interlocking branches. When it was not, they hugged the most heavily screened bank. After sloshing for a mile and a half, Cabtab stopped. He pointed at the bank, which rose to about three feet above the water. Here the creek swirled as if it were going into a hole under the surface. This, Cabtab explained, was exactly what was happening.

"There's a pipe four feet in diameter below the bank. It catches a lot of silt and mud, and we have to clean it out every few days. But it's open now. You'll have to hold your breath for about thirty seconds. You first, Gaston."

Evidently, Cabtab did not trust him not to make a break for it. That was all right. Duncan, in Cabtab's place, would not have trusted him either.

He got down on all fours, the water up to his neck, and launched himself downward. His fingertips felt the inside of the cold pipe. He pushed himself forward and dogpaddled, entirely submerged. His head kept bumping into the hard pipe, which, it seemed to him, must slant downward. Suddenly, he was half-out of the cold water and in an airy but dark chamber. He stood up slowly, his hand above him so that he would not bump his head. He could only straighten up partly until he had walked forward for about ten feet. The pipe sloped upward for three feet, then leveled out. He still could not stand completely upright. Behind him, Cabtab gasped, and his voice boomed and echoed. "Keep going. I'll be right behind you."

Now the smooth damp floor slanted downward, and suddenly his upraised hand had lost the ceiling. Footsteps sloshed and heavy breathing came behind him. "Keep moving," Cabtab said. A finger touched Duncan's back and pushed. He walked, not briskly, until light bloomed around. He was in a room ten feet long and eight feet high, its walls, floor, and ceiling of seamless material. The light came from the material, making the shadowless illumination he was used to in the city. Ahead was a door only five feet high and three feet wide. It had neither doorknob nor handle.

"Stop!" Cabtab said. Duncan obeyed. The padre passed him,

halted before the door, and muttered something Duncan could not understand. Doubtless he was not supposed to.

The door moved sideways, disappearing into the recess of the wall.

Cabtab turned, smiling, his back bent, and said, "The materials are rather recent, but they were placed in an old area. This used to be the hideout of guerrillas during the last days of the conquest of the United States. We had to do a lot of digging and a lot of stealing to get the materials."

He went through the door, ducking, and Duncan went after him. The hallway ran straight for twenty feet and then curved to the left. Its floor angled gently downward. After sixty more feet, they were in front of another door. This was taller than the first. Cabtab still had to stoop, though Duncan could straighten up, the ceiling two inches above his head.

"These were not made for us moderns," Cabtab said. "Our ancestors were mighty warriors but little fellows."

"Why haven't the ganks detected these hollows with magnetometers?" Duncan said.

"Oh, they have, they have," Cabtab said cheerfully. "But this whole area is honeycombed with these underground dwellings and forts. The organics know they're the legacy of the armies and the guerrillas of the old days. They've dug into some for archaeological purposes. Most of them, though, are under two thousand years of accumulated dirt and forest growth. Many are partially filled in where the ceilings collapsed. We've done some redigging and rebuilding here and there, now and then. By we, I mean not just us, the moderns. There have been many generations of outlaws here."

He turned and muttered something, and the door slid sideways. Duncan followed him into another hallway, which also curved and sloped downward. The air was fresh, which meant that some kind of ventilation was provided. He could see no vents in the wall and could hear no moving machinery.

"Ah, here we are!" Cabtab said. He stopped before what seemed to be a wall, the end of the tunnel. "We are being observed, of course," he said. He spoke a string of nonsense syllables, a code, then said, "They know me, but we have to go through the ritual anyway."

He chuckled. "Who knows? The ganks might capture me and then send my clone to get in here. Or I could be an angel—or a demon—which has assumed my appearance for good or evil."

Duncan did not know if he was jesting or not. As far as he knew, cloning had been made illegal a hundred subyears ago. However, he knew that the government was not above breaking one of its own laws. But a clone seemed like a lot of trouble and expense to go to just to capture a few daybreakers. Besides, it would take thirty or more subyears to grow from a baby to Cabtab's present age, and by then Cabtab would be an old man or dead. Yes, the padre was kidding.

The door opened and revealed a brightly lit large room. Just beyond the doorway were a man and a woman. She was short, no taller than five feet eleven, dark, very thin, young, and somewhat pretty. The man was about Duncan's height, middle-aged, fat, big-paunched, black-haired, brown-eyed, and big-nosed. Both held long knives, though these were not raised *en garde*. The man moved close to them, and Duncan wrinkled his nose. He was long overdue for a bath and clean clothes.

Cabtab introduced them. "This is a recent jailbreaker and daybreaker whom I fortunately met and rescued. William St.-George Duncan. Dunc, this is Mika Himmeldon Dong and Melvin Wang Crossant."

"Pleased to meet you," Duncan said. The two smiled, though coldly, and nodded.

"Well," the padre said. "Now for the truth mist."

Duncan said nothing. He had expected this. He followed the giant down the hallway while Dong and Crossant trailed him. They went into a small and sparsely furnished room. Duncan was invited by Cabtab to sit down on a folding chair.

"I won't say make yourself comfortable. But you won't be in it for more than ten minutes with the diluted mist we use."

Time enough to find out all they want to know just now,

Duncan thought. He was happy that the outlaws had gotten hold of the mist. That would ensure that their band would harbor no traitors or double agents. Unless, like him, they could lie after breathing the mist.

He awoke stiff and uncomfortable. The padre, smiling, gave him his hand and lifted him up. "Quite a story, my son," he boomed. "Puzzling, though. You seem to have been more than one person at one time. You also seem to have locked up in you a secret that the government very much wants you not to reveal to the public."

Mika Dong, standing by the padre, said, "That makes you very dangerous to the government." She paused. "And to us.
I don't think the government is going to stop looking for you."

"Am I too dangerous for you to let me stay with you?" Duncan said. He was hoping that she would say that he was not. If they would not keep him, they also would not release him. He knew where they were. That meant that he would be killed or, if they had facilities, perhaps stoned. In any event, he would have to be silenced.

"That isn't for me to say," Dong said.

Padre Cob said, "Pah!" indicating disgust, though with whom or about what he did not explain. He led Duncan, the others trailing them, into the hallway and down it for thirty feet. Then he went into a huge room with a low ceiling. There were a dozen rough-hewn wooden tables and benches in here, several small food-destoners, water-coolers, and some bunks. There were also about a dozen men and women and a boy and a girl about three years old. Duncan was surprised to see the infants. This was a hell of a place to raise children, he thought. Then, It's also a hell of a place for adults to live.

"Welcome to the Free Band!" Padre Cob trumpeted. "Such as it is!"

Duncan had assumed that the giant was the leader. He was so huge and had such a forceful personality that he seemed the most likely to be the chief. Duncan was mistaken. The tall man with the pantherish body and towering forehead above heavy prognathous ridges was the leader. He was introduced as Ragnar Stenka Locks. The Decider.

"Put on some clothes, Padre," Locks said in a soft but authoritative voice. "You look indecent."

"You're just jealous," Cabtab said. He laughed, but he walked out of the room. He was back in a minute wearing a rainbow-striped monk's robe with a cowl.

He grinned at Duncan and said, "Behold the band's Friar Tuck! Or vice versa, initially speaking!"

Locks made the rest of the introductions. There were so many names that Duncan could not recall them all then. The few he did remember were Giovanni Sing Sinn and Alfredo Sing Bedeutung, who told him they were brothers; a ravishing blonde, Fiona Van Dindan, who wore a body-fitting shimmering blue gown; and Robert Bismarck Korzminski, a short and slender mulatto with the longest fingers Duncan had ever seen. The band was composed equally of males and females. However, during the meal that followed shortly afterward, a man came into the room and whispered something in Locks' ear. He left then, though he slowed his step to look at Duncan.

The padre, sitting next to Duncan at the table, said, "That's Homo Erectus Wilde. On duty as lookout."

Duncan choked, coughed, drank some water, and said, "You're kidding?"

"Not his natal name, of course," the padre said. "He took it when he came of age, as is his citizen's right. He's our resident homosexual. He's hoping that you'll be of the same sexual compulsion. Nobody's told him different yet. Let him abide in hope and nourish his fantasies for a while."

Locks rapped a spoon against his glass. When he had silence, he announced, "Wilde reports that there is unusual activity by the organics in this area. He's seen twelve craft patrolling around here so far. One party has landed and is using listening devices. Quite near here."

The silence continued for a while. The two children moved closer on the bench to their mothers.

"No need to be alarmed!" Padre Cob said loudly. "They're looking for our guest, but they must be looking everywhere. They have no occasion to concentrate here. I predict they'll move on soon."

"The padre is right," Locks said. "Now, Citizen Duncan, you say . . ."

Duncan answered his questions as best he could. When the meal was finished, several men and women cleared off the dishes and took them into the kitchen. A TV set was trundled into the room. When the people were finished in the kitchen, the tape of Duncan's interrogation while under the truth mist was shown. After that, he was questioned again by Locks while the others listened. If they had any comments to make, they waited until after he was gone.

Duncan was then given a short tour of the living area and was instructed on what to do if the alarm sirens sounded. Mika Dong, appointed as his guide, explained things in a singsong voice. She never smiled. After a while, Duncan concluded that she still did not trust him. Or else she had taken a dislike to him. Or perhaps she was just a sourpuss.

Probably, it was that mysterious chemistry that decreed, statistically, that in any group of more than seven, one person at least would not like one of the others. Hundreds of tapes had been issued by scholars on this subject, each with its own theory of why this phenomenon occurred. There were thousands of tapes about the other side of this chemistry, instantaneous attraction, but these were much more in agreement about the causes. That, Duncan thought, was strange. Generally, most people could see why it was easier to hate than to love.

He shrugged. Perhaps he was wrong. Mika Dong was probably just suspicious of strangers.

At seven that evening, he went to the gymnasium, a vast room that had been used as an armory during the war. Here, though most of the band played basketball, the padre was lifting weights. Duncan joined him for a while, then, when he saw fencing equipment, stopped. He asked if anyone was interested in the sport and got Locks, the Decider, to test him. Locks was a good fencer, but Duncan scored five out of six points. Locks, panting, finally called it quits.

"You're damned good. Who was your instructor?"

"I don't remember," Duncan said. "The psychicist told me that I'd been a fencing instructor, but I remember nothing of that. In fact, I didn't even think of it until I saw the foils. Then how do I explain it? Something called me. I just had to get a foil in my hand."

Locks looked peculiarly at him but said nothing.

At nine, Duncan showered and then went to bed. He was tired after all his frantic activities and nervous strain; the adrenaline that had kept him going at a high pitch was dried up. He was shown by Homo Erectus Wilde into a large room fitted with bunks.

"A lot of space for just us two," Wilde said. He smiled. "Oh, don't worry. I won't bother you. I respect your rights. I was hoping, though, when you first showed up . . ."

After an uncomfortable pause, uncomfortable for Duncan, Duncan said, "You know my story. But why did you become an outlaw?"

"My lover talked me into it. He was a wild man, unlike me, no puns, please. He hated the constant surveillance by the government. He had some insane ideas about his right to privacy. I went with him just because I didn't want to be parted from him. Truer love had no man. And then . . ."

After another long pause, Duncan said, "Then?"

"The ganks surprised us. I got away. He got caught. So, I suppose, he's a stoned statue somewhere in a government warehouse. I kept hoping he'd be brought to the one close to here, but . . ."

"I'm sorry," Duncan said.

"Doesn't help much."

Wilde began weeping, and, when Duncan tried to say something, Wilde spoke fiercely. "I don't want to talk about it! Don't want to talk about anything just now!"

Duncan went to bed. Though exhausted, he could not sleep for a while. He had many questions to ask about this group. What was their main goal now that they were hunted day-breakers? Did they have any, other than staying out of the hands of the organics? What kind of life did they lead? Where did they get their food from? What did they do when they needed a doctor?

Thinking thus, he finally passed into a state in which he had many nightmares.

5

Duncan's first thought on awakening was depressing. He had escaped from one prison only to enter another. The organics were looking for him and probably would for a long time. That meant that he would be confined here until they quit searching. If they did so. He seemed to be so important to them that they might persist until they found this hideout. Once more, he would be in their grasp, and he doubted that he could ever get loose from it again.

Moreover, the people who had taken him in knew that he was fiercely wanted by the government. Would they finally decide, however reluctantly, to give him to the organics? No. They could not do so because he knew where they were. A spray of truth mist would make him spill all to the officials.

But what if the organics did find him out in the forest—dead? Then they would call off the search, and he would not have revealed anything about them.

That seemed the only logical course for his hosts to take. He could not argue against that.

He thought, I have to escape from the outlaws. The son of man has no place wherein to lay his head. The foxes in their burrows, the birds in their nests, are indeed better off than I am.

By the time he came out of the bathroom—running hot water for a shower, something he had not expected—he was no longer depressed. There was always a way out of a bad situation, and he would find it. Smiling, whistling softly, he walked to the dining room. Before he reached it, though, he was wondering why he felt so jaunty. Logic and its child, probability, were against any optimism. In that case, so much for them. But then he remembered what the psychicist had told him during a session.

"I don't know how you did it, but you created—built yourself, rather—a new personality. You selected, so it seems to me, the elements you wanted for the persona of William St.-George Duncan, and you put them together. You have this buoyant optimism and this belief that you can conquer anything, get out of the most impossible jams. That isn't enough. Belief, optimism, they can't overcome reality."

Duncan had replied, grinning, "But you told me that I don't have any plans to escape."

The psychicist had frowned. "It's also part of your persona that it can hide your thoughts from others. And from yourself when you don't want to know them. That makes you dangerous."

"You just told me that you weren't worried about me."

The psychicist had looked confused and no doubt was. She had hurriedly changed the subject.

I'm somewhat confused about myself, Duncan thought. But what difference does that make as long as my behavior isn't screwed up? Right action indicates right thinking.

Somewhere in his brain dwelt another person who was not one of the seven personae. Or a *part* of himself. It was doing the thinking for him, the thinking needed for his survival, anyway.

All human beings were unique in some respects. He doubted that anybody else had a persona deliberately put together of different character elements and selected memories so loosely, yet vitally, connected to his waking self. Or his dreaming self, too, perhaps. But that persona was not a self-programmed *robot*.

Breakfast was in the big room where he had eaten dinner.
Duncan was invited to sit at the great round table in the center
of the room with Locks, Cabtab, and other leaders. The priest,
who sat by Duncan, still stank of the incense his clothes had
absorbed during mass and several other rituals he had per-
formed early in the morning. He wore a sky-blue robe and
yellow sandals. Duncan asked him how he could blend all the
religions into a harmonious whole and appoint himself as its
vicar.

"No trouble of conscience or logic for me," Padre Cob
rumbled through a mouthful of toast and omelet. "I started out
as a Roman Catholic priest. Then it occurred to me that Catholic meant *universal*. But was I truly universal? Was I not actually
limited, confined by one church, which was not really universal?
Was I not rejecting other religions, all of which and every one of
which God must have founded, put on Earth through the
minds of their founders? Would they exist if the Great Spirit
regarded them as false? No, they would not. Therefore, proceeding both on divine revelation and logic, which have never
before had anything to do with each other, I became the first
truly universal, therefore catholic, priest.

"But I did not found a new eclectic religion. I have no ambi-
tion to compete with Moses, Jesus, Mohammed, Buddha,
Smith, Hubbard, etcetera. There is no competition. I am that
who is. I was officially decreed so by God. Who is higher than
any priest, pope, or what have you. I became the unique
priest. I am elected and entitled to practice any and all religions and to serve God, humbly or proudly, as the case requires, in the capacity of Its, or His or Her if you prefer,
minister."

Someone at the table behind Duncan's sniggered.

The padre did not turn around. He put down his fork, placed
his hands in prayerful attitude, and bellowed, "Oh, God, forgive the doubter his many doubtless sins! Show him or her or it
the error of his ways and bring him into the fold! Or, if you
don't care to, make sure that he doesn't laugh in my face. That
will keep me from knocking him flat on his ass for showing such

disrespect to a man of the cloth! Save me from the sin of wrathful violence, however righteous it may be!"

There was silence for a while thereafter except for the clink of tableware and some loud chewing. Then the padre, having finished his breakfast, said, "Decider, what have you decided?"

Locks drank the rest of his milk, put down the glass, and said, "We'll talk about that . . ."

At that moment, a man walked swiftly into the room, went to Locks, and said something softly into his ear. Locks rose and called for attention.

"Albani tells me that the organics have started drilling just above us!"

Duncan heard gasps and someone said, "God help us!"

"There's no need to get overly alarmed," Locks said. "The organics are probably doing it in many places. They've probably started probing into a number of randomly selected areas where they know underground chambers exist. At least, I hope so. You will gather your flight packages and be here in five minutes. Make as little noise as possible."

Duncan stood up with the others at the table. He smelled the stale sweat of the man Wilde had referred to as "Downwind," Mel Crossant. Duncan turned to see him and Mika Dong glaring at him. She spoke in a low but intense voice. "If it wasn't for you, this wouldn't be happening!"

"Knock that off!" Padre Cob said. "When we picked *you* up, you put us in some peril! Don't forget that! Yet we welcomed you!"

Neither Crossant nor Dong replied. They walked away, though they were talking to each other. Dong stopped once to glare again at Duncan.

The priest, putting a hand on Duncan's shoulder, spoke gently. "They're terrified, so they're taking their fright out on you. Of course, that's no excuse for their despicable behavior."

"I don't think they're the only ones who feel that way," Duncan said. "I regret putting them in danger, but what else could I do?"

"Don't worry about it. We stay together, free or captured. See you in a few minutes."

He strode away, the hem of the robe swaying around his bare massive calves. Duncan sat down. He had nothing to take with him. For a minute, he contemplated deserting by the same route by which he had entered. That would, however, be a foolish self-sacrifice. With the woods swarming with organics, he would be quickly found. That might cause them to quit pursuing the others, but how would that help him? It would not, and he would soon be stoned and forever a statue in some government warehouse. These people had taken him in with full knowledge of what might result from their hospitality. Besides, why should he feel bad because some of his hosts had panicked? They would get over it, and he would go to . . . to do what? He did not know at this time what he hoped to do. Whatever it was, it would be more than just hiding out like a rabbit from a fox. These people might settle for that. He would not.

Brave words. He might have to send them sneaking back to where they had come from.

Presently, Ragnar Stenka Locks returned with a large plastic sack attached to his back and one held by hand. This he gave to Duncan to carry. Shortly thereafter, the last of the band, Fiona Van Dindan, straggled in. Her form-fitting electric-blue gown had been exchanged for a yellow tee shirt and Lincoln-green shorts. Locks told the two children that they must be quiet and do whatever they were told, though their parents had already done this. Wide-eyed and grave-faced, they nodded that they would. Locks kissed them on the tops of their heads and said, "I know you will. You've been through this before."

As he turned away, Duncan, who could read lips, saw him mutter, "Hell of a life for kids."

With the brothers, Sinn and Bedeutung, walking about twenty feet ahead of the band as scouts, they all went down the hallway. Duncan wondered what the organics would do when they broke through into the chambers. They would know at once that they had been recently occupied and would try to

chase the refugees down. Undoubtedly, by then, the outlaws
would be safely hidden someplace. At least, he hoped they
would. He whispered to Wilde, who was walking beside him,
"Does this happen often?"

"Last time was about seven submonths ago. We got away OK,
but they filled in the chambers and halls with dirt for two miles.
It only took us two months to empty them again. Gave us something to do."

After a mile of winding tunnels, their way lit by electric
torches, the band had to get down on hands and knees and
crawl for about a quarter of a mile. This narrow pipe traversed,
they were able to stand up again. The padre, who was the rear
guard, rolled a circular door from the recesses across the entrance. He dropped a bar across it but said, "Won't take them
long to burn through that."

After going down another hallway, they turned to the left and
went down a straight corridor for about sixty feet. Here it
seemed to end; dirt had spilled out onto the floor from the
caved-in wall. Bedeutung and several others used shovels to
remove the wet damp earth for several feet and to reveal a small
round section of wood. Bedeutung pried it open with a little
crowbar. A narrow shaft with a wooden ladder lay under the
trap door. All filed down the ladder, the padre the last to enter.
He had piled dirt around and on top of the door, and when he
closed it above him, dirt, it was hoped, would cover the door.

By the light of the torches, the band went down along a
down-angling tunnel, their shoes muddied by earth mixed with
water. Here Duncan saw the first of the many human bones and
skulls he was to note along the route.

"There were a lot of bones in the area we went through,"
Wilde said to Duncan. "We've cleaned them out, but I think we
should have left them there. They made the areas look unoccupied."

Duncan saw, now and then, masses of rusted metal.

"Arrowheads, swords, spears, proton guns," Wilde said. "The
Americans put up a hell of a fight, but they lost. The under-

ground forts were sealed up and monuments put over them. Outlaws reopened them a long time ago. Most of the monuments above in the preserve have been neglected; you still come across them half-buried, surrounded by trees."

Occasionally, the wall looked as if it had been half-melted. These areas were darker than the light brown of the other areas.

"Flamethrowers did that," Wilde said. He shuddered. "It must have been awful."

They came to the end of the metallic-looking material. From there, a tunnel had been dug through the rock and earth and braced with wooden beams and uprights. This led straight for fifty feet. At its end was a pile of large rocks. Sinn removed some to expose a trap door. Moving air flowed from the shaft, very welcome to the band, who had begun to suffer from the hot, unmoving, oxygen-poor air. After going down a rusty metal ladder, the band passed through a long passageway made up of some rubbery stuff interspersed with hand-dug tunnels. The air, Wilde said, came from a machine connected to a narrow pipe that ran from the tunnel and curved up into a hollow tree. The air-conditioner had no moving parts and was run off a wheel driven by falling water in a nearby natural cave. This did not generate much electricity, but it was enough.

Locks ordered a rest. Thankfully, all sat down except the leader and Bedeutung. These went back down the tunnel. Sinn applied a large disc attached by a wire to a small black box attached to his belt. He listened through earphones for a while, then took them off. "Nothing above that I can hear," he said.

Duncan drank from a canteen he took from his pack. He had no sooner put it back than the earth trembled under him, a roaring came from the far end of the tunnel, and some dust swirled from it. Locks and Bedeutung appeared from the cloud. The leader's teeth shone white in his begrimed face.

"The shaft's plugged up," he said. "They won't be able to follow us."

"Yeah, and we can't go back if the organics block us off ahead," Wilde muttered.

Crossant, sitting close enough for Duncan to smell him, said, "We shouldn't be in this mess."

"Whine, whine, little dog," Wilde snarled. "God, I get tired of your bitching."

"Shut up, you . . . you *it*!" Crossant snarled back.

"Ah, ha!" Wilde cried. "I knew you were prejudiced."

"All of you, quiet!" Locks said.

"Yes," the padre rumbled. "There comes a time when head-knocking is in order, God forgive me for saying so. We have more weighty issues at hand than your childish bickering. Throttle down or get throttled."

Wilde got up and went to a place distant from Crossant to sit down. Duncan followed him. He said, "Dong and Crossant, what's their background?"

"Their story, you mean? Why're they here?"

Wilde chuckled.

"It's not because of political principle. They're petty thieves, well, maybe not so petty. They were Wednesday's citizens, and he was a TV producer, game shows, and she was his executive secretary. Then he got this stupid idea, he's not very bright, to fix it for some contestants to win if they paid him off. Dong was his live-in, and he talked her into collaborating with him. They did all right for a while. The contestants split their prizes with him. Or, if the prize was extra credits, they transferred half of those to him.

"The inevitable happened. Crossant's superior caught on to what was happening. He confronted him and said he'd not turn him in if he and Dong split with him. He also wasn't very bright. Crossant got mad, attacked him, and knocked him out. He and Dong were caught dragging the unconscious man across the roof of their apartment building. They must've intended to drop him over the edge, make it look like an accident. More stupidity. The organics would've used the truth mist on every suspect; in fact, on anybody who was involved in the game show.

"The woman who caught them was the building manager.

She stopped them and then started downstairs to report them. Crossant and Dong compounded their crime by knocking her out. By then it was apparent even to them that they'd gotten in too deep. So, instead of taking their lumps, a trial, a sentence to a rehabilitation institution with maybe freedom in a few years, they fled. We found them wandering in the woods starving and just about ready to turn themselves in to the ganks."

"Why did you take them in?"

"We take in anybody who's on the run. That's our inflexible rule. If it wasn't, they'd not have let me in. I'm not a political refugee either."

"But those two are potential murderers. The only thing that stopped them was being observed in the act."

Wilde shrugged. "Everybody's a potential murderer. *I*'ve thought of killing Dong and Crossant. But, of course . . ."

"Fantasizing murder isn't the same thing as doing it."

"No. But those two were in a peculiar, a unique, situation. They won't be in it again. And, maybe, they've learned their lesson. However, it's an axiom that TV people never learn by experience."

Locks gave the order to push on. Sinn had reported that he could detect no aboveground noise. His detector was not sensitive enough to record the ordinary sounds of the woods, bird calls, people walking on the ground. It could register any drilling.

While they were traveling through the tortuous, sometimes dangerous passages, Duncan had to ask Wilde something that had been bothering him since their conversation.

"Any group, even outlaws, has to have rules and laws for its own organization. What do you do with those who create such dissension that you just can't put up with them? What do you do to someone who's killed someone in your group? What're the punishments for crime?"

Wilde snorted, and he said, "Oh, we do what we so vigorously protest against the government's doing. We stone them."

Duncan said, "Ah!" and was silent thereafter for a long time. Where would the band have access to a big stoner?

6

After passing slowly through a labyrinth of caverns, crawling
sometimes, wading up to their waists in swift-moving, icy, and
numbing water, they entered another tunnel complex. Some
sections of these were separated at their junctions because the
two great earthquakes of ancient times had moved them apart.
This band, or perhaps previous outlaws, had dug through and
shored up the spaces between the ends of the great pipes. After
walking for three hours, they went through a pipe that ended in
another natural cave abounding in stalactites and stalagmites.
Here they stopped for the night. They drank from a small
stream winding Styx-like through the darkness, ate cold food,
and then got into sleeping bags. The floor was rough, sloping,
and hard, but they slept soundly.

Duncan's turn at watch came an hour before the others were
to get up, so he did not slip back into his bag. A half-hour after
renewing their journey, they were back in another cave complex
and wading in a corridor with flowing water up to their ankles.
Wilde explained that the stream had been deliberately diverted
from a cavern creek into the complex.

"The water will remove our tracks and the odor molecules
associated with it."

"But they'll figure we used the stream to do this," Duncan said. "So they'll just follow the stream."

"Yes, but what stream? The flow is channeled through all the side exits along this hall. Besides . . ."

He did not finish. Perhaps that was because he knew that Duncan would soon see what he had intended to say. Before they got to the end of the hall, Sinn turned into a room, and the others followed. Duncan stood with them while his feet became even more numb and blue in the water. Sinn and Bedeutung opened a wall section, revealing a palely lit closet. Its back section swung out to give entrance to another cavern. Beyond a stretch of stalagmites and stalactites, its water looking black, was a small river at least fifty feet wide. The band followed along its course while their feet sloshed and froze and drops of icy water fell on their heads. Duncan's teeth began to chatter.

Presently, they came to a dam made of large rocks over which the stream boiled and whirled. They climbed up alongside it on rocks forming a very rough staircase. Before they reached its top, twenty feet high, they were drenched with water that struck the rocks and soared up and over them.

"God, if we don't die of shock, we'll die of pneumonia!" Crossant muttered.

"That's all right," Wilde said. "You need a bath."

"How'd you like me to shove you into the river?" Crossant snarled.

"I'd loathe even that minor contact with you," Wilde said, grinning.

When Duncan got to the top, he stopped for a moment to wait for those behind. "Who built this dam?" he said to Wilde.

The padre, hearing him, said, "Who knows? Some of the earlier outlaws. Maybe a thousand obyears ago, maybe only a hundred. In any event, we owe them thanks and blessings."

"Why?"

"You'll find out very soon."

Sinn and Bedeutung had gone ahead. By the time the rest caught up with them, they were pulling together on a huge, heavily painted steel lever projecting from a slot in the cave wall. Locks ordered two men to add their weight, and the lever slowly traveled down to the bottom of the slot. While it was descending, the rock floor began to tremble. When the lever was all the way down, the floor was shaking, and a roaring came up from beneath it or someplace close to it.

Wilde, his teeth clicking, his body shaking, said, "Watch the river."

Others had their lights directed on it. Duncan saw the water sinking slowly. After a few minutes, its level was a foot lower and the noise and trembling beneath him had lessened.

"The tunnel complex is now flooded," Wilde said, grinning and shivering. "They won't be able to follow us. In fact, if all goes as we hope, they'll think the tunnels have been flooded for some time. Depends on how close they were behind us."

Duncan thought that the people who had constructed this trap must have taken a long time to do it. They had had enormous patience, had labored hard, and probably lost lives while building it.

"When we go back, we'll lower the buried gates and wait until the water runs out of the complex," Wilde said.

"If we get a chance to go back," Mika Dong said.

"You're just brimming over with high morale, aren't you? It's such a pleasure working with you through thick and thin."

"One of these days . . ." Crossant said.

Locks ordered the band to move on. The children, who had not complained openly but had been whimpering, were now covered with blankets brought from their parents' waterproof knapsacks. Duncan envied them. After ten minutes of wet and slippery passage, however, they climbed down a shaft made of vertical pipes. Rungs secured with rusty screws were spaced along the wall.

"Our forerunners had to carve this tunnel with great care," Wilde said. "They couldn't use heavy equipment because of the noise. It must have taken them a hell of a long time. How they did it without getting caught, we'll never know."

The tunnel went straight for three hundred feet, ending in a room just large enough to hold the band comfortably. Part of it was filled with boxes of supplies and a large black metal box attached to a cable. The cable ran into the rock wall.

Sinn pushed a button on a thick metal plate on one wall. Light filled the chamber. Several opened the boxes and brought out smaller containers, long and flat. They put thirty of these into the large metal box and pressed the controls on its panel. A second later, they removed the boxes to reveal trays full of food and bottles. These were placed, four at a time, inside the microwave oven on a table nearby. Though there were no tables or chairs for their dinner, no one complained. The food was hot and good, and the bottles provided wine and beer.

Duncan, his mouth full, spoke to Wilde. "How did you manage to tap into a power cable?"

"We didn't. The setup was as you see it. Our unsung heroes and heroines did it before we came along."

"But the power loss? Won't it be indicated at the control headquarters? It'll be traced . . ."

"Might be," Wilde said cheerfully. "But the power is taken off the system up there." He waved a fork at the ceiling. "You'll see why the monitors don't pay any particular attention to it."

Duncan decided to be content with this partial explanation. The electric heater in one corner was making him warm, and he was feeling sleepy. After he ate, he put the dirty tray into a large barrel and went into the narrow toilet unit in a far corner of the room. This also used electric power, stoning the wastes. These would be removed from the lower part of the unit and stacked in a corner for later removal.

He slept soundly in his bag and woke on Thursday. Though he was a Tuesday native, he knew that the organics of each day would be continuing the search. The days had a minimum of communication, but his case would demand that Wednesday leave a message for Thursday organics, and they would pass it on to Friday. And Friday would send it on to Saturday and so on.

Duncan was not surprised when a ladder was put up along-side a wall and Sinn opened a section of the ceiling. Sinn, carry-ing his sound detector, went up the ladder and through the opening. Five minutes later, he was back.

"No sign of activity. Looks clear."

The shaft above the ceiling was about forty feet high and so narrow that even if you slipped on the rungs you could brace your back against one wall and your feet on the other. The entire group went up, Duncan seventh from the lead. He came out into an enormous chamber, the ceiling sixty feet above him. Since no one had told him what to expect, he was startled. Thousands of silent figures in hundreds of rows extending as far as he could see stood in the room. Men, women, and chil-dren, lined as if for dress parade, though all were nude, some with open eyes, some with closed eyes. Around the neck of each was a cord from which hung a plaque. These bore the names of the stoned and the ID, biographical, and medical data in code.

Duncan needed no explanations. This was an underground government warehouse that stored those who had been stoned for various reasons. Among them would be people who had been dying of incurable diseases and had opted for stoning. Someday, when medical science could cure them, they would be destoned and given treatment. At least, that was the theory.

There would also be people who had died but had been im-mediately stoned. When the means for resurrecting them and curing them were available, they would be brought out of the warehouse. Or so they had been promised.

There might also be here criminals whom modern science could not rehabilitate. Whenever their particular drives could be eliminated and they would again become good citizens, they would be destoned. That was the officially proclaimed policy.

"This is a comparatively new storage place," Locks said to Duncan. "The oldest here go back to about three hundred obyears ago. We're in the oldest section, which means that no-body comes here."

The air was fresh and moving. No doubt it was electronically filtered, but that had not kept dust from collecting on the bodies or on the floor. The band was making tracks in the dust. Locks, seeing Duncan look at these, said, "We'll smoothe it out before we leave. Meanwhile . . ."

He waved his hand at the men and women running up and down the narrow aisles and at the two noisy children playing hide and seek. "It's not like outdoors, but at least they have room to exercise, and they're rid of the stale air."

Duncan did not feel so buoyant and free. These ranks of the dead—well, most of them were not really dead—which could be brought back to life in a microsecond, depressed him. From somewhere came the knowledge that, the last he'd heard, there were over forty billion of these stoned in such places all over the world. All waiting for a restoration of life and health.

Wilde, smiling peculiarly, said, "No way will there ever be enough medical people and facilities to handle these. And where would they go, where be housed, where get the food, etcetera, if they were cured? Meanwhile, millions more are added every year. It wouldn't matter if we had a different government, one that tried to bring them back into society. No government could handle them, and Earth isn't big enough to house and feed them. They'd all starve to death."

"In that case, forget about it," Duncan said. He turned to Locks. "It's evident that there are no monitors in this area. What about elsewhere?"

"Only the newest part, where the stones are brought in, is monitored. They're digging near that, getting ready to build another storage facility."

Locks grinned. "We're safer here than any place I can think of. They won't be looking for us here because they can't imagine we'd move so close to them. There's a ranger-agricultural-organics village only three miles from here. Come. I'll show it to you."

Before they started, Duncan saw a man, who had climbed a ladder to the ceiling, raise a section of it and go on through. Locks, following Duncan's gaze, said, "If it's all clear, we can go out into the woods. We need to get outside, especially the children."

Duncan, accompanied by the padre and Wilde, went with the chief down the central aisle of what he knew were not statues but could not help thinking of as such. After a mile of walking, they came to a wall. Locks opened a small door inset in one of the enormous closed gates. Beyond it was another facility. This, Locks said, had three subbasements below the main floor. It also held six levels, open on the sides, all containing the stoned bodies. After walking down the central aisle, Locks turned and went through row after row, stopping when he came to an open elevator against the wall. The four got onto it and went to the top of the level. A tall window here gave Duncan a view of the surrounding scenery. Apparently, the upper end of the facility projected from the ground. Below him, the ground slanted steeply a hundred feet, then leveled out and became a plain across which he could see another range of hills about five miles away. These were heavily forested, and there were many groves on the plain. But most of the land was for farming. In the center of the valley was a village of a hundred or so houses dominated by a white five-story building, square, its energy panels shining in the morning sun. Around it was a circular area ringed by white houses with green roofs. Their architecture, however, varied widely. The backs of the houses were on another circular street, across which were the fronts of other houses. The whole village was composed of streets that were concentric circles. Locks handed Duncan binoculars so that he could get a closer view. There were people moving around and in them, several small children playing in the yards, and men and women driving out of or into the village.

Sweeping across the valley with the glasses, Duncan saw at closer range the small farmhouses, the larger barns and silos, and various types of farm machinery moving out over the fields or parked within enclosures. He knew, though he did not know how, that the small houses were not for residency. They contained the computers by which the farmers remotely controlled the robot plowers, seeders, tillers, sprayers, and other machines. When the farmers were through for the day, they would drive back into town. There were, however, near the town, gardens that were the individual property of the farmers.

Here and there were cows, kept to provide milk for the locals and manure for the fields. There were also chickens running around inside enclosures. These were kept only for their eggs. Animals were no longer slaughtered for their flesh; beef and chicken flesh was grown in cloning factories. No doubt there was one here, but it would be underground.

Duncan handed the binoculars back to Locks. "Looks pretty quiet and peaceful."

The Decider smiled and said, "The organics and rangers are all out looking for us."

He pointed at the far hills. "Over on the other side is the intercontinental train line."

Duncan indicated the main road, a shimmering gray ribbon that ran straight through the woods, swerved outside the village, and plunged onward through the farms. "Is that used to bring in the stoned?"

"No. A government dirigible hauls them in. There's a mooring tower on top of this building."

"Could I go into the newest building?"

"Why?" Locks said.

"I just want to get the layout hereabouts. You never know when it'll come in handy."

"For escape, you mean?"

"Not from you," Duncan said. "I mean in case the organics caught us by surprise."

"Of course," Locks said. "Sure, why not? The monitors are set for detecting people trying to break in. They're not the least worried about the occupants breaking out. Though they should be."

They went down to the main floor and then through two gigantic buildings, each of which also contained twelve stories, before they got to the newest facility. Again, they took an elevator. Locks led them into an office complex where they sat around for a while in the most luxurious office. It was seldom used now but was provided with a stoner and plenty of food and liquor in stoned form. Using one of the stoners—these were everywhere throughout the facilities—they activated the normal molecular motion of some supplies and ate seafood, salad, and potatoes and drank beer and wine.

The only thing that kept Duncan from complete ease was the trembling of the far wall and a dull roaring. Locks told him that these were vibrations from the excavation operations near this building. "There's an army of workers out there."

Duncan drank beer and felt more relaxed. He waved his hand to indicate the computer wall screens and the instruction boards on the desks. "Could you use these without setting off alarms?"

"Sure," Locks said. "In fact, that's why I came here."

He swiveled his chair, set down his bottle of wine, and punched on the control board. "Luckily, no code is needed to activate this. The officials never dreamed that any unauthorized persons would be using this. After all, this is a little-populated rural area. Besides, you have to have the code to enter the building. Or so they think. First, we'll start the monitors and see what's going on outside."

Apparently this also did not need a code. He said, "T3C6. Command. Turn on the local area view monitors."

Immediately, the blank walls became screens, and Duncan saw the areas outside of each of the four sides of the facility.

Locks straightened up and said, "Oh, oh!"

7

The western screen displayed a silvery dirigible, its nose down, flying at about a hundred feet above the ground. It was proceeding slowly, its jet engines shining on the southern side, the locking device in its nose open. Duncan could see the tiny figures of the bridge crew behind the viewshield in the upper part near the nose.

"They're delivering another load of stoned," Locks said. He erased the recording of the recent activation and turned the power off. He stood up and said, "Get the trays and bottles. We don't want to leave any evidence behind."

The others followed him out of the office. Duncan said, "What does this mean?"

Wilde replied, "We have to hide for a while. It doesn't take them long, maybe two hours, to unload their cargo. But we'll lie low until tomorrow."

It was then that Duncan decided that he was not going to stay with this group any longer than he had to. It had no future. All they could do was run and hide and steal outdoors for a few hours in the open or into storage facilities. This was a rabbit's life, and he was no rabbit.

Nevertheless, for the time being, he had to be with the band.

Reluctantly, he went back down the shaft into the room at its bottom. He sat down on his sleeping bag, his back against a wall, and sourly regarded the others. This room was crowded, and the children insisted on running around—he couldn't blame them for that and felt sorry for them—and there was little to do except drink and talk. Now and then, he got up and went for a walk down the tunnel to stretch his legs. The third time, he was doing sitting-up exercises in the dark when a light blazed in his eyes. Though he did not stop his situps, he said, "Who's there?"

Locks identified himself. He sat down, saying, "Don't let me stop you."

Panting, Duncan rose and did some rope-skipping without a rope. He said, "I noticed you looking rather thoughtfully at me in the control room."

Locks kept the light on Duncan's face, half-blinding and completely annoying him. Duncan said, "You can shine that away from me and still see my expressions."

Locks chuckled and pointed the beam at the wall. Now Duncan could also see his face.

"You probably think we live a rather useless futile life, right? After all, what do we do except keep on the run? What use are we? We don't like the government, we resent being forced to live only one day a week, and we hate being observed all the time. But what do we do to break the status quo? Wouldn't we be more useful, and also far more comfortable, if we kept within the confines of normal life and used constitutional and legal means to protest?"

Duncan quit exercising and sat down. "Yes, I've thought that."

"After all," Locks said, "just what are we protesting about? Why kick against the pricks when there's so little to kick against? We are citizens of a society that has never existed before, a society in which not only does no one starve but every person has all the food he can wish for. Good food, good housing, good medical service, good educational opportunities. All the luxuries one could reasonably hope for. There is no war and no prospect of any. We're taxed, yes, but reasonably so. The rate of crime is the lowest of any society in history. There's only one lawyer to every thirty thousand people. Racism is dead. Women have full equality. Almost all diseases have been eliminated. Child abuse and rape are rare. The poisonous seas, land, and air our ancestors bequeathed us have been cleaned up. The great deserts are being restocked with trees. We have as near a Utopia as is possible, given the irrationality, greed, stupidity, and self-centeredness inborn in so many people."

"You make a good case for loving our government," Duncan said.

"It was some ancient author, don't remember his name, who said that you should hate every government currently in power. By that, he meant that no government is perfect and citizens should strive to rid government of its flaws and evils. By those, I mean not just institutionalized faults but those people in power who take advantage of the faults to advance their own interests and those who are incompetent."

"Sounds correct," Duncan said. "But is it necessary that the government keep such a close eye on its citizens, never stop looking over their shoulders? Isn't that a quality to hate?"

"Ah, but the government says it's absolutely necessary. It prevents crime and accidents, and it enables the state to ensure peace and prosperity. By knowing what every citizen is doing at every moment of the day—most of the moments, anyway—that he is outside his house, the state has the data to ensure that its citizens are safe and that raw materials and finished goods flow in the proper traffic routes all over the world. It—"

"I don't need examples or a lecture," Duncan said. "What are you getting at?"

"Everyone over twenty-five years of age who can also pass an examination on knowledge of history and political conditions can vote. There are three major political parties and a hundred minor ones. The votes are registered from the voters' homes—"

"No lecture," Duncan said.

"I was just trying to demonstrate that our government is the first really democratic government. The state is run for the people by the people. Or so the government claims. If the people aren't satisfied with the way the state is run, then they demand and get an election so they can change the administrators or change the laws. So the government claims.

"But the people in power control the computers that report the results of the elections. Why is it, then, that for the past two hundred obyears, the voters have always voted to maintain the close monitoring of themselves? Why do so many of the world government officials stay in power? Why is there always a definite majority of votes in favor of these candidates?"

"A lot of people believe that the computers don't give the correct numbers," Duncan said.

"Yes, many do believe that. So many that it seems odd that the majority opinion isn't reflected in the vote tally."

"The government takes polls now and then to investigate just that belief. These always show that there aren't that many people who believe that the results are fixed or that there's fraud involved."

Locks smiled and said, "What's to keep the opinion polls from being fixed?"

"I'm not arguing with you that they are honest. Only . . ."

"Only?"

"What can we do about it?" Duncan said.

"Apparently, nothing. There's not enough desire for reform to cause riots, strikes, a revolution. Maybe over half of the population is convinced that changes should be made and that the present administrators—rulers better defines them—should be ousted. But they don't have any real grievances, not like the ancients did, anyway. Even if they're irked by certain restrictions, why kick a hole in the boat?"

"Why, indeed?"

Duncan was silent for a moment while Locks stared at him. Then he said, "I'm like a newborn who nevertheless has memories of past lives. It seems to me . . ."

He wrinkled his brow and chewed on his lip for a few seconds.

"I wish I could remember why the government is so hot to get hold of me. However, I do remember that I've had doubts about other things than election frauds. One . . . wait a minute . . . now it's coming. The state keeps hammering on the thesis that the earth must never become overpopulated again. No couple is allowed to have more than two children. In view of what happened to the world in former eras, that seems like a very logical and necessary restriction. But a lot of us . . ."

Duncan looked as if he was straining his mental muscles. Locks said, "A lot of people. . , ?"

". . . are not sure that the population statistics are correct. They may be overhigh. If the truth were known, the government might have to allow more than two children, three, at least, to each pair of parents."

"The truth is," Locks said, "at least, my information is, that the present global population is two billion. Whereas—"

"The official statistics say eight billion!" Duncan said loudly.

Locks was not so much shocked that he did not wonder how this outlaw, isolated from the data bank systems, could know this. "Two billion," he said. "What was the second thing bothering you?"

"With only two billion people, there's no reason to maintain the daykeeping system! It should be abandoned. We can all go back to the ancient system of living every day of the week. It would have to phase in gradually, of course. Seven times as many houses would have to be built. Everything would have to be increased by seven, food supplies, transportation facilities, power supplies, everything. It'd take a long time to do that. There'd be a hell of a lot of problems but nothing that couldn't be solved. Then humanity could get back to the natural system, the way of living meant for people. I . . ."

He wrinkled his brow again, was silent for a moment, then said, "It seems to me that I knew . . . somebody told me . . . that the daykeeping system breaks up the circadian rhythm for humans. Whereas people used to sleep eight hours or so a night without a break, now they often have to sleep four hours or so, then get up and get the other four hours as they can. This has resulted in far more neurotics and mental breakdowns than the government allows the public to know. In fact, the crimes of passion, so called, have been increasing for quite a while. But the public isn't informed about that. It's fed false data, and the news media are kept from reporting many of these cases."

"We're guaranteed freedom of the news media," Locks said, "whereas, in fact, we don't have it. But the government is very subtle about its repression. The state has the guile of the serpent, the wisdom of the dove.

"One thing hasn't changed, though. The majority of the population has always been conservative. That seems to have been true from the beginning of the history of government. The daykeeping system has been with us so long that most people regard it as natural. The way things should be. Even if the government wanted to go back to the old system—it doesn't, of course—it would have a hard time convincing the majority that it should be done."

By now, Duncan knew that Locks was not just talking to pass the time. He said, "You're far more than you appear to be, aren't you?"

Locks grinned. "You mean I'm not just the leader of a bunch of scraggly and pathetic misfits? What do you think I am—in reality?"

"I think you belong to an organization that sent you out here as a sort of recruiting agent. And an agent for an underground railroad. If somebody like me comes along, you send him on to . . . I don't know where or what."

"Very good," Locks said. "I'm not going to tell you any more about that just now. You won't be informed until the last possible moment in case . . ."

"I should get caught before you can carry out your plans?"

"Exactly."

Locks rose and stretched. "Yes. See you. Oh, you won't, of course, talk about this to anyone else?"

"Of course."

"Meanwhile, if I can get back to the data bank office, I'll try to find out why you're wanted so badly. If, that is, I think I won't trigger off any monitor alarms."

"I'd sure like to know," Duncan said.

Stiff from sitting, Duncan began exercising again. He was balancing himself on his hands and doing pushups when he saw the blazing eye of a torch down the tunnel. He was upside-down when the light stopped. Crossant's whine came from behind the glare.

"For God's sake, Duncan, what are you doing?"

"Certainly not balancing an eel on my nose," he said. He lowered himself until his nose almost touched the floor, then propelled himself upward with his arms, bent his legs, landed and straightened up. Wiping the sweat off his face with his arm, he said, "And what are you doing here?"

Dong's high-pitched voice said, "Locks told us to get you to help us. We have to bring in some supplies from the cavern."

The light moved closer. He saw something dark and blurry lash out from behind the light, and the light blinked out along with his mind.

He woke up confused, gasping and choking, whirled around in darkness, and, as his senses cleared, he realized he was in water. He swam desperately, not knowing if he was going up or down or horizontally. Something hard struck him in the left ribs. The agony made him choke even more. But he was able finally to cry out just before he was dragged or hurled under the water again. So . . . he had awakened on the surface. Of what? Whatever the kind of stream, the icy water numbed him and made him sluggish.

Despite this, he strove to make his arms and legs move, and he then was above water and gulping air. Not for long. Something knocked on the back of his head, driving him under, causing him to gasp and to take in water. His flailing hands felt hardness above him. Stone. For the first time, he knew that he was in an underground stream and that it was now speeding through a narrow tunnel. His shoulder scraped against rock, something seized him and spun him around, and then, blessed relief, his head rose into air again.

That lasted for a few seconds, perhaps. Violently, he hit stone once more, this time on the right ribs, and he was submerged. He tried to swim upward, hoping that the river would have passed through the tunnel or borne him into a chamber with air above the surface of the water. His hand felt rough stone just before he was sucked down. This time, he had run out of air and hope. A bell clanged in his head; streaks of light seemed to shoot before his eyes; his throat had caved in on itself; he was going to die in a very few seconds.

Abruptly, both air and light were his. He fell out into brightness, burst with the waters from a hole, tried to straighten out so that he would not strike the foaming boiling pool below him in a belly-flop, but failed. The impact of water hurt, and his lungs, which he had thought emptied, whooshed air out. Nevertheless, he rose and swam toward the high bank that had appeared on his right. Carried by the current toward a rapids, he managed to seize the root of a tree projecting from the eroded mud bank and clung to it. Pain and cold had made him as weak as a newborn. The world waiting for him, however, was that of the dead.

While he clung to the root, he looked at the hole from which he had been launched. It was about twenty feet above the pool and near the base of a seventy-foot-high limestone cliff. Beyond that rose the slopes of higher hills, though how far away he could not tell. The stream was hemmed in by clay banks; the forest angled upward sharply. Many of the trees were growing out at a forty-five-degree angle. These, he supposed, were the products of the biolabs.

Wherever he was, he was not near the entrance into which the padre had led him.

He looked the other way. The current a few yards away had carved out a small bay in the bank. The force of the creek was less there, and the bank was about two feet high. Perhaps . . . He let go of the root and swam as fast as he could, not fast at all, to the tiny bay. It took him some time to drag himself up the bank. Several times, the mud loosened in his grip, and he slid back. Panting, too tired to move all the way over the edge of the bank, his feet in the water, he lay in this bent and perilous position for a long while. When his breathing was close to normal, he clawed the rest of the way, pulling his legs up onto the ground. While he rested again, he thought of Dong and Crossant and why they had done this to him.

They were mean-spirited, and they certainly had not liked him. Those were not reasons strong enough to make them murder him. Murder? Crossant had knocked him out and could have broken his skull in with the club if he had wished to do so. Instead, they had dragged him into the cavern complex and pushed him into the underground creek. They must have known that the stream did not go far before it reached the outside. They had counted on his drowning, on the water finishing their dirty work. His floating corpse would be seen by a satellite or by the organics. The hunt would be called off, and the band would be safe, for a while, anyway.

No. His scenario was not quite faithful to reality. Locks would wonder if Duncan had deserted the band. He would become suspicious of Dong and Crossant since he would know that they had gone into the tunnel. He would doubt that Duncan, knowing that he was going back to civilization soon, would have run off and so abandoned the only hope he had to get away from the miserable underground existence. Locks would subject the two to the truth mist.

Knowing of this possibility, they would not have returned to the band. They had gone back into the tunnel complex to hide for a while and wait until enough time had gone by for Duncan's body to be found. Then they would take refuge in the forest.

Or did they intend to come out as soon as possible, let themselves be captured by the ganks and ask for amnesty after having told their story? They might get it, even though they would have to go to a rehabilitation center. After all, they had eliminated Duncan and betrayed the rest of the band. Of course, the organics would despise them as traitors, but Dong and Crossant were used to being despised and, perhaps, thrived on it. Maybe they had done this to him because they had not done anything despicable for a while and needed spiritual nourishment.

He laughed weakly at that thought and wondered if he was getting delirious. However, delirium was usually accompanied by a fever, and he was very cold. He wished he could crawl into a patch of sunlight coming through the branches and warm himself there. The thought that a satellite might detect him kept him in the shade.

He rolled over, shaking, and hugged himself. The wet clothes were keeping him cold. He should take them off. No, he was too tired. His body heat would dry them off. By the time the sun had gone a few degrees—it was now halfway between zenith and set—he would be comfortable and would have regained some of his strength.

Then what?

The woods were quiet except for the far-off cawing of crows and a squirrel angrily chattering at something, probably the crows. After a minute, a large black fly buzzed close to his head. Duncan swatted at it; it zoomed away. A half-hour passed. He closed his eyes and wondered if he would be safe if he slept for a while. His head ached badly where the club had struck him. His ribs pained him, and the back of his left hand hurt where skin had been scraped off. The cold and the danger had numbed him to the injuries. Now that he was becoming dry and warm, he was suffering too much to sleep. Despite which, he was getting drowsy.

At that realization, he forced himself to sit up, groaning from the pain of his battered ribs. Maybe he had a concussion. If that was so, he had better get up and walk. He did not want to die in his sleep.

He started to get to his feet but stopped in a crouch. The voices of Crossant and Dong were coming faintly from somewhere.

8

From behind a bush, Duncan watched the two. They were about sixty feet away, half-obscured by tree trunks, sitting with their backs against a giant dead oak. By their legs were two large packs. No doubt they had picked these up from some cache on their way out. That meant that they might have been planning their flight for a long time. That they talked loudly might indicate that they did not care if the organics did find them. Indeed, they might hope they would.

Though he could hear the voices, he could not make out the words. He crawled to the left, out of their sight, and circled. Moving slowly, half-bent, he got to a bush close behind the couple. He could not see them, but his ears caught everything.

Dong was talking shrilly. "No, I say we look for him. He can't have been carried too far by the creek. We find him, and we stay with the body until we're picked up."

Crossant whined, "That might take too long. For all we know, he's been swept far away. Or . . . well . . . he could've been snagged in the cave. His body might not come out for a long time, if ever. I think it's smart to push on until we're seen. We don't have to have the body as evidence. One spray of mist, and they'll know we're not lying."

"I want to see the son of a bitch dead," Dong said.

"God, you're vicious!"

"Look who's talking! Who hit him with a club?"

"Yeah! And who talked me into doing this?"

"Oh, shut up! Anyway, what's the difference who did what? We're both in it."

"Deep as it comes," Crossant said. "We're in it up to our necks. Which are going to be wrung if they come after us. I say we get the hell out of here."

The *they*, Duncan understood, was not the organics but the outlaws.

The two continued quarreling while Duncan crawled on and around until he was in a position to see them from the front. His eyes widened when he saw the huge hole in the tree a few feet above their heads. That was the entrance through the hollow trunk to a tunnel. The entrance they had used as an exit.

All he had to do now was to wait until they left. Then he would go to the band and warn it. However, Dong and Crossant might be picked up soon. That would bring the organics quickly down on the outlaws. The two should be stopped. How? He was weaponless and weak. They had big knives in sheaths attached to their belts, and they might have proton guns in the packs.

A few moments later, a crashing sound nearby brought both to their feet. Their hands dived into the packs and came out clutching the butts of pistols. At the end of a six-inch barrel was a globe of shimmering white metal.

Dong's voice came faintly to Duncan. "If it's the organics, they'll shoot if they see the guns."

"There're bears and other dangerous animals here," Crossant said, his voice even shakier than hers.

Presently, the cause of the noise appeared. It was a four-legged beast about six feet high, appearing at first sight to be a pygmy elephant. Its curving tusks, however, identified it as a forest mastodon, descended from the product of a bioengineering laboratory. A thousand obyears ago, using mastodon fossil cells as templates, the engineers had grown six hundred of these and released them in some of the forest reserves. It was one of these, soon joined by a dozen others, that faced the two humans.

"Don't panic," Dong said. "They won't attack unless they feel threatened. Just stand still."

She spoke so quietly that Duncan could barely hear her. Crossant said something out of the side of his mouth too low for Duncan to understand.

He was by now working his way back toward the oak. The mastodons might have glimpsed him or they might just have been wary of human beings. Whatever the cause, their leader trumpeted shrilly, turned, and went smashing through the bushes toward the south. The others, also trumpeting, trotted after her. Under cover of the noise, Duncan ran through the vegetation. By the time that the last of the hairy gray beasts had disappeared, he was standing behind the oak. In his left hand was a branch, a thick piece of dead wood.

"Let's get the hell out of here," Crossant said. "Some of them might've had implanted monitors."

"So what?" Dong shrilled. "We want to be found, don't we?"

"Well, I'm not so sure now," the man said. "It's going to be pretty rough for a while. And I was just thinking that maybe they'll decide we can't be rehabbed. You want to end up in the warehouse?"

"Coward! Snivelbrain!" Dong shouted. "Oh, why couldn't I have tied up with a real man?"

"Yeah, and you're a real woman. Let me tell you, bitch—"

Duncan came swiftly around the tree and struck Crossant, who was leaning over to pick up his pack, on the head. Dong had turned away, apparently in disgust at Crossant. One hand was clenched; the other held a gun. She whirled at the sound of the blow and Crossant's grunt. She paled, her eyes wide, and that second of hesitation was long enough for Duncan to strike her wrist hard with the club. The gun fell, and she ran, an arm dangling, into the woods. Duncan started after her, then stopped. He was not up to a short chase, let alone a long one.

He picked up her weapon, adjusted it to extreme long range by rotating a dial just ahead of the trigger, waited until Dong appeared between two trees, and squeezed on the trigger. A violet beam spat. It touched the back of her right thigh, and she crumpled. At this distance, the charge had probably not penetrated deeply. She was up and hopping on one foot but stopped when he shot again. This, hitting where he had aimed, burned a piece of bark from a tree trunk close to her. He shouted, and she stopped, turned, her face white and twisted, then sat down on the earth.

Crossant groaned and started to get to his feet. Duncan hit him on the head again, though not as hard as the first time. After putting Crossant's proton gun and knife in his belt, Duncan walked to Dong. She sat there, silent, her features crumpled with hate and pain. He threw the stick in front of her.

"Use it for a cane."

When they got back to the tree, Crossant was regaining consciousness. His skin, already pale, became even whiter when he realized what had happened.

"Back from the dead," Duncan said cheerily. He took one of the packs, got some bread, cheese, and a can of self-warming soup out, and a spoon. While he ate, one hand near the gun, he did not speak. Crossant broke the silence by pleading that Mika had talked him into doing what he had never wanted to do. Duncan told him to shut up. After finishing the meal and restoring the spoon and empty can to the pack, he said, "Now we go back."

He waved the gun. "You two first. Don't try anything. I'll shoot both of you if just one makes a false move. Or a true move, for that matter."

"They'll kill us," Crossant said.

"Not when there's a stoner handy," Duncan said, grinning savagely. "I heard enough to know that Locks doesn't believe in killing except as a last resort. You'll end up stored with the others in the warehouse. Who knows? You might get lucky. Maybe somebody'll find you two, three hundred years from now and destone you."

"That's the same as killing us," Crossant said, and he groaned.

"Take your choice."

Weeping, begging, the two put on the backpacks. Duncan handed the man a torch and told him to lead into the hole.

"I'll follow with my torch," Duncan said. "Remember, I'll shoot both of you if either one of you tries something. Now, lead on. Downwind."

Crossant wiped his nose with his sleeve and turned to climb into the entrance. Both he and Dong screamed. For a second, Duncan was confused. Then he saw the bearded face of Padre Cob in the hole, looking like a bear just awakened from hibernation.

"Ho, ho, ho!" the padre boomed. "By Saint Nicholas, what goodies do we have here?"

He climbed ponderously out. He was still dressed in the monk's robe, but he carried a proton gun with a barrel a foot and a half long and a large charge chamber. "I thought you might have taken this route," he said to Crossant. To Duncan, he said, "You look as if you'd been chased through the ten hells of Ti-yu. What happened?"

Duncan told him. The padre said, "You're a very lucky man, William. I hope your good fortune rubs off on all of us. Except for these vermin, who are, alas, human, and must be treated as such."

"What does that mean?" Duncan said.

"It means they won't be shot. They'll get a chance to be rescued someday."

It took forty-five minutes to get to the room at the bottom of the shaft. Duncan was surprised to find that it was empty.

"Except for those looking for you, they all went back up there," the padre said. "The latest shipment has been stored, and the airship has departed. All's clear. For the time being, anyway."

Two hours passed before the search parties could be notified that the missing were found and all had returned. There was another delay when Crossant and Dong insisted that Duncan was lying. The truth was, they said, that Duncan had tried to desert and they had followed him. He had managed to sneak up on them and overpower them. They only gained a little time. Locks told them that he would use the mist on all three. Crossant acknowledged then that Duncan's story was not a lie.

"You're pathetic," Locks said. He signaled to the men appointed to carry out the sentence. They seized the two, and forced each, screaming and struggling, into a cylinder. Duncan was glad that the children had been taken away. Even he, the victim, was sick at what had to be done.

The doors were shut, and the padre pushed two buttons on the panel of a console. A second later, the doors were opened. Crossant and Dong, harder than rock now, fell outward, their fists raised before them, frozen in the act of striking against the door windows. They were dragged to the shaft and pushed over the edge. Four men went down the shaft to drag the two into a tunnel.

"We could have put them with these," Locks said, waving his hand to indicate the silent ranks. "But they wouldn't balance. They'd fall over. Besides, who knows? The government might decide to send in auditors. They sometimes do that. We wouldn't want them to find those two. They'd know this place was being used for purposes other than official. And that might lead them to look around until they found the trap door."

Later, when he was able to speak to Duncan with no one else around, he said, "I'll tell you tomorrow some of what we're going to do with you. Provided, of course, you volunteer to do it."

"I'm ready for anything."

"Good! But it's not something we can prepare for overnight."

When bedtime came and the band went down to the room to sleep, Locks was absent. Duncan thought that he must be in the data bank room, completing the operation that had been interrupted by the appearance of the dirigible.

He slept long and, from his stiffness on awakening, hard. He remembered one terrifying dream in which Mika Dong and Mel Crossant, stoned, moving as if on wheels, had come out of a fog and pointed accusing fingers at him. Their eyes glowed as if lit by fire. He rose, groaning, though his headache was almost gone, and cursed himself for the nightmare. Rationally, he should have no regrets, no knifecut of conscience. But he, like all citizens, had been conditioned from infancy to loathe violence. Which did not keep the government, he reminded himself, from using violence in its dealings with criminals. And he, according to what the psychicist had told him, had once been an organic who had killed several people.

Feeling much better after exercise and breakfast, he went with Locks and Cabtab to the data bank office. The Decider turned on the computers and indicated a wall screen. This showed three photos of Duncan, face-on and the right and left profiles. Beneath the photos was the biographical data.

"I want you to look closely at this before it's printed as an ID card," Locks said. "If there's anything you object to or if you see any discrepancy, anything that might cause you trouble, we'll change it before printing."

Ten minutes later, the machine tongued forth a ceramic card.

"It looks valid," Duncan said.

"It is. The data to validate it is in the bank. But if somebody gets suspicious and starts tracking it down, you're in trouble. It'll take time to invalidate it, though."

"So now I'm David Ember Grim."

"Yes. A citizen of the state of Manhattan and a computer specialist, second-grade, who's been on loan to the agricultural complex of Newark, New Jersey. Your application to migrate to Los Angeles has been accepted. Tuesday's Los Angeles is just now receiving immigrants of various ethnic-national mixes from selected states in North America and India. These will replace the fifty thousand being sent to China. You'll be in the twentieth group to go from Manhattan. It's up to you if you want to go express, stoned, that is, or travel on a passenger train. That's slower, but you'll be able to see the country."

"Passenger, for sure," Duncan said. "I've never been out of Manhattan. Until recently, that is."

"You'll have all the documents needed for that tomorrow. It

takes my man in . . . never mind . . . longer to arrange that. You
have two weeks to memorize the details. Meanwhile, we have
several members working on the mystery of why you're so badly
wanted. It's very slow, delicate, and dangerous work. If the data
bankers think it's too touchy, they'll quit the search. Getting
codes isn't at all easy, and it's usually done by corrupting the
code-keepers. That's easier and safer than trying to hack into
them. Relatively safer, that is. It's all dangerous. In fact, we
wouldn't be sneaking in where angels fear to tread if we weren't
convinced of your importance. Something's made the government frantic to find you. Ironic, isn't it, that you don't know
yourself what it is?"

Duncan nodded, and he said, "Two weeks? Obweeks?"

"Obweeks. Fourteen normal-sequence days from now."

"Meantime, the organics are in a frenzy. One of these days
they're going to think of looking here no matter how ridiculous
it might seem to them that outlaws could be holed up here."

"That's a possibility we're considering. But we have to stay
here until the hunt dies down."

"It won't."

Duncan thought about what would happen if Locks was captured after he, as David Ember Grim, had left. Locks would be
subjected to truth mist, would reveal all, and the organics would
go after citizen Grim.

Locks rose from the chair. "Let's take a walk to the new section. I always like to look over the latest consignment. There
might be a candidate there, a recruit. I've not found anyone so
far I've wanted to take a chance on. Still, new faces, new hope."

On the way, Duncan said, "What do you know of the facilities
in that village I saw from the window yesterday?"

"Station NJ3?"

"You didn't say what its name was. Is there a biolab there?"

The three were in an ascending elevator. Locks squinted at
Duncan. "Yes, there is. A rather large one. Why?"

"Do you know the layout? Have you ever scouted it?"

"You've got something up your nose, haven't you? A brain-
bug?"

"Maybe."

"No, we haven't gone near it. Why?"

"Could you get its layout through the data bank? Without rippling any monitor?"

The elevator stopped, and they got out. They were in a room even larger than the one they were living in. This, however, had row on row of open cubes rising to the ceiling, which was at least a hundred feet up. There were elevator shafts between the vertical rows of cubes, and each was occupied by about fifty stonees.

"Yes, it could be done. And would, if the returns were worth the risk."

"If we could get a detailed plan of the building and if it could be entered, would you do it? Provided, of course, that the results might far outweigh the danger?"

Locks moved one side of his mouth. "Well. . . ?"

"It takes about sixty seconds to scan completely a human body and to store the data. That data can be used to duplicate the body. Under special conditions, forced growth, etcetera, a duplicate can be grown in a week. The biologists have never succeeded in making a duplicate that lives more than a day or two. There are always slight flaws in the duplication because the scanner is not perfect. Those many little flaws result in a dead body or one that soon dies. It looks on the surface, skinwise, you might say, just like the original. It's useful only for scientific experiments. It—"

"By God!" Locks said. "I see what you're driving to, I think! You want us . . ." He put his hand on Duncan's shoulder and began laughing. Between explosions, he said, ". . . to make a duplicate of you and then put it someplace . . . oh, my!"

"Where the ganks will find it and will think I died. It'll have to be somewhat decomposed, not enough for the fingerprints or retinaprints to be lost. When they find that, they'll . . ."

"It's a great idea, a wild idea, I should say. It'd be splendid . . . only . . . how the hell could we pull it off? How're we going to get into the lab, and if we do, how're we going to set it up so that the lab people ignore the body growing in their vat?"

"Let me think about that."

"You're serious, aren't you?" Locks said.

"Not until I figure out a workable plan."

"I'll chant for that," Padre Cob had rumbled behind them.

By then they had come to the area where the latest consignment had been set up. Fifty of them stood on the lowest level of a chamber, thirty men and twenty women. Locks took his time looking at the faces and reading the plaques hung from chains around their necks. Duncan walked slowly by them, wondering what had brought them to this state and place. He did not bother to read the plaques. And then he stopped before one. The woman was short, five feet eight inches high, slim-bodied with small perfect breasts. Her short black hair was sleek, reminding him of a seal's fur, and her open eyes, large and brown, also recalled a seal's. The face was delicate-boned, high-cheeked, and triangular.

Duncan bent down to see the inscription on the ceramic plaque.

PANTHEA PAO SNICK.

The lines beneath were in code which seemed familiar but which he could not quite comprehend. They trembled like heat waves on the edge of his mind, shimmerings almost ready to form into definite images. And the face. It, too, shaped something. What?

"Come here, will you?" he called to Locks. "Read this for me."

"You know her?" Locks said.

"Not quite, but it seems to me I should."

Locks frowned. "I can read the ID number. The rest . . . it's in a code I never saw before."

"Isn't that peculiar?"

"Damned peculiar. There's something special about her."

Locks removed the plaque. "Let's take it up to computer. Maybe we can find what it's all about."

But, after the code had been fed into the machine, the screen displayed: ACC DEN.

"Access denied," Locks said, and he turned the machine off.

"I hope that isn't reported. If they get curious because a request issued from an unauthorized site . . ."

Locks asked Cabtab and Duncan to leave. "I trust you, but what you don't know you can't tell the ganks."

Ten minutes later, Locks called them back into the office. He was smiling. "I put in a request through a certain channel, and my contact got some data. Snick was an organic detective-major, a Sunday citizen, but she had a temporal visa to operate in other days. A temporary temporal. That's all my informant could find on her aside from the usual biodata. He couldn't get what case she was working on. But—this is significant—she just disappeared from the bank. Nothing current on her. My informant didn't pursue the search. He was very careful; he didn't want to warn the monitors; he was afraid to push his search too far."

"Why don't we destone her and ask her?" Duncan said. "That's the logical thing to do."

"I don't know she's that important," Locks said.

"How're we going to find out unless she's questioned?"

"I'll think about it."

Duncan decided that, if Locks wouldn't do it, he would.

9

On Thursday, the weather conditions at 11:00 P.M. were just what the band had been waiting for. Having seen the predictions on the TV in the warehouse office, Locks knew that no better situation would be coming again for at least two weeks. He and six others, Duncan among them, were huddled under trees near the edge of the road. The sky was dark except when veined by lightning, and rain fell heavily. From behind the trees, the outlaws could see the pale water-veiled lights of the village, a mile to the north. No vehicle beams were visible. The inhabitants were inside, sleeping until close to midnight when they would rise to enter the stoners or do whatever they wished to do before they must end their activities.

Locks stabbed a finger at the lights and led the others out into the strong wind and heavy rain. Clad in rainproof hats and coats taken from the warehouse, they trudged, heads down, behind Locks. They cut across a meadow, turned left when they reached the road, a four-laner which had very little traffic even in the daytime, and left it after a quarter of a mile. Skirting a copse of beeches, they approached the two-story stone bio-laboratory. The solar panels atop the octagonal building formed a many-angled bonnet.

Locks had obtained all the information about it via his computer informant. The building aboveground formed the living quarters of the scientists and technicians. The work facilities were undersurface. There was no security because there was no need for it, or so the officials had assumed. In this relatively crime-free society and with the isolation and small population, why lock the doors? What was there to steal? Why would anybody dare to thieve when there were so many forest rangers and at least a dozen organics nearby? Nevertheless, Sinn scouted the entrance area. He looked through the door, opened it, entered, and was gone for about a minute. When he came outside, he said, "Coast seems to be clear."

If the data that Locks had received was correct, Thursday's personnel would go to bed to resume their interrupted sleep. At 8:00 A.M. they would descend to begin work. It was possible, however, that some people might come down to work immediately after leaving the stoners instead of sleeping. One or more of them might have an experiment that he could not stay away from.

The seven went down the silent hallway to the stairway entrance and walked down it. The lights came on automatically as they progressed. When they entered the first room, these sprang into hard brightness. Bedeutung was stationed just inside the door, a proton gun in his hand. Locks sent Sinn on ahead to guard the other stairway entrance to this area.

After passing through the large room with its equipment, strange to these laypersons, they came into another twice as large. Locks, a penciled map in one hand, led them by equally unfamiliar and often exotic-looking machines and vats in which animals in various stages of fetal development floated in a clear liquid. They stopped at a corner occupied by a long vat holding only fluid. Near it was a large coffinlike box with a transparent lid.

"That's it," Locks said to Duncan. "Take off your clothes and get into it."

Duncan stripped and climbed into the machine. He lay down

on a soft transparent bed and stared upward. The padre, grinning and muttering the last rites in Latin, closed the lid. Duncan could hear nothing after that. He lay still as Locks had instructed him the day before in the warehouse. Though he could not see Locks, he knew that the man was now adjusting the controls of the scanner near the box. Locks was looking at a paper on which were the operating instructions given to him by his informant.

Abruptly, two machines, one at each end inside the lid, began moving on little wheels toward each other. They met soundlessly in the middle of the lid and backed away from each other. When they reached the ends of the lid, they again rolled out toward each other. Beneath him, two similar machines would be doing the same thing. After the superior scanners above him had come together thirty-five times, Locks tapped on the lid. He made a whirling motion with his hand, and Duncan rolled over on his side. A few minutes later, he turned onto his other side. Presently, Locks opened the lid.

"OK. Get out and dress."

While putting on his clothes, Duncan said, "That's it?"

"That's it," Locks said. "Every molecule of your body in its proper relationship to every other molecule has been recorded. The growth process has already started."

He pointed to the vat in the corner. Something fuzzy and tiny was now suspended in the middle of the fluid. Within an hour, it would be much larger and with a definite shape.

"Thursday will believe it's Wednesday's project," Locks said. "They'll run off the data concerning it and find an order from Wednesday and an officially registered description of the project. Wednesday will get an order that seems to have originated from Thursday. The other days will check up the order and will find that this is Thursday's order. Only Thursday will think that it's Wednesday's."

The whole thing would be blown if somebody checked out the validity of the order. Why should they? The orders were in proper form and and just one in a sequence of the interdiurnal events. Or it would seem to be.

"Let's go," Locks said. "The sooner we get out of here, the better."

Duncan tarried for a few seconds. That thing in the fluid-filled vat would be his near-duplicate in seven days. Sometime near the end of Wednesday, it would look to the naked eye just like him. If it were to be scanned then, the data register would reveal tiny differences, the sum of which would be a big difference. Big only in that the duplicate could not live long because of the many flaws. But, someday, so the scientists claimed, the flaws would be eliminated, and long-lived adult duplicates would result. These, however, posed ethical and philosophical problems the solving of which was for the future—if ever.

Padre Cob was grinning like a kid who had just gotten into the cookie jar. He said, "This bucks up my morale. Now, we're not rabbits. We're rats. Oh, ho, ho, ho! That's quite a promotion, isn't it? Rats, not rabbits. One step up in the band's evolution. But I'd rather be a rat. They have more fun!"

"Maybe we'll be wolves someday," Duncan said.

"Wolves, like everything else, only exist because the government permits them to exist," the padre said. He was frowning; his joy had evaporated.

"What we've done tonight we can do tomorrow on a big scale," Duncan said.

Cabtab smiled again. "Or die like men, not rabbits or rats!"

Duncan did not reply. It seemed to him that it was far more important to live like a man. How you died did not mean much unless it benefited the living.

They returned to the warehouse, hung up their rainclothes, and rejoined the group in the oldest building. Duncan would have liked to share his experiences with those who had stayed behind. They would have enjoyed it and would have wanted to celebrate. But Locks had insisted that the fewer who knew about it, the better. The others had been told that the seven had been in the central computer office during their entire absence. Locks had said that he was just gathering data. If some of the others wondered why so many had to be there with Locks, they said nothing.

The Decider, however, had not entirely lied. Before the party ventured out, Locks had gotten as much information as possible from his informant about the search for Duncan. The news was unsettling. The ring was closing in, and many outlaw refugees had been found.

"The center of this ring is the storage facility," he told Duncan. "Sooner or later, probably sooner, the organics will figure out that we've had the chutzpah to hide here. Then . . ."

"How soon?"

"I don't know. But I think we'd better try to get away on the surface. If we could sneak through the ring . . ."

"If they could find me," Duncan said. "I mean, that body . . . they'd probably give up the search. You're no priority. But do you have the time to wait?"

Locks bit his lip and rolled his eyes. "I don't think so. Under other circumstances, I'd take them out at night and try to get outside the search area before daylight came. We could make ten miles on foot even with the children along. But if any of us got caught, well, they've seen you. And I don't know where we could hide you. If you went with us, you wouldn't be able to get on the train for L.A. It's very important, though not vital, that you do. Also, we couldn't give them your duplicate, and so they wouldn't call off the hunt."

Locks grinned with pain. "The Decider reeks of indecision."

"We can have our cake and eat it, too," Duncan said. "If you want to take the chance, but anything we do is chancy."

He told Locks the plan that had formed in his mind like crystals precipitating while Locks had been talking. They argued quietly for a while, not so much because Locks was against it as to work out the problems. Then Locks, satisfied that Duncan's idea had more possibility for success than the others, called the band around him. He explained what he wanted it to do. There were more arguments and some strong protests. Eventually, after an hour and a half of wrangling, he did what he seldom did. He put it to a vote, and the majority were for Duncan's plan, though many were not enthusiastic.

"Very well," Locks said. "We won't wait until the organics get very close. We'll do it now, take our time, clean up the place and do everything that's necessary."

That unsettled some of the band, and there were more protests. Faced with acting at once, the realization of their helplessness while the scheme was being carried out struck them hard. They could do as Locks wished but surely not right now. Wait a while.

"No!" Locks said loudly. "Damn it, no! We might not have the time to make you look like the others. We have to make us look as dusty as them and put dust on the floor, too. That'll take time and care. We can't predict just when the organics will get to this place. They might come tomorrow. They might get the bright idea that we have come here, and they'll leapfrog, send a unit here."

Though some still grumbled, all obeyed. Duncan went with a crew to haul Dong and Crossant out of the cave and up the shaft to the facility. Then they had the unpleasant task of destoning the two. They were rendered unconscious immediately by squirts of the truth mist and taken to the latest facility. The wheeled robots from the unloading area were used to transport their bodies. Dong and Crossant were laid out on forms that adjusted them so that they would stand upright when they were stoned. The forms were slid into a horizontal stoner, and power was applied. The bodies were removed by the robots' pincer-tipped arms and carried back to the old facility.

Meanwhile, half of the band, chosen by drawing lots, had been stoned by the other half. Robots then placed the rigid and cold bodies in gaps in the rows. Evidently, at various times in the past, some stones had been removed, though for what reason was unknown. Sinn and Bedeutung returned from the ionic rooms behind one end of the facility with bags of dust scraped off the collectors. They proceeded with the delicate job of putting just enough dust on the newly stoned.

"Damn, this is complicated," Locks said. "I hate complicated plans. One step goes wrong, and the whole structure falls down. Simple is best."

"Agreed," Duncan said. "But simple is out."

Padre Cob and the beautiful Fiona returned from the new facility with the ID plates they had made in the new facility. They hung these around the necks of the bodies, and Sinn and Bedeutung blew dust on the plates.

"If the organics are fiendishly thorough," the padre said, "and if they check out every plate against the records, they'll expose the fraud. We'll be sunk."

"They won't do that," Duncan said. "They'll be looking for living beings. They'll know we've been here, no way of covering that up, but they'll think we fled."

By then, Locks and two others came back from the data bank office. The Decider said, "I erased all records of the use of the computer, and we cleaned up the place, wiped off all prints."

When the time came for Locks to be stoned, he put his hands together in front of his chest and bowed. "So long, Bill. I'll be seeing you."

"If all goes well," Duncan said. He shut the cylinder door and pressed the POWER button on the box behind the cylinder. The only living being in the vast and silent building, he got onto the platform on the robot's rear and pushed the button that initiated the program. The long arms of the robot raised as it rolled forward. Its pincers closed on the immensely heavy body of Locks inside the cylinder, lifted it, and withdrew it. Turning its wheels, the robot carried the body to a gap in a row and deposited it standing. Duncan punched the rest of the instructions to the machine. Having already set the timing on the box connected to the cylinder power cable, he entered the stoner and closed the door. For six seconds, he stared out the round window. The robot was waiting. It would open the door, remove him, and place him in the gap in the row designated as SSF-1-X22-36. There he would stand, the fake ID card around his neck, until the robot, per instructions, returned six days from now. It would open the door of the stoner designated SSSF-413B, then go to Duncan, lift him, carry him to the cylinder, insert him, and close the door. That should be at 6:30 P.M. next Wednesday. At 7:00 P.M. the timer on the box would turn on the destoning power. And he would step out and begin the work of destoning the others.

After the machine had put Duncan in the proper place, it would lift the box, full of dust, from the platform in front of it and would sprinkle the dust over Duncan and over the tracks it had made. It would continue to do this until it entered the new facility, where there was no noticeable dust. Before it re-joined the other robots in their storage place, it would put the dust box in a shelf in another storage room.

Duncan was not even aware that the power had come on and he had been unconscious for six days. Eyes still open, he stared out the window at the robot a few feet from the door. Its square green body with the round many-eyed head and whirling an-tenna atop it was advancing now. Its arm reached out, and the door swung open. He stepped out, muttering, "Either it's OK, or the robot is screwed up."

"ZY," he said. "What is the date and the time of day?"

A digital display on the "belly" of the robot flashed: WED D7-W1 MO VAR 7 p.

Wednesday, Day-Seven, Week-One, Month (of) Variety 7:00 P.M.

So, either the organics had not gotten here yet, in which case they might enter at any moment, or they had come and gone. A glance at the many footprints on the floor showed him that they had been here.

Ignoring the dust on himself—the robot had put on too much—he swiftly checked that the others in the band had been undisturbed. He expected that they would, since, if one had been found, all of them would. But he had to make sure. Hav-ing ascertained that they were still standing in their proper places, he walked through the warehouse and through two oth-ers to the new facility. This he went into cautiously, because, for all he knew, the organics could be unloading another shipment of stonees. All was quiet, however, and a swift exploration of the offices showed that these were also unoccupied.

On his way back to the oldest facility, he stopped before the stonee named Snick. What in hell bothered him about her? What made his curiosity rise like undigested food in his throat? The logical answer was that he had known her, and not slightly. Logic then demanded that he revitalize her and find out what was scratching at some door in his mind.

Not now. He had a lot to do in a short time.

10

"They plugged it up all right," Padre Cob said.

He, Duncan, and Locks were standing by the trap door opening onto the shaft. The square hole was filled with a whitish solid substance.

"What do we do now?" the giant said. "Our food supply is gone, and so's our escape route."

"The storeroom has plenty of food," the Decider said. "But if they should make a recheck sweep, we've no place to hide. It won't matter for a while, anyway. We're moving out tonight."

"You changed your mind?" the padre said.

"Yes. We can't stay cooped up here. It's getting on everybody's nerves."

Locks sent four people to destone the amount of food and medical supplies needed for ten days. When they came back, he explained what he had in mind for the band. Some objected because they were exposing themselves to capture.

"Sure," he said. "But when aren't we? As soon as the organics find Duncan's body—his duplicate's, I mean—they'll go back to normal routine. Meanwhile, we'll be holed up elsewhere, and we'll be able to get out into the open, breathe the fresh air, roam the woods, shoot the state's deer, enjoy life day to day as God decreed it."

"Until we get caught," someone muttered.

"That's the dressing on the salad of life," Padre Cob said. "The piquancy of danger. Where else can you get it but in the wilds?"

Later, when Duncan and Locks were in the data bank office, the latter said, "I think time is running out on us. One of these days, one or more of us is going to get fed up with this way of living. We're not as happy as we all pretend, you know, and someone's going to surrender to the ganks. Once that's done, the rest of us won't have long. The worst part of it is that the ganks will know all about you then. The hunt will be on again."

"I know," Duncan said. "But what else can we do?"

Locks had turned off the computer after getting his final instructions from his informant. He rose from the chair and said, "The weather is almost what we ordered. Let's make sure everything's ready and we've left no evidence of having been here."

In two hours, the seven who had made the first raid on the biolab would make the second. Having some time to spare, Duncan went to the new facility and stood for a while before Panthea Snick. Her face was stirring up something in him, a faint pleasure. Behind that, he was sure, was a stronger feeling. Of what? Whatever it was, it could only be determined by awakening her. He was still thinking of this when the group left the new facility. The sharp immediacy of the mission cut out all thoughts of her. He walked head down through a strong wind. As on the first raid, the only lights were those from the building windows. Following the same route, the seven entered the biolab and stationed the same guards as before. Locks erased the data concerning the growing of Product HBD-10X-TS-7° and entered the orders for its removal by Wednesday. Thus, when Thursday awoke, it would find this data in the diurnal-exchange bank. This was limited to those transfers of information which were extremely important.

Wednesday would get a separate order saying that Thursday had removed the duplicate. The danger was that someone might investigate and expose the double entries, but this was not likely to happen. Who in one day cared what the other day did if it seemed legitimate and did not interfere with the smooth operation of one's own day?

By the time that Locks was finished with the computer, the still-alive but unconscious duplicate had been lifted from the vat by the overhead crane, put into a shower to wash off the fluid, dried, clothed, and put into a bodybag. This bag had been brought from the facility because a missing bag from the biolab stores might cause an investigation.

When he looked upon his own not-quite-dead face, Duncan felt somewhat remote, as if both he and the corpse were not a part of reality.

"That's not the face I see in the mirror," he muttered. "It has nothing to do with me."

Nevertheless, he was relieved when the bag was zipped up to the duplicate's nose.

After the fluid that had dripped on the floor was mopped up, two men carried the body out on a stretcher that had been brought from the warehouse. Duncan was the first through the door to the outside because, for some reason, he felt personally responsible for the duplicate. It was as if he was conducting his own soul to hell. Just as he swung the door out, he saw through the window a figure advancing toward him. It was a few feet away, lit by the interior light, vague in the darkness and the rain. Beyond it were some flashing red and orange lights.

The man wore a transparent slicker that was so thin that it could be folded and put easily inside a shirt pocket. It could be opened very quickly by pulling on both sides to break the weak magnetic hold. This took only a second, but Duncan had slammed against the door to open it and had run out by the time the man had the slicker unlocked. The organic also had to unstrap the holster before he could snatch out the proton gun. He was just bringing it up when Duncan's head slammed into his chin. They went over, Duncan on top. He reared up and chopped the man in the neck with the side of his hand. The second blow had probably not been needed; the man was limp and silent.

Locks was by then beside the two. He bent over and said, "What the hell is he doing here?"

Duncan stood up, his head hurting slightly. "He's an organic." He pointed at the small canoe-shaped two-man air-craft hovering a foot above the ground, its lights flashing. "I don't know what he was doing here, but he must have been returning late from a patrol. He saw the lights here and came down to investigate. But he couldn't have been too suspicious or he'd have had his gun ready."

The others had by then arrived. The two men lowered the stretcher to the ground. Sinn said, "What do we do now? This sure tears it!"

The Decider stood while the rain beat upon him, chewing his lip and staring into the darkness as if the answer was walking toward him from the night.

Duncan dropped to one knee and felt the man's pulse. When he rose, he said, "He's still alive." He spoke to Locks. "We could put him in a stoner. He won't be able to tell his story before next Wednesday. By then . . . No, that won't work. He'll tell what he saw, they'll investigate. They'll find out what we did."

Sinn said, "He has to be shut up. Permanently."

"Kill him?" Duncan said.

"Or stone and hide him."

Duncan could see the pitfalls abounding in this idea. He said, slowly, "No. He has to be killed."

There was silence for a moment.

Duncan was the first to speak. "It has to be done. It also has to look as if he saw me—my duplicate, I mean—and went after me and in the struggle we killed each other. And it has to be some miles from here."

"Well," Locks said, "I hate it, but, as you say, we have no choice. However, how will it be explained? What was he doing so far away from here? He surely must have reported in that he was done with whatever he was supposed to do and was heading for home base."

That was easily checked by running the tape on his radio set. Sinn opened the canopy over the front seat of the aircraft, reached in, touched the controls, and started the recording. It was as Locks had said. The organic, Second-Class Patroller Lu, had reported to HQ that he was now coming home. His night probes had failed to find any signs of the refugee Duncan.

By the time that the recording was finished, the organic's arms and legs had been bound and his mouth gagged. Duncan said, "Fortunately, he didn't report the lights in the biolab. Run the coordinates again, Sinn, where he last called in from. The plane has to be found near there."

Locks, his voice lined with asperity, asked Duncan what he had in mind. Evidently, he was troubled because Duncan seemed to be taking over. His inability to see a way out of their predicament must also have made him angry at himself.

"I'll have to fly the plane to that area," Duncan said. "I'll take the duplicate and Lu along. And I'll have to set it up so that it looks as if I—the duplicate—jumped him. I'll have to kill both of them." He paused. "Unless somebody else volunteers for the job."

As he had known, no one wanted it. After a few seconds, he said, "Is that OK with you, chief?"

"It's the best we can do," Locks said. "In one way, we're lucky. We won't have to carry the duplicate for five or so miles in the dark and rain and then walk back. It'll take you a few minutes to get five miles from here. I suggest you arrange this . . . matter . . . near the road. You can follow it back; you know your way from here. We'll go back to the facility. The fewer there are of us outside, the better."

The padre had been silent until now. He said, "Is there no way we can avoid murder? It's against all my principles . . ."

"When you became an outlaw, you signed up to kill if you had to," Duncan said. "If you don't, you endanger everybody. Yes, it has to be done."

"Very well," the giant said. "But I insist on giving Lu the last rites before you take him away. The . . . other, too."

"Jesus Christ, man!" Locks said. "Every second we stay here, we increase the danger! Besides, that thing has no soul!"

"You don't know that," Padre Cob said. "I insist. You may go on if you wish." He opened the little black bag he carried and drew from it a crucifix and some objects the names and uses of which Duncan did not know.

Duncan checked out the cockpit instruments while waiting for the priest to finish the ritual. He was irked, but he would be wasting time arguing with Cabtab. He knew how stubborn the man could be. What irritated him most was that Patroller Lu was not a Catholic or of any religion. Anybody who practiced a religion was automatically barred from membership in the police force or in any government position. No matter. Padre Cob would administer the rites to Satan himself if Satan were unconscious. Duncan would not have put it past Cabtab to knock out the devil to prevent his protests.

Duncan looked at the panel chronometer. Wednesday's people had gone into the cylinders. In ten more minutes, Thursday's would be stirring.

After what seemed a long time, the padre's broad serious face appeared by Duncan. "It's done. May they find enlightenment when they arrive at the Great There."

Duncan did not ask him where *There* was. He said, "See you, Padre. You'd better get the hell out of here."

"Be sure to confess your awful sin when you get back!" the priest cried as the plane lifted up. "I can't give you absolution unless you sincerely repent: But who is going to absolve me?"

His words reached Duncan faintly. The plane was heading for the woods.

"For Christ's sake!" Duncan muttered, then thought that Cabtab would have agreed with the words of the phrase though not with the sense in which Duncan meant them.

Keeping the craft very close to the treetops but within sight of the road, Duncan flew for six miles. Near a deserted place, with no lights of town or house or vehicle visible, he lowered the plane between two large trees. When it had landed, he got out of the craft and dragged the organic out. The flashing lights were bright enough for Duncan to see that Lu's eyes were open. If he was scared, his face did not show it. That was going to make it harder for Duncan. He did not like killing a brave man. Come to think of it, he did not like killing anybody, cowardly or courageous. But, whatever his character, or characters, had been before he became William St.-George Duncan, he was now a man who would do whatever had to be done. Within certain limits. He could never kill a child.

Using the organic's proton gun, Duncan shot him once through the middle of his chest. Lu fell on his side. Duncan rolled him over and removed the cloth hand-and-leg cuffs and the gag. Putting these into a pocket, he scorched the side of Lu's right leg to simulate a near-hit. Then he climbed into the cockpit and steered the craft through the forest. After half a mile of slow going, he lifted it above the trees and sped along the road. Two miles from where he had left Lu's corpse, he landed the plane. After placing the limp body of the duplicate on the grass of the meadow, he stood above it and aimed the proton gun at the left knee. The ball at the end of the barrel spat a purplish beam; the clothing and the flesh exploded. Despite the heavy downpour, he smelled briefly the stink of incinerated flesh.

He knelt by the duplicate. Its face was serene. If its nerves felt pain, its brain did not.

He took the organic's long hunting knife from his belt and shoved the blade a few inches into the stomach. The wound would not be immediately fatal, but the duplicate would soon bleed to death. He pulled the knife out and threw it into the cockpit.

When the organics found the duplicate's corpse early in the morning, or whenever, they would look around for Patroller Lu. It would not take them long. Then they would try to figure out what happened. The scenario that Duncan hoped they would image would be thus: Immediately after reporting that he was coming home, Lu would have been surprised by the refugee, Duncan. Or Lu would have surprised Duncan. In either event, the two had struggled. Lu had shot Duncan, but the outlaw had managed to struggle with him. During the fight, Lu's proton gun had been wrested from him or knocked out of his hand. Lu had then used his knife to stab Duncan. But Duncan had gotten to the gun and shot Lu. After which, Duncan had flown off in the plane. He had pulled the knife from his wound, but, feeling himself sinking, had landed the plane. Before he had gotten more than a few steps from it, he had collapsed and died.

If the ganks accepted that, the hunt was ended.

Duncan strode through the rain across the meadow. The grass would leave no footprints, and the mud from his shoes would be washed away. If only no government vehicle came along, he would go unobserved. At this time of morning, it was unlikely that there would be any traffic. As he had hoped, no vehicles appeared. When he was within a mile of the village, he went into the woods. His progress was slower here, but it was necessary to be concealed. Finally, before dawn, he entered the new facility. Locks and Cabtab were just inside the door and waiting for him. In a monotone, Duncan described what he had done. Locks winced when told of the killing; Cabtab crossed himself and began chanting in Japanese.

"It's war," Duncan said. "He was a soldier, and he died."

"Would you like to confess now?" Cabtab said.

"Don't be ridiculous," Duncan said, and he walked away.

11

"If my feelings were easily hurt, they'd be throbbing with pain now," Duncan said.

"Why is that?" Locks said.

The padre answered for him. "Because, my dear leader, he is being shunned by all except you and me and perhaps Wilde. He has killed a man and did not do so in self-defense. Although, if you consider all the implications and ramifications, he did, in a sense, a strong sense, put an end to the organic in defense not only of himself but of all the band. He stated quite clearly that he might have to slay the man, in fact, probably would. Yet not one of us stopped him. So we are all guilty. But they won't consider that. He alone is the guilty one, the Cain who has murdered his brother, though . . ."

"So they shrink from me. They don't say what's in their mind, no open criticism, but they regard me as something of a monster," Duncan said. He shrugged.

"If a child had suddenly come upon us as the organic did," Padre Cob said, "would you have killed him?"

"No," Duncan said. "I wouldn't have been able to."

"And why not? A child could have exposed us. That was why you killed the organic, wasn't it? Because he could not be allowed to reveal that we were there? If you would spare the child, why not the adult?"

Duncan shifted impatiently in the chair. "Fortunately, I was not put to that test. In reality—"

"In reality," Locks said savagely, "Duncan could do nothing but what he did. He sacrificed the man to save the rest of us. You people are pathetic. Disgusting."

The padre ignored Locks. He said, "Doesn't it bother you any? No little bites of conscience?"

"I've had a few nightmares," Duncan said. "A small price to pay."

"Let's get away from the hypothetical and the philosophical," Locks said. "We have enough real problems."

"The hypothetical, the philosophical, the ethical, the fantastic, the imaginative are all parts of reality," the padre said loudly, and he patted his enormous stomach as if that, to him, embodied the real. "The sum is made up of the parts. The hypothetical, the philosophical, the ethical . . ."

"Let's stick to the point at hand," Locks growled. "Now, you want to go with Duncan to L.A. That's going to require a tremendous change in plans. I have to communicate with the informant, get his permission, and if I do, set up a new ID for you, get passes and visas, and all that. Are you sure that you want to leave us, Padre? You have a lot of people depending upon you for spiritual comfort."

"As I told you, Chief, I had a vision the other night. An angel appeared to me in a blaze of light, and it told me to get going, to leave this place and my flock and go forth. To wipe the mud of this desert from my feet and walk among the men and women of the great cities. My mission—"

"I know, I know," Locks said tiredly. "I heard you at least three times. Very well. If you get permission, you may go. But you know what your flock will say. You're a rat deserting a sinking ship."

"They don't have to stay here," Padre Cob said.

Locks swiveled around in the chair and began operating the computer. Duncan stood up. "I'm going to take a walk."

Once more he was standing before the gray figure of Panthea Snick. What was he going to do about her? Logic and circumstances required that he leave her just as he had found her. To destone her to ease the itch of curiosity and then to stone her again would be cruel. If she had an incurable disease, he would have to do just that and she might think that she had been vivified because her disease was now curable. She did not, however, look as if she had been in ill health. Probably, she was here because she had committed some crime. In which case, she could be recruited into the band.

On the other hand, one more member would make more problems for Locks. He had enough as it was. Duncan doubted that he would give permission to destone Snick.

"I have to know what it is about her that bugs me so much," Duncan muttered.

Have to overcame *should not*.

He went to the carrier-robot section, activated and programmed a robot and walked behind it as it carried the heavy figure to a stoner and deposited it within it. It did not take long to close the door and apply the power, then swing the door open. The woman stepped out of the cylinder, her face pale and wondering. Duncan said, softly, "Don't be frightened, Panthea Snick. You are among friends."

That was a lie of kindness, of course. There was no guarantee that anyone else would be friendly to her. Nor was Duncan sure he could be called a friend.

Her bewildered expression vanished, and she smiled.

"Jeff Caird!"

That was one of the names the psychicist had said was his basic persona. His feeling that he had known her was based on fact.

He led her to a table, asked her to sit down, and handed her a glass of water. "I'm a victim of amnesia," he said. "Maybe you can tell me who Jeff Caird is and who you are and how we happened to know each other?"

Snick downed the entire glassful, then said, "First, tell me where this place is and just how you managed to destone me?"

She was now in complete self-control. Gone was the look of confusion, and her color had come back. Her voice was crisp and authoritative.

He told her where the warehouse was located, but he said, "I insist that you answer my questions first."

That she wanted to argue with him was evident. Nevertheless, she must have decided that, for the time being, he was the master. She gave him a flitting smile and launched into a long tale, which he did not interrupt. When she was finished, he was silent for a little while. Then he said, "So, you're an organic. An ex, I mean. And you're here because certain government officials thought that you knew too much. They shut you up by accusing you of a crime you didn't commit and then framed you with false evidence and stoned you."

She looked impatient. "That's what I said."

Jefferson Cervantes Caird had been a citizen of the state of Manhattan, an organic officer, upright and dedicated, loyal to the government, and a distinguished fighter against crime. On the surface. Secretly, he belonged to an organization that was highly unlawful. It had its origin in Gilbert Ching Immerman, a biologist who had discovered a means for prolonging life far beyond the normal span. Instead of sharing it with all of humanity, he had kept it for himself and some members of his family. As the family had grown through several generations, it had formed a secret organization, the immermans. Later, it had started to take in members who were not of the family, though these were relatively few. Within two hundred subyears, the family had gained many powerful positions. By the time that Caird was born, there were members in many countries and some in the world council.

When Caird had become an adult, he had also become a daybreaker. Instead of going into the stoner at the end of Tuesday, leaving it the morning of the next Tuesday, he became a Wednesday citizen with a different name, ID, and profession. On each day of the rest of the week, he had a new ID and profession. His adoption of these personae had been so successful that he *became* each person, on its particular day, retaining only a shadowy memory of the others. To carry out the deception, he had to retain a certain link to his other selves. After all, to be effective in performing his courier duties in the organization, he must know something of his seven personalities, and what had occurred on each day.

But he had gone overboard. He had kept the separate "souls" too separated from one another.

That had resulted finally in each persona trying to gain complete control of the others so that these could be dissolved.

The struggle had not started until shortly before Caird had been caught after a frantic flight from the organics.

Before that, an immerman scientist named Castor had gone mad and had been imprisoned in a Manhattan rehabilitation institution. The immermans, afraid that Castor might reveal the existence of their organization, made sure that he would not do so after being put in the institution. They had arranged that only members of their organization would have close contact with him. But Castor had murdered his chief keeper, escaped, and then killed Caird's Tuesday wife. Castor meant to murder Caird, also, because Caird had been the arresting officer.

In his Wednesday persona, Caird was told by an immerman that he had to find and kill Castor before the nonimmerman organics caught him. Castor must not be allowed to expose the organization. Reluctantly, Caird had obeyed the order. Meanwhile, a Sunday organic, Panthea Pao Snick, had questioned Caird. She was, in fact, looking for members of another outlaw organization, but Caird thought that she was on his trail. Then he found out that his own people now considered him to be dangerous to them because Snick seemed so close to catching him.

As Bob Tingle of the Wednesday World, Caird had killed Castor while the madman was trying to murder him. At least, that was what the psychicist had told Caird he had told her during a session under the truth mist. Caird himself had only a shadow's shadow of a memory of that event.

Snick was sitting in a chair and drinking another glass of water when Duncan asked her if she knew anything about the rescue.

"Nothing."

She seemed to be rising out of her shock and disorientation. Her large brown eyes were clear now. And beautiful. They seemed to be appealing to him, but that surely was his subjective impression. What was going on behind those eyes might be something different.

Duncan said, "I was told that I found you in a cylinder, stoned, where Castor had put you. Apparently, he was saving you for torture and mutilation before he killed you."

The woman shuddered.

"But the immermans got you, too. They destoned you, drugged you, and then used the truth mist on you. When they were done with you, they stoned you again. You were unconscious all that time. That's why you don't recall anything that happened during that time."

"I was looking for a subversive named Morning Rose Doubleday," she said. "Then I stumbled across the existence of another group, yours. I was informed about Castor and told to keep an eye out for him. I didn't know then that he was an immerman. In fact, I hadn't even known that such a subversive group existed."

"I thought you suspected me of something when you questioned me," Duncan said. "I didn't know then that you wanted to use me in your pursuit of Doubleday because I was a data banker."

"An immerman named Gaunt, a cell-section head, conducted the questioning of you. He wanted to kill and mutilate you to make the organics think Castor did it. That'd divert suspicion from us. I objected. But I was overruled. Then Castor showed up, and after he was killed, the organics came. I had to run. Next day, Thursday, as Charlie Ohm, I was summoned to the Tower of Evolution."

He was silent for a few seconds. Then, shaking his head, he

spoke softly. "I don't know what the hell I did in the Tower. The psychicist skipped that part. She did tell me about my flight and capture."

Snick smiled and said, "Oh, I can tell you some of what happened there! That's only because my interrogators told me about it, though what they knew was based on speculation. Or so they said. I wish, though . . . I wish . . ."

"Wish what?"

"That they'd not told me. If they'd kept quiet, I wouldn't have known so much, and thus I wouldn't have been a danger to them! They wouldn't have decided it'd be best to accuse me of a false crime so they could stone me and get me out of the way."

"What was the charge?"

"They accused me of being a member of the immermans!"

She rose indignantly from the chair, her eyes even larger, her face twisted. "Me! One of the immermans!"

"How could they do that?" Duncan said. "The mist would prove that you weren't."

"I know! I demanded that they show me the interrogation recording. They did so, and there I was, unconscious and admitting that I did belong to the immermans and had been secretly working for them for a long time!"

Duncan was more than puzzled. Something was buzzing in his head as if someone wanted him to open a door.

"But you said . . ."

"Yes, I said I was innocent! I was! I am! What they did was to insert a computer simulation into the recording!"

"A simulation of you confessing while under the mist?"

"Of course!"

"But an examination of the recording by specialists would prove that the section was simulated! Didn't you demand that?"

"Of course I did! And it was denied me!"

Duncan was not as shocked as he had expected to be. Perhaps, in one of his personae, probably that of Caird the organic, he had heard of such duplicity. Or—he hoped not—had been involved in such.

"All right," he said. "What were you told that made them decide not to trust you, to put you away?"

"I was asked, while I wasn't misted, though they must've asked when I was misted, too, if I'd ever heard of the *longevity factor.*"

The buzzing in Duncan's head stopped. The door had been opened. But the shadowy images flitting through were too thin and misshapen for him to know what they meant.

"Longevity factor?"

"I don't know—as yet—what it means, what it implies. It must have been significant. The woman who asked me about it was immediately told to shut up. She got pale. Not red, as if embarrassed, but pale, as if terrified. She was told to leave the room. They weren't very smart about it. If they'd been cool, said nothing, I wouldn't have thought anything of it. I replied that I'd never heard of such a thing. It was true. They knew I was not lying. Nevertheless, that's the only thing I can think of that made them decide to stone me. Somehow, they thought that, just by their mentioning the longevity factor, I'd become dangerous."

She was looking around at the stoned figures while talking. She stopped, rose from the chair, and said, "My God! That's the woman who asked me about it!"

Duncan looked at the stonee she was pointing at.

"And the two by her side! They were in the room, too!"

"I think," Duncan said, "they knew too much. They must not have been trusted enough. Whatever it was, let's find out."

He was not eager to destone even one of them, however. Bringing Panthea Snick to life would probably cause enough trouble. Any more unauthorized destoning was going to upset Locks twice as much. So be it. That was too bad. Let him burn. He, Duncan, was asbestos. If he was not, he would certainly find out.

"Which one seemed to be in charge?" Duncan said.

Snick indicated the woman, a tall blonde with a rather hard face.

"Then she might know more."

Duncan got a robot into operation. A few minutes later, the woman stepped out of the cylinder. Snick seized her from behind, and Duncan sprayed truth mist in her face. She struggled to free herself and to hold her breath while doing so. Duncan helped Snick restrain her until the woman slumped, her head hanging forward. After they had placed her on a table, Duncan swiftly interrogated her. She readily answered in that soft and slurred voice, seldom emotion-charged, that those under the influence used. Detective-Captain Sandra Johns Bu, however, could only report that her superior, Detective-Major Theodore Elizabeth Scarlatti, had ordered her to question Snick about what she knew of the LF, or "longevity factor." Scarlatti did not explain what that phrase meant. Nevertheless, Bu had paid heavily for her slip. Shortly after Bu had been commanded to leave the room, she was taken in for questioning. Wholly bewildered, frightened yet angry because she knew she was innocent, she had denied knowing anything of the LF. Then truth mist had been administered to her. She had awakened suddenly in the cylinder, where she had been seized by Snick and Duncan.

"And so back she goes into stone," Duncan said.

A few minutes later, Bu was standing once more in the silent ranks.

"We don't know any more than we did before," Duncan said.

"Not quite true," Snick said. "We know that you know or at least knew something about prolonging life. You were not a scientist in any of your seven personae. Therefore, you must have been given that knowledge. Perhaps you shared it with the other members of your organization. Whatever . . . the government has not made public the existence of your group or of the LF. It's desperate to keep it secret. It's also desperate to get hold of you, and that must be because you know what the government doesn't want the public to know."

"I already figured that out," Duncan said. "Question. How do I find out what I know, yet don't know?"

12

Duncan had been right. Ragnar Locks was angry.

"You had no right to bring her into the band! Especially when you're just about to—"

He stopped because Snick was within ear range. He did not want her to know that Duncan would be going under another identity to Los Angeles.

"She was my only means to find out why the government wants me so badly," Duncan said. "That reason is very important. Anyway, she's no danger. She can't go to the organics and tell them about us. She wouldn't, anyway. She hates them now."

"It was for nothing," Locks said. "You still don't have any idea of why they want you."

"I have a clue, and that's more than I had. Look. She's very well trained, a highly competent organic who knows the ins and outs of her field. I think she ought to be given a new ID, too. She could go to Los Angeles with me."

Locks' face got even redder, but he choked back his retort. He threw his hands up and walked away. Duncan winked at Snick. She was pale but managed to smile slightly. Shortly thereafter, Locks returned, much calmer.

"I'll be glad to get rid of both of you," he said. "OK. If it can be done, she can go with you."

Two obdays later, it was done. On Tuesday morning, at eight
o'clock, Duncan, Snick, and Cabtab were in the town of New
Ark, New Jersey. This was near the old city of Newark, which
had long ago disappeared, overwhelmed and buried by ac-
cumulating soil and heavy forest. Even those buildings that had
survived the siege and the burning and had been preserved as
monuments had in two thousand obyears been covered over. A
plaque on the station wall commemorated it as the site of the
prison camp for New York and New Jersey criminals after
Wang Shen's forces had conquered the eastern United States of
America. It was near here that twenty-three thousand criminals,
including all known Mafia, had been executed. This had happened, as the plaque noted, before the beginning of the New
Era and its stoning techniques. Capital punishment had long
ago been abolished. In theory, anyway, Cabtab pointed out to
his colleagues.

"Wang Shen can't be accused of racial or national discrimina-
tion. All felons convicted of murder, extortion, rape, and drug
dealing were executed throughout the world. The Great Clean
Sweep, Wang Shen called it. However . . . ho! ho! ho! . . . there
were just as many criminals in the next generation. That, of
course, was just the start of the New Era. In the third generation, government propaganda, you can call it conditioning, if
you wish, had reduced the number of detected criminals by
three-quarters. Then the number of detected criminals rose
during the following generation because the invention of truth
mist made it impossible for a criminal to lie. After that, well, no
society that existed previously had been so crime-free. Not that
there aren't still some. Take us, for example. Ho! ho! ho!"

Duncan looked around uneasily. Cabtab's loud laughter and
his three chins and huge belly were attracting attention. Nobody was staring at them; the citizens were too polite to do that.
Nevertheless, they were glancing sidewise at Cabtab and moving away. Though the station was crowded, there was an unoccupied area ten feet in diameter around the three.

"I think," Duncan said, "we should quiet down."

"What?" Cabtab said. He looked around. "Oh, yes, I see."

"It would help if you started to diet, too," Snick said.

"I've done more than enough by getting rid of my religious artifacts," Cabtab said softly, his face red. "That was a tremendous sacrifice, though no one else seems to appreciate that."

"You're no longer a preacher," Snick said sharply.

"Not according to my ID. But if you take the preacher from the church, you can't remove the church from the preacher. Wherever I am, there is my church."

"Try to keep quiet about it, then," Snick said.

Cabtab prodded her in the ribs with a huge horny thumb, and he laughed loudly. Snick winced.

"Now, now, let's not get too organic. You're no longer invested with great authority. I don't have to jump at your command."

"I think," Duncan said in a low voice, "that we should quit any such talk altogether. Remember, we're not who we were. Act accordingly."

"Quite right," Cabtab rumbled. "I'll strive to be a good little boy from now on."

They were standing near the north entrance of the building. It was a towering structure that looked like a cross between a pagoda and a Gothic temple. Its white walls, exterior and interior, were inlaid with scarlet twelve-sided alto-reliefs bearing bright-green globes. The four main entrances were two-story-high arches, open at the moment because the three sectional doors had been withdrawn into wall recesses. The main room had a domed ceiling two stories high. There were about a hundred people beneath the ceiling, sitting on benches, walking around, or standing in groups. The inevitable giant TV screens were placed here and there on the walls so that the occupants could keep up with Tuesday's news, the train schedule, or the current hi-pop shows.

The three went to a bench and sat down. Shortly thereafter, another area was cleared around them. Duncan bit his lip. Cabtab was not, just now, anyway, an asset to him and Snick. However, he was not the only unsocially obese person there. And being fat was not a crime, though the attitude of most people and of the government was that it bordered on illegality. Certainly, the obese were often hounded by agents of the Bureau of Fitness and Standards. TO LOSE IS TO GAIN was the official slogan. Lose fat and gain health, respect, and a longer life was what the state meant. FOR THE GREATER GOOD OF THE PEOPLE BECOME LESSER.

Cabtab's new ID was that of Jeremiah Scanderbeg Ward, and the fake data bank file was spotted with frequent reprimands and small fines by the Bureau of Fitness and Standards. Which must have caused whomever had made up the file a lot of work, Duncan thought.

Snick's new ID was Jenny Ko Chandler. Duncan's had for some reason been changed from David Ember Grim to Andrew Vishnu Beewolf. He would have preferred Smith or Wang or even Grim, but the unknown data banker who had put the ID into the files must have had a compelling reason to choose Beewolf.

"Here comes the train," Cabtab-Ward said.

It was actually fifty miles away, as indicated by a wall screen. The TV monitors along the route, however, showed the bullet-shaped cars rocketing by. Estimated time of arrival at New Ark: 2.5 minutes. The porters were already moving out large robot-carriers, the platforms of which were jammed with stoned people. These were passengers who preferred to ride safely, invulnerable to the most terrible crashes. Also free of the boredom, anxiety, and inconvenience of travel. On the other hand, they would not enjoy the sights of the countryside or of the unfamiliar cities the train would go through.

The wall screens announced that boarding time would be in ten minutes. The crowd picked up their travel cases and moved out into the open area between the station and the "tracks." Duncan stood behind the safety railing near them. The tracks were actually a narrow highway of synthetic metal on the ground and enormous vertical hoops of metal placed at forty-foot intervals above the road. Presently, the train, now moving

slowly, appeared around a hill. It took some time for the end of
the mile-long series of fifty-foot-long cars to show. The lead car,
its radar antennae rotating, floated five feet above the shiny
gray roadway. When the train stopped, the end car was four
thousand feet from the station. Then the chain of vehicles sank
slowly to the roadbed.

Whistles blew. Porters' voices rose hoarsely. The screens on
poles near the safety railing flashed instructions. Duncan and
his companions got into line. The doors of their car slid open,
and conductors stepped out. They wore Lincoln-green uniforms, tunics that came halfway down to the thighs and caps
that had not changed for two thousand obyears. A wide scarlet
patch on their breasts bore two crossed steam-locomotive insig-
nias. Just above the visors of their caps was a gold-colored metal
circle bearing a green globe.

The conductor at Duncan's entrance, a tall dark woman with
a big motherly bosom and a wicked stepmother's face, spoke
loudly. "Step right up! Move it! We have a schedule to meet! No
farting around!"

Duncan slipped his ID card into the slot and his right thumb
into a hole. The conductor looked at the screen showing vital
data and his destination. It flashed a short code indicating that
the data was correct and the thumbprint was Andrew Vishnu
Beewolf's. Three short whistles issued from the machine; its
screen flashed: ID CERT.

Duncan removed his card and hurried into the car. The information had been transmitted from the scanner to various
data banks all over the world, checked with the records, and
found not wanting. Snick and Cabtab also passed the test. The
first of many to come, Duncan thought, as he sat down by a
window. Panthea was on his left, Cabtab across from him. The
fourth passenger was a middle-aged man, only six feet tall, thin,
large-eyed, and long-faced. He wore a very fashionable hat,
sporting two yellow antennae. His rainbow-colored tunic was
also current, knee-length and with a scoop that went almost to
his navel. He wore a neck-chain from which depended a large

metal image of an ant. Before the train started to move, he introduced himself in a high-pitched voice.

"Doctor Herman Trophallaxis Carebara, late of the University of Queens. Immigrant to the State of Los Angeles, Lower California Division. And you, if you please?"

Duncan introduced himself and the others. Carebara church-steepled his hands together before his chest and bowed slightly each time Duncan said the names. Snick replied in kind. The two men just waved a hand to indicate that they acknowledged the introduction. A subtle expression passed across Carebara's face. Duncan interpreted it as dislike of their informality.

"I am a professor of entomology, specialty formicology," Carebara said. "And you, if you please?"

"Entomology? Formicology?" Cabtab said.

"The study of insects. My specialty is the study of those insects known to the layperson as ants."

"I'm of theologian genus, of the street preacher species," Cabtab said, grinning. "My mundane professions are garbage collector, waiter, and bartender. My female sister-in-spirit is a medical technologist, and my brother-in-spirit is a data banker. We are all New-Jersey born and have never been out of this state."

"Very interesting," Carebara said.

By then, the doors had been shut, the PA had told the passengers that the train was leaving on schedule, which they already knew, and a conductor was moving his wheeled machine down the aisle. He was requiring the passengers to give him their ID cards so he could check them out again in his machine. That, Duncan thought, was unnecessary, redundant, and time-wasting, not to mention annoying. But the regulations demanded it, and there might be a very very slight chance that someone unauthorized had slipped onto the car.

He glanced out the window. The train was now five feet above the roadbed and accelerating swiftly. The giant rings were flashing by, and the meadows, farms, and forest were whipping past. He wished that the car were not moving so fast.

He liked to see the countryside and the little towns in detail. Such hurry was really not necessary. The train would have to stop when it came near the border of the Central Standard Time Zone. Why couldn't it just amble along and push ahead, as it were, the next time zone?

"My main studies have been in the communication codes of ants," Carebara was saying. "That is, in the forms of recognition and exchange of information, ocular, physical, and chemical. Signs and scents. My special specialty, if I may call it that, is mimetism. That is, those nonants, those insects who pass themselves off as ants. Beetles that look like ants, behave like ants, and live off of ants in their very midst." He smiled and said, "Beetles that are freeloaders, bums, spongers, parasites. They give nothing, and they take all they can get."

Cabtab rolled his eyes and drummed his fingers on the armrest. Snick sighed. Duncan, however, was intrigued. He said, "Just how do they do that?"

Carebara smiled, delighted that he had at least a mono-audience.

"The main form of communication in an ant colony is by odor. The members give off pheromones, scents that identify them as belonging to the colony. The parasites have evolved through millions of years of evolution, have adapted their bodies to give off pheromones similar enough to the ants' to fool their hosts. They beg food from the ants by drumming on the hosts' bodies with their antennae and stroking the mouths of the ants with their legs. Whatever it takes to get the ant to disgorge its food. The bums also eat their hosts' larvae and eggs. Some do, anyway."

He settled back, closed his eyes for a moment, and smiled. He was pleased with himself. When he opened his eyes, he said, "Essentially, the parasites have evolved to the point where they have broken the ants' codes. The sensory and olfactory codes that ants use to do work, defend themselves, or cooperate in attacking other ants or intruders. The beetles, fifth columners, in a sense, infiltrate, settle down among their hosts and live high off the hog, as it were.

"In this, they differ from their human counterparts, the revolutionaries, the subversives, the malcontents, who want to overthrow the government so that they can rule. No insect wants to overthrow its government. No ant ever rebelled. And the beetles . . . they don't care about changing the system in the colony. Why should they? They, if you'll excuse the colloquialism, have it made."

Cabtab, who had gotten interested in spite of himself, looked at Duncan and winked. "Perhaps there's a lesson for us in our learned friend's discourse," he said.

Duncan ignored him and spoke to Carebara.

"It's basically a matter of breaking the code?"

Carebara nodded and said, "Yes. Formicologists now know exactly how the body chemistry of the mimetic beetles matches that of the hosts. We formicologists have been working with biochemists for a long time on that subject. You may have seen TV documentaries or read tapes about our work in making synthetic species, most of which, unfortunately, are short-lived, even for those of the entomological persuasion. Yes?"

Snick and Duncan nodded.

"Two out of three isn't bad. Well, my colleagues at the University of Lower California, Los Angeles, have done splendid work on both natural and synthetic mimetic beetle parasites. They invited me to come to L.A. to collaborate in their research. Since emigration also brings with it more credits, better housing, more perks, as you well know, no doubt they are your main reason in emigrating, otherwise, why tear up your roots? Ah, as I was saying, for these reasons I left Queens for the first time in my life."

"Yes, we wanted a somewhat better life, too," Duncan said. "Also, our life has always been somewhat rural. We would like to try metropolitan living. Anyway, these synthetic mimetics. . . ?"

"Fire ants, as you laypersons call them, have recently become a menace again. My work, mine and my colleagues', will be to make mimetic beetles that will transcend the aims, if I may use that word, of the natural parasites. They will be genetically programed to eat the eggs and larvae of their hosts. But not openly so that their hosts become alarmed and eat them. Thus, we hope to wipe out or at least greatly reduce the numbers of the fire ants. However, the project may take a long time. Its long-range implications are that entomologists, in conjunction with biochemists, may be able to make many species that can control all those insects that are harmful to humankind. They may work out far better than the laboratory-made mutants we've used so far."

The conductor interrupted him, and after he was gone, the three outlaws shunted the conversation onto another subject. When Carebara, after futile efforts to rechannel it back to his ants, left for the rest room, Duncan spoke softly so that the neighbors couldn't overhear.

"Think he's on the up-and-up? Or is he an organic provoker?"

"He can provoke all he wants," Snick said. "We'll have to pretend we're just ordinary citizens, perfectly satisfied with the policies of the government, adhering to the official philosophy in every respect."

"He can't suspect us," Cabtab rumbled. "If he is an organic, I mean. I think he's just a professor, like he says. If he had any suspicions we were anything else than our cards say we are, the ganks'd be all over us."

"I know that," Duncan said. "Actually, the main thing I'm worried about is his boring us to death. He's a monomaniac."

"Of the deadly persuasion, you mean," Snick said, and she laughed.

"He has given me something to think about," Duncan said. He leaned back and closed his eyes. After a few minutes, he opened them to look through the window. The view was blurred now and would be for a long time. But it was being filmed, and the passengers could pull down an overhead screen and run the scenery in slow motion. Thus, they could barely see where they were but could view in detail where they had been.

13

At an average velocity of two hundred miles an hour, the train arrived in Chicago, State of Illinois, North American Department, at 1:30 P.M., Central Standard Time. Here the passengers disembarked and registered in rooms at the government-run Pilgrim's Progress Hotel. Later, they toured the city on a bus. The taped voice informed the sightseers that Chicago was now reduced to a twenty-square-mile horizontal area but extended as much as a mile, here and there, vertically. Lakeshore Drive was now five miles inland from the original drive because the level of Lake Michigan had risen fifty feet. The entire city, in fact, was ringed by a seventy-foot-high lakewall.

The screen in front of the bus showed a map of the ancient limits of the city, a shocking sprawl, and the present limits. Where there had once been miles and miles of ugly factories and even uglier houses and apartment buildings were farms, forest reserves, artificial lakes, and recreation lodges.

Duncan and his companions went to bed early, rose at 11:30, went into the hotel cylinders, and came out the following Tuesday at ten minutes past midnight. After sleeping again, they rose at six in the morning, breakfasted, and boarded another express at 7:30 A.M.

Twelve hours later, having been sidetracked for three hours, the reason not explained, the train pulled into Amarillo, State of West Texas, at 7:30 P.M., Central Standard Time, 8:30 P.M., Mountain Standard Time.

"We should have taken the straight-through," Snick said. "I'm weary of traveling."

"What? And miss seeing this great country?" Duncan said.

"I also could have missed having a paralyzed ass."

"There's a disadvantage to everything," he replied. "The advantages in this situation more than make up for the drawbacks. At least, they do as far as I'm concerned."

They were walking to the station entrance when she stopped and pointed into darkness at a complex of winking lights in the air. The reflection of the city lights vaguely outlined a long dark shape.

"Going by airship would have been more fun."

"Only a privileged few are allowed to travel unstoned in them," he said. "If we'd taken that, we'd have been just a part of the cargo. Anyway, dirigible travel is even slower."

"Yeah, I know. I'm just tired, and I want to get to L.A.," Panthea said.

The country around Amarillo was hot and humid and rampant with farms or large groves of jungle. But the city was domed, and the air within was fresh and comfortable. Duncan was delighted with the citizens' garb. They had preserved the Western tradition; everybody looked like a cowboy or a cowlady. He doubted, however, that the original Texans would have admired the enormous brightly colored codpieces of the men or approved of women whose breasts were more often uncovered than covered by the jewel-sequined leather vests.

The following Tuesday, the train arrived in the State of Los Angeles. The last four hours were in the dark, but the screens showed the landscape as viewed in the bright sunshine. Because of the delays, unexplained, and an hour's stop so the passengers could stretch their legs along the rim of the Grand Canyon, the train arrived at the terminal station, Pasadena, at 7:30 P.M. The three spent an hour in line waiting for their new ID cards because of a computer breakdown. The cards were just like the old ones except that they contained data re their status as citizens of the State of Los Angeles, Lower California Division, North American Department. After this, the passengers were bused to the Immigration Department Hotel, where, after the procedures for immigrants were explained to them, they were free to wander around until half an hour to midnight.

Duncan, however, went to bed at nine. Though tired, he could not sleep. The narrow room was too confining, and Cabtab, on the bunk beneath his, snored loudly. For some reason, he rejected the use of the morpheus. Perhaps he felt he was getting too dependent on it. Visions of the journey kept flashing on the monitor of his mind, especially those of Arizona and New Mexico. At least a quarter of the area of these states was covered by enormous solar panels, the power from which furnished twelve states with light and heat. Interspersed among the gigantic sunflashing structures were jungles. The Southwest had always had a hot climate, but the rains of twelve thousand obyears ago were returning. The soil, where not shadowed by panels, had given birth to a vivid green and tall tangle that looked like lowlands Central America.

The rainclouds that made vegetation flourish also made the Southwest less sunny, but clear skies were frequent enough to justify the solar panels—so far.

Phoenix had been a collection of great domes connected by transparent passageways. The domes were polarized against the sunlight when necessary, and the mountains around it had long ago been leveled. The debris had been piled twenty miles away to make a new landmark, Mount Remove.

Duncan finally oozed into a sleep shot with dreams fractured by near-nightmares. These were not so much "personal" as "historical." They seemed to osmose from his ancestral memories, which, of course, did not exist. Nevertheless, there was no other explanation, which did not mean that there was none. They might have been evoked by the documentary he had watched while on the train, though something else could have been their midwife. Whatever their cause, and no one knew what thousands of single items formed a flashing-by complex to screw the dreams upward to the conscious of his unconscious, they formed a forward-speed pageant.

Perhaps it was the journey across the continent that pushed the RERUN button.

History was a nightmare, and his nightmare was history.

Who could have predicted that, in the early part of the twenty-first century, gunpowder and rocket fuel would be unusable in war? Or that in World War III internal combustion engines could be rendered inoperable? Or that the chief weapons would be, in the early stages of the war, swords, spears, crossbows, gas-powered guns, lasers, and steam-operated machine guns? That airplanes could not be used and lighter-than-air craft were too vulnerable? That tanks had to operate by nuclear fuel or coal?

Who could have foreseen that the chairman of the Communist party of China, Wang Shen, would see the potential in this change of transportation and weaponry and would declare war on the U.S.S.R.? Or that, in twelve years, using the armies of the conquered countries, Wang Shen would conquer the world and establish a world government? Or that his son, Sin Tzu, would found the New Era, an age that renounced the ideologies of communism and capitalism except as they applied to his brave new world? Or that, before he died, he would use the invention of "stoning" to build something completely unique in history. The seven-day world.

Air and water and earth were now clean. Immense forests had been planted to restore the oxygen–carbon dioxide content of the atmosphere, though that had taken a thousand years and the oceans were still rising. The tropical belts of rain forests were even larger in area than they had been in the early nineteenth century.

No one was now hungry or badly housed, and education was available for everyone. No one had to go without medicine or doctors or hospital care, all of which were of the highest quality possible. Armies, navies, and air forces were like dinosaurs, extinct. The last war had taken place two thousand obyears ago. Murder, assault, rape, and child abuse still existed, but the rate of occurrence was the lowest in the history of humankind.

All of this had, however, been achieved at a price. It had cost the most for those involved in World War III and the formation of the New Era. But there were those now living who believed that they were also paying a price. None of the great benefits of the New Era could exist without the seven-day system and the smothering surveillance of satellite, sensor, and police, the last euphemistically termed the organics.

Or so the government claimed. But men and women like Duncan thought differently. The highly artificial seven-day world had been around so long that it seemed natural to most citizens. These truly believed that it was absolutely necessary for the greatest good of society that every person be closely watched so that no one could escape punishment for crimes against society. The heavy surveillance was sometimes irksome or inconvenient, but the resulting safety and ease of mind made this more than just endurable. And if truth mist made it impossible for anyone to get away with lying, wasn't that the way it should be?

The government officials were also required to be misted before being employed or if their conduct was in doubt. But what if those who did the misting lied about the results?

Images exploded from the dark, and faces spun out of the blackness that lies at the base of all thought, out of the dark emptiness that somehow gives birth to fullness. Faces spun by, the faces of his forefathers and foremothers who had fought in the great battles of Canada and the United States of America. All were twisted with the heat and red of fear and bravery and battle, and all were smoothed out into pale death. Some were North American Caucasians; some, Asiatics, Africans, Europeans, and South Americans. Duncan was descended from those who had shed their blood for Wang Shen and also for the United States, ancestors who had tried to kill one another.

Then the final war to end all wars was ended, and the survivors struggled to live and to have children and to keep their children alive. Children were crying, their faces drawn and fearful, their hands stretched out for food, when Duncan was snapped from the nightmares by the wall-screen alarm.

"Oh, God!" Cabtab moaned in the bunk below Duncan's. "Another day! Before it ends, we'll be in L.A. What then? More of the same?"

The padre had also been having nightmares.

14

Los Angeles, however, looked that morning like a pleasant, and in some respects erotic, dream.

Duncan and his companions had gone through more admittance procedures, this time at the Immigration Department in L.A., and then had taken the elevator to the top floor. This was on a level with the peak of Mount Wilson, where long ago an observatory had stood. Now the governor of Los Angeles lived in a mansion there. The three had a splendid view of the Pacific Ocean, which filled the great basin. The old metropolis had disappeared under the waves, most of it buried in mud or washed away. It was the third city to be built there, the first having been destroyed by fire in World War III and the second tumbled by the Great Earthquake and then burned.

Now, rising from deep-sunk pylons, many varicolored towers glittered in the clear air and bright sunshine. These were interconnected by bridges at many floors, and a four-level bridge led through a great cut in the Hollywood Hills to the valley beyond. Pedestrians, bicyclists, tricyclists, electric buses, and a few electric automobiles filled the bridges.

Westward, the sea and the sea-filled basin flashed with thousands of automated freight vessels and manned craft. Eastward, the water-surrounded towers and the interconnecting bridges gave way finally to the foothills of the mountains. Southward, the sea-girded towers extended for fifteen miles. The Baldwin Hills were a thousand years gone, used for fill in the dikes that had kept the ocean out until the second great earthquake. To the north, only four towers rose into view from beyond the Hollywood Hills.

"Beautiful," Snick murmured. "I think I'm going to like it here."

"It's the citizens that make a place beautiful," Duncan said. "Ugly citizens, ugly city, no matter how fabulous the architecture and how clean the streets are. Some of the locals are going to be very ugly indeed if they find out who we really are."

"There's where we'll be living," Cabtab said, pointing to the west. "The La Brea Complex Tower, twentieth floor, west super block neighborhood."

At that moment, a woman who had been standing near them, though not within earshot, approached them. She was about thirty subyears of age, of middle height, pretty, dark-skinned, and with blonde hair and blue eyes that had probably been dark before depigmentation. She wore a tight cerulean-blue blouse and skirt, nothing beneath, and yellow, very high-heeled shoes. Her handbag, canary-yellow with black spots, was shaped like a leopard. A tiny black right-handed swastika, marking her as a Buddhist of the Original Gautama sect, was tattooed on her forehead.

Duncan looked at her because it seemed obvious that she was going to speak to them. Instead, she passed them, but she slipped something into his hand. He pushed back his impulse to call after her, turned so that his back was to the pedestrians, and looked at the card.

WILL MEET YOU THREE AT 9:00 P.M. AT THE SNORTER. RUB THIS.

Duncan read it three times, then slid the palm of his hand across its face. The words disappeared. He stuck the blank card into a pocket and whispered what he had read to his colleagues.

"Where in hell is the Snorter?" Cabtab said.

They went to a directory booth around the corner, and after Duncan questioned the machine, its screen glowed the answer.

"It's a tavern near the west rim in the west block neighborhood of the La Brea Complex."

"We can read," Snick said.

"God save us from the snippy," Cabtab moaned.

Panthea ignored him. "Well, we have been contacted. Let's go to the complex and get settled in. Tomorrow we'll be busy with job-adjustment."

The directory told them what buses and transfers to take. They rode over bridges that were probably swaying in the wind but gave no indication of doing so to those on it. The bridges ran from building to building, sometimes through them, sometimes around them. The pageant of street traffic and the beautiful sailing boats far below them would normally have held their interest. They, however, were concerned about the message.

Cabtab, who had taken an empty bench behind them, leaned his head between them. He whispered, "I hope they'll let us in on their main purpose, what they hope to accomplish. I don't like working in the dark."

"Don't get too nosy," Duncan said. "It's dangerous."

"Damn it!" Snick said. She was biting her lower lip and frowning. "It's so unjust! I only wanted to be a very good organic, the best I could be. And I don't want to be an outlaw!"

"Those are dangerous feelings, too," Duncan said. "Best to keep them to yourselves. I know nothing of the people we have to work with, of course. But I'm sure they want enthusiasm, fanaticism, probably. You show reluctance, kick against the pricks, and you might end up stoned again and deep in the ocean where you'll never be found."

"I know that, but I hate injustice! I just . . . oh, well!"

She was silent during the rest of the trip.

Duncan did not speak much nor did he really appreciate the stimulating views from the high bridges. He was zeroed in on his feelings for Panthea Snick. This dark and pretty little woman with the sometimes abrasive personality was not somebody he should be so strongly attracted to. Yet he was. So what was he to do about it?

At this time, he did not know how she felt about him. Probably, she was not at all attracted to him. But why not ask her if she was?

No. That might put her off. He would wait. Let her feelings for him, if they were at all favorable, develop.

The trouble with that attitude was that he was not as patient as he would like to be. Take just now, for instance. He would like to lean over, put his arms around her, and kiss her.

He looked away from her and said, softly, "Ah!"

"What?" Cabtab said.

"Nothing."

The bus halted on the tenth floor of the La Brea Complex Tower. The three, their bags in hands, got off. They walked along the gently curving exterior through the thick flow of people wearing brightly colored clothes until they came to a public lobby. Inside this enormous chamber with its many shops, they took an elevator to the floor. Leaving the cage, they walked to a moving strip, one of many which ran down the center of the circle forming this level. After half a mile, they worked their way across the moving walks to a stationary walk on the edge of the strips. They entered another huge room, one partly devoted to the reception of immigrants. They got into a line before a desk and eventually were interviewed by an official. Having satisfied her, they took a bus to their assigned apartments. Duncan's was large and on the outer wall of the tower, giving him an excellent view. The seven cylinders in his apartment held Saturday's through Monday's occupants; the others were empty. Evidently, the Wednesday, Thursday, and Friday immigrants had not arrived. The ID plaques of the cylinders indicated that two were from Wales, one was from Indonesia, and one was from Albania. This accorded with the little that Duncan knew of the national makeup of the new tenants of the west super block. Most immigrants had come from these nations, but the faces were like those he knew in Manhattan and New Jersey. Most citizens of Earth had both Chinese and Asiatic Indian ancestors, and it was said that the faces of Congolese citizens looked just like those of Sweden. That was something of an exaggeration, but it was near enough to the reality to be believed by everyone.

The global melting pot begun by Wang Shen was well on its way to boiling. Nationalism and racism were wiped out, though, some thought, at the price of variety. The immigrants brought here, mostly unmarried or childless, were supposed to marry and have children whose mixture would be even more complex than those of their parents. The index of mixture that had already occurred was apparent from the languages that the majority of newcomers spoke. Welsh had long been extinct; most people in Wales spoke Bengali, a language that would itself be dead in two generations or less. Albanians spoke a descendant of Cantonese. Both groups, like everybody else, could also use Loglan, the synthetic worldwide speech, though only when they had to do so, and all had learned English in school. The Conqueror, Wang Shen, and his son had had a great love and admiration for that tongue. As a result, one-fourth of the world had been born to it. Unfortunately, Indonesian English, for example, was not always completely intelligible to speakers of Norwegian English, even though the mass media of the world used Standard English.

VARIETY WITHIN UNITY.

That was one of the most-displayed government slogans, one that school pupils heard from kindergarten on. The trouble was that the government had been getting from the beginning of the New Era more variety than it wanted. And the varieties had not always been desirable—from the state's viewpoint. As Padre Cob Cabtab had once said, "The outlaw slogan is: OR-NERINESS IS NEXT TO GODLINESS. He who kicks against the pricks hurts the bureaucrats. Let him who denies this fall into a latrine."

Duncan went out by himself to shop for clothes at the nearest store. He came back with twelve outfits, folded them, and placed them on a shelf in his personal closet. They occupied a space six inches square and a half-inch high. Afterward, he ate lunch with Snick and Cabtab at the nearest dining hall, a room large enough to hold two thousand people. It was almost full, not because the food was so excellent but because the locals liked to gather here for socializing. Duncan, looking around, spotted at least ten men and women who he believed were organics. Though they were dressed like civilians, they had the slightly withdrawn, contemptuous, and weary expression of the policeperson. Bad actors, he thought. He and Snick lacked that attitude that soaked upward from the organic soul and oozed from their flesh.

It was not true that once a cop, always a cop. Or was he just fooling himself? No. After all, though some of his former personae had been establishment-loyal, others had been anti-establishment. In his present and, he hoped, last incarnation, he certainly was against the government.

At one o'clock, he went to the office of the super block leader, Francisco Tupper Min. After cooling his heels for an hour, his neck getting hotter with every minute of delay, he was admitted into the presence of the august personage. The squat, enormously overmuscled, and shaven-headed Min rose from behind his desk and greeted Duncan with an apology. He held out his huge hand, and it took Duncan a few seconds to realize that he wanted to shake hands.

Min laughed—his voice was very high-pitched—and said, "Our customs in L.A. are different, Citizen Duncan. We pride ourselves on being progressive, pioneers, always in the forefront of the new. But we have gone back to *some* ancient customs. Why worry nowadays about spreading disease by handshaking when there are none to spread? This bowing and holding your hands prayerwise is too formal. Shake hands, touch, feel human warmth!"

Duncan took the hand and felt a powerful pressure. It intimated that Min could have crushed Duncan's bones if Min had wanted to. But Min was too good a politician to humiliate any voter.

Not that, as Min pointed out, Duncan was one just now. He had to wait six submonths and pass an elector's examination before he could send in his vote through a computer.

"I always have a tight schedule, but I keep to it," Min said. "Sit down. Have a drink. No? Well, you're an understanding man. You perceive how busy I am and don't want to waste my time . . . and yours, too. I thank you for that consideration. As I was saying, in normal times I'd have plenty of time to get acquainted with you, and I plan to do so after all these pressing issues are disposed of. I like to know all about my blockers, not just from the files, but from eye-to-eye meeting. I want them to be more than just data on a screen."

Bullshit, Duncan thought. There's no way you could know two hundred thousand people intimately.

"Anyway, as I was saying, this flood of immigrants, the present election for block leaders, and there's the big experiment coming up. The particular items of the experiment will be voted on two days from now, subdays, that is. It's—"

"Big experiment?" Duncan said.

Min stared at him as if he could not believe his ignorance.

"You mean you haven't heard about it?"

Duncan shook his head.

"It's been on all the channels, night and day."

"I haven't even looked at the news," Duncan said. "There was something on the dining hall screens, but the noise was so bad I couldn't hear it. Anyway, I just got here."

"It's been on all of Tuesday's channels for some time now," Min said. "In fact, this is such an important experiment, if it's voted in, that is, that I don't doubt it's been transvised to all the other days."

"What?"

"The world and national governments have long been concerned by the many complaints about oversurveillance of people. A lot of people all over the world have organized protest groups. And the government, as you well know, is very sensitive to civil rights."

Min, Duncan noticed, did not even smile when he said that.

"On the other hand, Citizen Beewolf, the government has to keep as its first rule, its upmost and everpresent, the greater good of the people. It doesn't believe that a relaxation of surveillance will benefit its citizens."

Taped speech number 10A, Duncan thought.

"However, since there has been so much objection, even though the government regards it as ill-founded if not basically trivial, the government has decided to make a test and find out what will happen if surveillance is lessened to a certain extent. This is to be an experiment, so it won't be conducted worldwide. Only a few cities will be chosen for the experiment. Los Angeles is one of these."

"Any reason why L.A. was picked?"

Min smiled widely and gestured violently. "Because we're one of the most progressive cities in the world, of course!"

Duncan wondered if that was correct. It seemed to him that the government should pick out the less liberal metropolises for its experiment.

"However," Min said, "it's not determined that this test will be run. Today's election day, and if the majority of the voters are against it, the experiment won't be run."

"Ah!" Duncan said.

"What do you mean by that?"

"Just an exclamation."

"I'm surprised you didn't know about it."

"Why would I?" Duncan said. "I come from New Jersey. I doubt that any city there is big enough to be in the experiment."

"That wouldn't matter. The news has been on every Tuesday area. You should have seen it on the train screens, if no place else."

"I didn't."

Min had quit smiling. Eyes narrowed, he thrust his ball-shaped head forward on his massive neck.

"You're not one of those who ignore the TV, are you? Every citizen should keep himself well informed."

"I was busy looking at the countryside," Duncan said. "This is the first time I've ever been out of New Jersey. In fact, anywhere more than ten miles from New Ark."

If Min wanted to check that, he could consult the data from Duncan's ID card. He probably had done so before Duncan came into the office.

"Welcome to the big world, Beewolf. May I call you Andrew? Last names are so formal. I like to think I'm the buddy of every person in my block. A sort of father, too."

"Andy is fine."

"Since you don't seem to know about the election, I suggest, Andy, that you bone up on it. You can't vote for block leader yet, but you *are* entitled to vote on the surveillance issue."

"I'll do that, of course," Duncan said. "Meanwhile, I have to get a lot of things done before I go to my job tomorrow."

"Yes, do that." Min put out his hand. "Good luck to you, Andy, and may you be happy here. You have any problems, my screen is always open."

15

The Snorter was a half-mile walk from the apartments of Duncan (Beewolf), Cabtab (Ward), and Snick (Chandler), though none of the three lived less than a quarter-mile from each other. They met in the courseway, thirty feet wide and thirty feet high, near the entrance of the tavern. It was eight in the evening, and the election results had been displayed on the news screens. Seven million, three hundred thousand, one hundred and eleven had been in favor of decreasing surveillance. Approximately three million had voted against the measure. Three million, two hundred thousand and one had neglected to vote. Apparently, the election had pleased everybody in the neighborhood; all seemed drunk with joy. Now they were on the way to the tavern to get really drunk.

The three moved through the wide doorways into an immense room divided into four compartments by walls reaching halfway to the ceiling. In the center of each was a huge four-leaf-clover-shaped bar encircled by a dance floor, and outer rings of tables and booths. Here and there were huge pots holding the beautiful pimalia, a synthetic tree. The walls were filled with screens displaying the news and various shows. Though their sound could not be heard above the uproar, no one cared.

"They're mad with the foretaste of freedom," Snick said. "A freedom they didn't even know they didn't have until some radicals pointed it out to them."

They were threading through the mob toward a table against the wall.

Cabtab apparently did not hear her. Duncan was close enough to catch the words. He said, "You talk like a gank."

"No. I'm just being rational. Does that make me gankish?"

They sat down, Cabtab saying, "This looks like the last table open."

Duncan looked at a wall screen. "Twenty minutes to go."

The padre leaned forward so his lips could be close to their ears.

"You think she'll show? This is a hell of a place to talk subversive. You have to shout to make yourself heard."

"It's the best place," Duncan said. "Who the hell can overhear us?"

A sweating and tired-looking waitress appeared after ten minutes. "Sorry, folks," she said. "Tonight's bedlam and chaos."

Snick ordered a limewater; Cabtab, a beer; Duncan, a bourbon. The waitress disappeared into the yell and the swirl. When she showed up twelve minutes later, spurting out of the crowd like a grapefruit seed, she looked even more harassed. Just as she reached them, she was shoved against the table, and her tray fell. The drinks splashed onto Snick and Cabtab. The waitress, snarling, picked up the tray, turned, and banged the man behind her over the head with the tray. Protesting that he was innocent, the man punched the waitress in the belly. Cabtab, bellowing, shot from his chair and hurled himself against the man. A woman, shrieking, fell over the waitress, who was on all fours and in agony trying to get her wind back.

Duncan was not able to follow clearly the train of events after that. The entire tavern seemed to explode into fist fights, face-clawing, screaming, and war cries or shrieks for help. He, like any sensible person, of whom there seemed to be few there, got down on his hands and knees and crawled to the wall. He reached out and pulled the table, which was now on its edge,

toward him as a shield. He expected that Snick would join him.
But, looking around the side of the table, he was amazed to see
her chopping a man in the back of the neck with the edge of her
palm. Then she went down under a woman who had jumped
on her back. A man staggered backward and slumped against
the table, jamming Duncan against the wall for a moment. By
the time he had shoved table and body out from him and
looked again, he could find neither of his companions. Somewhere in the hue and din, though, the padre was thundering
threats of mayhem.

What would Henry V do in a situation like this? Duncan
thought. He would sally forth and get a black eye, a bloody
nose, a broken jaw, a concussion of the skull, and possibly a
wrenched back and injured kidneys.

What would Falstaff do? He would stay behind the table and
rationalize his cowardice, which he would call discretion.

Duncan compromised by leaving the shield of the table but
crawled close to the wall, the exit his goal. If Snick and Cabtab
had any sense, they would get out, too. The organics would very
soon be swarming into the place with their cattle prods and stun
mist. They would arrest everybody and then, to separate the
sheep from the goats, would administer truth mist to the sus-
pects. Though the ganks were required by law to confine their
questions to the particulars of the situation in which the sus-
pects had been arrested, they did not always do so. Anyway,
when Snick and Cabtab were asked to identify themselves after
breathing the mist, they would give their true names. These
would be checked inside a few seconds against the organic data
bank, and their name would not be mud. It would be stone.

Their stories would also expose Duncan.

"Damned fools!" he muttered. He stopped because a falling
woman's head had slammed into his ribs. Grunting with pain,
he scrambled on as fast as he could.

"No, you don't!" a man yelled at him and kicked at him.
Duncan shot forward, grabbed the man's ankle, and yanked.
The man went down but was stopped halfway by impact against

two struggling men. Duncan let go of the ankle and squeezed the man's testicles. The man's knee came up hard against Duncan's jaw. For a few seconds, Duncan did not know who he was or where he was. But he recovered enough then to start crawling again. He could hear whistles shrilling faintly. The ganks were coming.

He rose, shoved an entwined and bellowing male couple away and plunged, head down, through the fray. Bleeding, panting, he fell out through the door, got up, and ran across the courseway into a store. The screen over the door advertised it as Ibrahim Izimoff's Candy and Legal Drugs. He and the proprietor or clerk were the only ones in the place. The tall pudgy middle-aged man, pale-skinned, sporting bushy purple-dyed sideburns, said, "What in hell is going on over there?"

"A stupid brawl," Duncan said. "Is there a back exit?"

"Sure. Several. Just a minute. I'll close up the place and go with you."

Another Falstaffian, Duncan thought. He did not want to be anywhere near the place when the ganks started arresting. He could be pulled in as a witness.

"You Izimoff?" Duncan said.

"Yes. You Beewolf?"

"For God's sake!" Duncan said. "You the one supposed to meet us?"

"Not exactly. I was going to get your orders to you. Come on!"

"My colleagues are still in there," Duncan said. "If they get arrested . . ."

He went to the door and looked both ways down the courseway. Here came the men and women in green, running, blowing their whistles. But there were only five. Many more would soon appear.

Just before the first one, slowing down, reached the entrance, Cabtab, pulling Snick along with one hand, charged out of the doorway. His leviathan body slammed into a gank and knocked her down. The second to arrive, a big man, was floored by a huge fist. Cabtab, roaring like a lion, plunged across the courseway. Snick, now trailing along by her arm, her toes scraping against the floor, was dragged like a bundle of grain. The third gank to get there, a tall well-built woman, tried to spray stun mist in Cabtab's face. He quit bellowing because he was holding his breath. His fist shot out again, tore the can loose from the gank's grip, and with it still clenched, hit the point of her chin.

Others spilled out of the tavern and formed an unplanned barrier between the padre and the two remaining officers. But from right and left down the courseway a horde of green uniforms was running toward them.

Izimoff had by now turned out all the store lights. Duncan held the door open until Cabtab and Snick were inside. He shut it but could not, since it was a nongovernment store, lock it.

"For God's sake, let's get out of here!" Izimoff said, and he ran toward the back. There was enough light from the courseway for Duncan to see Cabtab's and Snick's puffed lips, swollen eyes, and bloodied scratches.

"Another fine mess you've gotten us into," Duncan said.

"Hell with that! It was fun!" the padre said.

"I'm sorry now," Snick said, panting, "but I worked off a lot of my anger. I would've preferred to do it on the ganks, though."

They hurried out through the store behind Izimoff's, causing some stares from the few customers and clerks, and into 10AB3 Courseway, also known as Welcomewagon Avenue. Some of the wall screens between the stores were already displaying the riot, the newspeople having arrived close on the heels of the peace officers.

Izimoff, puffing, sweating as if he were in a sauna, led them quickly down the courseway for a hundred feet. He turned into another store, went to the one behind that, and came out on a courseway that was part business, part residential. After they had gone a hundred yards, he stopped before a filigreed and rainbow-colored door that matched his frilly rainbow-slashed garb. He inserted his ID card into a slot, and the door swung inward. When he stepped inside, the lights went on.

As he led them down a hallway, he said, "First, we get rid of your bungs and bruises."

That was quickly done with medicine from the communal cabinet in the bathroom. In twenty minutes, the sorry faces were half-healed.

"Modern medical science," Izimoff said as he took them to the living room. He sighed. "Would that we could cure all social ills with stuff from a bottle." He stopped and waved his hand. "Sit down. Make yourself comfortable. I'd offer you a drink, but I doubt you need any more."

"We may stink like booze," Snick said sharply, "but we never had a chance to get even a single sip."

"Well, I don't stock any liquor," Izimoff said with a hint of smugness. "And I'm not about to break into the personal closets of the other days. Anyway, I don't think you should stay here long. I hadn't planned to bring you here. I was just going to venture into that den of iniquity long enough to pass on the data I'd been ordered to give you. And I have to get back to my store. I'm not supposed to close it until ten. I may be fined if the ganks notice it's shut. I can plead I was worried about the brawl, didn't want the drunks coming into my place and smashing things up. Also—"

"That's irrelevant," Snick said. "If we have to get out quick, you'd better give us the data."

"Oh, yes, of course," Izimoff said somewhat stiffly. "Though, I don't know. The situation has changed. There's no telling what consequences this unfortunate brawl may have. Maybe I should wait until I hear from my contact. He might reconsider the plan, a different approach now that the frame has changed. Maybe he wouldn't want you to have the data. God knows we're all in danger now that you've attracted the ganks' attention."

He pulled a piece of tissue paper from a pocket and wiped his forehead.

"Everything happened so fast, I doubt very much the ganks

could ID us," Duncan said. "For God's sake, man! We've been left in the dark too long as it is. We're thirsty for at least a little information, and we're eager to do something for the organization. Anyway, if you disobey orders, you may find yourself in hot water with your superiors. Come on. Give. Then we'll be on our way as soon as the bruises and cuts have healed."

"I don't know what it is," Izimoff said.

"What?" the three said at the same time.

"I mean it's on a card. I was going to give it to a young fellow who works part time for me. He was going to give it to a waitress, pay her for doing it, and she would give you the card when she served your drinks. You'd read it, and then rub it so the data would be destroyed. The brawl broke out just as I was about to hand the card to the young man. I told him to disappear, and—"

"You allowed the card to get into the hands of nonmembers?" Snick said. "I can't believe it. What if the brawl had started after the young man was in the tavern but before he could give it to the waitress? It'd be floating around in there, and you can bet your fat ass the ganks would soon have it."

"There's no need to be insulting," Izimoff said. He mopped his forehead again. "I was ordered to get the card to you circuitously. Not to deliver it personally. Now that's been shot to hell. You *know* me. That's why I'm reluctant to give it to you now. I know I'm going to be blamed for this even though there was no way I could avoid this frame."

"What could they do now?" Duncan said. "Kill you?"

Izimoff widened his eyes, rolled them, and said nothing.

"What kind of an outfit is this?" Duncan said.

"Oh, no! They wouldn't kill me, do anything like that, for God's sake!" Izimoff said. "But I might get chewed out, might get punished in some way. I don't know. What do I know about how they punish their members? I'm isolated, just one cell contacting another cell now and then. I don't even know the IDs of the cells I've met. They don't know mine, either, of course. I've never ever met anybody at my store or apartment. If only that riot hadn't happened!"

"You must've been approached by a recruiter," Snick said. "You've been to meetings, haven't you? You've been indoctrinated, surely?"

"Yes, but it was in a dimly lit room. Everybody was masked and our voices were transmitted through synthetic-audio devices. I've been to two meetings so far. Both places were in gymnasiums used also for church and synagogue congregations. Each meeting lasted half an hour. We swore an oath . . ."

He pulled out another piece of tissue. "I'm talking far too much. Stress. I thought I'd handle it better. You won't report me, will you?"

"Not unless you don't give us the card," Duncan said. His look at Snick said, I hope the other members are made of better stuff.

Izimoff removed a stiff gray rectangle from his pocket. "Here you are."

Duncan took it. Snick and Cabtab got up and stood behind him to read it. He rubbed his thumb on the corner marked by a thin angling black line. A sequence of phrases in English sprang into being on the white surface.

YOU WILL BE NOTIFIED SOON.

"What is this crap?" Duncan said. "Of course we expect to be contacted soon. We know that."

He glared at Izimoff.

"Is this what we risked our lives for?"

"I don't know," Izimoff said, backing away. "I don't want to know what it says. Please rub it again and give it back to me."

Duncan did as requested. Izimoff slid his thumb back and forth over the card as if to make sure that the message was destroyed. He glanced at the wall-screen clock. He groaned softly. It would be fifteen minutes before the faces of his unwelcome guests healed and they could leave.

"This is stupid!" Snick said. "Your organization is stupid!"

"Don't say that!" Izimoff said, holding out his hand, palm up, apparently to bounce her words, tennis-ball-like, back at her. "They're very cautious, but they wanted to encourage you, to let you know that you weren't being ignored. At least, I think they do. I didn't read the card, but from what you said it's evident what was written."

Cabtab gingerly touched the area around his left eye. The swelling and redness were almost gone.

"That our friend here is overly nervous and the sender of the card is not too bright doesn't mean that the entire outfit is a bunch of nellies and morons," he said. "Anyway, what else can we do but stick with the course outlined? We can't very well resign. Whatever they are, they wouldn't allow that."

"You may be sure of that!" Izimoff said.

They did not talk much thereafter except for a few comments while watching the news. They saw the organics carry the unconscious bodies of the arrested into vans and drive away. Then they saw some of the brawlers in the organic precinct house being arraigned. The questioning by the organics was not shown; that was always kept from the public. That the news media had been allowed to film any of the proceedings was proof that the ganks regarded this as just a mass drunk-and-disorderly incident. The media people were permitted to interview a few of the discharged as they left the precinct.

Media Interviewer (MI): "Just a minute, citizen. May we ask your name and what you're charged with?"

Citizen: "Screw off!"

MI (to another man): "You look like a cooperative citizen. Would you describe for our watchers just what happened in the Snorter?"

Citizen, smiling with puffed lips: "Garble, garble."

MI: "That's perfectly all right, citizen. We understand." (To a third, a tall big-shouldered woman with long black hair in a mess and a damaged cheek): "Citizen, would you say something for the audience? They're eager to get the details of the fracas at the Snorter."

Citizen: "I wasn't there. The ganks pulled me in because my husband and I were having a little disagreement. If you'd like to hear all about that bastard . . ."

MI: "Thank you. Oh, here's a man who looks as if he has something interesting to say. Citizen, would you . . .?"

Duncan pointed at another man slipping past the camera, his head down and his hat pulled low. "Hey, isn't that Professor Herman Trophallaxis Carebara? The ant-man we met on the train?"

Snick leaned forward, her eyes large. "Yeah, that's him. But what's he doing there? Did you see him in the Snorter?"

"No, and he shouldn't have been there. He said he would be living in the University Tower."

Snick shook her head. "Do you suppose he's a gank, and he's shadowing us?"

"We can't suspect everybody," Duncan said.

16

This meeting with the leader of the cell was not much like what Izimoff had said it would be like.

Only Duncan and the man who had summoned him were present. If, he thought, it was a man. The small bare room was lit by a very feeble light, and the person was wearing a mask, a wide-brimmed hat, and a figure-hiding cloak. Also, the round device strapped over his or her mouth not only distorted the voice but might have deepened it considerably. His own device made him sound as if he had just breathed in a lot of helium.

Since the room had been swept for monitoring bugs, the darkness and distorters seemed to Duncan to be unnecessary. Also, why were Cabtab and Snick not here?

He asked why.

"We have our reasons," the voice-at-the-bottom-of-the-well said. The cloak swirling, the person rose from the chair swiftly and began pacing back and forth, its hands locked behind its back. The baggy pants kept Duncan from observing whether the legs were male or female.

"I don't mean that you can't ask questions," it said. "If you didn't you'd be dull, too dull for us to want you. But you must understand that many of your questions won't be answered. If they're not, don't persist in asking them. Understand?"

"Understood."

"When we hold mass meetings—mass? four or five at the most—we deal with general issues. We never talk about the particular projects of the members in these meetings. Unless, of course, it's a project in which a number have to assist one another and delicate synchronization is needed. That doesn't happen very often. Just now, we have in mind a special project for you. But first, this."

The hand that came out from under the cloak held a blue spray can.

"We administer this at all first meetings and then at random from time to time. We can't be too careful. You understand?"

"Certainly," Duncan said. He could not keep from wondering if the can contained something other than truth mist. What if the organization had decided that he was a danger? How easy it would be to spray poison instead of what he expected to breathe. There was nothing he could do to stop them. If he refused, he would be done away with anyway.

The can hissed. He felt wetness on his lips, nose, and eyes and sucked in the sweet-smelling cloud. At least it had the violets odor of the mist. It would do no good to try to hold his breath until the mist was dissipated. It was working through the skin and into the bloodstream now. There was enough to produce a half-consciousness that would make him breathe naturally.

He awoke to find the dark figure standing close above him.

"So . . . it's true, then."

"What?" he said. His wits still had not come back in full force.

"That you can lie when under the mist. I was told you could, but I didn't believe it. Not really. All my probing failed to get from you anything except that you were indeed Andrew Vishnu Beewolf, and everything you told me fitted with your ID card. The items that aren't on it, personal things that the organics might question you about, these all came out as if you could be none other than Beewolf."

Again, the person strode back and forth, hands behind its back.

"I don't understand it, but there it is. It's a unique talent.

Incomprehensible! Genetic? Or a skill you taught yourself? Never mind. It doesn't matter. Well, yes, it does. If others could be instructed in how to do it, what a splendid advantage we'd have!"

The figure wheeled and pointed a finger at him as if it could shoot a ray that would drill him and make the truth pour from the hole.

"Did you *learn* how to do it? Or did it just seem to come naturally?"

"I taught myself through experimentation," Duncan said. "But the ability seems to me to come, as you put it, naturally. So I really can't answer your question."

"Unfortunately, you can lie, so I don't know whether you're telling the truth. It wouldn't do any good to subject you to the mist again and ask you."

Duncan was sure that the person had already put that question to him. Why was he or she lying? Was it just because the members of the organization were so accustomed to deceit that they lied when they did not have to? Or did the person have a good reason for doing so?

I've wondered this before, Duncan thought. I must have done it quite often when I was Caird and six others.

His singular talent also had its disadvantages from the viewpoint of the organization. If he could lie to the organics, he could lie to them. Which meant that he could be an infiltrator. He could not be fully trusted, but they could not refuse to use him. He was a tool such as neither organic or subversive had ever had.

"Does this group have a name?" Duncan said suddenly. "I'm tired of thinking of it as just the organization or outfit. It's hard to identify with something nameless."

"Ah, yes, Homo sapiens demands labels, tags, titles. Otherwise, it's at a loss. Do you really have to have a name?"

"I'd feel more comfortable."

"Very well. During this submonth, it's RAT."

"This month. You change it every twenty-eight days?"

"It could confuse the organics."

That was not so, Duncan thought. Any member caught and questioned would just reveal all the names that had been used.

"RAT?"

"Rebels Against Tyranny."

"I see."

"I don't like it because it implies only destruction. We're that, but we're also builders. Rebuilders. Constructive. However, that doesn't matter now. What does is your project. Listen carefully."

Thirty minutes later, the person said good night to Duncan and, taking both voice distorters with it, went through a door. Duncan, as instructed, tore his mask into strips and put them in his pocket. He left by another door, stepping into a hallway that led to a noisy gymnasium. He turned left and went out a side door into a courseway. Going by a public trash can, he dropped the strips into it. At 10:00 P.M., he boarded a bus. Ten minutes later, he got off at the corner near his apartment. He had tried to detect a shadower but had failed.

The work assigned to him was, he was sure, a small part of a grand plan. He was not supposed to know how it would mesh with the work done by many others. He was just a gear in a vast underground machinery, which, he hoped, was not a Rube Goldberg. Well versed in history, though he did not know why he was, he knew that revolutionaries were much better at tearing down than at carpentry. Not always, it was true. But they seemed, generally, to have been motivated more by the lust for power than the desire to make a better society, though all certainly would have denied this. The genuine rebuilding had almost always been done by those who had pushed aside or liquidated the first generation of militants.

He was working for a group that had not enlightened him about how it would achieve its ultimate goals. Perhaps, after he had "proved" himself, he would be told much more. If he was not, he would find it hard to keep working with enthusiasm. Unfortunately, he could not quit the RAT if he lost his zeal. Once joined, forever joined.

Maybe.

As a data banker, he would have the way open to establish a new identity if he wished to do so. The danger was that the RATs would, if they were keen enough, know this. And they would have set up a monitoring alarm system to warn them if he tried to do that. On the other hand, he could arrange a monitoring system to detect their monitors. But they might have anticipated that and inserted a monitoring of his monitoring system.

This could go on indefinitely and result in an electronic hall of mirrors.

He laughed, though he did not feel as if his funny bone had been tickled nor was he exuberant. Nevertheless, there was a streak of absurdity in the fantasized situation. If there was a God, It must be laughing at those made in Its image. Or perhaps It was so disgusted that It had long ago left this universe. Or perhaps, being all-powerful, It had canceled Itself and no longer existed. Never mind the contradiction in that It was also always and forever infinite and eternal. Those attributes could be erased if It wished to do so.

Duncan entered the door, which opened onto a hallway lined by apartment doors. His ID card, inserted into the slot in the door, released the lock. The lights came on as he went from room to room. He stood for a while looking through the ceiling-high window at the view. Los Angeles was splendid with lights radiating from every tower and bridge, from boats and ships in the water below, and from airships and airplanes. It was a wondrous sight, and one that should not be stained by worry and pending troubles. The metropolis glowed as if it were a beacon for beauty, hope, and love. These should come flying in like moths. But . . . flies and buzzards were also pulled in by light. The citizens of this magnificent place had everything to make them both contented and happy. That was the theory. The facts were otherwise.

"It's always been that way," he muttered. "Yet, if grief, hunger, hurt, insanity, neurosis, physical sickness, and frustration could be made quantitative, wouldn't it be true that there is far less now than there ever was? Wouldn't past societies regard ours as a near-Utopia?"

Homo sapiens was never satisfied. At least, some of its members never were.

Loneliness certainly was as endemic as ever—judging from his own experiences and what he knew of others'. At this moment, he was standing in a shower of it, and he had thought himself extraordinarily impervious to such feelings. Lonely . . .

Which led him to think of Panthea Pao Snick. He would like it very much if she were sharing this apartment with him. He desired her and envisioned with delight living for a long time with her. He was, to put it mildly, in love with her. Why, then, had he not told her so? Easy to answer that. She had given no sign that she had for him any other emotion than that felt for a close colleague. He was not even sure that she had that. He should find out just what she did think of and feel for him. Perhaps she was as inhibited as he. After all, she was, had been, an organic, and they tended to be very careful about revealing their personal attitudes. Besides, there really hadn't been much time to express any such thing as budding love.

"I must have had some such feelings for her when I was my other personae," he said aloud. "Why would I feel this way about her now? It's been all too sudden; it must have sprung from previous experiences, which, unfortunately, I don't remember."

He mixed himself a drink, then turned on a wall screen for messages. That the screen was blank made him also feel blank. Sighing, he made dinner, then set about cleaning up the place so that the Wednesday tenant would find nothing to complain about. Moving from room to room, he half-saw and half-heard the news. The details of the issues in the referendum to be put before the people were shown in print and then repeated by newscasters. The items were to be voted upon separately, then the final referendum would be placed before the citizens. Meanwhile, those against and for it would be making their pitch.

Having finished the cleaning, which did not take long because he was seldom home long enough to dirty it, Duncan entered the stoner.

17

Duncan sat in the center of his own workroom in Boda Lab, the Bureau of Data Assimilation, Los Angeles Branch. The chamber had a twenty-foot diameter, and its walls were lined with ten-foot-square screens. His workdesk was circular and held twenty smaller computers and their monitors. His powered chair moved on a track along the inner perimeter of the big O. Four hours each workday he sat there; the rest of the day was his for whatever he wanted to do. Go home or shopping or sailing or bowling or looking for a lover or put in two hours of volunteer work for a bureau project or for his own research project.

At this moment, he was gathering information on a task assigned by his immediate superior. This was a small part of a very big program that had been going on for several subyears. Duncan did not think it was important, though his supervisor had stressed that it was very much so to the government. Duncan resented it because it was one more delving of the government into the private lives of its citizens. He did not know why it should be in any way needed nor what its final goal was. His supervisor was also ignorant of the goal, but that, he said, did not matter.

"A perfect state can't be achieved until it has complete information," Porfirio Samuels Phylactery had said to Duncan. His depigmented leaf-green eyes seemed to glow as he waved a hand that had been depigmented into light and dark stripes. The "zebra effect" was much in fashion among those who had the credits required for the treatment.

"It's true that much of the data we've accumulated may not be used for a long time. But when it's needed, it'll be there. Let me tell you, Andrew, I've seen long-stored and never-called-up data suddenly needed for a project. And it's there, waiting to become alive and vital, summoned within a microsecond, springing into being and service, fitting into the program. It doesn't have to be laboriously and time-consumingly worked on while other parts of the program lag because the data isn't ready. It's hidden treasure, and a push of a button or a spoken phrase brings it out like uncorking a genie's bottle. It's simply fabulous! So don't ever think you're just on a makework job. You're being very useful. If not for this generation, then for the next. But probably for this generation!"

That last sentence was not very arguable. Since the average longevity span in subyears was eighty-five, most of this generation would live approximately 595 obyears. The rest of what he had said, though, was 50 percent crap and 25 percent chaff.

And 24 percent doubtful.

"You're right, boss," Duncan said, nodding and smiling. And, he thought, he was lining up at the head of ten thousand generations of ass-kissers. But he was not doing this to curry favor and advance himself for material gain. He was playing a role.

So what else was new?

Phylactery left the room, his walk very springy, sallying forth to encourage any who were dubious, discouraged, or misled. Duncan gave the broad striped back the finger, a gesture that had probably originated in the Old Stone Age, if not before then. Feeling a little ashamed of himself at his childish act, Duncan settled down to work. Currently, this was setting up the computer complex to match the PEI (personality element index) of citizens subclassed as having a high ratio of SC (self-centeredness) to other character traits. High SC was defined as immaturity characterized by the possessor's expecting others to arrange their schedules and interests according to the wishes of the POSS (possessor) and for N-POSS (nonpossessors, that is, those socially involved with the POSS) to do many things for the POSS that the POSS was quite capable of doing for himself or herself. There were, of course, many other subsubelements integral to the HI SC POSS.

All but saints, whose existence the state denied, were self-centered to some degree. But the HI SC POSS firmly believed that he or she was the axis around which the entire universe turned.

Duncan's summary of data already collected re this superclass established that not a single one of the three billion under study believed that he or she was anything but normally self-centered. (*Normal* was not as yet clearly defined in the official psychicist catalog.)

Since the founding of the New Era, the government had been stressing in every way it could think of the desirability of cooperation and self-sacrifice for its citizens. The results were coming in now, showing that N.E. (New Era) citizens were much more cooperative and socially aware than citizens of previous societies (though there had been no substantially scientific studies of these traits in pre-N.E. citizens).

However, at least 20 percent of this generation were still HI SC POSS. According to the projections made by the government a hundred obyears ago, there should now be only 1 percent of the "incorrigibles."

The failure to respond to state education and propaganda must, therefore, have its origins in genetic patterns.

Since the CH COM (chromosomal complex) of every citizen was in the data bank, it was comparatively easy, though not always quickly done, to match the individual's CH COM against the HI SC POSS index. Eventually, when enough subjects had been matched to make the study significant (in a statistical sense), it could be determined (it was hoped) that certain chromosomal patterns would be shown to be responsible for high self-centeredness.

The next step?

The government had not stated this.

It was obvious to Duncan, among many others, that the present research into the alteration of chromosomal patterns before birth would be greatly stepped up. Goal: to change the undesirable patterns to desirable ones.

Just how this could be done in more than 4 or 5 percent of the unborn Duncan did not know. There just were not enough doctors and technicians to work on more than this percentage. Meanwhile, the studies had not yet been done and probably would not be for another 20 subyears or 140 obyears.

At the moment, the digested results of the study on the ratio of HI SC among zealous bridge players, homosexual males, and surgeons were being displayed. The implications of these could have been left up to the computer, but the human brain was still better in sensing subtleties and implications than the machine. Some brains were.

Duncan had the computer compress the results even more, and rotating his chair, read the desk and wall screens. Then he had each display produce voice. While listening to the verbal scan, he also considered what he would do after workhours. But he soon concentrated again on the present task.

Among the eighty million zealous bridge players, sixty-five million had a high SCI (self-centered interest index). The comparison group, eighty million citizens chosen at random, eliminating bridge players, showed that only twenty-nine million had an SCI of similar intensity. The comparison group also excluded male homosexuals, surgeons, politicians, priests, rabbis, ministers, and mullahs. Duncan had no idea why the last four groups were barred. Perhaps the government ideology prevented any consideration of "holy men and women" as non–self-centered. Or perhaps they were excluded because they were irrational and thus not fit subjects for this kind of study. If this was so, then the study was invalid in this respect.

It was possible that the entire project was based on invalid or unscientific premises. After all, the conclusions of the bureau interviewers that the individuals interviewed and studied were highly self-centered were grounded on subjective judgments.

Duncan shrugged. He had a job to do, and any comments he made about its ineffectiveness would only cause him unwelcome attention.

He switched the displays to the results of data drawn from 100 million male homosexuals. The SCI was even higher, 820 million being credited with an upper level "negative" rating. But the "social cooperation" ratio, placed on the screens at his order, showed that only 50 million of these were anywhere in the "antisocial" bracket. Of these, only one-eighth were labeled as "dangerous." And of the fraction, only one-third was marked as "superdangerous." But when Duncan considered that the SUPDAN classification could result from such minor crimes as spitting on the public sidewalk more than three times or fisticuffs in a tavern, he was not sure of its validity.

Also, the cause and origin of homosexuality had long ago been established as purely genetic in all but 3 percent of the cases studied—three billion during two subcenturies. The nine chromosomal complexes responsible had been identified, and they could, in nine out of ten cases, be altered successfully in prebirth individuals. Two factors, however, had kept the government from passing laws to make the alteration mandatory despite the strong insistence by various heterosexual organizations that it should. First, the homosexuals vigorously objected. Despite all evidence to the contrary, the gay groups insisted that their sexuality was not genetically determined but was arrived at by choice, by the exercise of their free will. Second, the much more powerful determinant, the government wished to keep the population at zero growth or less. The more homosexuals there were, the less the population increased.

However, the government had made it illegal for homosexuals to beget children parthogenetically or through surrogate mothers. The official reason given for this was that, if homosexuals could not have children, homosexuality would die out. The

enraged gay groups had not been able to budge the government from this position. They pointed out that most of the
children born to homosexuals before the ban was imposed had
been heterosexual and that at least 10 percent of the children
born to heterosexuals were homosexual.

The government paid no attention to this reasoning or to the
discrepancy in its own logic.

There was nothing new in this kind of logic for any government, past or present, Duncan thought.

He ran a comparison of the chromosomal complexes thought
by most geneticists to be responsible for the high SCI in homosexuals to corresponding areas in bridge zealots. This had been
done by others, but he wished to study the matchings himself.
Perhaps he could detect something that the others had failed to
observe. After a while, he tired of that and took his lunch hour.
This was spent mostly in the bureau gymnasium, twenty minutes at weights and fifteen at jogging. After showering and then
eating lightly, he went back to work for an hour, then went
home.

That evening, he came back to his office. The guard noted
the time of his entry. Since his supervisor would also check the
roster of overtime workers, Duncan had to spend some time in
continuing the comparison search. That would justify his presence there. But after an hour's work, which would satisfy Phylactery that Duncan had not been just goofing off, Duncan set
up the codes ensuring that his illegal probes would erase themselves at the first monitor alarm or probe by anyone else. Then,
using the codes given him by the dark figure at the meeting, he
put in an inquiry for a name. MARIA TUAN BOLEBROKE.

The figure had said, "I'm in a position to get the access codes,
but I can't use them myself. I'd be too open to exposure. You
use them, then do what I told you to do after you get the data. I
do have some data, however. Here's the little I know on the
subject."

No codes were unbreakable, though it was dangerous to attempt to crack them. There were too many safeguards. How-

ever, codes were set up by human beings, and some men and women were, unlike the codes, accessible. That was the theory, which sometimes worked out in practice.

Duncan asked for the file on Maria Tuan Bolebroke. Challenged by the computer, Duncan gave the second code needed to get entry. But he was challenged again. Having spoken the third code, Duncan was admitted to the file. He studied the information on the screens until he had memorized all that he might need. It was against RAT procedure to run off a printout.

After he was sure that the data were locked into his mind, he gave the code that would erase all records of the procedure from the data bank. This, too, had been given him by the masked person in the gymnasium. Possession of all these codes meant that the mysterious stranger had a high position in the bureau and was also probably an upper-level organic, a "traitor." Though Duncan was curious about the person's identity, he resisted the impulse to try to track him down. He could have asked for the IDs of all the top-security officers of the local bureau, but, even if he did not trigger alarms by doing this, he still would not know the face and voice of his superior.

"Forget it," he muttered.

Still, the figure had gestured vigorously and probably with a definable pattern. If he could get hold of videos of the top officials while talking, he might be able to identify the figure. Which having done, what would he do then?

"I'll keep it in mind, anyway," he said. And he wondered why he often talked to himself. It was not a desirable trait. Since he had assembled the personality of William St.-George Duncan, he would not have chosen the habit of thinking out loud. Was there a leak way down there, a rupture in one of the buried personae? Was the talk bubbling out like wine from a goatskin long ago sunken in an ancient gallery?

Wherever those psyches were, they had not been cut off entirely. A good thing, too. Otherwise, he would not have been able to work as a data banker. Beewolf knew nothing of that profession. Well, yes, he did. The leaks from the others were just as much a part of Beewolf as his body even though these were not in his ID card or the GOV DTA BNK.

"I have a leaky personality, but they're good leaks in that I need them very much."

He resumed his concentration on Maria Tuan Bolebroke. His orders had been to learn all he could about her. Then he was to get acquainted with her, become familiar with her if he could, and, if possible, be her lover. That might not be so difficult since she had had twelve in the last two subyears, and Duncan was the physical type she preferred. Once he had gained her confidence, he was to try to get her to reveal certain codes. How he did that was up to him.

Duncan did not believe that, even if he could be on intimate terms with her, he could last long enough as her lover to get out of her what the RAT wanted to know. Her turnover rate was too high. Putting in all the time required to get something from her that she would probably not give seemed ridiculous to Duncan.

He asked for and got information about her routine and habits. This did not set off a block-access notice. He read the report, and he smiled. Why not take his own course, a much quicker one?

At lunch hour the following Tuesday, he was a few paces behind Maria Bolebroke, BODA LAB, Supervisor Class 3-M, as she walked to a restaurant near the bureau offices. Sunlight, piped in via optic fibers, made the great curving courseway bright. The crowd was clad in many-colored clothes except for the nudists, many of whom had striped skin of various loud colors. All were in a hilarious mood because of the coming surveillance-free period. When the vote on the exact items of freedom was concluded, their liberation would begin. That, however, was at least a subweek away.

The joyous mood of the people should tell the government something, Duncan thought. Though there was little official complaint from the citizens, their attitude now showed that they must have resented, even if unconsciously, their peeping-tom overlords. Just what all these L.A.-ers planned to do when the watchers quit looking, Duncan did not know. Did they think they could do anything they liked?

Maria Bolebroke was alone, and Duncan hoped that she would not be meeting someone in the restaurant. If she were, she was safe from him for that day. He let out a little sigh of relief when she took a tiny one-person booth in a corner. He got a table already held by Cabtab across the room. Snick was sitting at a nearby table with five of her coworkers. She glanced at Duncan and after that did not look his way.

"Expecting company, citizens?" the waiter said.

"No," Duncan said.

The waiter pressed a button at the end of one seat, and the seats slid in on themselves. The table area also shrank as the outer end dropped down and then moved under the other part. A flunky, at the waiter's gesture, brought a folding table and chairs and set them up to occupy the space vacated by the reduced booth.

Duncan and Cabtab gave their orders, Duncan's eyebrows rose when the big man requested only a small salad and cottage cheese.

"My boss demanded that I lose sixty pounds in six months," Cabtab grumbled. "Otherwise, I'll lose some credits and perks."

"Don't cheat," Duncan said.

"I won't. But the other day I saw on TV that a new product is coming out soon. It's mostly good-tasting bulk and very few calories. I could stuff myself on that. The only trouble is that some people have side effects when they eat it. Dizziness and diarrhea, the report said. I suppose it'd be just my luck to be one of the afflicted."

"Pray to God to give you willpower to stick to the diet."

"Yeah? Which One?"

"Try all of Them."

"I don't know," Cabtab said somewhat gloomily. "I've been doing a lot of thinking lately. That is, I have when my roomie isn't chattering away. The Great Ear-Bender, I call her, though she certainly has enough good qualities to almost make up for her verbosity. Anyway, as I said, I've been thinking. Worshiping all the Gods should reinforce the quantity of good returns. But Jahweh and Allah and Buddha—who isn't a God, by the way, but he likes being prayed to and He is, in a way, an agent for the Universal Equilibrium—and Woden and Thor and Zeus and Ceres and Ishtar and the Living Mantra and Jumala and Vishnu and—"

"Spare me the entire list," Duncan said. "I understand what you're saying."

"Do you? I don't. Anyway, the theory is that praying to all of These multiplies the powers of your prayers and enforces manyfold the divine interest of the divine capital, the celestial output, you might say. But . . . what if a prayer to one deity cancels a prayer to another? What if all my prayers blend to make one big null? Then where am I? Maybe I've been wrong all these years and wasted my life, not to mention the lives of my disciples. It might be—"

He stopped while the waiter put the water and food on the table.

"Anything else, citizens?"

"No, thank you," Duncan said. When the waiter had left, Duncan leaned across the table and spoke softly. There was not much chance that they could be overheard in this babble of speech and laughter, but the two who had just sat down at the table by them might be carrying narrow channel audio-detectors. They looked harmless, and he thought he could spot organics by their expression, that ghost of power shining from their faces. He could be mistaken, though. Why take a chance?

"I didn't know you had a lover."

"I wouldn't exactly call her a lover," Cabtab said. "She's attractive and very interested in my theory and practice of theologically covering all bets and touching all bases. But I really think what attracts her is my large apartment and extra credits, not to mention my near-Samsonian sexual prowess."

"What's happened to you?" Duncan said. "No offense, but I'd expected that your big ego would avoid such demeaning self-reproach or self-doubts."

"I don't have a big ego!" Cabtab said. "I'm just a realist; I see things as they are. But I'm human. I depend on my environment to keep me physically well. Physically well; mentally well, as the slogan goes. As long as I eat as much as I need, my soul flourishes. But when I'm forced by this picayunish pygmyish society to diet, to lose the sheathing and the armor as necessary to me as a shell to a crab, then I suffer. I also languish, dwindle, shrink. The body loses substance, and so does my soul. Food is my sun. Without a sun, how can I have shadow? The shadow is my soul, and . . ."

Cabtab had been talking too loudly despite Duncan's warning gestures and expressions. The couple next to them were undoubtedly listening in. Though Cabtab was not saying anything subversive, he certainly was expressing some rather eccentric ideas. That was not against the law any more than expressing dissatisfaction with the government was illegal. But organics reported everything that might indicate a potential for eccentricity or a malcontent. Cabtab was not in a situation in which he could bear investigation. Nor, for that matter, was he, Duncan.

He gripped the giant's wrist and said softly, "Eat. We may not have time enough."

Cabtab shook his head, blinked, and said, "I must learn to be more humble. Perhaps then the Gods will be in a better mood to listen to me."

Jesus! Duncan thought. In this age, a primitive polytheist!

Through a mouthful of cottage cheese, Cabtab said, "I would apologize if I really thought it was necessary. But I am, above and below all things, a preacher. I find it very hard, you have no idea how hard, to refrain from and pour concrete over my God-given natal desire to tell people the Truth and attempt to sway them toward it."

"Time to go," Duncan said. He had been switching his gaze from the adorable Panthea Snick—his chest ached when he looked at her—to Bolebroke and back again.

"She's going into the P and S."

Snick had been chattering away with her companions, but she had been keeping an eye on Bolebroke. She got up from her table at the same time that Duncan rose. They walked toward the restroom at a leisurely pace. Before they could reach the entrance, their quarry's Titian-red hair, arranged in a Tower-of-Babylon coiffure, had vanished. Duncan went down the curving hallway into the big room. Two men were standing by the urinal; a quick look under the batwing doors of the stalls showed that only one had a pair of female legs in it. The doors that Bolebroke had entered were still swinging.

Duncan stood before the urinal and made some comments about the forthcoming election to distract the two men. Snick, not hesitating, withdrawing her sprayer can from her handbag, entered Bolebroke's stall. If Bolebroke objected, Duncan did not hear her. The two men left, but a third came in. Duncan stood resolutely by the urinal, saying something about prostate trouble to the man. He had to have some excuse to linger there.

Snick did not take long. She stepped out of the stall about sixty seconds later. Duncan sealed up and followed her out.

"How'd it go?" he said.

"I sprayed her face just as she opened her mouth. She passed out immediately. I asked her about the codes, and she gave me the answers as if she was taking an exam."

"You gave her a hypnotic suggestion to forget the whole incident?"

"Of course! She won't remember it. She'll think she fell asleep, if she notices the passage of time. I told her not to notice it."

"It was just a rhetorical question," Duncan said. "You don't have to be so snappish."

"I'm nervous. But I feel good, excited."

"Sure. So do I."

They stopped talking. Snick rejoined her companions. Duncan went to his table. Cabtab said, "It went well?"

"Like castor oil down a goose."

They finished eating, went to the register, slipped their cards into the slot, and left. That evening, Duncan stopped off at the Snorter, slid onto a stool by Snick, and asked her for the codes she had gotten from Bolebroke. After a few minutes, pretending that he had failed in his hit on Snick, he left. He would have preferred to spend the evening with her and some time in bed before stoning time came. He could not because, other factors aside, he was not to appear to have more than a casual relationship to her.

At ten o'clock, shortly before closing time, he went into Izimoff's store. The last customer was just leaving. Duncan strode to the counter and asked for the nonprescriptive drug Wild Dreams. When Izimoff, who was sweating even more than usual, handed the bottle to him, Duncan gave him the codes. They would, Duncan supposed, be recorded by some device that Izimoff was wearing as a decoration. Perhaps it was concealed in the Laughing Buddha dangling from a chain around his neck.

Izimoff looked surprised. "I was told you probably wouldn't have the data until the end of the month, if then."

"I work fast," Duncan said.

"Yeah, I guess you do. Meet your supervisor at the Wetmore Gymnasium, that's in the east block, at 7:00 P.M. tomorrow. The supervisor said I was to pass this on as soon as you gave me the data. The supervisor's going to be surprised, though."

"Tell him it went off without a hitch. There's nothing to worry about. She—he'll know who she is—isn't even aware we got the data."

"I wish I knew what was going on!" Izimoff said.

"So do I," Duncan said. He picked up the bottle. "Be seeing you."

"Oh, wait a minute," Izimoff said. "You ever used those before?"

He pointed at the bottle.

"No."

"Better read the warning on the label. Sometimes, rarely, but it does happen, you get nightmares instead of pleasant dreams. If that happens, don't take any more, and be sure to notify me. I have to report such occurrences to the Drug Bureau. They need the data for their statistical summaries."

"For God's sake," Duncan said, "I just bought it so I'd have an excuse to pass the data on. I don't take nonmedical drugs."

Izimoff wiped the sweat off his forehead with the back of his hand. "Sure. I'm just nervous."

"It's dangerous to be too nervous," Duncan said. "I don't mean that all the danger's from the organics."

He left while Izimoff stared wide-eyed at him. No doubt Duncan's words had made him even more anxious. Duncan, however, was only trying to warn him, not to upset him. He felt sorry for Izimoff at the same time that he felt that Izimoff was a misfit.

On the way home, he jogged at a moderate pace, passing or being passed by others. The last buses were in the courseways to take people to their apartments so that they would have plenty of time to get ready for stoning. An organic patrol car, a small green three-wheeled electric vehicle with a topless frame, drove slowly by him. The man and woman in it gave him a quick look. Nothing in that; organics did that to everybody.

Just as he was nearing the door of his apartment and going by a brightly lit store, he heard a woman call out across the street.

"Caird! Jeff Caird!"

For two seconds, he failed to recognize the name. Then it drove through him like a car through a barricade. That was the name of one of his personae, the name of the basic person that he had been.

He ducked his head and strove not to break into a run. He stopped before the door and slipped the ID card into the slot.

"Caird!" the woman called out even more loudly.

Duncan turned. The woman was walking across the courseway now. She was in civilian clothes, but her bearing and expression told him that she was a gank. She was almost as tall as he, was slender, and had a long though rather pretty face. One hand was in the folds of her purplish silver-sequined robe.

"Caird!" she said again. "Don't you remember me? Manhattan? Patroller-Corporal Hatshepsut Andrews Ruiz? Hattie?"

18

Her face rode by in his mind like a duck in a shooting gallery. It rose, flopped over, rose, flopped over. Flashes of her in various places appeared like a holograph beamed at random. Though he did not recall much about her, he remembered enough to know that she knew him well. What was she doing here? Visiting? Immigrated? It did not matter.

He forced a smile. "I'm sorry. You're mistaken. I'm Andrew Vishnu Beewolf. Do I look like this . . . Caird?"

Ruiz was not so sure now. She stopped a few paces from him, squinted, and said, "A natural clone. I was shocked when I saw you. I thought for just a minute . . . you can't be! Caird's dead!"

"I'm sorry to hear that."

His heart was beating hard, and his body seemed to be about fifty pounds lighter. If this kept on, he would be floating off the sidewalk.

"You needn't be. He was a traitor, a subversive. He—"

She stopped, probably because she was revealing more than she should.

She quit smiling and said, "ID, please."

He looked up and down the courseway. No one else in sight.

"Sure." Then, "Are you an organic?"

She nodded and reached with the other hand into an inside pocket. Duncan did not give her time to pull the card out. He slammed her on the point of her chin with his fist, lunged after her as she staggered back, and chopped the edge of his hand against the side of her neck. She fell heavily, her head striking the soft and springy courseway.

It took him three seconds to carry her limp body into his apartment. After removing her ID card and her proton-accelerator handgun, he went to his personal closet. He came back with the illegal can of truth mist and spurted a cloud on her face. That would guarantee that she would be unconscious for fifteen minutes. But he had little more than an hour to decide what to do with her.

"Could've bluffed it out," he muttered. "Only she wouldn't have been satisfied. She would've run my card against Caird's file. And that would be all, brother. Damn it! Why'd I have to run into her?"

Actually, if the encounter had to happen, it was best that it take place as it had. If she had seen him anywhere else, he might not have been able to attack her without causing public attention.

He considered giving her a posthypnotic suggestion to forget the whole incident. But she would awake with a sore jaw and aching neck that would make her more than just suspicious. She would go to a psychicist who would run the passage of time just before, during, and immediately after the unexplained blankness. The psychicist would see to it that she recalled everything, including the tactile and audio data she recorded while knocked out and while under the mist. He could not take that chance. What was he to do with her?

If she disappeared, the organics would investigate. Undoubtedly, she had reported in every half hour, and HQ knew that she was last seen in this area. This area would swarm like a hive next Tuesday. Every citizen here would be questioned. If the organics suspected anybody because of "suspicious behavior," they would subject that person to the mist. He could lie, but if they really dug into his ID, followed it back to birth—and the bastards sometimes did—they might find something smelly. And there could be only one conclusion to that even more deeper search they would conduct.

It was too late to try to get a message to his supervisor. Besides, he had gotten into this mess, and it was up to him to get out of it. First, find out where and when she had known him. Also, get out of her if she knew anything about him that he did not; that is, about his personae in Manhattan.

Ruiz, now lying on a sofa, her eyes closed, replied promptly to his questions. She had served under him when he had been Detective-Captain Jefferson Cervantes Caird. She did not know what underground organization he had belonged to, but she had been in on the manhunt before he had been exposed and imprisoned. She had also taken part in the hunt after he had escaped. She knew that his corpse had been found in New Jersey. That data had been transmitted to the Manhattan organics officials. She had learned that only because she had been Detective-Major Wallenquist's lover for a while.

Wallenquist. A broad fat face floated before him. Wallenquist had also been his superior. But that was all that Duncan could remember about him.

What else had the major told her? After some very specific questions designed to get the information out step by step—a person under the mist answered with a minimum of data and had to be interrogated carefully—Duncan knew all that she knew. Unless he had failed to ask the proper questions. Wallenquist had once said something to her about Caird's longevity. When Ruiz had asked him what he meant, the major had told her not to pursue the subject. Forget what he had said if she cared anything for both of them.

"Was Wallenquist frightened when he told you about Caird's longevity?" Duncan said.

What in hell did his life span have to do with the organics?

"He was upset," she replied tonelessly.

"How upset? Frightened? As if he had said something he should not have said?"

"Yes."

"Wallenquist never referred to Caird's longevity again?"

"Never."

"What did you think of that comment and his reaction?"

"Not much. I did not know what he was talking about."

"Did you ever hear anybody else say anything about it? Did anybody make a comment that reminded you of what Wallenquist said?"

"No."

"Did you ever hear of, see, or read anything that suggested that Caird might not be dead?"

"No."

That was that. Now, what to do with her?

It was fifteen minutes to midnight. The wall screens had been flickering bright orange and emitting a soft hooting. They were warning Tuesday that it was time to enter the cylinders. Some people would already have set the controls so that they would be stoned before the time limit. Thus, if he activated the power to his own cylinder, it would be indicated in a data bank. But that would not draw attention.

He could stone her, open a window, and drop her body out of it. At this late hour, probably nobody would notice it. She could lie under the mud under the waters around the tower for a long time. Maybe forever, though he doubted that. The bottom was periodically dredged. When? He would have to find out. The way his luck was going, it would be tomorrow.

When he had only five minutes to go, he decided that he would put off the problem until next week. He dragged Ruiz into the cylinder with him, bent her down at his feet, and waited for the power. After what seemed a long time, unconsciousness came. He had just closed his eyes, or so it seemed, when he opened them again. He looked through the cylinder window to make sure that no one else was in the room. Though there should not have been, he was always careful to make sure. Satisfied that things were as they should be, he pushed the door open. Stepping out over Ruiz, still asleep, he went to a wall screen. He spoke Snick's number after telling the machine to blank out the video.

Snick, looking very sleepy, responded immediately.

"A.B.," Duncan said. "You alone?"

"No, I'm not," she said. "But he's in the bathroom. What's up?"

For a few seconds, Duncan could not reply. Fury seized him and made him speechless. Then he envisioned a hand coated with ice gripping his brain and heart, and he literally cooled down.

"I need you at once," he said. "Emergency. Can you get away without causing suspicion?"

The sleep had cleared off her face as if it were a film of water under intense heat. "Sorry, can't," she said.

"Then I'll get . . . Never mind. See you later."

He cut her off, and, breathing faster than he wanted to, called the padre. Cabtab bellowed, "Who the hell is this? Waking up a man from his vital sleep?"

Which meant that Cabtab had gone directly from the cylinder to his bed.

"Big E," Duncan said. "Can you get over here at once?"

"Certainly, my man," the padre said, his voice softer. "Can you tell me. . . ?"

"I can't," Duncan said, and he cut off the screen. Ten minutes later, the padre, dripping wet and angry again, showed up.

"Damn automatic courseway sprayers," he thundered. "Why don't they clean the streets at midnight when nobody's abroad instead of waiting until Tuesday has begun? There's no escaping the sprayers; they shoot from the sides, the ceiling, and the floor!"

"The sanitary corps has to have some fun," Duncan said. "OK, here's the situation. I need your muscle, not your brains, to help me."

He had already restoned Ruiz, hoping that the surge would not be noted at the city power records department. It would be recorded, of course, but it could be overlooked. Or, if seen, the observer might be too lazy or too busy to trace the location of the surge and send somebody to inquire about it. It was chancy, but there was nothing else Duncan could do.

Oh, yes, there was.

He could have cut Ruiz up and put her down the garbage dispenser. That, however, he would not do.

Together, Cabtab and Duncan pulled and pushed the very heavy body to Duncan's personal closet. After they had removed some materials and goods from the shelves and stacked these in a corner, they took out shelves and piled them on top of the stuff. Then, grunting and sweating and swearing a little, they got Ruiz into the space they had made.

"That's just temporary," Duncan said. "If they start looking for her, and they will, we can't have her here. We've got to get rid of her very soon."

Cabtab wiped the sweat from his forehead. "How soon?"

"The next ten minutes would be fine."

"We might get her out through the window by then. But there's too much danger somebody'd see her fall. Anyway, I think the ganks would drag the bottom around the tower as a matter of routine."

"They won't like it," Duncan said, "but we have to contact RAT. They'll have the people and the means to make her disappear."

"Izimoff's our only contact, and I know by God's little green apples he won't like it."

"Too bad," Duncan said. He activated a wall screen and put in a call to Izimoff's apartment address.

"How'd you know that?" Cabtab said. "I thought we were only supposed to get to him at his store."

"I asked the city directory. I thought we might have an emergency."

After a minute, Duncan gave up. "He's either not home or using a sleep machine."

He hesitated for several seconds, then called Izimoff again. Though he did not like doing it, he left a message for Izimoff to call him at his apartment. Since he and the padre had to wait for the return call, he decided to get breakfast for both of them. They ate and showered and then sat around talking about various ways to transport Ruiz far from this area. None seemed to have much chance of working.

"The ganks won't bother getting individual warrants for house search," Duncan said. "They'll get a blanket warrant. They'll apply the override code to all the door locks in a certain area and turn that inside out. This section may be the first they'll go to."

"We got until nine before they'll know she hasn't checked in at her office," Cabtab said. "We might have another hour or so after that while they're trying to find out why she hasn't reported in."

"I'd say more like twenty minutes. They don't screw around."

Duncan thought fiercely for a minute, then said, "I don't like to do it, but we have to rouse Izimoff. After all, there's no reason for anybody seeing us there to make a connection between us and Ruiz. Anyway, we have to do it."

Even at this very early hour, buses were available. They took one to within four blocks of Izimoff's and walked the rest of the way. Number 566, Fong Avenue, was a scarlet-and green-striped door in a curving row of apartments. Duncan pressed the bell-button and tried to look nonchalant as some pedestrians passed. So far, he had seen ten people on the street. One of these was, statistically, a gank in civilian clothes. One out of ten.

Duncan kept his finger on the button. After sixty seconds, he said, "Either he's gone or he's out like a candle in a windstorm. Or he sees us but doesn't want to let us in."

Cabtab glanced up and down the street to make sure no one was watching him. Then, standing where he would be seen by Izimoff's monitor, he gestured frantically. If the man was watching, he would know that his visitors were not here to just pass the time of day.

"Let's go," Cabtab said. "Maybe he's dead."

They went back to Duncan's apartment. Over coffee, Duncan said, "It's up to us. There has to be some way."

The doorbell gonged. Duncan put on the monitor and saw outside the door a woman with a high coiffure and wearing a scarlet cloak. Her face was long and narrow but good-looking. Her lipstick was black.

He said, "Who is it?"

"It's a big E," she said. "Let me in."

Duncan told the door to unlock. He met the woman before she had gotten a few paces into the front room. "Who're you?"

She smiled swiftly and said, "Best you don't know."

She pulled a card from the pocket of her cloak, looked at it, and said, "You're Beewolf. And he's Jeremiah Scanderbeg Ward, right?"

"How'd you know?"

"Never mind that. I can't stay long. I've been sent to say that your message to Izimoff has been deleted, so don't worry about that. And . . ."

She wet her lips.

"And. . . ?"

"Izimoff is dead."

That startled him. Cabtab said, "My God!"

"Died early this morning. The authorities don't know that yet. I've been sent to inform you of this because of your message to him. Do you have something that should be passed on to your superior?"

"I'll say!" Cabtab blurted. "Only . . . how'd he die?"

"I wasn't told anything about that. What's the message?"

"There'll be hell to pay," Duncan said. "Two people disappear on the same day . . . the ganks'll be frothing at the mouth."

"Two?" the woman said. "What do you mean two? And what do you mean disappear?"

"I'm not entirely a dummy," Duncan said. "The RAT killed Izimoff, didn't they? They distrusted him, he was getting too nervous, and he was too unstable."

Cabtab said, "You're jumping to conclusions, Andrew. How. . . ?"

"Maybe," Duncan said. "But I've had some experience with subversives. Izimoff behaved as if he was insecure and afraid. He was a weak tool, if appearances can be trusted."

"You're paranoid," the woman said.

Duncan shouted, "Maybe I am! But I'll bet. . . !"

"Take it easy," Cabtab said softly, but gripped Duncan's shoulders from behind with hands like a robot's. "You'll make them think you can't be trusted either."

Duncan took in several deep breaths and envisioned sunny green meadows on which fauns and nymphs gamboled. The flush gone from his face and his breathing slower, he said, "Yeah. OK. Maybe I am too suspicious. You'll have to admit that with the kind of life we lead suspicion breeds like bacteria in pus."

"Very poetic, my friend," Cabtab said. He took his hands away. "What's the message, woman?"

"I'm authorized to give it only to Beewolf," she said. "You'll have to go into the next room, and you, Beewolf, must promise you'll not reveal it to him."

"Promised," Duncan said, thinking, it depends on what you have to tell me. Also on whether or not it'll put Cabtab in jeopardy.

The padre, looking indignant, his mouth moving soundlessly, left the apartment.

"Here's what I was told to tell you," the woman said. She spoke for approximately a minute. Duncan's eyes widened while listening. Otherwise, he gave no sign of the effect her words were having on him.

"Repeat that," she said.

He gave it back to her word for word.

"Good," she said. "Now, what is the emergency?"

Her eyes widened, and she became somewhat pale under her dark skin. When he had finished, she said, "My God! I don't know! This is something my superior'll have to decide! I'm not authorized to take any action in this kind of situation. Besides, I don't have the slightest idea what to do!"

"Then you'd better get your ass in gear," Duncan said. "Can you get in contact with your superior at once? We can't stand any delay."

"I think I can."

She wheeled and started for the door, then stopped, and turned again. "What time do you go to work?"

"In two hours and five minutes."

"Wait here. If you don't hear from us, make some excuse not to go to work."

19

Cabtab strode into the room like a disheveled and cross lion looking for a fight.

"Is the bitch gone?"

"She's just doing her job," Duncan said, "though I doubt she knows what it really is. But then I don't either."

"Perhaps I was too hard on her, unjust," the padre said. "I'll search my soul and determine if I was. If so, then I'll have to find some means for forgiving myself. And forgiving her for provoking me."

"There are more important things to consider."

"Nothing is more important than the state of the soul."

"With the possible exception of the belly," Duncan said, looking at Cabtab's huge paunch.

"Soul and belly are inextricably twisted together," Cabtab said. "He who untangles them is free."

"Of what?" Duncan said, gesturing impatiently. "Listen. She said a crew from the Transportation-and-Shipping Bureau will be here soon. At least, they'll seem to be T-and-S workers. Maybe they really are. That doesn't matter. We have to get Ruiz ready for them. They don't want to spend any more time here than absolutely necessary."

"What do we have to do?"

Duncan told him, and they set to work. After destoning Ruiz, they bent her body so that she was in a fetal position. After taping her so that she could not straighten out if she suddenly regained consciousness, they put her into the cylinder and turned the power on. Then they dragged her out, wrapped her with a sheet, and put tape around that.

During the time-oozing fifteen minutes that followed, Duncan saw an organic patrol car pass slowly down the courseway. The TV camera on top of the vertical pole set in the rear of the vehicle revolved like the head of a one-eyed owl. The driver and his buddy were talking animatedly about something.

Duncan was glad that the law permitted only government monitoring cameras at courseway junctions and on patrol cars. If, as the government desired, every block had a monitor camera, the incident with Ruiz and the visit of the RAT agent would have been recorded. As it was, the presence of the T-and-S crew would be seen at various intersections and possibly noted by patrol car cameras. However, he was sure that authorization data for the crew would have been put into the gank data bank. Just how much investigation the authorization could bear he was not sure. He would just have to trust that it looked authentic. Of course, it was highly possible that no gank would bother to check it out.

"We're not just walking a tightrope," he muttered. "We're running on it."

"What?" Cabtab said.

Duncan did not have time to repeat. The doorbell gonged. After looking at the door screen, Duncan spoke the open-sesame that admitted the crew. This was two men and two women in the orange-and-black coveralls of the Transportation-and-Shipping Bureau. They had arrived in an orange-and-black zigzag-striped van, and two were carrying a large wooden box between them. They had to stoop to get the top of the box under the top of the doorway. One of them was operating a four-wheeled semirobot carrier. When it had passed through, Duncan closed the door.

It took a few seconds to load the sheet-wrapped body into the box. Duncan did not have to say a word. Apparently, the crew had been given instructions on their task before leaving their HQ. Whether they had also been told not to talk or were just surly because of the early hour, Duncan did not know. Even the crew chief was silent when she held out her hand for Duncan's ID card. He, also wordless, handed it to her. She inserted the card into the flat case hung from a long chain around her neck, held it there for less than a second, and handed the card back to him.

Duncan watched the door screen as the box containing Ruiz was hoisted up on the platform to the level of the van floor. The van had been drawn up far enough to one side so that he had a partial view of its interior from the rear. He could see half of another object, covered by a sheet, on the floor. That, he was sure, was Izimoff, also in a fetal position. When the van got back to the T-and-S HQ—if it was going there—Izimoff would be put into the box with Ruiz. Where the box would go from there, he did not want to know. He had enough to worry about. It might be a few hours before the ganks learned that Ruiz and Izimoff had disappeared. After that, this tower, and especially this level, would swarm with organics. Now that he reconsidered it, it seemed inevitable that they would wonder just what was in the box. And they would also be calling on him to ask why he had shipped out something in a big box.

He inserted his card into a slot in a wall-panel control board. Per his spoken instruction, the screen displayed the data recorded during the T-and-S transaction. It showed what he should have expected and also revealed that his superior had expected him to be intelligent enough to get his instructions from the card itself. Someone in the organization had used a card identical to his to petition for an apartment closer to his work. According to the card, his petition had been granted, and he was to move into his new apartment before he went to work.

Somebody in a high position in the government had moved very swiftly this morning. He must have had a duplicate of Duncan's card handy. Probably he had duplicates of everyone's in the RAT. Predating the data, he had made it appear that Duncan had put in his request the previous Tuesday and that it had been reviewed and passed the same day.

So, Citizen Andrew Vishnu Beewolf, like it or not, had to move. Immediately. His personal possessions would supposedly be in the box furnished by the T-and-S Bureau. The crew would have taken it to his new apartment. There, they would have waited just long enough for the supposed personal property to have been removed from the box and placed on the floor. Then, with Izimoff and Ruiz still in the box, the crew would have taken the box on out to some government warehouse. He still had a problem. His PP, his personal possessions, had to be gotten out.

Cabtab was about to leave, but Duncan told him what he had to do. They began removing the stuff from his closet and from his PP bathroom cabinet. When these were put into two large duffel bags, they washed the cups and dishes, put them in a kitchen cabinet, and walked out. By then the courseways were beginning to fill up with people on the way to work. The two got onto a bus, rode to the new apartment, and went inside it. Duncan's card had the new entry code; the old one would be erased today in the data bank.

Cabtab dropped the duffel bag on the floor.

"You should look around," Duncan said. "It might pay you to be familiar with the layout some day. You never know."

Cabtab grunted, but he did walk slowly through the rooms. Duncan put the bags into his PP closet; he would arrange the stuff therein on the shelves later. The wainscoting and the funiture were lemon-yellow, the choice of Monday's occupant. Duncan would turn the controls to select the colors he wished. The walls were blank; it was up to him to display whatever he wanted on the screens. He could pick designs or scenes from tapes or create his own still or moving pictures. The uncarpeted floors were cloned oak, but a twist of a control could give him the shade of varnish he preferred. Decorating was simple and swift unless the decorator had trouble making up his mind.

The chairs, tables, and sofas could be quickly altered in color or mixtures thereof, though reshaping all of them would take at least half an hour. And they had to be put back into the conventional form before stoning time. Duncan seldom bothered with that. He rather liked the frail and delicate appearance of neo-Albanian furniture.

The living room had French windows that opened onto a balcony. The view from here was as good as from his old apartment, which in no way except a slightly different angle of sight differed from the new. That this place was closer to his job was the only advantage. If he had tried on his own to get a transfer, he would have had to wait for a subyear or more. Getting it so quickly, even if he had not wanted it, proved that one needed connections in this society to obtain something ordinarily unobtainable. It had always been so in every society and age.

"So long," Cabtab said. "My blessings, son."

"Thank you, Padre. I'll meet you at the Snorter unless I can't make it because something comes up."

"Blessings on your sex life, too," Cabtab said, and he left.

Duncan lingered a moment to look at the faces of those he shared the apartment with but would never talk to. Then he hurried to the bureau. The next phase of his task was correlating the self-centeredness indices of chess players, TV actors, and electronic engineers. While engaged in this, he glanced often at the wall screen displaying the news channel. By quitting time, he had seen nothing on it about Izimoff and Ruiz. That, he well knew, though he did not know how he knew it, meant nothing. The ganks were probably sitting on the news. *Probably.* Ever since he had escaped from the Takahashi Institution, his life had been an obstacle road of *probablys, perhapses,* and *ifs,* all looming up suddenly in the dark. He knew almost nothing about the organization for which he was expected to die if it was necessary. It might kill him if he did not carry out its orders satisfactorily. Murky and uncertain described his situation as it had been and now was.

He tensed. Here came another uncertainty, a dangerous one.

The man who had just been talking to a coworker was now heading his way. Though Duncan did not know what the man was thinking or what he intended to do, he was sure that he was an organic. Though in civilian clothes, he had that cold, hard, and somewhat withdrawn nimbus. It was a thin cloud that only long-time criminals and other organics could see.

I should be charitable, Duncan thought. That look comes partly from self-defense. Your typical gank is always wary, suspicious, cynical, and coiled to respond to attack. Though, statistically, very few are physically or verbally threatened. Most citizens are too afraid of them. With good cause.

Duncan rose from his desk as the man, shorter than Duncan but massively muscled, approached. Stopping at the rim of the circular desk, the man said in a frogdeep voice, "Citizen Andrew Vishnu Beewolf?"

Duncan nodded and said, "Yes."

The man held up the ID card suspended from a purple chain around his columnar neck. "Officer Rhodes Terence Everchuck, First-Class Detective-Sergeant, Domestic-Immigration Bureau. Do you wish to run off the data for verification?"

"No need," Duncan said. He smiled, but Everchuck's broad red face did not crack.

"I just have a few questions."

Duncan played the anxious citizen. "What's this all about?"

He did not expect an answer and did not get one.

Everchuck pulled a printout from a breast pocket in his purple gold-slashed robe. Looking down at it, he said, "I have here a copy of a request from you, transmitted to the Transportation-and-Shipping Bureau, for one box of your personal possessions to be removed from your canceled apartment and delivered to your new address. I also have the request and authorization for your removal to the new address. I also have the verification records of your transfer to the new address and of the delivery of the box containing your PP to that address. Did such delivery take place at the time stipulated or at any other time or was it not delivered?"

"It was delivered per schedule, and I moved to the new address, which is 421 Everhopeful Courseway," Duncan said. "Is there a problem, Detective-Sergeant?"

"In that case," Everchuck said, glaring into Duncan's eyes, "what did you and your companion, Citizen Jeremiah Scanderbeg Ward, have in the two bags you carried from your old address to the new address?"

Duncan had expected to be questioned about the contents of the box. But he also knew enough to know that the gank might hurl an unexpected and seemingly irrelevant question at him. He smiled, and he said, "The box wasn't big enough to hold all the PP. I put the extra stuff into the two bags."

"Why didn't you have the T-and-S workers transport those, too?"

"I made an error. I only requested that one box be transported. I thought I could get all my PP into one box. If I'd asked the T-and-S crew to carry the bags, I would have had to make another request. By the time that had been granted, it would have been next Tuesday. You know how these bureaucracies work. All the red tape . . ."

"Are you criticizing the government?"

"Oh, sure," Duncan said easily. "That's my right and duty. That's democracy. Do you deny me that right and duty?"

"Of course not," Everchuck said. "That wasn't my intention. Why did you feel it necessary to get the aid of Citizen Ward to help you carry the bags?"

"Two were too heavy for one man to carry."

"You misunderstand me," the organic said. "Why did you select Citizen Ward to help you? Why him in particular?"

"He's a good friend. It wasn't easy to find somebody who'd come over at that ghastly hour and help me."

"Do you know that Citizen Ward is a religious?"

Duncan shrugged, and he said, "Sure. But he doesn't work for the government. He has a right to be a religious."

"Yet you associate with him on an intimate and friendly basis?"

"I'm not a religious," Duncan said. "You know that. You've checked out my ID."

"You knew him in New Jersey?"

"You know I did."

Now, Duncan thought, now is the time for the completely unexpected, the disconcerting, the knocking-off-balance. The whammo.

"What happened to Ruiz and Izimoff?"

Duncan made himself look startled. He said, "Who?"

"Detective-Sergeant Hatshepsut Andrews Ruiz and Citizen Ibrahim Omar Izimoff!" Everchuck said harshly.

"I don't know," Duncan said. "You say . . . happened? I don't know what you're talking about. I never heard of this Ruiz. Izimoff . . . I do know that an Ibrahim Izimoff is the operator of a store across the courseway from the Snorter."

He paused, then said, "The Snorter's a tavern-restaurant."

As if Everchuck did not know that.

"You deny that you know what happened to them?"

"I told you I don't even know that anything did happen! Come on, Sergeant! What is this all about?"

"Would you agree to a truth test?"

"Of course," Duncan said. He held his palms out and up. "I have nothing to hide. I don't know why you're dripping all over me, but if you think I'm guilty of something, you spray me all you want. We can do it here, right now. I waive any interrogation in the precinct building with lawyer and authorized officials present."

Everchuck did not ask him to repeat his words into a recorder. The organic was carrying all he needed to record in a pocket, no doubt.

Now was the critical moment, critical for Everchuck, anyway. If the organic thought that he was bluffing, he would use the mist. If he was just poking around and had no real well-grounded suspicions of Duncan, Everchuck would not bother with the mist.

"This is just a routine investigation," Everchuck said.

"Sure, but I'd like you to mist me anyway," Duncan said. "I don't want to be even a remote suspect. I'm through for the day, plenty of time. Let's do it now. Won't take long."

"That's a very commendable attitude, Citizen Beewolf," Everchuck said. "But I don't have time to waste."

"What did happen to them?" Duncan said.

Everchuck swung around and walked away.

20

Duncan entered the Snorter at 5:00 P.M. He threaded his way among tiny tables until he saw Cabtab and Snick in a booth. They looked up at him, said hello, then went back to their argument. Duncan pressed the button on the table to indicate that an unserved customer was at the booth.

The padre drank deeply from a huge stone mug, put it down, and said, "No, my dear Jenny, I disagree strongly, even though I am a devout religionist and thus am in a strange position. But strange only at first glance. I maintain that the present government policy toward religionists is not harsh enough. A fierce repression and persecution of the religious population weeds out the hypocrites, the lip servants, the people who profess to believe in certain religions only because they have been raised in them or have a need to belong to a social group. Repression and persecution separate the wheat from the chaff. The only ones left after these are applied, the wheat, the gold melting from the dross, the truly devout, should be prepared to pay the price for their belief. They should welcome a chance to be martyrs and so express their worship of God."

"I don't see you rushing out to be crucified," Snick said sourly.

"That's because the government doesn't really give you a chance to be a true martyr. It's insidious. It doesn't prohibit the practice of religion. It just brands it as superstition, in a class with astrology or belief in a flat Earth or in good luck charms. You may worship, but you cannot gather in a church to do so. The only churches still standing are museums or have been converted to profane uses. The members of the faith, whatever it is, Christian, Jewish, Muslim, Buddhist, must gather in gymnasiums or any suitable building not used for secular purposes at that time. A street preacher may give his sermons outside buildings, but he can't preach except in designated public areas and he can't stay in one area for more than fifteen minutes. After that, he must move his soapbox to another clearly marked area."

"I know that," Snick said. "You're getting away from the main theme. Your insistence that the government should ban any religious practice whatsoever is absurd. If the government did that, it could no longer claim to be truly democratic and liberal. So it doesn't forbid worship. It just frowns on it, and with good reason. It makes it inconvenient, doesn't encourage it, you might say. And, of course, the children learn in school what an absurd and irrational thing religion is."

Cabtab drank more beer and burped.

"What do you think, Andrew?"

Duncan had been half-listening, his gaze on a display of the referendum results. The people had voted overwhelmingly to eliminate during the test period all surveillance except that absolutely necessary to ensure public safety. Duncan was surprised by that. If his theory that the government gave false data about the popular vote was right, then the majority should not have been registered as against surveillance.

"I don't know and don't care," he said. "The present system seems to me to be fine. Nobody's hurt, and the organized religion can't get any power in government. There's a strict separation of church and state. Enough of that. I have something important for you."

When he had finished telling them about Everchuck's visit, Panthea Snick said, "It seems routine. But you never know. Anyway, there's nothing we can do about it. Just be even more careful from now on."

"Careful we don't screw up because of the ganks?" Duncan said. "Or because of RAT? Don't you see the implications of what happened to Izimoff? If we become a danger to RAT, or it thinks we are dangerous even if we aren't, they'll expunge us as quickly as we'd brush cookie crumbs from our shirt."

"It has to be that way," Panthea said. "It's only logical. They're in a very fragile position. They can't take a chance on weak or uncertain personnel."

"Jesus, Thea, doesn't that bother you?"

She sipped at her sherry, then said, "Yes. But I knew what I was getting into when I took the oath. You did, too."

He drank some bourbon and said, "Not really you didn't. None of us did. We don't have the slightest idea what RAT stands for except they're antigovernment. That's pretty vague. What are their ultimate goals? What kind of government do they want to establish? What chance do they have of overthrowing the government? How big is their organization? Is it just a small bunch of pissants playing rebel? Or is it something really big and powerful?"

He sipped on the bourbon again, put the glass down, and said, "I'm really tired of blundering around in the dark and barking my shins."

Snick did not reply because of the uproar swelling through the tavern. Everybody was on their feet, cheering, screaming, clapping their hands. Duncan saw that they were all looking at the news displays. These were rolling the printed data re the new rules and regulations. The newscasters' heads, inset in the upper righthand corners, were repeating verbally the printed text. At least, Duncan assumed they were. Their voices could not be heard because of the customers' yelling.

Duncan leaned across the table, his head close to Snick's and Cabtab's. He said, loudly, "I don't know why in hell they're so happy! The satellites can't monitor them except when they're out of the towers, on the bridges, or in boats! And it's not like there're monitors everywhere inside the towers! Why don't they drop the surveillance in cities like Manhattan? That'd mean something! There the streets are observed by the satellites!"

"Maybe the government's just cautious, and, if this experiment works out all right, the open cities will also be tested," Snick said.

Duncan scowled. "They don't want it to work out."

She threw her hands up. "What could happen? The citizens aren't about to go ape."

"They won't have far to go if they do," Cabtab growled. That was a strange thing for the tolerant padre to say. Perhaps he was momentarily irritated by the monkeylike shrieks and hoppings-around of the customers. Duncan looked at the display again. All citizens were to run off a printout of the "new order" and to study it so that they could behave themselves accordingly. He made a mental note to do that when he got home. There would, of course, be about 13 percent of citizens who would not obey. The two-thousand-obyear governmental campaign to condition all adults to become politically conscious and enthusiastic participants had never succeeded. It would continue to fail because of the statistically determinable numbers of the born non-political. A small part of these were the philosophically apolitical; the rest, the genetically indifferent. Secretly, the government must be pleased with this, though overtly it encouraged and harangued the electorate to be active. That many PVHs (political voidheads) made it just that much easier for the state to push its programs.

"I shouldn't have said or even thought of such an unkind and derogatory category," Cabtab said. He drank deeply, then continued. "One should never generalize, not even one born to generalize, which I am. It was unworthy of me, although what I said had more than a germ of truth to it. Nevertheless, even if it were wholly true, I should not say it. Instead, I should pray for the misbegotten masses, the churlish common people, the asses who pretend to be Homo sapiens. After all, am I in any respect better than they? I do not throw stones. I throw mud, yes, but mud can't hurt and it's easily washed off. I—"

"Think I'll go home," Snick said. She rose. "This kind of talk is getting us nowhere. It bores me. I have a headache, and I'm tired. You speak of mud, Padre. I feel like I'm stuck in it. Worse, sinking in it up to my neck."

"Too bad," Duncan said. "I was hoping to meet your new lover."

He regretted saying that, but it was too late.

Panthea Snick looked surprised. "I don't have a lover, old or new. Not that it's any of your business."

"But you said . . ."

"I said? Oh, I see what you're referring to. I said that I had someone in the apartment. He wasn't a lover, just a visitor."

She smiled and said, "Are you jealous?"

Duncan opened his mouth but shoved back down his throat the impulse to deny her accusation. Now was not the time to conceal how he felt for her. Now was the time to get it over with, confess.

"Yes, I am," he said.

"You're *not* in love with me?" she said.

She did not look as if she were surprised but as if the thought might have scuttled across her mind before she helped it on into oblivion with a mental kick.

"Yes, I am."

She swallowed before saying, "I didn't know . . . you never showed anything . . . any sign of . . ."

"Now you know."

"For God's sake!" Cabtab said loudly. "What kind of courtship is this? This place . . . the noise . . . the crowd . . . is this a romantic scene, the place to declare one's love?"

"Don't be embarrassed, Padre," Snick said. "It just happened. Anyway, I'm glad it was here, not when we were alone."

"Why is that?" Duncan said.

She leaned forward, her hands on the the table, her face close to Duncan's.

"Because it's easier to say what I have to say. I'm sorry, Andrew, but . . . I like you, in fact, I admire you. In some ways, you're my hero. You did rescue me from the warehouse; you brought me back to life. But . . ."

"You don't love me."

"I have a certain affection for you."

She straightened. "That's all. I don't love you. I don't desire you, I don't lust for you. I don't want to hurt your feelings, either, though there seems no way not to. There it is. An honest answer."

"Thank you," he said. His voice sounded firm to him. Thank God, it did not betray the trembling inside him.

"Does this make a difference?" she said. "I mean in the way we work together, in . . . You don't hate me, do you?"

"I'm a little numb," he said. "I don't know what I feel. It's a shock, though it shouldn't be. I had no right to expect you to feel the same about me. I certainly never saw you do anything, say anything, or act in any way to make me think you might feel like I do. No, I don't hate you. And I'm sorry, you don't know how sorry, that I told you. I should've waited for a better time."

"There wouldn't have been any. I'm sorry."

She patted his hand, turned, and walked away. He did not watch her; his gaze was fixed on the table.

Cabtab said, softly, "Is there anything I can do to help you?"

"Yes," Duncan said even more softly. "Leave me alone."

"You're not going to get drunk and possibly get into trouble? Remember, you can't afford to attract the ganks' attention."

Duncan stood up. "No. I'm going home. What I'll do there, I don't know. But nobody's going to see me whatever I do."

The padre looked alarmed. "You're not thinking of killing yourself?"

Duncan laughed, and then he rammed back a sob.

"No. Jesus! This is stupid! Whoever would've thought of it going this way?"

"It's the dark night of the soul. Believe me, I've been there before. If only I could help you . . ."

"See you tomorrow," Duncan said, and he stood up and walked away. The padre was wrong. His soul was in no dark night. Everything shone brightly but crooked, as if the light rays were bending at many different angles around him. The light was not only searingly bright; it was cold, very cold.

21

Early next Tuesday morning, Duncan sat in the kitchen. He was nursing a big cup of steaming coffee and an even larger and warmer emotional wound. His breast ached. Tears welled. Images of the mighty bull elephant trumpeting with agony and fury at the spear sticking out of his ribs, of the lion licking the blood from a paw shattered by a bullet, of the sperm whale bristling with harpoons rising under the whaleboat and tossing it into the air fast-forwarded on his mind screen.

Then, when drinking his third cup of coffee, two times too many according to the Bureau of Medicine and Health, he laughed. It was a low laughter grinding with pain. But it was also shot with the pleasure of self-mockery. The images were all of noble and impressive beasts suffering from wounds. Why not envision a cockroach limping along, its pasty guts hanging out, after being half-squashed by a human foot? Why not a fly buzzing desperately in its struggles to free itself from a web? Why not a stinkbeetle the tail end of which had been snipped off by a closing door? Or a rat that had eaten poisoned cheese?

He laughed again. Events and feelings were being reclassified and hence falling into their proper slots. He wasn't by any means the only human ever to have been rejected, nor was this the first time it had happened to him.

His philosophical satisfaction was great, and his historical perspective—he being the subject of the history—was correctly aligned. Despite which, a few seconds later, he was hurting just as badly.

Ah, well. He would ride it out. Time did not heal all wounds, but time did make them not so painful and usually managed to bury them deep. He busied himself, after eating lightly, in cleaning up the apartment. When he left it, he found himself in a crowd of elated pedestrians. Though this was not a holiday, it seemed to be. Everybody, except himself, was chattering and smiling, happy because today was one of freedom from the monitors. The satellite eyes were turned off, and the ganks were sulking in the precinct stations. A heavy burden of which the citizens had not been aware was lifted. Or so, Duncan thought, they thought. Did they really believe they had complete license to behave like children?

Perhaps they did. When he got to the bureau, he saw that no one was working and that the supervisors did not seem to care. In fact, these were just as manic as their underlings. They stood around outside their offices talking, though with other supervisors, not the workers, and they drank coffee and laughed and joked. Shaking his head, Duncan went into his enclosure and sat down. Though no one else had even turned on the power to the computers, he activated his equipment. Now, what was he supposed to do?

That made him frown. His duties were hazy, somewhere in his mind but apparently skipping about, not ready to settle down and put their shoulders, as it were, to the wheel. He swore. Somehow, he had become infected with the over-buoyancy and giddiness of the others. He decided that he would ignore it. But, though he stared at the screens, he could not summon any concentration. And, when several colleagues suggested that they go out and have a drink, he said, "Sure! Sounds like a great idea!"

What the hell am I doing? he thought as he walked with the group past a gaggle of supervisors. These did not even seem to notice that the data bankers had deserted their posts and that many were leaving the office. Duncan, like his cronies, walked past the machine in which he was supposed to insert his ID card when he left the premises during working hours.

Outside, the group stood for a moment talking about where the best place to celebrate would be. They had trouble making themselves heard above the cries and laughs of the pedestrians and the passengers on the buses and the cyclists in the courseway. By the time that his colleagues had agreed that the Snorter was the nearest tavern and therefore the best, Duncan knew why the courseway was so jammed. The stores were empty; the clerks and customers who should have filled them were all outside. At the moment, that did not seem strange to him. Of course, these people did not want to work any more than he did. And, since the overseers were out in the crowd, why shouldn't they be?

Getting to the Snorter was not easy. They had to push through the jam. Taking a bus would not help them. These were by now halted in the press. Even if the vehicles could have moved, the drivers had also left their posts.

"What's going on?" Duncan shouted to Wark Zoong Cobledence, a woman who worked at the enclosure next to his.

"What do you mean?" she yelled.

"Ah, forget it!" he screamed. Which he did at once.

By the time that the group had reached the Snorter, it had only five left out of the original ten. They dived into the tavern, giggling and chortling, then lost some of their zest. The place was jammed with customers, but the waiters had not shown up or had left shortly after doing so. For the moment, the crowd was stymied. They milled around chattering or shouting as if their voices would summon the waiters. Then a woman walked behind the nearest bar, grabbed a glass from under the bar, and filled it with whiskey from a wall spigot. She downed the three-ounce drink, choked, and, eyes tearing, said loudly, "Drinks are on me!"

Others joined her to act as bartenders who were also their

own best customers. Some people made an effort to pay for the drinks by inserting their cards into the proper slots, but they were pushed away and jeered at.

"Today's Freedom Day!" Padre Cabtab bellowed. "Let everything be free! Or, if you insist, on me! But don't ask me my name!"

The crowd in the room thinned somewhat as others went to the remaining rooms, where the same thing happened. Presently, everybody was more or less drunk, mostly more, and having a very good time. Duncan and Cabtab, huge brandy goblets sloshing over the brims with World Joy bourbon, the second-best in the world, found a booth. Two more patrons, uninvited, sat down by them. One was a very dark and good-looking woman wearing only a purple-and-rose dressing gown. She said that she lived down the street, had not eaten breakfast, and had stuck her head out of the door to see what was going on. On impulse, she had decided to go into the street and get in on the merrymaking.

"So, here I am, ready for everything and anything!"

Her fingers tightened gently on Duncan's crotch.

This, for some reason, neither surprised nor disturbed him.

However, the man who had sat down with her did surprise Duncan. He was the thin man with the big eyes and the green hat with antennae whom Duncan had met on the train from New Jersey. Professor Carebara. Who, Duncan remembered with a jolt, he had seen briefly on TV after the big brawl at the Snorter. Carebara's face seemed even longer and narrower and his huge eyes almost insectine. He wore yellow calf-high boots, red kneebreeches, a blue swallowtail coat, a ruffled white shirt with a cataract of light-green lace at the ends of the sleeves, and a green hat shaped like an ancient Puritan's. It sported two foot-long purple antennae.

Padre Cabtab said, loudly, "What are you doing here, Professor? Slumming?"

Carebara sipped his wine, then said, "Of course not. I come here sometimes to check on the ant population."

"Ants?" Cabtab said. "What ants?"

"You haven't seen any? I'm surprised. The bureau's had a lot of complaints. They're everywhere, they live in the spaces between the walls, in warehouses, any place where they are not likely to be disturbed. They're a recent mutation of a species the scientific name of which would mean nothing to you. Suffice it that they're what laypersons call garden ants. They seem to have adapted wonderfully to what should be a hostile environment. They eat anything that can sustain human life, and they also eat other insects, including cockroaches. They—"

"Cockroaches?" the padre said. "What cockroaches?"

"There are plenty in L.A., though they tend to thrive in the residences of the minimum-credit blocks. The dropouts are very careless about cleaning up, despite all the government has done to educate them in the extreme need and urgency of sanitary living. In fact, I suspect the minims deliberately act like slobs just to defy the government. Anyway and however, I am not interested so much in the ants themselves, though they do present certain bizarre and fascinating features, as I am in the mimetic parasites that have moved in with them. These, too, are recent mutations, and they . . ."

Duncan quit listening. The woman who had sat down with Carebara had slid under the table and was now doing something that erected the professor's ants far above Duncan's mental view. Cabtab leaned over the table, ignoring Carebara's lecture, and said, "What's she doing down there?"

"I don't want to talk," Duncan said. His face twisted; he gasped; it was over. Then it was the padre's turn to grab the edge of the table, roll his eyes, groan, and gasp. A few seconds later, the professor stopped talking, and his face, usually deadpan, bent like a bow, twitched like the skin of an animal dislodging flies, and he uttered a long aah! After which his eyes became less huge, and he resumed his lecture, though not from where he had left off.

"Who is she?" Duncan said.

Carebara did not reply. Duncan squeezed the professor's thin shoulder. "Who is she?"

"I don't know," Carebara said, looking angry. "Why don't you ask her?"

The woman crawled out from under the table, reached up, took the padre's goblet, drank, and went on all fours to the next booth. Duncan half-rose and watched the expressions on the face of the woman seated on the outer edge. Her companions, a woman and two men, seemed to be aware of what was going on. They laughed shrilly and made remarks that the woman paid no attention to. Presently, hands clenching the table edge, her head thrown back, eyes closed, she moaned. Duncan sat down and turned his head away.

"No one objects," he said.

"Why should they?" Cabtab said.

Duncan had no answer to that.

"A very generous and democratic woman," the padre said. "I toast her." He lifted his goblet, saw it was empty, and banged it down. "Waiter! Waiter!"

"You forget there aren't any," Duncan said. "I'll get the drinks."

He got up from the booth but could not resist looking under the booth next to his. The nameless woman was now occupied with the man next to the woman she had first attended. Duncan shook his head, whether in admiration or disgust he did not himself know, and pushed through the crowd around the bar. They gave way without protest until he tried to squeeze between a man and a woman.

"Who do you think you're shoving?" the man said. He wore a dark orange hat shaped like a castle and had a long beard separated into many strands tied by buttercup-yellow ribbons.

"Just trying to get a drink," Duncan said mildly. Much of the tension, irritation, and uneasiness that had been swelling up these last three days had left him. And the whiskey also helped make him feel mellow.

"Don't take any crap from him, Milo!" the woman shrilled.

She lifted her arm above the mob and poured her vodka over Duncan's head.

"That's a waste of good booze!" the man growled, and he hit, not Duncan, who had thought he was going to get the fist, but the woman.

Duncan brought his fist up close to his chest—he had no room to straighten the arm out—and caught the man under the chin with it. Then he half-turned and jerked the back of his elbow into the woman's solar plexus. She quit laughing, doubled up, then fell to the floor. The man Duncan had hit staggered back but not far because of the press of bodies. Bellowing, he lurched toward Duncan, who ducked. The man fell over the woman, who was just trying to get back up, and Duncan slammed his knuckles against the man's cheekbone. All his mellowness was gone.

The room exploded. The fighting did not spread out from where Duncan, the woman, and the man were. It seemed as if it was not the contact of fists that started the brawl but the idea of a brawl. That flashed through the big rooms with the speed of thought, and the philosophical concept became realization. Inside a second, all the patrons were either trying to strike, scratch, or kick someone or else attempting to fight their way out of a fight. Duncan did not have long to contemplate the speed with which the tavern became a gladiator's delight. Something very hard, probably the bottom of a thick mug, slammed into the back of his head. Half-senseless, he fell to his knees. Descent seemed like a good idea then. It was certainly an irresistible one. He went down on his face, groaning, the impact softened by a woman's leg. A man fell heavily on Duncan's back, rolled off, but did not get up. Duncan stared at the bloodied face near his and decided that it made sense to stay on the floor. His vision began to clear, but the pain in the back of his head got worse. Meanwhile, feet banged into him, though not very hard. No one was trying to hurt him; the blows were accidental. Nevertheless, unintentional kicks can cause pain.

He made another decision. He would get out of the place and

to home, where he could treat his injuries. That would not be done without more bruises and bloodshed. But if he stayed, he was going to get hurt more, anyway.

And where were the organics? Why hadn't they come charging into the place, spraying everybody with unconscious-making aerosol, quieting the hullabaloo to a whisper? The age-old complaint that the ganks were never there when you needed them was certainly true just now.

No sooner had he gotten on hands and knees than a woman fell backward over him on his right and a man fell onto the back of his legs. These, however, did not stay on top of him. Cursing, screaming, and hitting—including two blows on Duncan's back—and all in all having a very good time, the two left. Only to return and to fall on him again. He struggled up. A knee banged his nose. Blood gushed out onto the hardwood floor below him. He got back down, rolled over, pulled out a piece of tissue paper, and held it to his nose.

"To hell with it! I'll just stay here until this blows over!"

He could not resist kicking a man who was struggling with another just in front of him. His heel drove into the man's crotch. Screaming, bent over, holding his testicles, the man was hit on top of his head with his antagonist's interlocked hands. Then the antagonist stumbled over Duncan and shot into the small and ever-changing space between the legs of two grappling men. The knees of both rammed him in the ears and rendered him momentarily unaware of the fickleness of geometry or his pain. Duncan, despite what he had decided a few seconds before, got on all fours again. By then the space above six inches from the floor had increased somewhat. A lot of people were lying down, by choice or not. Even the noise level had lowered, though someone entering the Snorter just then would have thought that the place sounded like the halls of hell.

High above the rest rose the bellow of Padre Cabtab. Duncan glimpsed him lifting a kicking woman high above his head. The arms bent and the woman shot forward and felled three men with her body. Duncan rose again, plowed through the crowd toward the priest, had to defend himself against a man and then a woman, got by them with some bruises and scratches, and suddenly was in a comparatively open area near Cabtab. The padre had just made some more space by hurling a man against two others and flooring all three.

"Glory to the gods of battles, Jahweh and Woden!" the padre yelled. His face was a blaze of joy smeared with blood. "This is wonderful spiritual and physical therapy!"

"Let's get out of here, let them be happy," Duncan said.

Then he saw Panthea Snick, whom he had not known was still in the Snorter. Her robe had been torn off, leaving her wearing panties and high-heeled shoes. One shoe, anyway. She was beating a woman over the head with the heel of the left shoe. Both were bleeding here and there, and she had a big blue mark over one eye.

"Follow me!" Duncan shouted hoarsely. He staggered up to the two females and pulled Snick away. The other woman fled, holding her head with both hands.

"It's me, Dunc," he said while Snick writhed in his two arms. His nose was buried in the back of her hair, which smelled of perfume, whiskey, and blood. "Let's go!"

The woman who had run off came back with two men. They advanced, spreading out to take Duncan and Snick from three sides. But Cabtab barreled across the floor, leaping over bodies, and slammed into one man, who was bowled over against the next. All three went down. Only Cabtab got up. The woman, shrieking, fled again.

"Out we go," Duncan said. He turned and bore Snick, screaming, her arms and legs waving, through the door. Cabtab followed him.

Outside was even worse, and Duncan wondered briefly if he should go back into the tavern. There were dozens of battlers slugging it out in the courseway and scores of bodies, some moving, some not, on the spongy black-and-scarlet-striped floor of the way. The noncombatants were either making love in various ways or feverishly betting on the battlers.

Snick suddenly went limp. She said, "Put me down. I'll be all right when I get some clothes on."

He released her.

"I think we should get out of the ways," he said. "My apartment is the closest place."

He looked around. Where were the ganks? Where were the ambulances and the doctors? Probably busy elsewhere. They just did not have the numbers needed to handle what must be a citywide riot. Plus brawl. Plus orgy.

He motioned to the padre, who was standing near the door to the Snorter. Cabtab did not seem to notice the gesture; he was looking upward at the ceiling courseway, which was a display of a deep blue sky and some wispy wind-driven clouds. Duncan called the padre's name, but Cabtab did not acknowledge it. His eyes were wide, and his face had the most joyous expression Duncan had ever seen. It made Duncan uneasy. No. Scared.

Cabtab suddenly lowered his gaze, his mouth working angrily but his face keeping the same "caught" expression. He lifted his hands and tore off the neckchains holding the dozen or so religious symbols. The crucifix, star of David, crescent, Thor's hammer, voodoo idol, and other figures flew up and out, falling into and on the crowd. Next to fall was the padre himself. He toppled stiff and straight as a tree sawed through at the base of the trunk and hit the slightly yielding sidewalk hard. Duncan ran toward him, pushing some spectators out of the way and jumping over bodies. By the time he reached Cabtab, the man had lost his rigidity and was vibrating every which way. He was not having an epileptic seizure; his eyes were wide open and bright, and he was talking rapidly. However, the language was one Duncan had never heard, and he was familiar with the sounds of the twenty still spoken on Earth.

A moment later, Snick, sealing up a robe she must have taken from one of the unconscious women, was by his side. "What's the matter with him?" she said, breathing hard. "He looks like he's had a vision."

"I think you're not far off the track."

Duncan jumped to avoid being knocked over by Cabtab's explosive rising from the sidewalk. The padre had lost much of the rapt look, but enough remained to shine forth. The molecules of his face seemed to have rearranged themselves into new features. If Duncan had not known that the man had to be the padre, he might not have recognized him.

"No more the ancient gods!" Cabtab howled. "They have gone and will not return! If indeed they were ever here! No! Yes! People, gather around me! I bring good news, perhaps the first you've ever heard! Honey for the ears! Meat for the soul! Gather around, and listen to me! I speak to you not as Padre Cabtab but as the loudspeaker of the Just-Born God! I am the display screen of the Divine!"

"Padre! Padre!" Duncan said. "Don't you know me?"

He pulled on the man's robe, but the giant pushed Duncan's hand away as if it were an irritating fly.

"I know all men and women and children!" he bellowed. "Listen to me, you whom I know and whom the Just-Born God knows beyond knowing! Listen to me! Hear! Drink in the truth! Then act! Do what the Just-Born bids you do through me!"

"He's crazy!" Snick said.

A few people, Duncan saw, had walked over to listen to Cabtab. The rest had not heard or were ignoring him. If he was doing what most of them were doing, he would not want to stop it to listen to a preacher.

"Crazy or not," Duncan said to Snick, "the ganks'll take him in when they come. You know what that means. They'll spray him, and they'll find out about us."

Duncan would rather have taken less violent and public action. There seemed at the moment nothing else to do. He stepped toward Cabtab, his arm raised, his hand formed to chop with the edge against the padre's lionlike neck. But Cabtab, as if warned by a voice heard only by him, wheeled. He was still babbling nonsense, but his eyes showed that he was completely aware of Duncan. His fist shot out against Duncan's chin. Duncan reeled, flailed his hands for support that was not there, and glimpsed a vast darkness in the middle of which a tiny but slowly ballooning sun flamed. The next he knew, he was face down on the pavement, and Snick, kneeling by him, was asking him if he was all right.

Helped by Snick, Duncan got to his feet. He shook his head as if trying to clear it, though his mind was not clouded, and he said, "There's nothing we can do except get out of here."

Snick, pale under her dark skin, said, "What do you mean we can't do anything?"

"I wish I knew what I mean. Take my word for it. There's nothing we can do unless you want to kill him."

Snick was too astonished to say anything. She was still wordless while Duncan pulled her along by her hand through the crowd.

22

After they had showered in Duncan's apartment, they went to the living room and drank some wine. He had put on fresh clothes; she had cleaned the robe she had taken from the unconscious woman. They sat silent for a while. Panthea watched the screen covering the wall opposite her, a scene from the great Chinese novel *All Men Are Brothers*. It depicted a marketplace in ancient China; soldiers with spears and swords were moving through the crowd looking for the hero, Ling Ch'ung, who was disguised as an old peasant. From Snick's expression, she was not really seeing the scene.

At last, after swallowing some wine, she said, "What do you think happened out there?"

She waved her hand at the door.

"The ganks released some kind of mental-emotional-deinhibiting gas in the tower's air-conditioning system," he said. "I don't know if that's true, but it's the only explanation I can think of."

"How could they get away with it?" she said. Obviously, she did not believe him.

"*They* will be conducting the investigation. Other departments will also be in on it. What difference does that make? The government's behind the mess-up. It caused it, and it'll issue the results of the investigation. There won't be any mention of a gas or whatever it was that drugged all those people, including us. The government will blame the whole thing on the license caused by the absence of surveillance. It'll conclude that too much freedom is dangerous, and it'll back up its conclusions with statistics on the damage and the injuries and deaths in L.A. Not to mention the other cities where the experiment took place. The government will fill the news stations with the reports for a long time. It won't let the citizens forget about it. I don't doubt that it will also press for even more surveillance."

"Maybe," she said slowly, "you're wrong. Maybe the people should be monitored closely for their own good. It's possible that the idea of so much freedom went to their heads, and they reverted . . . no, reverted isn't the right word, they exploded. They became like the pre–New Era citizens. You know how much crime there was in the old days."

"For God's sake!" Duncan said. "You were a gank. So was I. We're both very disciplined. Do you think that just the idea of being unobserved would affect us like that? We did things we wouldn't normally do; so did most of those people. We had to be drugged. There's no other explanation. Why do you think all the experiments were run in closed cities like L.A.? Because they're the only ones where the gas could be used effectively! The gas would be ineffectual in open cities like Manhattan. It would dissipate too quickly in the outside air, and the buildings there have their own air-conditioning."

Snick began weeping. Duncan understood why her tears were flowing. Despite what the government had done to her, she had believed that it was a mistake made by the officials. They had misjudged her; they had not condemned her because of secret policy. She had been a faithful servant and had not done anything wrong. They had been wrong in thinking that she was a danger to the state, and surely, some day they would find out that they had made a mistake and would right the wrong. She had joined the outlaws because it was her only way to stay destoned and do something to make the officials see the light. Just how she was going to do that, she did not know. But as long as she was living, acting, not a frozen statue, she had hope.

He waited until she had quit sobbing before telling her what he thought. She said nothing in reply; she just nodded several times.

"You realize what would happen to you if RAT found out what you really believe?" he said. "You'd be stoned or killed."

She looked wide-eyed at him and said, "You. . . ?"

He shook his head. "I won't betray you. Besides . . ."

She waited a few seconds, then said, "Besides . . . what?"

"Surely you don't believe that anymore. You have to be convinced now that the government doesn't reflect the will of the people. Except where the government's brainwashed the people so that the people's will reflects what the government wants them to believe."

She wiped the tears and the makeup from her face, blew her nose, and said, "No. But . . ."

"But?"

"RAT wants an absolute minimum of surveillance. It also wants to ensure that all information, all data, all statistics, everything, is free to the public. It wants to make certain that there is no distortion in the data, that all is given out, that there are no excisions, no half-truths, that the results of votes are truly given, that—"

"Who told you that?" Duncan said. "Nobody told *me* that."

"It wasn't anything specific I was told. I just got the idea from what he or she said when I was being interviewed. It was implied. Didn't you get the same idea that that's what the organization wants?"

"I had to surmise it. But so far, there's been very little definite said about the aims of RAT. We're swimming around in the dark with no idea of where the shore is or how deep the waters are. I think it's a hell of a bad situation we're in. The need for secrecy is so great, the organization is so vulnerable and fragile, and the system of cells is carried to such ludicrous extremes, you and I don't even know if we're in a truly revolutionary body. We're detached organs in the body, you might say. Unanchored livers floating around; uprooted kidneys trying blindly to find our proper place in a body we're not sure even exists. Maybe it's a mass of protoplasm trying to find a structure. I don't know. It's very frustrating!"

He looked at the screen over the front door.

"They're here."

Snick turned her head and said, "Oh!"

The front end of a green patrol car showed on the right side of the screen. In front of it three ganks wearing gas masks were spraying the faces of four citizens. These crumpled slowly to the floor of the courseway. Then a man and a woman jumped on the backs of two ganks and bore them to the floor. The other two officers shot spray from their cans at the struggling couples. The citizens became motionless.

Duncan laughed and said, "The gas must have residual effects. Otherwise, they would've submitted meekly. The ganks want to be resisted."

"Oh, God, what a mess!" Snick said.

Duncan told a wall screen to switch on the local news. He and Snick, sipping more wine, listened to the announcer and watched the scenes transmitted in from all over the city. Now and then, scenes from other cities where the experiments had taken place were shown. The same thing had happened there. Organics from San Francisco and cities in Oregon and Washington were being flown in to assist the L.A. forces.

"They'll have a hell of a time cleaning up just the litter before midnight," Duncan said. "Wednesday is really going to be pissed off. Oh, the reverberations of this will never cease."

"And the government will have its way," Snick said. "Still . . ."

"Yes?"

"I'm still not sure that we need a revolution. Just reform, that's all we really need, don't you think? If there was only some way to guarantee that voting was on the up-and-up and that the officials the people want were elected, what else really needs changing?"

Duncan shook his head again. "You'd better keep those ideas to yourself. And you'd better hope, devoutly, that your RAT superior doesn't ask you what you truly believe about its ideals the next time you're given truth spray."

"If there is a next time."

He did not have to ask her what she meant by that. The organics would take advantage of this opportunity to question everyone arrested. Stock Question Three would be: Do you belong to any subversive organization? If any member of RAT was picked up, and there were bound to be some—Padre Cabtab, for instance—Duncan and Snick would be exposed. They would not be able to tell the ganks much about the RATs next higher up in the organization. These would be safe—for a while, anyway. But three would be certain to be caught.

"Unless," he murmured.

"What?"

He told her what he had been thinking, then said, "Our only chance, and it's slight, is that RAT has someone high up in the government and that person will somehow suppress the information. The RAT would have to be present during the interrogation, would have to do the questioning, in fact. If somebody else does it, it'll be reported, and my hypothetical RAT wouldn't be able to block it. Those odds are too high against us. No, we have to do something now. What? I wish to hell I knew!"

It was then that the newsperson announced that martial law had been declared in Los Angeles. All citizens were to stay in their apartments if they were already there. All not at home were to go there at once. The only ones exempt were public servants whose positions were vital. While a part of the screen rolled these positions, the newsperson read them. During the next hour, except for some news about the process of the cleanup, the channel repeated only the same information. Duncan turned on other channels and found that all had been usurped for the same broadcast.

"Looks like you'll have to stay here until next Tuesday," he told Snick.

"Don't get any ideas."

"You mean about going to bed with you?"

She nodded, got up from the chair, and went toward the kitchen. He called after her, "I've got more important things to think about."

That was true, but if she had invited him to make love to her, he would not have hesitated to sidetrack the "important."

Trapped, he thought. Ensnared by love and by the government. The difference between the two is that my passion for her won't kill me. I don't feel just now that I'll ever get over loving her, but I know from my own experiences and those of others that I will. I may carry the pain in me, as I would an encysted tuberculosis bacteria, but I'll be able to function fully and healthily. More or less, anyway. But there is nothing now and probably never will be that I can do about her. She is only one person, but I'm incapable of solving my problem with her. On the other hand, the government is an entity, and it's arrayed thousands against me just in this area. But I may be able to do something about it.

He watched the news screen while he mentally scanned all the possibilities for escape. He could not go into the courseways today nor did he entertain long the fantastic idea of letting himself down a rope from the window or gliding—somehow— down to the harbor waters. He had to stay in the apartment until midnight, no witching hour but certainly stoning time. He did have the choice of going into his cylinder then or of staying out of it.

If he selected the latter, then what?

Whatever he did, he would have to talk Snick into doing it with him. If she got picked up and questioned, she would betray him because she could not help herself. That reasoning was logic-tight. But he knew that most people followed, not classical or symbolic logic, but that unanalyzable and invalid system of logic deriving from their emotions. First, the feelings; then, the rationalization. He rose to go to the kitchen; it looked as if Snick was going to stay in it. Just as he did, he saw the scene on the screen change. Now the camera was in front of the Level 20, Third Organic Precinct. The ganks were working hard and swiftly to unpile and carry the never-ceasing influx of bodies into the station. These were people who had been sprayed and brought in for later questioning, probably next Tuesday. The newscaster was saying that the number of "detainees" was far too large to be handled speedily. Most of them would be stoned in the precinct facility, their IDs would be recorded, and they would be transported to a warehouse. However, since there were too many for the precincts to handle, the emergency stoning stations scattered throughout the city were being used. The hospitals had already been filled, so all injured and dead, whether they were arrestees or unaccused, would be put into "suspension" until their turn came to be destoned. That, the newscaster said, might take until Tuesday after next. Or perhaps the time might extend until the third Tuesday.

"This metropolis has never experienced such a catastrophe," the newscaster said. "Not since the last great earthquake."

"Oh, hell!" Duncan said. There, among the bodies, was that of Padre Cabtab. A lift-robot had shoved its broad arms under the padre, who was lying face-up on the flatbed of a long many-wheeled trailer with many other unconscious people. Now it was raising the limp figure, whose arms dangled over the sides of the robot arms, was turning on its wheels and moving toward the twenty-foot-wide entrance. The camera zoomed in on Cabtab's profile, showing in detail the gaping mouth and the wide-open eyes.

"As I was saying," the newscaster, Henry Kung Horrig, said, "we've been unable to get many specifics about any of those brought in for questioning. I was lucky to get some data about the detainee you are now viewing. According to a high organic official, the detainee, whose ID has not been checked yet, but whose robustness is apparent, gave the arresting officers a very hard time. He knocked two officers unconscious, broke the arm of a third, and battered two more about the face and body before being subdued. The detainee was apparently preaching in the courseway, which is in itself a second-degree misdemeanor if the first offense and a third-degree felony if a second offense. He was exhaling a very liquorous breath, and, since he was apprehended outside the Snorter, a tavern, he may be one of those who looted its liquor supply. In which case . . ."

Duncan did not wait to hear more. Calling, "Panthea! Panthea!" he strode to the kitchen. She was sitting at the table by a big window and staring down at the harbor. Hearing him, she looked up alarmed. "What's the matter?"

He told her, then said, "Unless we're very lucky, we're done for. We have to do something, do it fast."

He noticed then that she had quit drinking wine. A large mug of steaming coffee was on the table before her. That was a good idea. This was not the time to scramble ones wits with alcohol.

"Let's not do anything foolish," she said. He sat down on the other side of the table, glancing out of the window while he did so. There were large freighters down there and many sailboats, their canvases flashing in the late afternoon sun. They seemed to be keeping to the prescribed traffic patterns. Apparently, the explosive sense of freedom that the organics claimed had afflicted those within the city had not affected those outside it. How would the ganks explain that?

Easy. The sailors were few and far between. They had not been touched by the mass hysteria in the towers.

"I'm not acting rashly. I've been thinking this out. The only course open for us, the only one with any chance at all, is to break day."

"And get caught on Wednesday," she said.

"I'm an experienced daybreaker. I doubt if anyone knows better than I do how to do it."

Well, not me, really, he thought. But those other men down there, those who keep feeding me bits of their memories—they know.

Panthea Snick was no longer looking at him. Her gaze was again outward, toward the ocean beyond the harbor. Her face was cast in a very thoughtful expression. It seemed to him that it formed an aching longing for freedom underlaid with hopelessness. He ached with the longing to kiss her and to tell her that he would give her hope. Anything she wanted.

There was a silence that he did not know how to break without causing pain. Yet it was as tedious as waiting for sap to ooze from a tree; it made him fidget and burn slowly with impatience. He wanted desperately to speak, but he knew that if he did so now his words would slide off her mind.

Finally, she turned her head toward him, sighed, and spoke.

"There's no use. We might as well turn ourselves in now and get the agony over with."

"How the hell could I have ever loved a pathetic creature like you?" he said. "You've got the spine of a sponge, the spirit of an empty whiskey bottle! Even if you know you can't win, you don't surrender!"

"Bullshit," she said tonelessly.

"It smells better than the dogshit you put out! You can't give up! I didn't, and I won't! If I had, where'd I be! Long ago stoned in a warehouse!"

"So you put off the inevitable? What's a few more days of living? What's the gain? Once you're stoned you won't remember that extra time you fought for. Was it really worth it?"

They were silent again, though, if Duncan's anger could have been expressed in radiation, he would have glowed white-hot, would have scorched her black.

After another silence, she said, "I don't know! The trouble is I really think I'm in the wrong! I deserve stoning! There's nothing essentially bad about our society. If the government lies or does a few things it shouldn't because they're illegal, it's for the good of the people."

"You're a born gank," Duncan said. "And I'm wasting my time arguing when I should be working out my plan."

"What plan?"

"I should tell you so you can tell the ganks when you turn yourself in?"

"Do you really have something in mind that has a ghost of a chance?"

Her face was still doleful, but her voice had brightened a little.

"Yes, but you have to promise you'll stay with me and do your best to help me."

"What if I can't?"

Then, Duncan thought, I stone you and get on with life, whatever kind it is, bad or good.

23

By ten that evening, Duncan and Snick were almost ready to start the first stage of their plan. If, that is, a hope that they could think of the correct action to take when situations changed could be called a plan. These situations could not be foreseen, and it was very probable that they would fall headlong into one from which they could not unmire themselves.

The initial steps would be easy. Wednesday's tenants, a man and a woman, would stay stoned. Though the destoning power was applied automatically, the cylinders had manual controls. These would be set at OFF, and Sebertink and Makasuma would not come alive. Duncan would then use their ID cards to get all the information he could about them from Wednesday's data bank. He and Snick, pretending to be these two, would have to call into Wednesday's places of work and make excuses for staying at home. Fortunately, Sebertink and Makasuma were not employed in the same business and location. If they had been, their superiors might have thought it peculiar that both had called in sick.

Duncan had already set up video-audio simulations of the man and the woman so that the persons who took the messages would see what they thought were Sebertink and Makasuma.

Also, fortunately, Duncan had much experience at simming. At least, he had the knowledge swelling in his memory. Rather, it was in the memory of one of his former personae. During what would be, they hoped, a brief exchange of communication, they would have to control the postures, expressions, and voices of the simulations. Duncan would coach Snick in the techniques.

"We'd better practice it for a while," Duncan said. "You be the person at work first. I'll manipulate the sims while you ask the kind of questions that might be expected. Then I'll be the work-person while you operate Makasuma's sim. This is just to learn how to work the controls. Tomorrow, we'll sharpen up the sims' images and go through several sessions before we call in. We'll have to get up early, though."

Tonight, by just inserting the cards into the wall-slots and asking for a display of the three-dimensional images of Wednesday's tenants, they would see on the screens all Duncan required to start "building up" the simulations. The first stages would be Sebertink and Makasuma greeting their bosses. After that, Duncan and Snick would have to improvise and do so swiftly and smoothly.

"I wish we had simsuits," he said. "That'd make it easy. We put on the face and body transponders, set the interface to register our body movements, expressions and voices, and these are translated into real-life outputs by the sims. The viewer at the other end of the transmissions sees the sims as if they were the genuine person. There's nothing hesitant or jerky or awkward about the sims."

Snick indicated the controls of the machine set on a table in the hallway. "This isn't supposed to be used for simulations. It's not built for that kind of operation. Can we really fool the viewers?"

"Yes, if the transmission is short enough, and the viewer is still dull from sleep. Or naturally dull and uninterested. If the viewer starts asking questions about Sebertink's or Makasuma's duties, some particular problem, we're sunk."

"We'll just have to make it short, pretend to be really sick."

"Yeah. And then we only have an hour or so to get out of here before a paramedic's here to check up on us."

"I still think we should avoid all this and leave shortly after midnight," Panthea said. "As you said, there are very few out then and the ganks might notice us. But the chances they'll stop and question us aren't high. They'll probably just think we're first-shift workers on our way to work. It can't take us more than ten minutes to get to the bottom of the tower, steal a boat, and be gone."

Duncan did not reply. She had already heard his argument that this Wednesday was not going to be like those in the past. Tuesday's government would have left a message informing Wednesday's of the unusual events today. Not that Wednesday would need that to know that it had inherited a hell of a mess. Tuesday had just barely been able, according to the newspeople, to stone all the injured and the arrested. The street maintenance crews had been pressed into assisting the organics and the hospital personnel in that task. The courseways were littered and stained, and considerable damage had been done in stores and taverns. To clean up, Wednesday would be calling for volunteers. If the computers reported that not enough had responded, all citizens in nonvital jobs would be drafted. Sebertink was a clerk in a sporting goods store, and Makasuma was a hospital pathologist. Both would probably be recruited for the cleanup. That might be after they reported for work, but Duncan and Snick could not report in as these two. If they went out soon after Wednesday was destoned, they might be picked up by ganks and told to join the work gangs. The ganks would not wait until the quota for volunteers had been filled. Anyone out that early would be questioned about their jobs, and, if these were nonvital, would be assigned temporarily to the sanitary and maintenance department. Before that happened, however, their IDs would be checked.

The only reasonably safe course for them was to go out when the streets would be filled with the S and M crews. Then they might be able to walk casually, or, perhaps, hurry as if they had an order to obey, and thus get through the ganks. But a gank might halt them and ask them what they were doing.

Duncan was not looking forward to the run, but it would take about ten minutes if all went well. He would have preferred going down the staircases from level to level to reach the bottom of the tower. These were seldom used since most people preferred the escalators or the elevators. However, the staircases were UVS, under video surveillance. The ganks had installed these under the pretext that people might accidentally fall down them, and if this happened, the medics could be notified at once. That made sense to the public, which had voted in favor of having them located there. Duncan was sure that, this time, the voting results had been reported correctly.

If he and Snick went down the stairs, they might get by unchallenged. It was highly probable, though, that they would be halted and asked to insert their IDs in one of the slots located every twenty feet along the staircase walls. The ganks would think that he and Snick were trying to duck out of the cleanup.

He looked at the wall screen that showed the courseway outside. The bright lights revealed a street littered with trash but empty of people. Shortly after midnight, the sprayer nozzles in the recesses in the ceiling, sides, and floor of the courseways would spurt out water for two minutes. The water and the loose and light objects on the street and sidewalks would be carried to the drains. Then hot air would blow from the nozzles by the sides of the sprayer nozzles, and two minutes later, only a thin film of water, which would quickly dry, would be left.

On that section of the courseway which Duncan could see, the spraying would take away everything except the handbag in front of the apartment door across the street and a dark stain on the sidewalk. It was then that he got the idea for getting to the bottom of the tower when he and Snick would be least observable.

"Thea!" he said.

Fatigued by lack of sleep and the hard hours of simulcasting, she must have nodded off. She sat upright in the chair, widened her brown eyes, and said, "What?"

"We'll go down the steps during the spraying period. The cameras will be covered with water, and the ganks won't even be careful to monitor them. They won't expect people on the stairs then."

"We'll get soaked."

"So we don't have to take a shower."

"We can't get to the bottom of the tower in two minutes."

"We'll run like hell. We're going down, not up."

"There's still not near enough time."

"We'll put grease on our asses and slide down the banisters. They don't have posts blocking the ends at each landing. We can zip nonstop down them. All the way."

She laughed so hard that she slid down off the chair. He was somewhat angered or perhaps embarrassed, but he was glad at the same time that she was laughing. At least she was no longer gloomy.

She remained sitting on the floor, her back against the chair, though she was no longer howling. After wiping the tears away with the back of her hand, she said, "You're crazy! Sliding down the banisters for twenty stories! That's what? At least three hundred feet straight down? Four hundred? Maybe five hundred feet on the banisters if you figure in the angle of the banisters to the vertical?"

"Four minutes. Four minutes before the water dries off the lens of the cameras. The first two minutes, the water protects us against the friction. More, considering the time it takes for the banisters to dry off. Three minutes. And we'll still have greased pants to provide lubrication. The grease won't burn off fast while there's water on the banisters. We could make it to the bottom in four minutes. Maybe less."

"And what if we lose our grip? Our hands'll have to be greased, too, and the water pressure is very strong. If we fall . . ."

She shuddered.

"Damn it! I'm going to do it with or without you!"

She got to her feet and looked up at him. She was half-smiling. Smirking?

"You certainly don't lack invention or imagination. It's awfully dangerous though."

"We're not in worse danger right now?"

She nodded and said, "I'll do it."

He grabbed her, pulled her close, and hugged. "Great!"

He released her quickly and said, "I'm sorry. I didn't mean to embrace you. I was just so happy."

"For God's sake!" she said. "I may not be in love with you, but I don't think you're repulsive, and I do think you're admirable. I liked the hug."

He turned away quickly, not wanting her to know that the brief closeness had given him an erection. He went to the wall screen, gave it verbal instructions, and watched the display of the area map. The closest stairway entrance was three hundred feet to the left of the apartment door.

The screen showed a man standing in front of the door. He reached out, and the doorbell gonged.

Duncan felt a tremor. Skinquake.

"Carebara! What in hell is he doing *here, now*? Any time?"

He frisbied off his mind the first thought that came, that Carebara was a gank. If he were, at least two others would have been with him, and a patrol car would have been parked in full view of the door-monitor. Organics always tried to overpower visually the potential arrestee before making the physical clamp.

Carebara looked as if he had not gone unscathed through today. Somebody had tied the antennae on his hat into a knot so tight that he had not been able to get it loose. His left eye was black and blue and shone with healing ointment. He did, however, look alert. More than that. Apprehensive. He kept turning his head to look right and left along the courseway.

Duncan told the screen to open the door and strode toward the door. It swung in with Carebara so close to it that his long thin nose almost touched it. His hat came off to reveal short spiky hair, dark brown and as hard-looking as a beetle's shell.

"No doubt you're wondering what I'm doing here?" he said.

He stopped walking, his mouth open. Pointing at Snick with the hat, he squawked, "What's she doing here?"

Then, "I tried to get you first. You weren't home."

"Two birds with one stone," Snick said.

"What're *you* doing here?" Duncan said.

"Your friend Ward has been arrested and stoned!"

"Cabtab," Duncan murmured. More loudly, he said, "Yes, we know."

"Then I don't have to tell you the implications, possibilities, and repercussions," the professor said. He looked around.

"May I sit down? It's been a hard day, and it's not over by any means." He glanced at the wall screen.

"Forty-five minutes before midnight. We have a lot to do."

His pronunciation sounded peculiar. It was as if he had acquired a speech impediment since they had last seen him.

Duncan waved at a chair. Carebara took it but stood up again almost at once. "No time to take it easy. In fact, it's imperative and vitally necessary, life or death, we leave at once. I'll explain on the way."

Duncan did not move. He said, "We don't go until we get some explanation. For one thing, are you a RAT?"

Carebara's big green eyes became even bigger. "Of course, what else? Though I must admire your caution; it's the best policy not to take anything for granted. Only . . . as of today, it's not RAT. It's Pooper."

"Pooper?"

The professor's face squeezed out annoyance.

"No. It's my Georgian accent."

He spelled it. "P-U-P-A. Pooper."

"Pupa. The form of the developing insect before it becomes a mature adult."

"Yes."

Duncan did not have time to ask him what the initials stood for and was not sure that he cared.

"Let's go as you are," Carebara said. "Just bring along whatever's in your bags. Your IDs too, of course."

"No," Duncan said firmly. "We don't stir unless we have some idea of what you have in mind."

Carebara glanced again at the digital time display.

"All I can tell you is that Ward has been arrested and that it's not likely that the situation can be rectified. Therefore, you two have to take refuge. I'll take you to a place where you'll be safe. I can't tell you more because that's all I know. Come on!"

"You know more than that," Duncan said. "For instance, it's obvious you're rather highly placed in RAT. I mean, PUPA. Were you assigned to watch us from the time we got on the train to L.A.? Ride herd on us?"

"I'll tell you about that on the way. If we waste time here, we may not be able to get to . . . where I'm taking you."

As if it was an afterthought, he reached into his shoulderbag, saying, "Oh, yes. One for each of you. I already have mine in place."

His hand came out of the bag and opened. In the palm lay two cone-ended and shiny black cylinders. Each was a quarter of an inch long and one-sixteenth of an inch wide. With his other hand, he picked up one and held it out. Duncan leaned close to look at it. Now he could see that the cylinder had two flattened-out sides.

"Press a flat side against the skin just above the gum ridge," the professor said. "It'll stick there, won't come loose until you push it off with your finger. The flat side will tear loose then, and you'll swallow the powder that'll spill out of the container. It doesn't matter whether you have time to swallow all of it or, for that matter, any of it. A little bit will do the job even if it gets no further than the surface of your tongue. Here. Take one, but be sure to use your thumb and finger on the cone-ends only. Don't touch the main body."

Duncan took one of the capsules and held it up a few inches from his left eye.

Snick said, "Job? You mean by job it'll kill us."

"I have one in my mouth, too. Here. Stick your finger in my mouth if you don't believe me."

"Oh, I believe you have a capsule there," she said. "But how do I know that yours is filled with poison?"

"For God's sake!" Carebara said. "You're insanely suspicious! Why would I try to trick you?"

"That is something we can't know," Duncan said. "You can't blame us if we don't trust anybody. We've no reason to do so, not with all that's happened to us. Tell me, just how do we get the capsule out of our mouth without breaking it open when we're safe from arrest? I'll be damned if I'll keep it there for the rest of my life!"

"You fill your mouth with a liquid that'll be given you. It loosens the adhesive on the flat part. Hold the liquid in your mouth for a minute. The pill'll come free then."

"Why should we commit suicide if the ganks catch us before we get to your safe place?" Duncan said. "They've got Ward. If they do find out he's a RA—PUPA, I mean . . ." His voice trailed off. Then he said, "I see what you're getting at. Ward doesn't know you're a PUPA. He'll expose us but not you. And if all three of us are dead, then the ganks can't trace beyond us and Ward. But they will investigate all your known associates. One of them, at least, maybe more, is bound to be a PUPA."

"That one will die, too," Carebara said. "Look! We cannot waste any more time! Are you coming with me or not?"

The professor must have orders to kill them here and now if Snick and he refused to obey orders. That was why Duncan had stayed very close to Carebara since he had entered the apartment. If Carebara put his hand inside his robe or his shoulderbag, he would not get the pistol out very far. Or, perhaps, the professor had orders to get rid of them, and he did not intend to leave the apartment with them. Snick could be right. The capsules could dissolve immediately, and so would the lives of Duncan and Snick.

Snick walked over to Carebara and removed the other capsule from his open palm. She dropped it into her shoulderbag. Duncan put his capsule into his shirt pocket.

"We'll go with you," he said. "But—"

"You're ordered to affix them in your mouth!" Carebara said loudly and shrilly.

"I don't even know what position you hold in the organization," Duncan said. "You may be my inferior in rank. We go without the poison in our mouths, or we don't go at all."

Face red, eyelids blinking as if they were the wings of a heavy beetle trying to fly, Carebara stepped back. Duncan stepped forward. The professor took another step away from Duncan, who kept the same distance between them. Carebara stopped when he felt the door behind him.

"Get away from me!" he squeaked.

"Which is it?" Duncan said.

Carebara's right hand shot into his open shoulderbag.

24

Carebara did not have time to withdraw whatever he was reaching for. Duncan drove his knee into the man's crotch, seized his wrist, and twisted it. He stepped back and yanked Carebara forward with the arm. The professor fell forward hard on the floor. His hand was empty, and he was too busy yelling and writhing with pain to attempt to draw the weapon out from the bag. However, when Duncan pulled the bag from Carebara's shoulder and looked into it, he did not find the expected proton pistol. There was a small unmarked can, which he supposed was what Carebara had meant to use. He pointed it at the man's face, pushed the button, and a violet-colored mist sprayed over Carebara's face. He gasped once, his eyes closed, and he quit yelling and jerking.

Duncan had stepped back as he shot the mist, but he caught a whiff of it.

"Truth mist!" he said.

Carebara might not have intended to use it for its primary purpose. After all, he had no time to interrogate them. He had just wanted to subdue Duncan. Or, perhaps, he had meant to knock both of them out when he found out that they would not put the capsules into their mouths.

Duncan looked at the wall time display. Forty-two minutes until midnight. In twelve minutes, the first flashings of the streetlights and the wall lights in the residences would notify the citizens that it would soon be time to enter their cylinders. The sirens in the courseways and the buzzer alarms in the residences would add their warnings.

"Get his feet," Duncan told Snick.

She hastened to help him, and Carebara was quickly laid out on a sofa. The sofa was told just where to swell so that the professor's head was propped high. Snick placed Carebara's right arm across his chest so that it would not dangle and be filled with blood.

Duncan pulled up a chair close to the sofa and sat down. He leaned forward and spoke in a medium-loud and authoritative tone. "You, Doctor Herman Trophallaxis Carebara, will answer all my questions fully and truthfully. Do you understand me?"

Carebara's lips barely moved. His "Yes" was very weak.

"Speak more loudly and enunciate clearly," Duncan said. "Do you understand me?"

The professor's reply was clear.

"Is Herman Trophallaxis Carebara your natal name?"

"No."

"What is your natal name?"

"Albin Semple Shamir."

Snick bent down close to Duncan's right ear and whispered. "Is all this preliminary stuff necessary? We don't have much time. Why not ask him for the essential data?"

Duncan frowned, then said softly, "You're right. But I have a couple of questions about his background in the organization."

Duncan asked them and learned that Carebara had been recruited ten obyears ago. He had gone from Atlanta, State of Georgia, to the State of New Jersey. Though he had taught entomology ever since he had gotten his Ph.D., he had also been a secret agent for the organics. That position had enabled him to protect the subversive organization and to aid its plans.

Duncan asked him again if he was loyal to the organization.
"Yes."
"Who is your immediate superior?"
"I don't know."
More questioning revealed that the person who gave him his orders was masked and spoke with a voice distorter.
"What were you supposed to do with us?" Duncan said. "I mean, where were you ordered to conduct Duncan and Snick?"
"Where?"
"To what place?"
"I wasn't."
"Ah!"
Duncan leaned back and looked up at Snick.
"Now we're getting somewhere!"
But he was not.
"Were you ordered to kill Duncan and Snick?"
"No."
"Were you ordered to knock them out with truth mist?"
"No."
"You were not told to take Duncan and Snick to another place? To meet your superior?"
"No."
"You were not told to kill Duncan and Snick or to make them unconscious?"
"No."
Panthea Snick said softly in Duncan's ear. "Remember, the subject replies rather literally. Instead of asking about both of us, ask him about just one of us. Yourself first."
"To what address were you to conduct Beewolf from his apartment?"
"I was to take him to 173A Pushkin Plaza, Level 25."
"To what address were you to conduct Chandler?"
"I was not ordered to conduct her to any address."
"What were you ordered to tell her when you went to her apartment?"

"I was ordered to order her to go to 173A Pushkin Plaza, Level 25."

"She, that is, Chandler, was to go on alone to 173A Pushkin Plaza?"

"Yes."

"Then you were to come to Beewolf's address and to conduct him to 173A Pushkin Plaza?"

"Yes."

"What were you to do when you and Beewolf got to the plaza?"

"Hand Beewolf over to somebody."

"Who was the somebody?"

"I don't know."

"How was this somebody going to identify himself to you?"

"The somebody would know me."

"But you would not know him?"

"No."

"After you met the somebody and that person took Beewolf into custody, what were you to do?"

"I was ordered to go home."

"What is your home address?"

"It is 358 Orange Courseway, Level 17, University Tower."

"Was Chandler to wait at 173A Pushkin Plaza until you and Beewolf came there?"

"I do not know."

Duncan looked at Snick, raised his eyebrows, and shrugged. It seemed strange to him that Snick would be sent by herself to the plaza. If she were picked up by the ganks on the way, she would have no excuse for being out. She should have gone with Carebara to Duncan's place. As a secret organic officer, Carebara would only have to flash his ID to any curious ganks, and they would have let him and his companions go without further questioning.

A cold thought made him shiver.

What if some PUPAs had been waiting for Snick to leave her apartment after Carebara had told her where to go? They might have had orders that Carebara did not know, orders to take her to some place and dispose of her. She was a danger to the organization now that Cabtab would probably expose her true identity. So am I, Duncan thought. But I'm valuable to PUPA. I have the ability to lie under the mist, and I might be able to teach the techniques to PUPA. Also, there is that other reason why the government regards me as such a peril to it.

He rose and strode toward the front door. Snick said, "What is it?"

He did not reply. He opened the door and stuck his head out. At first, looking along both sides of the courseway, he saw no one. Then a second sweep revealed several vague figures under the canopied entrance of a store far to the left. He stepped back in, released the door, and walked back to Snick. Looking anxious, she said, "What now?"

"Two PUPAs—I think." He told her of his suspicions.

"Get rid of me?" she said. "Why? I'm not a novice, an amateur. I'm valuable, too."

"Maybe not from their viewpoint," he said. "Anyway, I don't intend to stay with them. They're just too callous and casual about knocking off their own members. That policy is, I suppose, responsible for their having escaped detection so far. PUPA is like an ant colony, as our friend Carebara might say. The good of the whole leaves no room for consideration of the individuals. They'll be sacrificed to ensure that the group as an entity doesn't suffer. But we're not ants. Still . . ."

"Still what?"

He held up his hand for silence. Facing the nearest wall screen, he asked for a display of the entry code to the apartment door. Then he ordered that a new code be inserted.

"It's just temporary," he said to Snick. "I suspect that those two ganks have the entry code to this apartment. Yours, too. Now they can't get in."

He looked at the time display.

"They should be trying to enter soon. They don't have much time, and they're probably wondering why the hell Carebara hasn't come out with us."

"Why would they know that I'm here?"

"They must know we're friends. When they didn't find you in your apartment, they figured you came here. Or maybe they don't know. In any event, they're worried about me and the professor."

He walked to the sofa.

"Let's get him into a cylinder. Might as well use mine."

While she lifted Carebara's legs, she said, "The ganks'll find him, and he'll spill everything."

"I don't care! I have no loyalty now. PUPA deserves whatever it gets. We won't be around."

She said nothing while they placed Carebara in a more-or-less fetal position in the cylinder, closed the door, and turned on the power.

The walls flashed on-off with orange, and the phone buzzer rang. Both Snick and Duncan were startled. Before Duncan could ask who was calling, the wall screens displayed large black letters: C. YOU HAVE FIVE MINUTES. These lasted for perhaps five seconds, then the screens resumed their normal appearances.

"They're waiting for him, for him and me," Duncan said.

"Why don't they ask to speak to him?"

"Too cautious, I suppose."

Though they were in a very tight and dangerous situation, Duncan grinned. Even if he had wanted to go to 173A Pushkin Plaza, Level 25, he could not do so. The two down the street must have orders to get Snick, and if she came out, they would follow their orders. Which meant that he would have to defend her. But, since he had no weapons to do that, he was staying inside the apartment.

"All we can do is wait them out," he said. "They'll have to leave soon. Even if they're ganks, they won't have an excuse to stay unstoned."

Looking at the wall screen that showed the courseway, he said, "Get some grease, if you can. If there isn't any, butter will have to do. And get some cloths, anything we can hold in our hands to protect against the friction."

"You're really serious about sliding down the banisters?"

"I'd rather fly down. You know how we could do that?"

"Don't be a smart-ass."

"Smart or not, I'm trying to save our asses."

Then he said, "Oh, oh! They're not waiting anymore! They're here!"

Clearly visible in the bright light, the two men were standing before the door. They were of medium height but well-muscled, both wearing cone-shaped hats with wide floppy brims, loose sleeveless robes that fell to the ankles, no socks, and moccasins. One was dark and had a broad and high-cheek-boned face with dark eyes with slight epicanthic folds. His black hair was spiked and greasy-looking. The other had a long nose, lobeless ears, thick lips, and round eyes. His skin was striped a la zebra mode. Though his eyes were blue, Duncan suspected that they had been depigmented.

The unstriped one reached out and pressed the doorbell.

"We won't answer," Duncan said.

After the doorbell gonged seven times, the unstriped man said something in a low voice to his companion. Both reached into their shoulderbags, and each pulled out a proton gun.

"They're going to blast the lock mechanism!" Duncan said.

Snick grabbed her shoulderbag, spun, and ran toward the back of the apartment. Duncan did not think that she was deserting him. He knew her better than that. Whatever her doubts about the rightness of the revolutionaries' cause or her indecision about how to escape, she would react properly to an immediately dangerous situation. She would be going to the kitchen to get knives and whatever else she could for their defense. He was as sure of that as if he had read her mind.

Duncan could not see the bright spot of the laser beam used for aiming, but he knew that it was now on the slot into which his ID card had to be inserted to activate the lock. There would be no time for Snick to return with the knives, which he doubted they could use advantageously at the door. He told the sofa to extend its wheels. It raised up, and he got behind it and drove it forward, his hands on one end. It slammed into the door just as smoke curled from the midsection and the metal melted.

"Wheels down!" Duncan said, loudly. He turned, snatching up his bag from the sofa, and ran toward the kitchen. Having to push the sofa out of the way would at least momentarily delay the two. Now, he had to get to Snick before they could see him well enough for a shot. Near the entrance to the kitchen he dived because it seemed to him that they should be inside by now or at least have opened the door wide enough for one of them to have a good view of him. Just as he began sliding forward on the floor, the lights went out. Snick must have told the computer to turn them off.

He rose swiftly. There was illumination, not very strong, from the lights of the nearby towers and from the levels above and below this apartment. There was also the bright light from the courseway. The invaders had left the door open.

Snick, a shadowy figure, handed him a long thin knife. She whispered, "I told the electrical power not to go on unless *I* say so."

She giggled. "If they kill me, you're going to have a hell of a time getting the lights back on or phoning out. Nobody can call in, either."

The soft illumination from the courseway was suddenly cut off. The men must have realized that it silhouetted them and made it difficult for them to see into the kitchen.

"They don't know if we have a gun or not," Duncan said softly. "They won't charge on in."

He told the large table to extend its wheels. It rose swiftly, the mechanism silently turning over the wheels in the grooves in the legs. It dropped them onto the floor and then raised the ends of the legs. He pushed the table to one side of the kitchen door, turned the table onto one side, and shoved it across the doorway. The invaders would be able to see that the entrance was blocked because of the twilight glow from the window. They would know they had to push it ahead to get into the kitchen—unless they tried to leap over it. He doubted that they would try that or that they would stick their heads around the side of the door first.

"They won't take their time," he said. "Time's as important to them as to us. More important, in fact."

He got down on all fours and crawled behind the shield of the table to the other side of the entrance. He rose to his full height.

One of the men called, "Beewolf! Chandler! Where's Carebara!"

Duncan raised a finger to his lips. Dark as it was, it was still light enough for Snick to see the gesture.

"Come on, Beewolf! We know you three are in this apartment! No one's come out! Carebara wouldn't be hiding from us. What did you do with him? Where is he?"

The silence was as thick as the darkness.

"We just want Carebara and Chandler," the same man called. "We have no orders about you. Give them up now! Now! Or we come in after you! We'll shoot if we have to!"

These two would be in a PUPA cell, and they would probably have been kept as ignorant as he and Snick. But their cell must be bigger, their information base wider. Otherwise, how would they know about Carebara?

He wondered if they knew how important he was to PUPA. Would that data, if they knew it, keep them from harming him except as a last resort?

He got down on his hands and knees and, pushing his shoulderbag ahead, moved a few feet backward. It would not do for them to make an accurate guess about just where his voice was coming from. Not if they meant to shoot him if forced to do so.

"Carebara is unavailable!" he said, and he crabbed sidewise and then lay flat on the floor. His bag was within reach.

One of the men cursed softly. There was another mutter, two voices this time.

"We don't have time for that crap!" the second man said harshly. "Give up Carebara and Chandler, now! Or we come in shooting! I mean it!"

"And kill Carebara, too!" Duncan said.

Holding the bag, he rolled away toward the center of the kitchen.

"And also kill me!" he said. "Your superiors wouldn't like that at all, you morons! You know what they do to people who screw up!"

The first man cursed quietly again.

"Besides," Duncan said, "we have guns, too! We don't want to use them, but we will! You charge on in, we kill you!"

Duncan rolled away toward his right, half-rose, and moved his hand to indicate that Snick should back away. She nodded, and she moved away from the wall a few feet. Duncan gestured that she should lie down. Instead, she got down on her hands and knees. His violent signs told her to go all the way; she lay flat, her head turned toward the entrance. Her knife was still in her hand.

"Sure, you got guns!" the first man said loudly. "Why didn't you blast us when we came through the door?"

"Because you're PUPA," Duncan said. "We wanted a chance to reason with you."

"No time, and we got orders!" the first man said. "I give you three seconds, you and Chandler, to come out! Keep your hands high! We can see your outlines!"

"Toss your guns in first so we'll know you can't shoot us!" Duncan said.

"Sure, we'll do just that!" the second man said, and both laughed.

Duncan crawled over to Snick. His mouth close to her ear, he said, "When I give the signal, like this—" He raised his hand, fingers straight out, then chopped up and down, "—you say something loudly, then roll to hell fast toward the other end of the room. That way. If they fire, scream as if you'd been hit."

She nodded.

"Wait. I have to get back to the other side of the door."

Having resumed his former position and location, he brought his hand up and down several times.

She spoke loudly, "Go to hell, you bastards!"

As Duncan had expected, the two men guessed her location from her voice, though they could not know its exact area of origin, of course. The air crackled, and two holes appeared in the wall and made smoking holes in the floor. Screaming like a wounded puma, she had spun away as soon as she had finished speaking, but the closest beam was only a few inches away from her. Her scream stopped as if blood had choked her throat. Then the violet lights came again, this time spaced wider and higher. But she had kept on rolling.

"Wednesday'll have a hell of a mess to clean up!" Duncan said. He rolled away, too, but the men did not fire. Evidently, they were not sure that he was lying when he had said that he was extremely important to PUPA.

"Chandler!" Duncan called softly, but not so softly, he hoped, that the two men would not hear him. "You all right?"

Then, shrilly, "You goddamned murderers, I'll kill you!"

There was some more muttering from the hallway. The first man called out then, "Cut out the crap, Beewolf! We're not some thick-headed civilians you can fool!"

"You killed her!" Duncan shouted, and he rolled toward the wall until he was against it. Face close to the floor, he inched along to the center of the doorway behind the table. He turned over and reached into his shoulderbag. His groping fingers found the can of truth mist, and he took it out and placed it on the floor by his right hand. He did not intend to speak any more. The two would make a rush very soon. They could not afford any more time.

Nevertheless, they did not come. Or, if they were creeping up, their moccasins were making no noise. Perhaps they were very uncertain about his status in PUPA, and they were not so sure that they had not hit the woman they knew as Chandler.

A beam of violet shot over Duncan, causing him to jump inside his skin. It came, however, not from a proton pistol but from a small flashlight. It played over the darkness past the table on its side and onto the window beyond. Then it was withdrawn. But it could be that it was being used to search for Carebara. They should be able to figure out that Carebara might not be in the kitchen and had been put inside a cylinder or a PP closet.

While one was searching, the other would be waiting, his gun pointed toward the kitchen door.

Snick was busy, though moving slowly enough not to make noise. She carried a small table to the side of the door and placed it so that it could not be seen from the hallway. He wondered what she was up to but said nothing and made no signs to her. She put another, but smaller, table on top of the first. Now, she was putting a chair by the stacked tables. Now, she was stepping up onto the chair. Now, she was placing a foot on the edge of the lower table. Duncan could see the gleam of flesh; her bare feet looked like white mice.

He sweated heavily, and he brushed the acid liquid from the corners of his eyes. When Snick had stopped the power, she had also cut off the air-conditioning, but even if it had been icy cold, he would be sweating.

Duncan bit his lip, hoping that she would not slip or make any noise that might cause the man to shoot at its area of origin. At the same time, he was straining his ears to catch the sound of advancing footsteps. Since the floor was tiled and the men wore moccasins, he was trying to hear steps only because his instinct made him. However, if they were as tense as he, they might be breathing heavily enough to be detected.

Snick had room to stand up, but not much. She was facing toward the wall, her thighs against the edge of the table top, her toes on the edge of the lower table. She raised one leg, bent it, and rolled over very slowly. The table rocked beneath her. Not enough to go on over. She was on her knees. Then she was standing, poised, the knife gleaming much less brightly than her feet.

She must be planning to leap from above on the first to venture through the doorway, but her launch platform was very unstable.

He heard, very faintly, one of the men say something to the other. It sounded as if the speaker was some distance away. Duncan abandoned the idea of moving the table to one side and crawling out into the hallway. The chances were far too high of his being caught by their flashlight beam.

They would be getting desperate now. They had orders to kill Snick but none on how to deal with him. For all they knew, Duncan and Snick, Beewolf and Chandler to them, did have guns. Carebara was going to stay in the cylinder, and when his body was discovered by the Wednesday people or perhaps by Thursday's, he was going to be in a very bad situation. He would be arrested no matter what story he told or how high he was in Tuesday's organic force. One whiff of truth mist would make him tell all.

Midnight was coming fast. Conditioned to be in the cylinders before then, the two men must be panicked. Also, if they were found unstoned by Wednesday, they would be in as sticky a plight as Carebara.

In the next few seconds, they would either try to make some sort of deal with their quarry or charge on in.

He crawled back to the other side of the doorway, moved the table back, and extended his arm through the opening. His hand held the can of truth mist. He expected them to hear the slight hiss as it expelled the cloud but hoped that they would not identify the noise. When they galloped on in, they would run headlong into the mist. Breathing it in, they would be instantly numbed and be slowed down, though he doubted that they would inhale enough to make them completely unconscious. If he had miscalculated, if they were far enough away and did not attack immediately, the mist would dissipate and be harmless.

Having squirted out at least half the can, he withdrew his arm and moved the table back. It was then that he heard the soft hissing. He cursed. They were doing the same thing he had done!

The table slid backward as a man collapsed over it. Duncan

bellowed, "Hold your breath, Thea!" though he knew that he was too late and, by breathing, would become unconscious, too.

As his senses dimmed, he saw another dark figure sail, shouting, over the man lying folded like a tablecloth on the edge of the barrier. He also saw Snick leap, the knife dully gleaming, heard the top table fall onto the floor, and then . . .

25

He awoke startled, stiff and sore, though a few seconds passed before he was aware of his physical condition. He was lying on a soft bed. On the ceiling was a huge screen displaying a scene from the movie *Peer Gynt*, though he did not remember when he had seen it or who he was then. Gynt had been running through the mist-filled night on a moor studded with many firs charred to the trunk by a forest fire. He had been pursued relentlessly by balls of thread, thoughts made physical and animated. Then he had come upon a sinister old man, the Button-Molder, who carried a box of tools and a big casting ladle. The molder had told Gynt that he had been looking for him and that he was going to melt down Gynt in his ladle. Gynt was a flawed button, a casting missing a loop. Gynt was arguing that he was not a bad fellow at heart. Though he had been many selves, few of them admirable, the real Gynt was at the core, and he was worth saving from destruction.

The Button Molder: "But, my dear Gynt, why all this fuss/Over a technical point like this?/Your self is just what you've never been./So, what's the difference to you if you get melted down?"

What, indeed? Duncan thought. And he forgot the scene and

felt pain and bewilderment because he did not know where he was.

He half-rose, groaning because of his dull headache, and sat on the edge of the bed. He was in a long curving room with a single continuous window from wall to wall on the west. Bright daylight came through it though the sun was not in sight. The splendid furniture shone, furniture that told him that he was in the apartment of a high official. In one of his rooms, anyway.

At the other end of the large room was another large bed, and in it lay Snick, eyes closed, on her side and covered to the waist with an electric-blue blanket. The screen above her was displaying some movie that he could not identify at this angle and distance. Soft voices issued from it.

He rose and staggered to the window. A canoe-shaped organic aircraft floated by about a hundred feet away. Beyond it were the peaks of some towers and the upper parts of bridges. A freight dirigible moved majestically within his view. He walked close to the window, which became black. When he stepped back, the window lightened, though not enough for him to see very far. Another two steps back, and the window was so clear it did not seem to be there. Evidently, its material polarized when a body of a certain size got within a certain distance of it.

That confirmed that he was imprisoned, and the window would keep any aerial passengers from seeing him or he them. Not, he thought, that there was any chance that anybody flying by would respond to his signals for help if he was visible.

There were two doors, both closed, in the room. He pushed on the nearest; it would not give. The other, however, swung easily inward to reveal a toilet bowl, several sinks with faucets, soap, towels and washrags on racks, and a massive white-and-green-streaked marble sunken bathtub. He relieved himself standing up, though he was so shaky that he felt like sitting down. The toilet automatically flushed when he stepped back from it.

After drinking a large glass of water, he looked into the mirror behind the black and red onyx counter. He saw a weary and red-eyed Duncan. His clothes were the ones he had worn when he had passed out. He washed his face and hands, dried them, and was just about to open the door when it swung in. Snick stood in the doorway, her mouth open, and then it narrowed for her to say, "Oh! Thank God! It's you!"

"More or less," he said. He was thinking that it might not just be coincidence that the movie was *Peer Gynt*. Perhaps whoever had brought them here knew more about Duncan than Duncan cared for him to know.

Snick was still alive, and that might mean that their captor intended to allow her to keep on living. He looked at her as she brushed past him, pulled down her panties, sat down, and relieved herself mightily. Though he wanted to talk to her at once, he was driven out by the stench. He did some setting-up exercises to exorcise the stiffness of body and legs, though the effort made his headache worse. He was aware that he was being watched and wished that the observer would enter and tell him what was going on. He would like to get things over with quickly. That, however, was not to be. A buzzing sounded from the wall near the door. He stood up, turned toward the sound, and saw a seemingly seamless section of the wall rotate on a central axis just as the buzzing stopped. The other side, now this side, presented a semicircular shelf on which were two trays covered partly by napkins. He went to the section and found, as he had expected, two breakfasts. He lifted the tray, and the section rotated to its original position. Though he tried to see through the opening, he could make out nothing but darkness.

He and Snick had plenty to eat and drink. Eggs, bacon, toast, cereal and milk, orange juice, coffee, and vitamin pills. The protein, of course, would be relatively cholesterol-free. He called out to her to come enjoy, but, hearing the shower, he decided he would begin the meal by himself. Snick was certainly being cool about this, despite her seemingly painful puzzlement when she had come into the bathroom. He would have preferred to talk about their situation first. Not that that would have helped them except to ease some tension.

It was evident that PUPA, despite the danger of being caught, had sent out a party to his apartment. It would have had no trouble destoning Carebara after midnight. Snick's orders to the lights to stay extinguished would have been automatically overridden by Wednesday's circuits.

Snick came out of the bathroom, holding her clothes and shoes in one hand, her body dry but her black straight hair still somewhat wet, shining like a seal's fur. She walked across the room to the cylindrical cone-topped cleaner on a table in the corner. Its surface shimmered with colors passing from violet to blue; tiny gargoyles stuck their heads out at irregular intervals. Its owner, Duncan thought, must have paid a lot of credits for it.

Snick put the clothes and shoes inside it, closed the door, pressed a button, opened the door, took the clothes and shoes out, and put them on. Duncan, watching her, ate with decreasing appetite. Though the ancient modesties had been done away with because of their psychically damaging effects, he suspected that she was deliberately moving her nude body, exaggerating her motions, to excite his lust. Frustrate him since he could not expend it on her. Why had he fallen in love with the sadistic bitch?

On the other hand, perhaps he was giving her motives she did not have.

She sat down at the table across from him and began eating. Then she wrinkled her nose, said, "Phew!" and stared at him. "You didn't bathe or clean your clothes. You stink like a skunk."

"Why don't you sit over there then?" he said, stabbing his fork to indicate a sofa.

She took her tray away and sat near the window. "I'm sorry, but you were spoiling my breakfast. You can't blame me, can you? Wouldn't you feel the same if I was dirty?"

"I have more important things to think about," he said. "Also, I got sweaty and dirty trying to save your ass."

"Yours, too," she said. She looked around while chewing bacon and toast. "You woke up before I did. What do you think about all this?"

"PUPA got us here, how I don't know. We'll find out soon enough, when they're ready."

"They must've questioned us under TM."

"You, yes. They probably didn't bother with me unless they wanted to determine if I could really lie."

"Maybe you didn't want to then."

"Maybe. I don't know myself what I say. But my subconscious really works for me. Behaves as if it were conscious."

"You must have a hell of a cooperative subconscious."

"Eight of them," Duncan said. "I'm a man of many parts. But I did too good a job on myself when I became Duncan. I can't consciously summon the others."

After he ate his meal, he cleaned his clothes while Snick looked at him nude. He wondered what her thoughts were. After showering and dressing, he came out of the bathroom. Snick was playing with the window, stepping close to it to make it blacken, stepping back to make it transparent.

"We must be on the top floor or near it, judging by the other towers," Duncan said.

"Yes, and we're in the same tower."

Duncan asked the wall screen for the time and the date. It displayed nine o'clock in the morning of Wednesday. His suspicion that they might have been stoned for a long time was not valid. Unless, that is, the owner had for some reason ordered the wrong time and date to be shown.

Why would he? Duncan thought. That's crazy. I'm getting so I don't believe anything I see or hear or trust anybody.

The buzzing sounded, and the wall section rotated again. Snick got up and put the trays on the shelf. The section turned, taking the trays with it. Duncan had started to protest that she should not do their captor's work for him. But what the hell. If they wanted another meal, they would have to deposit the dirty dishes. The citizens were conditioned to be neat, clean, and orderly. Duncan himself had had to restrain his impulse to get rid of the trays.

Snick had just turned away from the wall when the door to the apartment opened inward. Snick stopped walking, Duncan started to rise, thought better of it, and eased back down in the chair. A man and a woman, both in street clothes, entered. They stopped and half-turned, proton guns in their hands. A large, dark-skinned man of middle age walked in. He was also in civilian dress, but it looked expensive, and he was unarmed. He stopped between the two armed guards. A huge, big-bellied and many-jowled man in a brown friar's robe entered. Behind came two men, holding guns.

Duncan sprang to his feet and shouted, "Padre! Padre Cabtab!"

Cabtab bellowed with delight, opened his arms, and said, "Come to Papa!"

Snick, smiling, started toward him and Duncan, grinning, began to rise. The male guard said, sharply, "Stay where you are!"

Snick halted; Duncan sank back down.

"All three of you," the man said, gesturing with the gun. "Over there. The sofa."

Duncan hugged and was hugged by Cabtab on the way to the sofa. The padre gave Snick a big kiss on top of her head and squeezed her shoulders. "I thought you were a goner," she said.

"I may well be yet!" he roared. "We shall see! Our host has treated me well so far, but you remember what the spider said to Miss Muffet!"

The middle-aged man looked at Duncan with very light blue eyes that contrasted weirdly with his dark skin. He had very heavy black eyebrows, prominent epicanthic folds, a large and hawklike nose, rather thin lips, and a massive chin. Duncan thought that he had seen him before but could not evoke any memory. However, he did feel uneasy. There was something about this man that threatened danger, and Duncan did not believe it was just because of this situation.

The man sat down in the chair Duncan had vacated. He church-steepled his fingers and said, "So, we meet again."

Since the man was looking directly at him, Duncan knew that he was being addressed.

"You have the advantage of me," Duncan said.

The man smiled and said, "In more ways than one."

He put his hands on his thighs.

"Now, the question is what do I do with you? And your friends?"

"Maybe if you told us why we're here, we could help answer that," Duncan said.

"He looks like you," Snick said quietly. "He could be your grandfather."

The room was wavering as if seen through very hot air in a desert. A voice was calling to him, a very faint and far-off voice. Something, no, some things, were fighting far down inside him, roiling his stomach, no, not his stomach, his mind. But making him sick.

The air became clear again; the voice died out. He still felt vaguely sick in his stomach.

The man frowned and said, "You remember?"

"No," Duncan said. "I . . . something . . . I don't know what. I was affected . . . I felt strange. I don't know why."

"You may go crazy," the man said but did not elaborate. Duncan knew, somehow, that the man would not explain his statement.

"The mess in your apartment was cleaned up," the man said. "But there was no time to replace the door. The Wednesday tenants did not report for work. The organics investigated and found the tenants still stoned and the lock on the front door burned out. Your cylinder was empty. The mystery will never be cleared up, I hope, but Wednesday left a message for Tuesday reporting the situation. You are done as Andrew Beewolf. And

Snick is done as Chandler. A few Tuesdays may pass before it's noticed that Padre Cabtab, known as Citizen Ward on Tuesday, is missing from the warehouse. The organics will assume that Chandler and Beewolf fled this city. But they'll know that somebody destoned Ward and spirited him away. Perhaps they'll tie all three of you together. It should be easy to find out that you were together at the Snorter more than once. Where the backtrail will lead, I don't know yet, of course."

"Are you PUPA?" Duncan said.

"In a sense, I am *of* PUPA and in another I *am* PUPA."

"The leader," Duncan said. "The head."

"Yes."

"You must have a reason for keeping us here instead of just getting rid of us."

The man lowered his eyelids halfway.

Looks like a sleepy hawk, Duncan thought. Or one thinking about past strikes with great pleasure. Or future strikes with even more pleasure.

Two courses of action were open to the man. He would find some use for his captives and they would stay alive for a while, perhaps for a long time. Or he would have them stoned and hidden or killed and hidden. Whatever would happen, it was going to be determined this morning.

"I'll be honest with you," the man said. "Snick and Cabtab are superfluous and could be a danger to us. It's not that I don't trust them—to a certain extent. Snick revealed her doubts about the morality of our purposes, and that makes her unstable from our viewpoint. However, if she swears that she will not betray us, she won't. That much we learned about her.

"Cabtab is unstable in that he really believes that he is in some sort of communication with God. He may be for all I know, but God has His purposes, and we have ours. He might swear that he would never betray us, and he would be sincere. But if the spirit came upon him, the Spirit of God, he would say, then he would obey the voice of God. And if God told him to betray us, he would."

He switched his gaze to the padre.

"Isn't that correct, Cabtab?"

"You already know that," the padre said.

"So we have a morally uncertain ex-organic and a theologically certain street preacher as agents. Not what I call stable agents. We also have you, Beewolf, a man of many parts, as you said, and a man who knows far more than he realizes. A man who can be very valuable to us; he can teach us the technique of lying while under the mist. He also knows something else he doesn't know, but that will remain suppressed, I hope.

"In any event, he can be used to great effectiveness. Not in the field, however. He'll have to stay hidden and teach the rest of us. Not all of us. A few key personnel. Will he do that? *Can* he do that? Does he know how he did it? He was under TM but said that he did not know how to teach it. Did he lie then? Or was he or whatever it is that speaks for him when he's unconscious telling the truth?"

"I really don't know," Duncan said.

The man smiled. His eyes were still half-hooded.

"Someone in you does know. We'll find out somehow just who that persona is. If we don't . . ."

"Yes?"

Duncan spoke clearly and loudly and bravely enough, but he felt cold from the very center of himself. He also felt as if a finger tipped with a sharp claw were scratching at the rear of his hindbrain.

"It may be very painful for you," the man said, "I am not hinting at physical torture. The pain will be psychic, though that can also be physical. But if you . . . if we are successful, then you will be able to come out from hiding and take your place in society. Which place will be very high, I promise you. Meanwhile, we have your friends. I doubt you'll really cooperate with us if they are not safe or kept alive. So I promise you they'll not be killed. But I think it best to stone them for a long while. They'll be out of the way, hidden safely, and when the time comes, they'll join you in the good and free life you'll be enjoying."

Duncan glanced right and left at Cabtab and Snick. Their faces were blank, unless you considered a lack of expression as an expression. In this situation, it certainly was. They did not want to be stoned even under these conditions. If the revolution failed, they would remain frozen forever. If the man was lying, the same would happen. Their future depended upon how much influence Duncan had.

26

"I'd like to have all this clear and hard in my mind," Duncan said. "You want me to teach your people how to lie when misted. I can't guarantee that I can do that—"

"I know that," the man said. "We'll experiment."

"—but I'll try, I'll cooperate with you fully. That is, I will if you let my partners stay with me. I need them, if only to keep me company. It'll be a very lonely and frustrating life for me if I'm kept in one room or even have the run of the rest of the rooms in this apartment. I won't be able to function 100 percent without them. If you did stone them, I'd hold that against you. Though I'd know that their lives depended upon my success, that'd be an extra burden on me. Worrying about them would squeeze the juice out of me. I'd resent you, hate you, if you want the truth.

"They should be allowed to live and to live with me. They'd be helpful. Their lives hang on helping me do what you want me to do."

The man smiled, and he said, "That's what I thought you'd say. That's why I didn't get them out of the way at once. Very well. They can stay with you, but I expect the fullest cooperation from them. If any of you, and that includes you, Jeff . . .

Andrew . . . try anything, any trick, any attempt at escape, all
three of you will go into the cylinder. You're getting your
chance now, but I won't give a second one.

"You understand that?"

Duncan nodded, and so did the other two. Snick sighed softly,
and her hands squeezed Duncan's gently.

The man had said, "Jeff." And Duncan had once been Jefferson Cervantes Caird, a Tuesday organic. Did the man know that
Snick had told Duncan that? He might not have specifically
questioned Snick on that point. But he would probably expect
that, since Snick had known Caird, she would have told Duncan
all she knew about him. The man, however, had not shown any
sign of chagrin at the slip of tongue. Either he did not think it of
significance or he was a good actor.

Could he, Duncan, somehow summon up a full-blown Caird,
question him, get the answers he needed, and then push Caird
back down into whatever dark abyss he now occupied? Or
would it be too dangerous? Would Caird fight to regain control
and to topple Duncan back into the abyss?

Would it make any difference if Caird did? Would not he,
Duncan, be also Caird?

No. They were separate identities. Duncan was as horrified of
losing his control as . . . as Caird must have been when he lost
his. No. Caird had voluntarily, eagerly, in fact, become six other
personae. He must have had enormous will power to overcome
the same searing panic that Duncan felt at the idea of dissolving
and letting Caird take over. No. It was not really a dissolution. It
was a repression, a retreat into a rathole in the brain, in a
manner of speaking. Or it could be said that Caird became
semistoned. That was a better analogy. Half-stoned but still able
to send out thought waves when, through some neural mechanism, Duncan wanted certain memories. Some memories were
provided, though they were not always clear. Other memories
just would not be transmitted.

Duncan became aware that the man and the guards were
staring at him. Snick squeezed his hand again and said, softly,
"What's the matter?"

"I'm sorry," Duncan said. "I didn't hear you. I was thinking of something. What did you say?"

"I didn't say anything," the man said. "You looked rather peculiar, as if your mind had gone to Mars. Are you subject to fugues?"

"No, not at all," Duncan said briskly. "I was thinking about working out techniques for lying while unconscious. Also, I was wondering if you would tell me your name. Not your true one, of course, any name by which we would know you. *The man* is too impersonal, too indefinite."

"Is that what you were really thinking about? Or are you trying to route me onto some other subject-track?"

"I would like to have a name."

"Labels and names seem to be vital to humans. Very well, you may address me as Citizen Ruggedo." He chuckled as if at some joke known only to himself.

Citizen Ruggedo rose from the chair. He held his hand high in the air, and a wall displayed the time and date: 9:00 A.M., Wednesday, D2-W3, HOPE, N.E. 1331. Day-Two, Week-Three of the month of Hope, New Era 1331. It was as Duncan had thought. They had just slept through the morning from midnight to about eight o'clock and had awakened on the day immediately following Tuesday. They had not been stoned. Which meant that they had been drugged to ensure that they slept after the effects of the TM had worn off.

"This room will be your quarters," Ruggedo said. "If you and Citizen Chandler, aka Snick, wish to share it, you may. All three of you may live here if you wish."

Snick shook her head. Cabtab said, "I'd be happy to share it with Citizen Beewolf, but I imagine he'd rather have privacy."

"What say you, Citizen Beewolf, aka Duncan, among other names?" Ruggedo said.

"Complete privacy," Duncan said. "It's going to be crowded enough during working hours if this will also be where we try to figure out techniques."

"Very well. You, Chandler, will have your own room, though

it won't be nearly as commodious as Duncan's. The same for you, Cabtab."

"Since you seem to know my real name," Snick said, "you may as well forget Chandler."

"Your supervisor will be here at ten o'clock," Ruggedo said. "Snick and Cabtab will also be here at that time. I won't be here very often, I have work elsewhere, but I'll be getting reports about your progress at frequent intervals. Work hard."

He turned, and two guards followed him out. The others motioned to Snick and Cabtab to precede them. The padre said, "See you, Dunc. I'll be praying for you, Snick and me, for all of them, including Citizen Ruggedo. God, the Singular, will guide them if it so pleases It."

When the door had closed, Duncan went to it and pushed on it. As he had expected, it did not give, but he had to test it. He did aerobic exercises hard for an hour, his mind working on the future while his body automatically labored in the present. He alternated between scenarios of escape and self-questioning about how he could teach the techniques. By the time that the door opened again, he had envisioned nothing successful for either of the problems. Nor had he been able to summon memory of where he had seen "Ruggedo" before.

Snick and Cabtab, looking fresher than when they had left, entered. Duncan expected the guards and the supervisor whom Ruggedo had mentioned. To his surprise, no armed people came in. The person following Duncan's companions was Professor Carebara. He closed the door and said, "Good morning, Citizen Duncan."

"You're the supervisor?" Duncan said.

Carebara said, "Yes," and sat down in a chair. "Now—"

"What the hell?" Duncan said. "You're an insect specialist. What do you know about psychology? Am I just another bug?"

"No need to smart off," Carebara said. "You forget I'm also an organic officer. I'm very experienced at interrogating unconscious people. I majored in psychics at college before I switched to entomology. Homo sapiens is too maddeningly irrational for me. The class Insecta are free of neuroses, and I seldom get emotionally involved with their problems. Besides, no psychicists are available just now. I've answered your questions. Do you mind if we get down to work?"

"If I only knew how to do it," Duncan said. "I don't even remember how I became the I that I am now."

Carebara put his hands together and moved the palms across each other while his left thumb slid up and down the lower part of the right thumb. His green eyes were wide and bright; his expression, eager and confident. Then he pulled out of a pocket of his bottle-green jacket a small blue can. He rose, saying, "Lie down on that sofa." He moved the can. "Herein lies the truth."

"Jesus!" Duncan said, but he went to the sofa. "You think it's that easy? You were told the problem, weren't you? Your problem, I mean, not mine. You can't get the truth out of me with that."

"I've been thoroughly briefed," the professor said with a lofty expression. "I'm not an amateur. I've studied the tapes of your interrogation made after you were brought here. They revealed what you think you do know. Now, we'll find out what you think you don't know. But I don't expect we'll do it quickly."

Duncan looked up at the long thin face and the abnormally large eyes. "I wish you luck. But what I need is an archaeologist of the mind, not an entomologist, a bug-crazy gank."

"I don't mind your hostility," Carebara said. "I'm used to hate."

The can hissed. Duncan smelled the faint odor, as violet as its color. The last sense to go, his hearing, made him think that he had just been bitten by a venomous snake with fang-tipped antennae. When he awoke, the professor, Snick, and Cabtab were in the same positions. Carebara looked like a puzzled ant. His hands were placed on his chest, and his fingers wiggled like feelers.

I have to stop this, Duncan thought. He's human, not an arthropod.

"You can get up," Carebara said. "We'll have some coffee first, then run the tape. What I plan to do is to show you every session so you'll feedback me, and I, you. You know yourself better than anybody else, theoretically anyway, so you may be able to observe and analyze yourself and then perhaps synthesize a psychic key to open yourself."

"See what's going on, you mean?" Duncan said.

"Crudely but correctly phrased."

They watched the session three times, the professor and Duncan with keen interest, but Cabtab yawned the second time around and Snick got up and prowled during the third running.

"As you see," Carebara said at the end of the first showing, "I am concentrating on your most recent persona, Andrew Beewolf. I formulate the process as peeling an onion, if you don't mind so homely a metaphor. First, Beewolf. Then, Duncan. Then Isharashvili and so on back to Caird, the primal psyche."

"I hate to tell you," Duncan said, "but Beewolf is not a persona. He's a role. I was always acting as if I were Beewolf; I never *was* him."

Carebara looked both nettled and embarrassed. He said, "Then I should have ignored Beewolf and gone for Duncan's jugular?"

"Yes, though that's too violent an expression. Your gentle probes weren't going for the jugular. I'd call them tickles."

The professor looked indignant.

"You don't know much about psychicism. If the practitioner lays rough hands upon the patient's psyche, he may bruise, not evoke. It's like a worker ant of the Myrmecocystus species stroking the distended abdomen of a replete. The strokes must be gentle if the worker is to get the replete's honey."

Snick stopped pacing. Cabtab sat up. Duncan said, "What?"

"Certain ants produce a special type of worker called repletes. These are fed enormous quantities of honeydew or other kinds of sugary liquids. The replete stores the liquid in its abdomen, which, as time passes, becomes huge, larger than the body of the replete itself. Often the size of a large garden pea. The repletes hang from the ceilings of the nest tunnels and regurgitate the highly nutritious and energy-packed liquid to the workers when stroked on a certain area."

"Yes? And if the workers are too rough, they might tear open the swollen abdomen? Is that what you're saying in reference to my swollen psyche?"

"Not swollen. Many-layered. But each persona will be delicate and so requires a feather touch. That is, until the very core is exposed. Then a more vigorous but still cautious manipulation is demanded. Often, the patient suffers agonies. Of an emotional nature, of course. The child in us cries out and fears a beating even if none threatens."

Duncan did not reply. He was galvanized, though he did not move a muscle. A spark, such as that shooting off from two naked electrical lines touching, a brief flash, white, blue-edged, had swelled in his mind. Swelled? Swollen abdomen? Swollen psyche? The light had faded, but not before he saw the face of a child, ten years old or thereabouts, grinning at him while tears ran down its cheeks.

He sobbed, and he started to speak to Carebara but thought better of it. He did not want Carebara to know of this.

In ancient times, when criminals were hanged, they must have felt the shock of certainty and the not-to-be-sidestepped when the trap door dropped. That face. It was his. That, however, was not what had made his mind jump and hop as if it had stepped on a floor laid with hot wires. It was the realization that that child was not Jeff Caird. It was he, Duncan, and also Caird, but only in that it inhabited the same body.

Jefferson Cervantes Caird, whom he had thought was the original persona, was the original *creation*. He was the first to be conceived in the mind of the child, nourished in the womb of his imagination, brought forth as J. C. Caird. Thus, the child was the first of eight, not seven, separate psyches. Beewolf, of course, did not count.

"I said something?" Carebara said.

"That's twice today," Snick said. Though she had seemed impatient and bored, she must have been watching him closely.

"A flash of something. Gone. I can't even describe it."

Carebara rose. "I'll see you after lunch, say, two o'clock. We will start on Duncan then."

He started to walk away but stopped and turned back. "You're not lying to me, are you? Beewolf is really just a role?"

"How would I know?" Duncan said. "I'm unconscious then."

"You're conscious now, and you should know if you're telling the truth about as simple a thing as knowing if you're acting or not."

"I believe I'm telling the truth. Of course, I could be lying when I say that. The only way you can determine if I'm lying is to spray me. But if I'm sprayed, I may lie."

Carebara threw his hands up and, muttering, stalked out.

The child had a face but no name.

What had happened to make him disappear as completely as data erased from a tape? What magnetomental shiftings of polarity had wiped out—seemed to wipe out, since he was still down there—the memory of the child in Caird? And in the seven others? Or had they, too, had such thrusts of recall? Since he did not have all of their memories, how was he to know whether or not they had glimpsed the child?

"My friend!" Cabtab boomed. He was looking inside the seven-foot-high food-storage container still called the "fridge" though it did not depend upon cold for preservation of food. "Dunc! It seems to me that you're as screwed up as I was! I believed in a plurality of gods in this universe, and you believe in a plenum of souls in your one body. What nonsense I spouted! There is only one God, and you have only one soul! You're just confused, that's all, just as I was confused. Forget this gibberish about seven souls in your flesh. Act as if you only had one, and you will be whole and single again!"

"It's not that easy," Duncan said. "You had to have a mystical revelation before you abandoned your pantheon. Do I have to have one also? I could wait all my life in the darkness for one and die without the light."

"Revelation?" Cabtab said. "I didn't have any! One second, I was the priest of many gods. The next, as smoothly as stepping through a wide doorway, I was, am, the priest of the one and indivisible Lord of Creation."

"It took you a long time to rediscover what Pharaoh Akhenaten discovered eight thousand years ago," Snick said. "Do we have to talk about such superstitious crap?"

"Sister," the padre said, smiling ferociously, "you lack respect for the beliefs of others."

Duncan said, "Hold it!" and he raised his hand as if he were a traffic cop. "Let's not get into this kind of argument. We have, at the moment, much more vital things to consider. You're transgressing on his self-image, Thea. If you challenge the validity of his religious beliefs, you're threatening his identity. You're chipping away at it, making him less whole, in short, less than he thinks he is or different from what he thinks he is. You're accusing him of being wrong, and he must believe that he's right.

"In any event, we have to cooperate if we're going to come out of this alive. Also, need I remind you that we're being monitored? PUPA doesn't want dissension among its members. It has a way of dealing with people it thinks it can't trust."

Cabtab's face became less red, and he made a visible effort to relax.

"You're right, Brother Duncan. My apologies, Sister Panthea, for my violent reaction. But I advise you to watch your mouth in the future."

"You're a good man in many respects," Snick said. "You're brave, and you're dependable when it comes to swift action. But I'd just as soon you didn't press your goofy—"

Duncan shouted, "Thea!"

Cabtab bellowed, "At least I can make up my mind! You're not even convinced that PUPA is—"

"Silence! Both of you!" Duncan yelled. "I said you were being watched! Every move, every expression of face and voice, is being taped. Let's cooperate, for God's sake, and act like adults!"

"I forgive you, Sister Thea," the padre said.

"You forgive me?" she said. "Why, you theological shuttler! In one day you switch from pantheism to monotheism! You—"

Duncan shot out of his chair.

"That's enough, both of you! Get out! Go to your rooms! I don't want you in here until you agree to behave rationally! I have a lot of thinking to do! I need quiet! Out!"

"Just how do we get out?" Cabtab said. "We're prisoners, remember?"

The door opened, and two armed men entered. One gestured with his gun at Cabtab and Snick. "You two come along."

Snick went out quietly and swiftly. The padre said, "Bless you, my sons. You certainly are watching over us like guardian angels." He turned his head toward Duncan on his way out and, grinning, lowered one eyelid. There were no wall screens behind Duncan, and that slow wink probably would not have been seen as such by a monitor. Nor would a monitor have thought that Duncan's gesture of a moment ago was anything but a nervous action or perhaps a desire to get the stiffness out of his left hand. His companions had noted the signal for them to start a loud quarrel. Now Duncan knew that the activities in the room were not just being taped to be seen during a later running. The guards were observing everything that went on in this room as it occurred. They had orders to interfere in anything that looked suspicious or that might cause trouble.

He had suspected as much but had to make sure.

He did not think, however, that Snick and Cabtab's friction was all just acting. They were quite sincere about their religious attitudes; their anger had been real.

Putting that out of his mind, he concentrated on the vision of the child's face. That got him nowhere. After an hour, he quit trying so hard and let the thoughts come as they would. Perhaps, while he was being bathed in the stream of the unconscious, he would see the child's face float by, or something connected to it. Lunch hour came, and his meal appeared on the rotating shelf. He ate it without tasting the food. The sun came around the corner of the tower, and the window to the west darkened. He jogged from one end of the room to the other two hundred times and then skipped with an imaginary rope. After walking on his hands twenty times across the room and doing three hundred pushups, he showered. During this, he could not keep from considering the "problem" of identity, as it was called, though he regarded tackling it as a waste of time. But since he had made an agreement with himself to let his mind wander, let it go where it wished into whatever byways and crannies it wished for several hours, he did not try to focus on any of the immediate and genuine problems.

Cut out the philosophical flab surrounding the identity of the human. Forget the many thousands of books written about it and the thousands of tapes made about it. The identity of the individual Homo sapiens was, simply, his body, which included his "mind," his actions and reactions at any second of time. Or, if minute distinctions had to be made, at any microsecond. Never mind whether the identity was formed by heredity or by environmental influences or by an interaction of both. The causes of identity were a separate question.

A person was what he did and thought at any second of time. He was not the same at one time as he was at another time. Identity was the flux contained within the skin and the flux outside the bag of skin wrought by that bag.

There had once been a man named Jefferson Cervantes Caird. He had an identity, as all humans do, even the totally paralyzed and the idiot. It had changed from time to time just as the appearance of his body and the state of his mind had changed. Only the label, Jefferson Cervantes Caird, had not changed. Then, the label had become Robert Aquiline Tingle. On Wednesdays only. Tingle had not been just Caird acting as Tingle. Caird *became* Tingle every dawn of Wednesday. And on Thursday Tingle had *become* James Swart Dunski. On Friday,

Wyatt Bumppo Repp. On Saturday, Charles Arpad Ohm. Sundays, he became Thomas Tu Zurvan, the street preacher, Father Tom, a zealous religionist, quite in contrast to the other six personae, who were all agnostics or atheists. Mondays, he metamorphosed as a persona and therefore as an identity into Will Muchluck Isharashvili.

Yet these unique people had not entirely forgotten one another. Since Caird was a courier for a secret organization, passing from day to day to transmit messages from one day to the other, he had to preserve some memory of whom and what he had been. In fact, some memory of all the identities. But the key words were *not forgotten* and *memory*. The thread that he followed from day to day despite his change of persona was that of a limited memory of his other identities. These memories, in a sense, leaked through from the others and were only of a nature and degree to guide him in his subversive activities. These were voices from the six men buried within him, faint but strong enough, advice, phone calls, as it were, from temporary tombs.

One bag of skin could hold more than one identity. People with multiple personalities, for instance, had two or more personae possessing them from time to time. The difference between these severely mind-wracked people and Caird was that his possession by others was entirely voluntary and depended upon his consent. Except at the last, when, threatened by death, the seven had fought for control.

At this moment, Duncan was wondering if he could dissolve the identity as Duncan and return to that of Caird. Would he have to tackle and defeat each of the seven in chronological sequence, working backward in time to the primal Caird? Or could he bypass all but Caird? If he did get to Caird, then he would become him. He would know what that one secret was that the government thought he had. He would know how he had gotten into the early phases of this situation.

There was a good chance, though, that his captors would not desire that he become Caird again. Duncan suspected that the man who had questioned him Wednesday, "Ruggedo," would not like that. What he wanted was to discover Duncan's techniques for lying under the mist. That was all. Or seemed to be all.

Why had he disintegrated or buried that memory? Perhaps to make sure that, if captured, he would not be able to reveal it to the ganks. Or he might have decided that he was through with becoming other people. He might have thought that he could tolerate no more becomings. The psyche could endure only so many of them. There might be a finite reservoir of psychic energy, and he might have just about drained it.

At that moment, the door opened without announcement of entry. Carebara came in followed by Snick and Cabtab. His companions looked refreshed and not at all angry with each other. The professor said, "I've been thinking. We may be on the wrong track trying to get to a persona that knows the transformation techniques. We'll attempt a different approach. You'll stay conscious, and as Beewolf, try to invent your techniques. If you did it as Caird, you can do it as Beewolf. No matter what your persona, your ingenuity is the same, and so is the potential for invention."

You're following the wrong sugar-trail, ant-man, Duncan thought. But I won't tell you that.

"Very well," Duncan said. "Let's get to it."

27

The swimming pool was forty feet long and fourteen feet wide and the ceiling was ten feet from the floor. The room itself was fifty feet long and twenty wide. Though sounds did not echo and become amplified as in a much larger public pool, they still carried quite well. Duncan and his two colleagues were diving, thrashing, and swimming noisily while two armed guards watched them. Starting Thursday, they had been conducted to this huge room, which was part of the complex, for an hour's exercise every day. All three were nude, but the guards kept their eyes mainly on Snick. Duncan managed to whisper to her while they were treading water and Cabtab's mighty bellyflops smacked loudly.

"We have to find a way to talk privately. I have a plan."

A guard must have seen his lips moving. He shouted, "Quiet, you! No talking! Or your swimming privileges will be canceled!"

Duncan held up a placating hand, muttered, "May your dong fall off!" and swam away. Knowing that he was being observed by the wall and ceiling screens, he had held his hand over his mouth when he had spoken to her. It was possible that the monitors could lip-read.

Later, while Snick was diving from the board, and he was sure that the guards were not alert to what he was doing, he said softly, "Padre, I have a plan. Somehow we must discuss it."

"This isn't the place," Cabtab said, and he upended and swam to the bottom.

When the hour was nearly up, a guard blew a whistle and conducted Cabtab to the door of a dressing room. When the padre had dried off and put his robes on, he came out. Snick was sent into the room then. When she left it, Duncan entered. He felt more than just frustrated. The only occasions when all three were together were in the pool room, during the sessions, and when they were allowed to eat in Duncan's room. There was no time when they were not closely watched.

The sessions were notable only for their lack of success. Carebara's thousands of questions, his insistent and sometimes tricky probings, had not dented in the least Duncan's platinum-hard psychic shell. Snick and Cabtab had sincerely tried to help the professor, but their suggestions had been valueless. Even Duncan's ideas, inspired by watching the sometimes censored tapes of the sessions, had been without fruit.

Carebara was the most worried. He had not said so, but it was evident that he was desperate. Perhaps that was partly because his failure would cause him to be transferred elsewhere. He would have to be given a new ID and thus would be in a dangerous situation. Or, Duncan thought, Carebara might believe, with good reason, that he would be stoned and hidden. That course would be the easiest and least perilous for PUPA.

Going to the swimming pool every day gave Duncan the layout of part of the apartment complex. Cabtab's room, a much smaller area than Duncan's, was next door to his, north. Beyond was Snick's room, also much smaller. And beyond that and the hallway outside their three rooms was, apparently, a wall beyond which was the apartment of another government official or perhaps a hallway. The route from the three rooms to the pool went invariably south along the wide hallway. This was lined by blank wall screens before which were some marble pedestals topped by marble busts. Duncan recognized the faces

of Julius Caesar, Alexander the Great, Napoleon, Genghis
Khan, and Wang Shen. Wang Shen, the last of the world con-
querors and the greatest, unlike his egomaniacal predecessors,
had insisted that no statues or monuments be erected to him
and that any tapes made of his life or any shows portraying him
as a character reveal his face as little as possible. Nevertheless,
his wishes had not always been honored, and Duncan recalled
seeing his features now and then. Just where, he did not remember.

What Duncan found strange about the busts was that they
were of men who, excepting Wang Shen, were not admired.
Descriptions of their military exploits were kept to a minimum
in the history texts, and what was described was dealt with in
terms of revulsion. Yet the owner of this apartment must have a
high esteem for these bloody warriors. The very presence of the
busts told Duncan much about the man who had installed them
here.

The hallway along which the three prisoners were conducted
went straight south for at least sixty or seventy feet. Duncan
counted seven closed doors on his left before reaching the end
of the hallway. There, just before he turned left into another
hallway, was a very large door. Down the hallway, thirty feet
away, was another door to the right. The prisoners and the
guards entered this before coming to the end of the hallway.
Beyond was a sort of foyer. An arched entrance opened to the
swimming pool room, but the prisoners were instructed to go
into the door immediately to their right. This led to another
very narrow hallway along which were three doors. Each of
these opened to a small dressing room. When the prisoners
came out, they went through another arched entrance into the
huge room containing the pool, and, at the far south end, some
gymnastic equipment.

Once, Duncan had overheard two guards talking quietly as
they went down the hallway. One had said something about
"the hangar." Was there a big room in the apartment that was a
landing place for small aircraft? If so, the roof above it had to

open to admit the vessels. And, once, a door had swung open as they were going down the main hallway. A middle-aged but good-looking woman had come out of the large room. He had only glimpsed the sinks, tables, and the racks of knives, forks, and spoons before she stepped back in and closed the door. Her alarmed expression and the guard's growl at her to get back into the room told Duncan that she was not supposed to reveal her presence to the prisoners.

He surmised that she was just one of several servants permanently attached to the place. How many? He would never know until his plan became reality, but he would have to be ready for the appearance of an unknown number. The servants would also have their quarters, probably not far from the kitchen and the rooms of the master, Ruggedo.

Going north from the kitchen along the main hallway that led back to his room were five doors. One, he suspected, gave entrance to a storage room next to the kitchen. The others were probably entrances to the monitor room, the guards' living quarters and bedrooms and, perhaps, the guards' recreation room.

Somewhere in this complex should be a small hospital room for those not deathly sick. Ruggedo would not want anyone stationed here to go to the metropolitan hospital. There would be too many questions, too much to cover up. Which meant that a doctor would be needed. Probably, the doctor was a member of the PUPA and lived nearby in the tower.

Duncan and his colleagues were allowed to watch the newscasts of every day, and they could order any of 129,634 dramatic, comedy, adventure, and documentary tapes. But when Duncan asked for a series of documentaries on the members of the WGC, the World Government Council, he was refused. No reason was given, though he requested one. That told him what he already suspected. Ruggedo was one of the council, and the prisoners were not to know that. Duncan had guessed that only an extremely powerful official could have such an enormous amount of living space for himself and also keep it a secret.

Even the governor of a state or member of a national governing council could not have such power.

Ruggedo was a member of both PUPA and the WGC.

Duncan asked himself—no one else to question—why a WGC official would be one of a subversive group. Or, probably, the founder and head of the organization. Did he not have as much power now as any human could have? The answer was that he wanted *more* power. He wanted to be the head person, not just one of the heads.

There might be additional reasons.

Where had he seen Ruggedo?

Though Duncan's impression of familiarity with him had been weak, it was not, he was almost certain, from seeing him on TV. That wispy memory could only have come from an intense face-to-face encounter.

Duncan wished that he had constructed his new persona with more access to memories of his previous selves. There were leaks, seepage of recalls, but they were not enough to help him. A more general reservoir of knowledge was available, but anything immediately identifiable with Caird and the others was cut off.

Meanwhile, Carebara had decided that verbal interrogation was not going to do the job by itself. He brought in a small machine with ten leads, which he attached to Duncan's temples, chest, wrists, upper arms, and penis. Using this machine, named the ATM, the professor could display on the screen changes in blood pressure, heartbeat rate, electrical skin fields, voice frequencies, and perspiration rate. He also required that Duncan keep his eyes open when he breathed in the truth mist. The dilation and contraction of the pupils were another indicator of truth-telling in the subject.

But when Duncan awakened after the first session with the ATM, Carebara looked disgusted.

"Any luck?" Duncan said. He grinned.

"I know you were lying sometimes," the professor said. "I have no doubt of that! Yet your pupils did not register that at all. You're a unique phenomenon, Duncan."

"Every human being is," Duncan said. He sat up on the couch and began pulling off the electrodes attached to the leads.

"You needn't look so smug," Carebara said. "If we don't get the answers to our questions, we may be in an undesirable situation."

"We?"

"You, I mean. If you're useless to us, and you have too much knowledge of us, well . . ."

"It won't be well. Tell me, Carebara, doesn't it bother you that PUPA so casually kills its own people if they become a nuisance or a potential danger to it? Doesn't that make your ethical skin, your moral nose, itch even a little bit?"

Carebara looked nervously at the nearest wall screen, and he said, "It's for the greater good."

"Godalmighty!" Duncan said. "Five thousand years of civilization, and you killers still can't come up with anything better than that!"

That evening, Cabtab and Snick were granted their request to spend a few hours with Duncan. The day before, they had pleaded loneliness to their guards, and the petition had apparently been sent on to whomever made the decision in such matters. Ruggedo, probably, Duncan thought. This morning the chief guard had told them that they could enjoy each other's company for a while tonight. He did not say so, but they knew that their every move would be watched and their conversation overheard. It would do no good to turn up the sound volume on the wall screen in the hope that it would make it impossible for the detectors to eavesdrop. The guards were controlling the noise level of the TV. Moreover, any attempt at covert communication among the three would mean that all visiting privileges would be stopped. Also, they would not be permitted to swim together again.

"Why not?" Duncan had said angrily. "How could we possibly escape from this place? If we want to fantasize about escape plans, what do you care?"

"Those are the orders," the chief guard said. He scowled and flared his nostrils. This latter characteristic had caused the prisoners to refer to him as Flapnose. The other guards were Flatass, Thinlips, Stripes, and Shifty.

That evening at seven o'clock Snick and Cabtab, escorted by Thinlips and Stripes, entered Duncan's room. When the guards left, Duncan said, "Tonight we're watching the old classic, *The Martian Rebellion.*" His back was to the eastern wall screens, and the wall strips above the long window on the west would not observe the rapid winking of his right eye. The padre's huge body, placed between Duncan and the western strips, blocked out the eye.

Snick and Cabtab did not wink back because the wall screens would have detected that. But Snick said, "OK," and the padre said, "Great! I love it. Can't see it too many times for me, though I abhor the violence in it."

"Sure you do," Snick said.

Duncan did not remember the code number for the movie, so he called up a list on the screen, stopped the rollup when the title appeared, and chose the code number of the first remake. Then he took the glass of Tennessee mash, Wild Radical, that Snick had poured for him and sat down between her and Cabtab. Bowls of popcorn, cheese curls, and various dips and crackers were on the coffee table before them.

Duncan sipped the liquor, bit into a cracker smeared with green pepper–guacamole dip, and said, "There's one scene I really enjoy in this."

"Which is?" Snick said.

"Oh, I'll let you guess, and you tell me what you think it is when the movie's over. On second thought, why don't I tell you when it happens."

As the opening music, Mulligan Tchakula's classic "Saint Francis Kisses His Ass Goodbye" swelled and the credits were flashing in orange letters in English and Loglan, Duncan thought about when he had first seen the movie. He had been eleven obyears old, and it had put an unsmoothable dent in his memory. Whose memory? Never mind that now. This remake had been first issued 245 obyears ago, the obyear he was born.

The revolt on Mars on which the movie was very loosely based had taken place forty obyears before he was born. Jerry Pao Nel, a captain in the Mars colony organics, and if the movie was to be believed, a raving, half-mad antisocial and fascist, had led an abortive revolution to free the colony from the Earth government and set up Nel's idea of a free society. The rebellion had taken a surprisingly long time to suppress, mainly because most of the colonists supported Nel and Earth had no military forces. In the end, Nel had managed to escape in a ship bound for an unknown destination, one of the stars supposed to have planets that might be inhabitable by Terrestrials. His cryogenically frozen body was undoubtedly still in the ship; it would be a thousand more obyears before it would come within landing range of any planet.

The movie, however, showed Nel dying during a fierce battle in the mazes below Syrtis Major. The three heroes, Moses Howard Kugl, Curleigh Estarculo Lu-Dan, and Lawrence Amir Bulbul, were staunch supporters of the Earth government, rebels against the rebels. Though they had actually played a small but vital part in the war against the uprising, the movie depicted them as having defeated the revolution with very little help from others. Nor did the movie mention that, after the war, the three had been convicted of large-scale data-bank embezzlement and chicanery and had been sentenced to rehabilitation centers for ten obyears. On the other hand, the writers of this version had a sense of humor and had shown the trio as the bumbling and accident-prone but very lucky clowns they had been in real life.

Duncan enjoyed seeing *The Martian Rebellion* again—it had been ten subyears or seventy obyears since he had last seen it. His pleasure was diluted somewhat by anxiety. He was afraid that Snick and Cabtab would not comprehend why he had stressed the one scene. Still, they had caught on quickly that there was something about it that he could not say openly. At least, he hoped that they had.

A few seconds before it was to appear on the wall screen, he squeezed their hands. "Watch this. You'll really enjoy it and perhaps profit from it."

Snick said, "Oh, I've seen it before."

Cabtab boomed, "I have, too, as I said. But it's a little unbelievable, you know. If everything had not gone just right, those three bums would have been killed. It could only happen once in a thousand times, not very good odds. However, they had to try it."

"Exactly," Duncan said. "They *had* to try it. They would not have gotten another chance at a situation like that."

"Yes," Snick said. "What if Nel had not entered their cell to interrogate them? They could have done nothing. They would have been executed, that would've been the end of them and maybe of the possibility of victory for Earth."

"But Nel did," Duncan said. "That made the difference."

At the same time the prisoners were being filmed, their voices were being frequency-analyzed. If these revealed any unaccountable excitement, any undue stress, the phrases associated with them would flash orange on the CRT. That would alert the monitors, and they would rerun the phrases for study. Duncan was hoping that the monitors would attribute any stress patterns to the movie itself. Since it was about a rebellion and subversive organizations, it would, of course, excite the three viewers.

When the scene was halfway through, Duncan squeezed the hands of his compatriots again.

"See what I mean?" he said.

Snick and Cabtab nodded.

28

Duncan had been in the apartment for ten consecutive days. The sessions with Carebara, now held two and sometimes three times a day, lasting from one to two hours each, had yielded nothing desirable. That is, they were unfruitful if Carebara was to be believed. It was possible that he was holding back information from his subject but reporting some progress to Ruggedo. However, Cabtab and Snick could see nothing but failure during their attendance. They were not always present, and Carebara could be censoring parts of the tapes taken during their absence. They did tell Duncan that the professor was beginning to use drugs more often. These were always administered, usually by syringe or by daubing liquids on his skin, after Duncan had become unconscious. He would not have needed their testimony to know that Carebara was experimenting on him with chemicals. His headaches after the sessions were more numerous and stronger, and he was quite often nauseated to the point of vomiting. Also, two days ago, a red rash with large watery blisters covering his legs, groin, and buttocks had appeared.

"Why don't you give up before you kill me?" Duncan said to Carebara.

"Kill or cure," the professor said cheerily.

Duncan yelled and shot his fist out. It caught the end of Carebara's pointed chin; Carebara staggered back and fell heavily on his back.

Duncan, swearing, his face red, picked up the open bag of medical tools and drugs and whirled the bag around by one end, syringe, bottles, cans, a stethoscope, and a box of gauzes flying out in every direction. Cabtab and Snick sat motionless, staring. His sudden rage had caught them as much by surprise as it had Carebara or, for that matter, Duncan himself. Duncan recovered quickly, though breathing heavily, and sat down on the main sofa. As he had expected, the door opened a few seconds later. Flapnose, Thinlips, and Stripes, each holding a proton gun, came in. These were, as always, set at stun power, though what was slightly stunning for one person might be heavily stunning for another. And a light charge hitting a skull might inflict permanent brain injury.

Duncan held his hands up in a gesture of placation. "You saw it," he said. "He provoked me, made me angry. I lost control for a moment. Under the circumstances, that's understandable."

"Shut up!" Flapnose said. He motioned with the weapon, and Stripes, a big woman with a blonde page-boy cut, knelt by Carebara. After holstering the gun, she opened one of the professor's eyelids, looked at the pupil, and then felt his wrist-pulse. Carebara groaned, muttered something, and tried to sit up. She pushed him back down, saying, "Take it easy, Citizen."

Though Carebara protested that he could get up and walk, Flapnose insisted that he lie still. The guard used the wall screen to summon a man and a woman. Duncan noticed that Flapnose did not use their names. The woman was the one who had come unexpectedly from the kitchen into the hallway. Duncan had never seen the man before. He supposed that he was one of the servants. The man unfolded a stretcher, and he and the woman rolled Carebara onto it, picked it up, and bore him out of the room. Probably, Duncan thought, to take him to the hospital room he had surmised was in the complex.

Flapnose, scowling, nostrils wriggling like a rabbit's, said,

"There'll be no more temper explosions, Beewolf. And from now on during the sessions one or more guards will always be stationed here."

"I didn't try to kill him!" Duncan said.

Flapnose did not reply. He ordered the other two to collect the objects spilled from the bag. Duncan was disappointed. He had kicked the can of TM spray under the sofa, but Stripes found it. Then the three left the room.

The guard named Flatass, Duncan thought, would be in the monitor room. There would always be at least one there. If that one considered that a situation had gotten out of control by the guards, he would call in help. Just how long it would take more armed PUPA to get to this place, Duncan did not know. That depended upon how close they lived to this area and also on the time of the call. If it occurred near midnight, very few, if any, would be able to come. He doubted that the guards were worried about this.

Duncan was worried. Not about whom the guards could get to help them but about his own lack of progress in the sessions. If Ruggedo became convinced that he, Duncan, would never be able to evoke the techniques for lying under the TM, Ruggedo would probably do away with him. Kill or stone him, Cabtab, and Snick. Somehow, he had to make the PUPA chief believe that keeping Duncan was going to be profitable.

So I don't remember how I made a new persona? Duncan thought. What's to stop me from recreating? Am I not the same imaginative, inventive, and uniquely endowed person as the others? The same in those senses, anyway. Why not try to rediscover the techniques? No. Rediscover was the wrong description. He could not dig into himself like some archaeologist of the psyche. He would be like the New Stone Age man who suddenly has a vision of growing plants and domesticating animals. He would invent the Agricultural Revolution of the psyche. Reinvent it.

Easier said than done. Nevertheless, for two days, when undisturbed, and when he should have been sleeping, he worked on the formation of a new persona. Since this was to have a short life and be born for one purpose only, to fool the inquisitor, he did not conceive the ID as a fully rounded man with a long history. It was not to be put into any data bank. It was designed only to lie.

Lying on the big sofa, his eyes closed, the screens cut off, everything outside his skin shut out, walled off, he floated in a darkness that extended to the boundaries, if there were any, of the universe. He was alone in the void, the space that lacked planets and stars and microscopic dust, lacked all matter, hence was not really a space since space could not exist without matter. Even his presence did not affect that universe, that nothing which had had boundaries but now extended into infinity. An infinity that was not infinity because infinity had to have a starting point even if it had no end. He, his presence but not himself, had no mass to bend, however insignificantly, space. He was just an image reflected by a no-mirror.

That image would be named Jefferson Cervantes Caird, but it would not be identical with the man about whom Duncan remembered very little. Unless, by coincidence, he chose some elements of character that were those of Caird number one. Though it would have helped Duncan greatly in his effort to remember the techniques for lying, he had been denied access to the ID data-bank file on all of the first seven personae. What little he knew of them had come from Snick and the tapes of the sessions. Carebara, no doubt, had consulted these files, but he would be mainly interested in whether or not Duncan recalled the techniques. Most probably, he was not going to question Duncan about his memory of the intimate details of Caird's life. Even if he did, Duncan could reply that he remembered only the techniques.

That may be true, Duncan thought. How do I know that I am creating these? Perhaps there is a leak from Caird, and I am displaying a mnemonic tape in my mind? Or one of my minds? That he had not the slightest doubt that what he was doing would work made this a strong possibility. His only lack of confidence was in the ability of anyone else to use his techniques.

Their formation seemed to him to be ridiculously easy. That, however, was because he was unique. A chance complex of genetic traits, never to be duplicated, combined with a unique family environment, made him the only one who could use his peculiar abilities.

Perhaps not. All he could do for now was to make something that would give Carebara and Ruggedo hope that he would be useful.

Now, toward the image of Caird II and yet at the same time away shot a bright blue dot in the dark abyss. No direction in this nonspace. Going anywhere in this medium—even nonspace was a medium—meant going everywhere. Now the blue speck swelled and filled all that Duncan could see and not see. It was a whirling filament twisted along its longitudinal axis, and its steady light had become a swiftly flashing blue. It wrapped Caird II inside it though Duncan could still dimly see him. Then it contracted, bringing the nonspace with it so that Caird II, glowing blue, was the only object that Duncan could see or even think about. How he was able to just think about it, and yet not think about what he was supposed not to be thinking about, he did not know.

The filament that had merged with Caird II had joined with, become one with, every cell of the body of Caird II. Seventy-five trillion cells now contained the same knowledge, had become identical data banks, insofar as knowing the techniques for lying were concerned. Within the nucleus of each whirled a blue filament that could not be detected by any chemical or electronic means. Or so it seemed to Duncan, and if the process worked, what difference if it could not be detected scientifically?

The blue filament held within its field all that Duncan needed to become Caird II.

Now the figure of Caird began rotating like the propeller of an ancient airplane, slowly, then faster, faster, faster, until it was solid glowing blue. And, as if an electromagnetic field holding it had been switched off, it shot forward. Also backward, sideways in three directions, and inward and outward.

It was gone. Wherever all those other images had sped to,

one had entered Duncan and was now dormant within him. But it could be raised, and Carebara would think that he had finally evoked Caird I.

He slept on the sofa until the buzz signaling the turning of the supper panel reeled him awake. The professor appeared forty-five minutes later accompanied by two guards. He did not explain why Snick and Cabtab were not present. Nor did he refer to Duncan's striking him. Duncan considered apologizing but rejected the idea. He had been justifiably angry, and though the law forbade physical violence in any situation except self-defense, Duncan felt that Carebara had gotten off easy.

He lay down on the sofa and was silent while the professor attached the electrodes and adjusted the controls of the machine. This time, instead of using the sprayer can, Carebara told Duncan to open his mouth. He held a tiny dropper above Duncan's tongue and squeezed the bulb on its end. Duncan felt the cold wetness and smelled the violetlike odor. He went under so quickly that he was not sure, when he opened his eyes, that the drug had taken effect. A glance at the digital time display showed him that thirty-five minutes had passed. Carebara, who had looked so glum and sour, was now smiling broadly.

Which doesn't improve his looks any, Duncan thought.

He sat up and said, "You must've struck something. A speck or the mother lode?"

"What?" Carebara said, blinking his big green eyes.

Evidently, he did not understand the reference.

"How did we do?"

Still smiling, Carebara rubbed his hands together, a gesture somehow similar to that of a praying mantis clicking its claws together before seizing its victim. Or was he recalling some other insect?

"We've found the right location. Now, we'll start digging."

"I'm not an ant colony," Duncan said. He asked for a glass of water; the drug always dehydrated him. Flatass brought it to him. Duncan said, "Thanks," and drained the glass. But his mouth was still a little dry.

Carebara sat down but was careful, Duncan noted, to do so in a chair a good distance from him. The professor said, "Let's run it now. You'll see what I mean."

Carebara fast-forwarded the preliminary boilerplate questioning required at every session. This consisted mostly of twelve questions needed to establish that the subject was indeed whom he said he was. Even though it had been proved many times that Duncan could lie and that the boilerplate was useless, Carebara proceeded by the book.

The professor had then gone through each ID, working backward, simply asking each for his name and citizen's overall code number. None had responded until he had requested Jefferson Cervantes Caird's. And then, while Carebara gasped, the information had been given. The professor had been so taken aback at his entirely unexpected success that he had been unable to speak for several seconds. Overwhelmed, he had not even checked for pupil sizechange or the machine's indicators for blood pressure and skin field changes. That made Duncan wonder if there had been any. But the professor, when he made his report for Ruggedo, would be sure to run off the records the machine had made at that time. Duncan was not really worried.

"How did you do it?" he said.

Carebara quit smiling. His hands came together on his chest, and his fingers wiggled.

"I . . . don't . . . know."

He put his hands onto his lap, leaned forward, and smiled again.

"What's the difference? I can determine that later. The important thing is that I was successful. It worked, whatever *it* was."

Watching his answers to the professor's excited questions, Duncan had to admit that it certainly seemed to have worked. One by one, he gave the answers Carebara wanted. At the end, he had revealed the outline of the techniques for making a completely new persona.

The wall screen displayed the code number of the taping and went blank.

"Now for the details," Carebara said.

"Tomorrow," Duncan said. "I'm far too tired to attempt that. I'm much more fatigued than from the other sessions. It wouldn't do any good to make another run. I'm just too pooped out."

Carebara looked disappointed, and he opened his mouth as if he were about to argue. He shut it, chewed his lip for a moment, wiggled his fingers, then said, "Very well. Tomorrow, shortly after breakfast, we tackle the details."

Duncan rose along with the professor. "I'm very excited, too. I was beginning to think it was hopeless. But you must've done something, something you don't realize, to have gotten through to the basic persona."

"Yes! But after we get the procedure programed, we have to make sure that the new persona can lie under TM. I don't know . . . the process seems so simple . . . maybe . . ."

"You're thinking that maybe not everybody can be taught it?"

"Yes."

"I'm sure that you won't have to try it out on too many people before you find someone who'll respond, someone who'll be able to do it as easily as I did."

Carebara, walking toward the door, the guards behind him, called back. "I've got a lot of work to do, a hell of a lot! I won't be sleeping tonight!"

Duncan was certain that Carebara would notify Ruggedo at once of his success. Whether that would bring Ruggedo here tomorrow, Duncan could only guess. He would come eventually. Then, if all went as Duncan hoped it would, he and Cabtab and Snick might escape.

How often did everything go strictly according to plan?

About once in ten thousand times, maybe.

Despite this thought, Duncan fell asleep at once. But not before saying good night to Caird II.

There was no reply. He had not expected one.

29

"You realize," Duncan said to Carebara, "that once everybody learns how to lie under TM, the government and the justice system will lose greatly. Subversives and corrupt politicians will no longer be detected so easily. Criminals will escape their proper punishment. Society will be plunged into the mistakes and errors, the chaos of ancient times. Of course, I'm just pointing this out to you as something to debate about. It may be that the ability of anyone to lie whenever he chooses is a natural right. Humankind has enjoyed the right and the privilege since it learned how to talk. Lying comes naturally and is perhaps a gift that shouldn't be taken away from people.

"On the other hand, look at how society has benefited or has seemed to benefit from the use of the truth drug. Justice is almost always done. The guilty almost never escape. The median citizen, knowing that he will assuredly be apprehended and punished if he commits a crime, refrains. The only criminals in the New Era are those who kill or injure because of a sudden passion or who are unintelligent enough to think they can escape the consequences of their crimes."

Carebara frowned, then gestured at the guard, Flatass, to carry Duncan's tray of dirty dishes to the wall panel. Flatass, a man with socially undesirable large buttocks, also frowned. He did not like doing a prisoner's work, but he obeyed.

"I wouldn't bother thinking about the problem," the professor said. "The knowledge of anti-TM techniques will be very restricted. Only a few will even hear about it."

Duncan smiled. "That's what I thought. The only ones who'll have that knowledge will be the very highest officials in the government."

"Right. And, of course, those who teach it to the officials."

Duncan smiled again. "How long do you think the teachers will be allowed to live or to go unstoned once they've taught all they know to a few officials?"

"Nonsense! That's ridiculous! Treasonous! Paranoiacal!" Carebara said.

"If you think it's so nonsensical, why are you pale?"

Carebara glanced at the wall screen, felt his throat, and spoke in a slightly trembling voice. "That would not be consonant with our high ideals."

"Ideals?" Duncan said, and he spoke no more on the subject.

"Let's get down to work," Carebara said.

"After I go to the bathroom. My bowels always move right after breakfast. They make an offer I can't refuse."

"Very well, but don't dawdle."

Duncan stood up from the chair. "What's the hurry? Is Ruggedo coming today?"

Carebara, his lips pressed together, looked away from Duncan.

"I didn't expect you to tell me."

When Duncan came out of the bathroom, he found that Stripes had also entered the apartment.

"One guard isn't enough?" he said. "What do you expect me to do while I'm unconscious?"

Carebara was still scowling. "It suddenly occurred to me that, if you can fake answers while under TM, you might also be faking unconsciousness."

"And you think I might try something? Like attacking you again?"

Duncan guffawed.

"Who's paranoiac now?"

He sat down on the sofa. "If you're really worried about that, all you have to do is check out my alpha waves while I'm passed out."

"Those can be controlled," Carebara said. "You're a very curious phenomenon, Beewolf. It's too bad, in a way, that you have to be kept here. You should be in some institution with extensive laboratory equipment and under observation by scientists far more competent than I am to study you."

He sighed, then said, "But that's not to be for some time. After the revolution, there'll be plenty of time."

"I'll still be a prisoner then?"

"That's not up to me."

Carebara attached the electrodes and pointed the antennae of the machine at various parts of Duncan's body.

"I have some questions to ask while you're conscious."

These, it was obvious, were designed to find out how much Duncan could recall of Caird's persona while he was in the awake state. That was easier for Duncan than he had expected. He closed his eyes and summoned up the image of Caird II, its feet tangled in long bloody glowing-red flesh-roots that trailed away into the abyss until they were lost in the darkness. Duncan became, in effect, Caird II, though he retained enough of Duncan to fake him when the professor addressed him as such.

Carebara was reading the questions from a list held in his hand. Duncan wondered if that had been prepared by Ruggedo. It seemed to him that Ruggedo must know far more about his previous personae than Carebara.

"What do you know of Charles Arpad Ohm?"

The question yanked Duncan from his reverie. It had leaped at him as if from ambush.

"Ohm?" Duncan said. "I only know what you've told me of him. He was my Saturday persona in Manhattan, a weedie, a bum, a drunk."

"That's all you recall?"

"Yes."

That was not true. Several faces had sped by that inner eye. His. Snick's. Ruggedo's. However . . . Ruggedo was named . . . was named. . . ?

"Are you certain?"

Carebara was looking at the wall screen on which were displayed in large characters the readoff from the machine. They indicated that Duncan was very relaxed and was just having a nice chat with a friend.

Carebara threw his hands up and said, "Pah! What use is it?"

"Yes, I'm certain," Duncan said. "What I know of Ohm is what you've told me."

Carebara resumed the questions dealing with Caird. Using only part of his attention, Duncan answered them automatically. Now and then, he was steered away from the mainstream of his thoughts by his inability to give the data Carebara asked for. Then he would say, "I don't remember," and go back to fishing for the elusive name. It kept hopping about on the edge of his mind like a deranged kangaroo.

Ruggedo? Ruggedo? Ruggedo?

That suggested something. What? Carpets? Individualists?

It had something to do with clocks. Watches? Timepieces? Digital displays? Chronometers? Chron . . . chron . . . chron . . . Ancient instruments for measuring time. Gnomons? A gnomon was . . . now he had it . . . a metal triangle or pin on a sundial. By the shadow that it cast on the dial, the time of day was shown. But what could a gnomon . . . a part of a sundial. . . ? Ah! Like a blank screen suddenly displaying a single huge word filling the screen flashed: GNOME!

But that was not quite it.

Gnome, gnome, gnome.

NOME!

The troll-like characters in Baum's Oz series, the mean, nasty, loveless creatures that lived underground. Their king was Ruggedo!

"What are you smiling about?" Carebara said harshly.

"It has nothing to do with you," Duncan said. "Next question, please."

"You haven't answered the present one."

"I don't know."

The chief PUPA was a sardonic bastard. He had chosen that name because Ruggedo was the monarch of an underground band. Baum's Nome king had dedicated his sordid life to invading and overthrowing the great and happy nation on the sunny surface of Earth, Oz. Oz was no danger to him and only wanted to be left alone. But Ruggedo could not stand the idea of all that easy living and joy. Besides, though he had in his dark and rock-shelled kingdom all the gold and diamonds that the most avaricious could desire, he wanted all that the open-air land of Oz possessed.

Duncan wondered if the PUPA Ruggedo was aware, when he chose the name to hide behind, that the Nome Ruggedo had always been foiled, his silicon-based ass deep in the mud and Glinda the Good's magical shaft driven all the way up it.

The people and beasts in Oz, all living things, including trees, were immortal. The fairy queen Lurline had cast a spell on the land that ensured that no one could grow older or die. Even if a man was chopped into pieces, he lived; the pieces twitched forever.

Immortality. That . . . the green idea was receding behind an ever-spreading barrenness, like the Deadly Desert that surrounded the land of Oz. "Jesus Christ!" he cried, and he sat up straight.

Carebara jumped and threw the list into the air. "What? What?"

Immortality!

The face of Ruggedo, its heavy-lidded eyes glowing bright as a traffic signal, its smile superior and all-knowing, had risen from the dry-brown barrenness. Like the ghost of Samuel called up by the Witch of Endor.

"Ohm!" Duncan said loudly.

Carebara, on his knees, looking for the list, which had glided under a chair, turned his head toward Duncan. "Ohm? What about Ohm?"

It was a measure of his mental resistance that Duncan's face did not reveal anything to the professor. The wall display showed a jump in blood pressure, a drumming of the heart, an electrical storm across his skin, a cataract of adrenaline in his blood, a nova of F-waves from the cerebellum. The professor did not see that, though he would when he studied the tapes later. By then, Duncan hoped, it would not matter. Meanwhile . . . he closed his eyes, visualized green fields, a white unicorn trotting across them, himself, goat-horned and shaggy-legged, atop the virgin the unicorn was heading for but would get to a few minutes too late.

He opened his eyes. As he had hoped, the readouts now indicated a man under no tension. That, of course, did not signify as much as it should. There were hundreds of thousands who could control the reactions to stress because of their many years of exercise in biofeedback. That was the main reason why, when the ganks administered TM, they seldom used physical/electronic lie detectors as auxiliaries.

"What about Ohm?" Carebara said again.

It had not been a trickle of recall. It had been a spurt, a geyser, rising and then falling and disappearing. So packed with images and words was the flash that Duncan could not see it all. Yet he had seen and remembered enough.

He, Charles Arpad Ohm, was in a secret apartment in the Tower of Evolution in Manhattan. Ruggedo was talking to him, but Ruggedo was Gilbert Ching Immerman, a man thought to have died a long time ago. Immerman was his grandfather and great-grandfather, and he was the founder and head of the subversive organization to which Caird and his six other personae belonged, an organization that had later been exposed and smashed. Somehow, Immerman had escaped detection and was still one of the world government councillors. Instead of abandoning his plans, he had organized another group. Or perhaps the remnants of the old group.

Immerman had made the biochemical integrocompound he called the immortality elixir, though it did not ensure life forever.

"Seven times prolonged!" Duncan murmured.

"What!" Carebara said. "I asked you about Ohm!"

"Oh," Duncan said. "There, just for a second, I thought I had some recall about him. But it faded away. I can't seem to bring it back."

Carebara looked pleased. "At last we're making some progress."

Immerman's elixir slowed the aging process by a factor of seven. Normally, a citizen who lived to be eighty subjective years old would live for 570 obyears. But an immer, one who took the annual drink of the elixir and whose normal lifespan was eighty subyears, would live to be 3,920 obyears old.

That was the other reason why the government had burned to capture him. Some of the higher officials, probably a very few of the very high, had learned that from the immers who had been caught. And the officials had kept the knowledge of the secret for themselves. Not only had they stoned all the captive immers, they had also stoned the lower-echelon people who might have found out about the elixir or might have heard rumors of it.

Snick had known nothing about it, but she had been brought to trial on trumped-up charges, sentenced, and put away in a warehouse.

Despite his effort at self-control, he was so angry that the screen showed a skyscraper blood pressure and a 20,000 Hz F-wave.

"Time to put you under," the professor said. "Open your mouth wide, please."

Duncan awoke an hour later, the electrodes removed from him. Carebara, looking puzzled, was standing over him. He handed a glass of water to Duncan after he had struggled to sit up. When Duncan had drained the glass, he gave it back to Carebara. After placing the glass on the end-table, the professor walked away without a word, followed by the two guards. As soon as the door had closed on them, Duncan got to his feet. He was very shaky. His mouth, despite the water, was so dry that he felt his tongue could scrape sparks off his teeth. His brain and his stomach were playing catch with a red-hot iron ball.

As he reeled toward the bathroom, he said, "The bug must've used TM four times on me. And drugs, too. That's brutal."

If, however, Carebara had probed into anything exciting, he was keeping it to himself. Duncan doubted that he had gotten any more than his subject wished to give. He would have a long list of procedures for creating a new persona, and that might bring Ruggedo—Immerman—running.

He forgot about that while he was vomiting his breakfast. After rinsing out his mouth, drinking more water, blowing his nose, and wiping his eyes, he felt somewhat better. He lay down on a bed and closed his eyes. Though he had meant to explore the results of the session, he fell asleep at once. When he woke, it was noon. He drank some coffee and ate some crackers and cheese. At one o'clock, the guards came to conduct him to the swimming pool. Despite still having a headache and feeling as if every molecule in body and brain was rubbing together, he followed the routine. Near the end of the hour, he felt much better. He was able to voice two words to Snick during one of Cabtab's bellyflops, and to the padre during one of hers.

"Tonight. Maybe."

Carebara came at two o'clock. "I think we're going to speed ahead now. It's not scientific to believe so, but I have a hunch."

"So much for your intuitive powers," Duncan said. "I haven't recovered yet from this morning. We're skipping this afternoon's."

"No, we won't," Carebara said, glaring. "We've got momentum. We're not going to lose it."

"I can guarantee that you'll be wasting your time and mine, besides making me sick," Duncan said. "You won't gain an inch unless I cooperate, and I won't. If I'm back in shape by tonight, we can try then. Otherwise . . . ."

Carebara bit his lower lip, wiggled his fingers, then said, "All right. We'll cancel this one. But you *must* be ready for this evening. It's very important."

Because Immerman will be here? Duncan thought.

"I'll take a long nap, use feedback to rid myself of the drug residues," Duncan said. "I'll try to be ready. But I think you're overusing the drugs, Carebara. Maybe you should bring in somebody competent to administer them."

The professor's face reddened, but he said nothing. A few seconds later, he and the guards were gone.

Duncan went near enough to the window to see the view clearly but not near enough to darken the plastic. The sun shone brightly on the white sails of the pleasure boats and the various-colored freighters. It flashed on the scarlet fuselage of a zeppelin and on the solar panels of the towers. A white gull angled downward fifty feet past the window.

But escape is easier at night, he thought.

At six, Carebara called via a screen.

"The session is put off until eleven."

"Why?"

"You don't need to know."

"Will Cabtab and Snick be here?"

"I can give you that data. Yes, they will. Orders."

Duncan smiled. There could be only one reason for the change of schedule.

30

Panthea Snick was lying unconscious, TMed, on a sofa. Care-bara was standing by her and saying, "Have you made a plan or plans for escaping by yourself from this apartment?"

"No."

"Have you made a plan or plans with others to escape from this apartment?"

"Yes."

Carebara looked delighted.

"With whom did you make the plan or plans to escape?"

"With William St.-George Duncan and with Padre Cobham Wang Cabtab."

"Oh, God, I knew it, I knew it! But how did they do it without speaking to each other? Listen, Citizen Snick. Answer my question in full detail. In what manner, verbal, written, or by screen, or by any other method, did you, Cabtab, and Duncan communicate the plan?"

"Ahh!" Duncan said.

He awoke, his heart beating fast, though the panic was receding swiftly.

His nap had lasted no more than three minutes, but it had been long enough for his hindbrain to display the scenario he dreaded. If his captors were supercareful, they would use truth mist on his friends. And they would know what they must not know.

It was five minutes to 11:00 P.M. He would soon find out if all the security measures that Carebara could take had been taken. It seemed to Duncan, though, that the professor would not think of that extreme procedure. Why should he? Every movement and every word of the three prisoners had been seen and heard or, at least, their captors would believe that this was so.

At one minute to eleven, the door swung inward. Flatass and Stripes entered, guns in hand. The former took a station by the wall of the bathroom. Stripes stood by the side of the north door. Snick and Cabtab entered, followed by the professor. Good! They had not been questioned about escape plans.

Snick sat at the opposite end of the sofa on which Duncan sat. Cabtab lowered his giant body gently onto a chair near Duncan. There was a delay of a few seconds, and Ruggedo—Immerman—walked in. He wore an elegant green robe slashed with scarlet, which, with his closely cropped hair and long slightly curving nose, made him look like an ancient Roman senator. Behind him came Flapnose.

Thinlips and Shifty were probably in the monitor room. Or one of them was standing outside the door, which was now closed.

Immerman nodded at Duncan and took a chair facing the sofa and about eight feet from it.

Flapnose stationed himself about three feet to Immerman's right. He stood with his arms hanging by his side; his gun was in its holster.

Carebara looked around for a few seconds as if he were not sure where he should sit or even if he should sit.

Immerman pointed and said, "Over there."

"Thank you, Your Excellency," the professor said. His face reddened, and he glanced at Immerman while crossing behind him. Though Immerman's lips compressed, he said nothing. Evidently, no one was supposed to use his title while in the prisoners' presence. Especially as that title was reserved for world government councillors.

Carebara would pay for that slip later.

Immerman stared at Duncan while his left hand stroked his stomach. A vision lightninged before Duncan, his grandfather holding a big Siamese sealpoint cat on his lap and petting it.

There was a long silence, then Immerman opened his mouth.

"Pardon me, Citizen Ruggedo!" Cabtab boomed. "Before we launch into the social amenities, may I have a drink? And would you like one?"

Immerman was slightly startled. He blinked, and he said, "You may get yourself one and you may get your friends one. I don't care for any. But . . ."

He looked severe.

". . . don't interrupt again. Speak only when I tell you to."

"I beg your pardon, Citizen Ruggedo. We're under some strain, and I thought a little liquor would ease it."

"Get the drinks," Immerman said.

Cabtab stood up. "Dunc, Thea, what is your pleasure?"

"I'll have a triple Wild Radical," Duncan said.

"A glass of Tokay," Snick said.

"Pardon me, Citizen Ruggedo," Carebara said. "Won't alcohol interfere with Citizen Duncan's proper functioning under TM?"

"I doubt it," Immerman said. "Anyway, that's about the only drug you haven't used on him. Perhaps his unconscious will be affected to our advantage."

Whatever Immerman had meant to say, he was going to keep it to himself until Cabtab had served the drinks. He watched the padre as he walked to the liquor cabinet, a tall and elegantly carved teakwood case placed against the outer wall of the bathroom. When Cabtab had passed out of Immerman's range of vision, Immerman looked steadily at Duncan. He had no trouble meeting his grandfather's eyes, but he wanted to watch Cabtab, so he shifted his gaze back and forth. Let the great man believe that he could outstare his prisoner.

Thus far, the scene in *The Martian Rebellion* had been re-enacted fairly closely. The furniture arrangement, though not exactly the same, was close enough. Immerman had allowed one of his prisoners to get up and go for liquor just as Nel in the movie had allowed Curleigh Estarculo Lu-Dan.

In the movie, the guard stationed near the cabinet had not moved away as Lu-Dan approached it. The guard, Flatass, however, took two steps away from the cabinet.

Stripes was still by the door, and Flapnose kept his station at Immerman's right. Stripes was watching Cabtab; Flapnose, Duncan.

Carebara cleared his throat and said, "Pardon me, Citizen Ruggedo. May I have a small glass of sherry?"

Immerman nodded. Flapnose said, "Cabtab, bring Citizen Carebara a—"

"I heard," the padre said.

He opened a little door beneath the counter and brought out a tray. He placed four glasses on it and poured out the liquor from the bottles on the shelf above the counter.

"Don't take all day," Immerman said in a husky and dry voice.

"Yes, Citizen Ruggedo. However, I propose a toast first. To our success and to the God Who Does Not Yet Exist."

Looking annoyed, Immerman turned his head and moved his body a little. "Don't try my patience!" he said loudly.

"Sorry, Citizen," Cabtab said. "With your vast indulgence . . ."

He raised his brandy tumbler, which was full of Duncan's choice, Wild Radical.

"A toast! May right and virtue triumph!"

He tipped the glass, and his adam's apple went up and down. He put his tumbler on the tray and turned to walk back across the room.

Duncan slid his buttocks forward on the sofa and moved his feet back so that he could raise his heels. His toes were pressed against the carpet, and his right hand was on the arm of the sofa.

He looked again at Immerman, and he said, "What do you intend to do with us after we're no longer useful to you?"

He paused.

"Grandfather!"

Immerman jerked slightly; his eyes widened.

"You remember?"

Flapnose had looked at Immerman.

Duncan glanced at Cabtab.

The padre was walking by Flatass. His head turned, and he spat a mouthful of mash liquor at the guard's eyes.

As in the movie, Duncan, reenacting Lawrence Bulbul Amir's part, leaped up and ran at Immerman. Out of the corner of his eye he saw Snick charging toward Flapnose. The chief guard's hand was on the butt of the holstered gun.

Duncan and Snick screamed to increase their captors' confusion and to slow their reaction the fraction of a second needed.

Others were yelling, too.

Immerman had gotten up from the chair just as Duncan's hands closed around his throat. He fell back, and the chair toppled over with Immerman against the chair and below Duncan. They rolled off the chair with his grandfather on top. Immerman, his face blue, tried to tear out Duncan's eyes. Then he slumped, though he was not yet completely unconscious.

Duncan rolled away and had started to get to his feet when Carebara, shrieking, fell upon him. Both went down, but the professor stopped screaming and went limp. Blood dripped down the side of his head from the wound made by Snick's gunbutt.

Snick, breathing hoarsely, said, "It's over." Then, "Oh, my God!"

Duncan rose shakily. Immerman was getting up. He groaned and fell on his face after Duncan kicked him in the neck.

Flapnose was on his back, his arms outstretched. His head was at an unnatural angle.

Duncan watched Snick as she ran across the room toward

Cabtab's prone body. He looked for Stripes and found her near the door, on her face, her gun some inches from her open hand. Cabtab had shot her after he had taken Flatass's gun from him. But she must have risen from the floor and tackled Cabtab from behind. Stripes had managed to ray the padre while they were wrestling. Then Stripes, badly wounded by Cabtab's shot, had fallen.

Duncan picked up Flapnose's gun, readjusted the dial from stun to high-burn, and walked to the corner near the bathroom.

Snick, weeping, looked up at Duncan. "He's dead!"

The beam had drilled through the padre's left shoulder and cauterized the wound. Not enough. Much blood had spurted from it.

"We'll mourn him later," Duncan said. "The other two guards must have notified the servants and God know who else."

He checked the other bodies. Carebara and Immerman were breathing hard. He did not care about the professor, but he had to have his grandfather alive and with a clear brain. With the spray-can of truth mist taken from Carebara's bag, Duncan squirted the violet cloud onto their faces.

"Stripes, Flatass, and Flapnose are dead," Snick said. "Flatass's neck is broken. The padre must've done it before he died."

"You broke Flapnose's neck, too."

"Yes."

They had Immerman as a hostage, but the guards could see and hear everything in this room. Whether he and Snick could overcome this great disadvantage remained to be seen.

"It went according to script," he said. "Only . . . Lu-Dan didn't die in the movie."

"Rewritten," she said. She laughed harshly. Duncan tensed, waiting for the laughter to become hysterical. She stopped it, and she began picking up the guns and removing extra charges from the pockets of the guards. When she had arrayed the weapons on a table and put the cylinders in the pockets of her robe, she handed him six charges.

"We don't need Carebara," she said, pointing at the professor.

"No, we won't kill him. We might need him."

The screen display indicated that four minutes had passed since Immerman had entered the room.

He gestured at her to follow him. When he was just inside the bathroom doorway, he stopped and turned. She halted outside the doorway so that she could watch the main door to the apartment.

"If their word was any good," he said softly, "there are no screens in the bathroom. You're blocking the screen behind you above the window. When you answer me, stick your head into the doorway just long enough to speak. Make it short. Here's what we have to do. We'll bring Immerman in here, and I'll close the door. You guard while I'm questioning him. For now, all I want from him is the layout of the apartment and the number of people in it. Also, the rooms they sleep in, and any codes that might be useful to us. I've got some other questions for him, big ones, but they'll have to wait. We must clear this place out and find out if any calls have been made to get outside help. Any questions?"

"Immerman?"

"Ruggedo's real name. Give you the details later. I'll carry him here. You guard that door. Yell if they bust in."

Duncan wasted no time. Though he did not know if the man was still comatose because of his injuries or had recovered from them, he began the interrogation. Apparently, Immerman would now be conscious if he had not been sprayed with TM. He responded at once, though weakly.

It took more time than he could afford, but a TMed person would not give requested data as if he were telling a story, would not, as it were, "spill his guts." He had to be led step by step. Nevertheless, Duncan got the arrangement of the rooms and the number of people stationed in the complex. Thinlips, whose name was Singh, and Shifty, whose name was Bottlejay, had been standing watch in the monitor room. The two servants, the woman named Pal and the man named Wisket, were or had been in their room.

Immerman had left Zurich two hours before on a government express rocket, had landed at Starshower Field, and had ridden in a small organic aircraft to the top of the tower. A door in the roof had opened at a radio-transmitted code, and the craft had landed in the hangar room. This was next to the main hallway, along which were other apartments—of other very high government officials, Duncan supposed—and was in the northeast corner of Immerman's apartment. The pilot, Wayne, was in the hangar or in the kitchen and was armed.

A world councillor, Immerman could skip the regular stoning times when he thought it was necessary, and he could ignore the time zones that restricted most citizens during travel.

Duncan stuck his head out of the bathroom and gestured to Snick to stand close to the doorway. He whispered his information to her, and she whispered it back to him so that he could be sure she understood the apartment layout. He went to Carebara's little bag and looked through it until he found a syringe and a bottle of sodium pentothal. Since he did not know how to prepare it to render a person unconscious for half an hour, he asked Carebara. Having done that, he made up the necessary amount and injected the professor. After which, he went into the bathroom and did the same to Immerman.

The pentothal, combined with the TM, would keep the two out for about forty-five minutes. Immerman, being much larger, would probably regain consciousness first. A few minutes earlier did not matter. Duncan hoped to be back before either awoke.

He spoke to Snick again from the bathroom doorway.

"I got the override code for the lights, sound, and monitors from Immerman. He's a cautious bastard. He's the only one who has all the codes for complete control of all the electrical equipment here. Just in case he had to make a quick getaway."

"That'll help us."

"Yes. I turned off the lights and all sound detectors except the receiver I need to control the power. The infrared is off, too. His people have IF view-equipment."

Duncan stepped out and spoke to the nearest wall screen. The code, the opposite of an "Open, O sesame!" resulted immediately in darkness. Now the monitors could neither see his room nor hear any sounds from it. They would, he supposed, not be wrapped in black for long. He had asked Immerman if there were flashlights available to his personnel, and he had replied that there were. They would be groping toward the cabinets holding these.

The exit door of his room was situated directly across from the storage room for food. This had no door opening to the hallway. The kitchen was just south of that, which meant that one or more people would be there, waiting for the prisoners to come out of their room. One of the guards' living quarters was just north of the storage room; its hallway door was ten feet north from Duncan's. Just north of the monitor room was the second guards' living quarters, and it had a hallway door. The final room was the guards' recreation area. This had no hallway door.

There were two women and three men out to get him and Snick. Singh, Bottlejay, Pal, Wisket, and Wayne. They could be stationed at any or all of the doorways on the east side. And some could be waiting in the entrances to Cabtab's room, just north of Duncan's room, or in Snick's, just north of Cabtab's, or in the storage room opposite the guards' recreation facility. If he were in command of the enemy, he would put at least two persons in the rooms directly north of his.

"Wayne!" Duncan said loudly. "Why didn't I think of that before?"

"What?" Snick said. "Oh, I see what you mean! Jesus!"

If the pilot had not yet taken the aircraft through the rooftop hangar door, he was trapped. But if he had left before Duncan had turned off all the power . . .

He did not have time to complete the thought. A dark bulk cut off the light from the towers coming in through the upper part of the window. Duncan could see the silhouette. It was long and slender, and the pilot and another person were profiled. Then the aircraft began to turn on its vertical axis; the vessel was rotating to point its nose at the window.

Duncan aimed at the pilot's body. His violet beam cracked at the same time as Snick's. One of them must have missed the target; a beam shot by Duncan only an inch away. He and Snick returned the fire, and there were five holes in the window, beyond which the canoe-shaped craft continued to turn and turn and turn.

"That was close!" Duncan said. "A good thing I turned the lights off!"

"Two down, three to go," Snick said.

31

"I didn't unlock our door before I turned the door power off," Duncan said. "Maybe they'll get courage enough to test if it's unlocked. But I can turn the power on to unlock the door without activating the light if I want to."

"Why don't we burn through both walls?" Snick said. "One of us can cut through Cabtab's wall and burn through the lock of my door. The other can cut through into Immerman's living room."

Duncan had already thought of that. They could outflank the flankers, but the three outside the room might have the same idea. However, he and Snick could not hide in the room, afraid to move because of what the enemy might be doing.

"All the doors that were open when the power quit will still be open," he said. "The others will be locked, including the only door to this complex. If they're in Cabtab's or your room or the storage room next to yours or in Immerman's living room, they had to cut their way in. We'll assume that they haven't done that yet or are in the process of doing that. Let's go through the wall into the living room and then through the wall into his bedroom."

He took a last look at the slowly pivoting aircraft with its dead passengers before he started work. With their guns on full power, they sliced out a rough square just high enough for them to crawl through. The stench of melting and burning treated cardboard, six inches thick, stung their noses and burned their eyes. After inserting fresh charges into the weapons, they got down on all fours. Duncan whispered the code word that would restore the lights but not the operation of the wall screens. He lunged through the hole, his weapon in his left hand. He had hoped that, if anybody was in that room, he would freeze for a half-second. That paralysis and confusion would give him the advantage.

If there had been anyone in the living room, he had been quick enough to drop behind a large piece of furniture. Duncan and Snick went cautiously, half-crouched, guns extended in both hands. A thorough tour of the living room and the bathroom showed that they were empty. Duncan cut the lights off, and another square was sliced through the wall. Again, the lights were turned on, and the same procedure was followed. They found that all the doors were locked.

After he had cut the lighting again, they used the illumination from the floor-to-ceiling windows to go to the southeast corner of the room.

"You cut the hole," Duncan said. "I'll watch the one we just cut. Maybe they've gotten into my room now and are trailing us."

Snick took about thirty seconds to make the new exit.

"I've got a half-charge left," she said.

"Use it till it's gone. We may need all we have."

He spoke to the wall screen; the lights flared. He had not expected anyone to be in the swimming-pool room nor was there. Nevertheless, he walked slowly toward the nearest edge of the pool. It was just possible, though it was ridiculous to think that anyone would do it, that a man or woman was standing in the water, his head below the edge. It would be an excellent ambush position. But who would do that?

No one, it seemed.

He felt a little foolish. Still, if he had shrugged off the idea and there had been someone there, he might be dead.

Once more, he cut off the illumination.

"They must be wondering what the hell's going on with the lights," Snick whispered.

"Good," Duncan said softly.

They were in complete darkness now and forced to feel their way along the wall. One hand trailed along its surface, the other probed ahead with the gun. After a few steps, Duncan stopped. The bulbous end of the weapon had scraped against something in front of him. By feeling, he determined that it was a bust on a pedestal. He made contact with six of these before the wall ended. When he activated the lights for a second, he saw that they were in a hallway and the archway to the foyer was ahead of him. In darkness again, he walked slowly through it, his shoulder barely touching one side. Once more, he ordered the lights to come on. The main door to the complex was closed. Was it locked? He pushed on it and could not budge it.

Snick following closely, one hand on his shoulder, he found his way back to the hallway, where he halted. It ran straight down the length of the complex to the wall of the next complex. The last room was the aircraft hangar, a rather large area with one door. He went down the hall, feeling with his right hand. No busts or small tables got in his way. When he had felt the third door slide by his fingers, he slowed even more. Then he touched the slight protrusion that marked the jamb of the fourth door. He told Snick to face the other way, gun ready, before he activated the lights again. When they came on, he saw that the door was closed. He quickly said the code that unlocked it, spoke the code that cut the lights off, and pushed. After he and Snick were inside, he evoked the lights again. The door had automatically locked behind him.

As Immerman had said, there was another gank air-patrol two-seater craft parked here. Grinning, Duncan got into the front seat, the pilot's. Snick, chortling, scrambled into the one behind.

"We're free!" she cried.

Duncan pressed the POWER ON button. He cursed. No indicator lights flashed, no digital displays glowed. Three more pushes on the button were equally fruitless.

"What's wrong?" Snick said.

"I don't know, damn it! I think . . . Immerman was right when he said there was another craft here. What he didn't say, because he didn't know it, was that the pilot removed some vital part before he took off. He must've done it just in case we did somehow get here. Or maybe he obeyed a standing order. Immerman wouldn't tell me about that unless I asked him. I'm not mechanic enough to know what's missing. If I was, I doubt there'd be a spare part."

He got out of the vessel and looked at the proton demicannon mounted on the prow. Its stand was welded to the frame, but the weapon could be removed quickly by opening two clamps.

"Weighs about forty pounds," he said. "I can handle it."

Sweating in the close, heavy, and unmoving air, they got the cannon down. Duncan removed two extra charges, bullet-shaped cases six inches long, from the supply canister of the craft. He jammed these into his kilt pockets and picked up the weapon in two hands.

"I'll set the lights so they go off and come on at one-minute intervals," he said.

Across the hallway was the door to the guards' recreation room. This, according to Immerman, was a large L-shaped room. Its door fell inward in four seconds, three to cut it out from the wall and one for Snick to kick it inward. The bulbous end of the cannon spitting violet streaks, Duncan walked into the room. The wall opposite the doorway looked like Swiss cheese, but the area was empty. Duncan walked by the swimming pool, not as big as the other. If there was anybody in the two guards' living quarters or the monitor room, they must know by now that their prisoners were free and behind them. Duncan did not care. He did not think he had much time left to

clear out the opposition and to question Immerman again. And
then do one more thing before getting out of here.

Snick went into the bottom part of the L. She burned out the
lock on the door that opened to the hallway outside Duncan's
room. Waiting until the lights had gone off, she pushed the
door out, got down on her belly, and looked around the side.
He could not see her in the dark, but he had told her what to do
and assumed that she was following instructions. Meanwhile, he
kept a watch on the hallway doors to the other rooms.

The room was suddenly bright. Snick's gasp came faintly to
him followed by three crackles and a woman's scream. Then
two more crackles, loud enough for him to know that Snick had
fired them. He started toward the doorway, but Snick wriggled
backward and stood up. Her smile was brighter than the lights;
she glowed.

"Got both of them! His shot came close, though!"

Duncan could smell the burned carpet. He said, "Who?"

"Pal, the cook. Took her left temple off. Got Singh, too, right
through the belly, but he came close. One inch closer, and my
head'd have a hole in it. I drilled both again to make sure."

"That leaves just one, Wisket," Duncan said. He paused, then
said, "You look happy."

"I'm killing subversives."

"For God's sake! We're subversives!"

"But they're the enemy."

He shook his head. "I'm not sure anymore who is or isn't the
enemy. OK. Did you see Wisket?"

"No, but that doesn't mean he's not behind one of those
doors."

He looked quickly around the jamb, then stepped back into
the room. Pal lay on her side; Singh, on his face. Apparently,
Pal had come halfway out of the kitchen doorway and Singh,
preceding her, had come all the way out. They must have been
planning to use the darkness to get near the guards' recreation
room. Since Snick had been on the floor, she had been a difficult target. She had also been faster. After she had felled them,
she had given them the coup de grace.

He would not want to face her in a duel.

"I saw that the doors of the monitor room and the two guards' living quarters were shut," he said. If there's anybody in there, Wisket, I mean, he's not going to get out unless he cuts his way out. If he does, he'll give us plenty of warning. We can smell it."

The lights went off.

"We're going into the hallway now. We'll move sidewise out of here, facing up the hall, south. I'll be on your right. At the count of three after you leave the doorway, we advance. You feel for the door of the monitor room. Wisket may have been trapped in there when I shut the door locks. The second door to the left."

"I know," she said.

"Just checking. I'll feel for Cabtab's door, and then I'll go a few feet further. I should be almost opposite the monitor room door then. When the lights come on, I'll be able to see from there if the door to the data-bank room is open or not. If it's closed, I'll nod at you. If it's open, I'll shake my head. We'll go on up to the data-bank room if the door is open. If it's closed, you cut out the lock to the monitor room. That'll be quicker and easier than going through every room again to find out if Wisket somehow got away from here."

"Got it."

"Let's go."

When the lights sprang on again, he saw that the data-bank room door was closed. He signaled her, and she walked, crouching, to the jamb of the monitor room entrance. Duncan motioned to her to lie down. When she was out of the line of fire, he pressed the trigger of the cannon. A violet beam spat like an angry cat as Duncan circled it around the area of the lock mechanism inside the door. When he was done, Snick reached up with her gun and struck the circle twice with the butt of the weapon. The circle fell inside the room. Then she reached out and rammed the heel of her palm against the door. It swung inward to the wall.

Wisket, if he was in there, had moved out of sight.

"Come out!" Duncan said. "All your buddies are dead, Wisket! You don't have a chance! Surrender, or we come in after you! I've got a demicannon, Wisket! I'll enfilade the whole room unless you come out, hands up, in four seconds!"

A deep but quavering voice called out. "I'll surrender if you'll give me your word you won't kill me!"

"Come out empty-handed! Toss your gun out first, then show me your hands! High against the jambs! No tricks! I have backup!"

"You promise not to shoot me?"

"I promise," Duncan said.

"What about your backup? I want her promise, too."

Evidently, Wisket was a cautious man.

Duncan nodded at Snick to give her word.

"I promise I won't shoot you!" she said.

"Is there anybody else with you?" Wisket called.

"How the hell could there be?" Duncan said. "You know how many of us there are. Come on, man! I'm in a hurry!"

"You said you won't shoot me," Wisket yelled. "I want your promise you won't harm me in any way. Otherwise, you'll have to come in and get me!"

His voice sounded as if it was coming from far back in the room. Before Duncan could shout at Snick to stop, she had rolled to a position facing the doorway. Holding the gun in both hands, she fired twice. A violet streak leaped over her and drilled a hole in the wall behind her. She rose and ran into the room. Duncan, cursing, followed her into it. Wisket was lying face down in the middle of the room.

"That was stupid," Duncan said.

"If I'd failed, yes, it would have been. I didn't, so it wasn't stupid. We'd have had to kill him anyway. You know that. We'll have to kill Immerman and Carebara, too, after we're through with them."

"I was going to let them loose, give them a chance to escape."

"And if they're caught by the ganks? They'll reveal everything, and our own chances of escaping will be very very small."

"You're a bloodthirsty savage," Duncan said.

At that second, he began to lose his love for her. Or it seemed to him that he did. He hoped so. He longed to be free of this obsession that no amount of logic had been able to banish.

"Well?" she said.

"You make sense."

"Good. Now, what do we do?"

"We get Immerman into the data-bank room as fast as possible. Then you stand guard by the door to this complex. They may have called for help. Take the cannon with you."

32

While Immerman was lying on a sofa in the monitor room, Duncan asked, as rapidly as possible, about the capabilities of the data bank. As he had hoped, it could be used to override all but some top-secret government channels, and it was linked to the world government, national, state, and local channels everywhere. His grandfather had secretly set up all these transmission potentialities a long time ago.

He paused for a moment to look at the wall screen showing the foyer. Snick was sitting in a chair, facing the door, the weapon propped on top of another chair in front of her.

"What is the name you now use?"

"David Jimson Ananda."

"What is the override access code?"

Immerman said, weakly, "IMAGO. ALWAYS."

Duncan asked him to spell it out. Then he said, "Are you the only one who can activate that?"

"Yes."

"What's required for access confirmation? Recognition of your voice?"

"Yes."

"Is anything else required for access confirmation?"

"Yes."

"What else is required for access confirmation?"

"The print of my left thumb. My right retinaprint."

Duncan asked him how these were registered. After Immerman had given him the data, he hoisted the limp body up and carried it to the chair in front of the main console. He propped Immerman up and punched the POWER ON button. He said, "Now, when I say *go,* you, Gilbert Ching Immerman, say, as loudly as possible, IMAGO. ALWAYS."

He placed the man's left thumb on a round unmarked plate on the desk and held Immerman's head up by the hair.

"Go."

"IMAGO. ALWAYS."

The screen, which had been displaying READY PER CODE INPUT, dissolved that. ACCESS CODE NOT COMPLETED replaced it.

A thin beam had shot out from the center of the screen. It fell on Immerman's neck, but Duncan moved his head until it shone exactly on Immerman's right eye. He pulled the eyelid up, and the screen flashed: ACCESS CODE COMPLETED. READY FOR INPUT.

Duncan was startled when the other wall screens began flashing bright orange and a low wailing issued from them. The first warning for today's citizens to prepare for stoning.

He ignored the distraction and told Immerman, step by step, what to tell the computer. Before he had gotten halfway through his instructions, a whistle came from the screen monitoring the foyer. Snick said, "They're burning through the lock!"

"Keep them out," Duncan said. "Do your best. I can't quit now. I can't help you until I'm through. I have to do this no matter what."

The results of "this" would be worldwide and very complex. Initiation was simple but required some time.

Immerman obeyed his every request as if he were a zombie, which, in effect, he was. What Duncan wanted to launch had been prepared long ago by Immerman. Though Immerman might have had something else in mind, he had set up the system so that it could be quickly done. At Duncan's command, Immerman repeated the instructions, and these were stored in secret data banks all over the world. At ten after midnight, all the wall screens in every house, apartment, and public building that were not tuned in to the public TV system at that moment would flash Duncan's message. At the same time, the printout mechanisms in every house, apartment, and public building would issue the message. He had avoided trying to transmit through the government TV. He knew that the screen displays would not last more than a few seconds before the censors cut them off.

Every private place and every public building except the government TV offices in this time zone would get the transmission. Every other time zone would get it at ten minutes after the day had started. Once the government recovered from the shock, it would be able to locate many of the banks and erase the messages. But some would get through. And even if the messages got to only one day, that day would make sure that the other days got the message. The citizens would see to that; they would leave the printouts for those who followed them. Some would, anyway. It was not possible for the government to go into every house and remove the printouts. It was a task that it would not even attempt.

Duncan's chief difficulty just now was in compressing the message. He did not have much time to formulate it, and he did not want it to be long. Short and simple but effective, that was what he needed.

Snick's voice came again. He looked up. The lock mechanism had been cut through, and the round section of the door around it had been knocked through. It lay smoldering on the carpet.

Snick's beam shot through the hole. If anyone had been standing behind it, he had a large hole in his belly.

CITIZENS OF THE WORLD!

YOUR GOVERNMENT HAS KEPT SECRET FROM YOU A FORMULA FOR SLOWING AGING BY A FACTOR OF SEVEN. IF YOU HAD THIS, YOU COULD LIVE SEVEN TIMES LONGER. THE WORLD COUNCIL AND OTHER HIGH OFFICIALS ARE USING THIS TO PROLONG THEIR OWN LIVES. THEY ARE DENYING YOU THIS FORMULA. HERE IS THE FORMULA.

This was not "deathless" prose or anything near it. He would have liked to have had time to compose a much better message. Given the more-than-pressing situation, he was fortunate to be able to get even this out.

The long and the hard part was making sure that the computer got the formula properly recorded. Immerman gave it from memory, and then, at Duncan's order, had the computer display it on a screen. He made the few corrections needed, and the data was stored.

CITIZENS OF THE WORLD!

YOUR GOVERNMENT HAS LIED TO YOU FOR A THOUSAND OBYEARS. THE WORLD POPULATION IS NOT EIGHT BILLION. IT IS ONLY TWO BILLION. RE-PEAT: TWO BILLION. THIS ARTIFICIAL DIVISION OF HUMANKIND INTO SEVEN DAYS IS NOT NECESSARY. DEMAND THE TRUTH. DEMAND THAT YOU BE AL-LOWED TO RETURN TO THE NATURAL SYSTEM OF LIFE. IF THE GOVERNMENT RESISTS, REVOLT! DO NOT BE SATISFIED WITH THE LIES OF THE GOVERN-MENT. REVOLT!

AUTHORIZED MESSAGE BY DAVID JIMSON ANANDA, AKA GILBERT CHING IMMERMAN. ALSO AUTHO-RIZED AND TRANSMITTED BY JEFFERSON CER-VANTES CAIRD.

When the officials saw Caird's name, they were going to be even more enraged. That was all right. Let them know that he was not dead.

"Tell it to repeat the instructions and the message," Duncan told Immerman.

A crackling from the wall screen made him look at it. The foyer door had been pushed open or, more probably, kicked open by someone who had then fled. Snick had fired a warning beam. He doubted that they would try to rush her through that entrance. They would cut through the wall at several places at the same time and try to flank her by coming in through other rooms. They would be cautious; they did not know how many defenders there were. Yet they did not have much time. The city would be astir at ten after midnight. Most of the citizens would go from the stoners to bed, but the first-shift ganks and workers would be out. If the tenants of these super-apartments came out into the hallway, they would notify the ganks. If, that is, they were not shot by the PUPA.

"Tell it to obey no more instructions from you or anybody else from now on," Duncan said.

Immerman said, "Z AND O-U-T."

"That's the cancellation code?"

"Yes."

He sprayed TM onto Immerman's face and carried him to the sofa. He said, "Goodbye, Grandfather. You're in a hell of a mess, and you deserve every molecule of trouble you get. You should have left me alone. But I'm glad you didn't."

He ran out into the hallway and to the door of his room. It was still locked, but the code word released it. He sprayed Carebara again, and then called in to the number provided for the nearest organic station. Ignoring the officer's demands that he identify himself, he said, "There've been several murders in Apartment Complex D-7, Level 125. There are murderers trying to get into the apartment! Hurry! They're trying to kill us!"

The sergeant was very angry. He was supposed to go off duty soon and enter his stoner. Only in the most extreme of emergencies could he pass into the next day.

"Your message is recorded," he said. "We'll have officers up there in three minutes. What is your ID? What is the situation?" Then, after looking at a display near him, out of Duncan's view, "There is no record of this apartment! What are you trying to pull?"

"Apartment 7-D, Level 125," Duncan said. "It may not be recorded, but it's here. You won't have any trouble finding it. Hurry, man! It's murder!"

He cut off the screen. The sergeant would now be looking at the screen to find the origin of the transmission, but he would fail. The override circuits would block off any channel for source search.

Duncan ran off a screen view of all the rooms. A section was almost completely cut through in the wall of the hospital room, and another had just been butted into the storage room next to the hangar. But the invaders would have to beam out the locks in the doors of these rooms to get into the hallway.

He called Snick. "Meet you outside the room by the hangar room. They'll be breaking out of that in a minute! They'll be in the hangar in a few seconds, too!"

She was there before he could arrive because he had been delayed by having to give the code to open the two doors of the dining hall. As he dashed into the hall, he saw her fire through the hole just made in the storage-room door. Screams came through it.

"The ganks'll be here very soon!" Duncan shouted. "I called them five minutes ago!"

The only reply was some groans.

Snick had gone on to the hangar door. Again, she fired just after the lock mechanism was punched out. Again, screams.

"The ganks are coming!" Duncan yelled. "They'll be here in a few seconds!"

There was a silence, then a woman said, "Sure, you brought them in."

A beam through the hole in the door made a crater in the opposite wall.

Duncan got down low and duckwalked past the door. He motioned to Snick to fire through the hole again. Staying to one side, she shot the beam at an angle. He half-rose then and shot through at a different angle. A man groaned.

"I don't care if the world falls down around all of us!" Duncan roared. "I don't give a damn! I'm not lying when I say the ganks are coming!"

He retreated down the hall and spoke to a wall screen. Now the taping of his call to the police would be shown in the storage room and hangar. He wished he had thought sooner of this confirmation.

Faintly, he could hear a conversation from the hangar.

Maybe they were going; maybe they were not. If they had any sense, they were running toward the stairway now.

He signaled Snick to kick the door inward. She did so, then sprang back. He went in with his gun crackling, and Snick was close behind him, but there was no one alive there. Two men, one almost cut in half, lay on the floor.

It was now ten minutes to midnight. The screens in the room were giving the final notice. They would be flashing all over the city, and the ganks would be swearing. They could not ignore his call, but they were so conditioned that they would feel very uneasy, if not panicky, because they were breaking day.

He told the one screen that had run the taping of his call to the ganks, the one that was not suffused with orange, to activate the opening of the doors in the ceiling. These slid away from each other, revealing a starry sky and bringing in cool air.

He started up the ladder, saying, "Leave the cannon here."

They climbed onto the roof. Everywhere, the towers and the bridges were pulsing orange and the sirens were wailing. The doors, acting on his instruction to close after sixty-six seconds, slid back together.

"We'll have to go down the stairway," he said. "It'll be tough, but if we hang on to the banisters, we might not get knocked down by the water sprays."

He laughed. "Too bad we couldn't have slid down on the banisters. Nobody'll be pursuing us. Not until we get down to the bottom, and maybe not then."

"What're we going to do?" she said, as she hurried along beside him. The warning lights and sirens had stopped now.

"I don't want to do it, but we'll have to take off for the wilder-

ness again. We'll hide until things change, until it's safe for us to
come in. There's going to be a hell of a lot of trouble for a while.
I'm betting on the people, what the historians call the aroused
masses. If they don't change things for the better, then you and
I are out of luck. But it's been pretty good for us so far. We've
had more luck than maybe we deserve."

"We made it," she said.

"We'll see how well we made it. God, I feel good! We've done
what nobody would think possible, including me!"

He whooped with joy at the stars.